# Blood Match

## Blood Match, Volume 1

Melinda Call

Published by Melinda Call, 2023.

BLOOD MATCH

**First edition. August 30, 2023.**

Copyright © 2023 Melinda Call.

ISBN: 979-8988376729

Written by Melinda Call.

# Table of Contents

# Dedication

This novel has been a labor of love for longer than I'm willing to admit. Let's just say answering machines were still very much a thing when I started writing. I hope you enjoy reading it as much as I have creating it, but within a much shorter timeline.

First and foremost, I need to thank my parents, J and Alice, who shared their profound love of reading and storytelling with me, while making sure I always had a book, or ten, to read. They also nurtured my hard work ethic and inability to back down from the challenges life threw my way. Without all of the above, this book wouldn't have existed.

*Blood Match* would have never made it into your hands without the unconditional support from both my husband, Russ, and daughter, Megan. They spent hours helping me work through storylines, correct dialogue, and make the characters more real (even if they both have a very different idea of how one particular character looks). Thank you both for believing in me especially when I had a hard time doing it myself.

I'm eternally grateful for my amazing group of beta readers who helped bring this story to life: Eileen B., Kara S., Megan H., Emma B. and many more over the years. Thank you, Sarah U., for helping me to not to choose the alternative ending to this book. Honestly, you should all thank her!

My third-grade teacher gifted me with a fear of commas, adverbs, and red pens. My editor, Brandi from My Notes in the Margins, made sure this book was as polished as possible. She was able to help me get past my fear of "the bleeding page" to make this novel shine to its full potential.

Last and certainly not least, thank you to my talented daughter, Megan, who created the book cover for this and the rest of the series. She almost co-wrote this series with as much help as she'd provided. She has her own art business so I appreciate every minute she took away from her passion to help build mine. Her work can be found at CryoMerch.com.

# Chapter One

Vampires. Creatures of the night. Romantic, immortal, dark, evil...

Lies. Fiction. In other words: Crap.

There are some evil ones, but we'll explore that more later. Vampires are nothing more than genetic mutants. Some say evolution; I say freaks of nature. How do *I* know so much about it? Well, I'm one of those genetic freaks. Why couldn't I have been lucky enough to get a mutation that made my eyes green or gave me cute dimples?

I'm not devastatingly beautiful, nor do I consider myself a hideous hag. Don't even get me started on those bat-faced things from the tabloids. An ex-boyfriend of mine once likened my hair to caramel but he associated *everything* with food. I've kept myself in good shape, more for my job than vanity, or at least that's what I kept telling myself. The only thing that gave me away for what I am, besides the slightly longer and sharper canines, are my eyes. All vampires have the same golden irises. Must be linked to our other messed up genes.

Other than that, I'm an average, mid-twenty-something Montana chick working for a living and paying taxes, all while I slowly beat down a mortgage. Don't get me wrong; there were some pretty sweet advantages to this genetic fluke. We have fantastic night vision, super sensitive hearing, and increased strength. All of which help me with my job in security.

Oh, please. I don't walk around a dark warehouse at night with a flashlight and a can of pepper spray. I'm a bodyguard for celebrities. In all honesty though, it's more like wannabe celebrities and spoiled rich kids, but in a few years, I might be protecting someone the general public would recognize.

1

Case in point, my protection detail for this particular evening was an up-and-coming singer. God, I hope he wasn't a whiny pop star or worse, a hip-hop joke. He had some cutesy stage name that for the life of me I couldn't remember, but I knew him from my paperwork as "Tom". Not what I considered a big security risk, but I protected whomever my company assigned. I'd only been with Geo's Security for a little over a year, which was still considered a newbie, thus getting partnered up or stuck with the cases nobody else wanted. This made my jobs easy, but it was difficult for me to stand out and get noticed.

So, I drove to babysit a probable no-talent jerk, living off a trust fund the size of Miami. For some reason, my client had requested getting to the club two hours before it opened, something about setting up. He was a one-man band. How long could it take? The reason didn't really matter. If he was at the club, I was there to protect him. I got paid by the hour so no complaints on the financial end of the gig.

The sun broke through the clouds and focused on a parking spot labeled 'Employees Only' which was too good to resist so I glided in and cut the engine. My baby was a midnight blue Mustang with two bold silver racing stripes that run from front to back, so new it still carried the new car smell. I inhaled and let the scent of leather and carpet cleaner wash over me before getting out.

From the outside, Club Opal looked like one of dozens on this end of town. As soon as I pulled open the door, I could tell there had been a major remodel since my last visit. Swanky luxury was an understatement. Soft lighting, black leather booths, and glass pedestal tables decorated the inside of the club. The floor was a random pattern of gray, silver, and black marble tile that gleamed even in the dim light from what appeared to be real crystal chandeliers. Everything was set up in circular tiers with the small round stage at the center, like some new wave chic coliseum. My usual work uniform was a pair of snug, yet unrestrictive black jeans and a long-sleeved white button-down shirt; my hair fashioned in a simple French braid down my back. It made me look like a waitress but that was part of the goal: to be there, but not necessarily noticed. Yet tonight, I was severely underdressed, so I stuck out like a sore thumb.

"We don't open until eight," a male voice called from my left.

Pulling my badge from my waistband, I held it up for the bartender. "I'm with the band."

He gave me a skeptical look as I shrugged off my leather jacket, so I continued, "Protection detail for Tom. Can you stash this someplace safe?"

"He's out back with Stacy," the bartender said as he took my coat.

Great. While I was gawking at some fancy club, my client could be getting clobbered in the alley. I was about to run back out the door when a hidden one on the opposite wall swung open, revealing the early evening light. Two people entered carrying various pieces of musical equipment.

The girl, Stacy I assumed, struggled with her load but otherwise looked determined. Tom, on the other hand, half-jogged down the stairs toward the stage lugging two guitar cases, a bulging duffle bag, and what looked like a collapsible microphone stand. After he deposited his things, he climbed halfway back up the stairs to help Stacy with the amplifier.

"Heavier than it looks," Stacy puffed, flipping a loose strand of hair and rolling her shoulders back in an attempt to show off her assets, which looked about as real as Barbie's. I rolled my eyes when Tom took the 'heavy' item she had been struggling with under one arm. His thick, dark hair was just long enough to brush the tops of his shoulders, and what a lovely pair of shoulders indeed. Those nice shoulders extended to the rest of his physique as well. Thanks to my enhanced vision, I could make out his features despite the dim lighting. No wonder Stacy was trying so hard to impress him.

Stacy continued babbling about how strong he was as she followed him toward the stage. Her tight-fitting cocktail dress, part of her 'uniform', made it awkward to descend the stairs. The ample amount of cleavage probably helped her tips, as must the low lighting. Her face was about as plain as her monochrome bottle-blonde hair, even with a pound of makeup and purposefully messy up-do. *Wow was I judgmental tonight!*

As Stacy continued to make a fool of herself, I descended the stairs from my side. Normally my heeled boots made nary a whisper but I didn't want to frighten the poor duo, so I put an effort into making my steps heavy. Stealth is not a vampire trait, just something I picked up during my security training. Both heads turned when I neared the bottom.

"We don't open for another two hours," Stacy huffed, placing her hand on a cocked hip.

"Arabella Simon, from Geo's Security," I offered, ignoring Stacy's less than friendly welcome.

"Hi, I'm Tom." He offered his hand to me and then flicked his eyes back toward Stacy. "I mean, Tómas River."

I took his proffered hand and gave it a nice squeeze. "Nice to meet you, *Tom*. I'll be your protection detail for the evening."

Stacy glared at me until the bartender called to her from above. "Who's going to protect him from you?" she muttered under her breath.

Obviously, she didn't know much about my kind, or maybe she did and wanted me to hear. Either way, I'd keep an eye on Ms. Stacy.

Tom turned back to his gear. "I still don't know why my agent hired you. No one is going to do anything to a nobody like me."

I shrugged. "Hey, I don't make the decisions. I just go where they tell me."

Tom flashed a brilliant smile. He had the look of a Hollywood star with his perfectly straight, white teeth and clear blue eyes. The club's lighting was a bit off but it looked like he also had a slight sun-kissed tan. If nothing else, I had some nice eye candy to watch over this evening.

I was still wondering why he needed to get here so early when he was done setting up in about half an hour. The sound guy showed up shortly after to adjust the stage lights and run through a sound check. Afterward, Tom sat down with his guitar and started practicing.

As soon as he strummed the first chord, I was mesmerized. The music was so clear but held a simple complexity making it sound more like three or four musicians rather than just one. The melody permeated my brain, making everything around me fade away. Just when I didn't think it could get any more perfect, he started to sing. Tom's tone was just a shade deeper than his speaking voice with a rich, warm resonance. I closed my eyes and let the music wash over me.

As quickly as the magic of the music had bewitched me, it was gone. My eyes popped open and scanned the club. I cursed at myself for getting so distracted. Several other employees had entered and I hadn't even noticed. I wasn't here for the show! I was here to protect this man, who if heard by the right person, would be right there with the big wigs of the music industry in no time. At least I could say I heard of him first. I made a mental note to ask for his autograph after the show so people would believe me.

Tom had been adjusting his chair and mic stand when my gaze swung back to him. When our eyes met, he smiled again and shook his head in what looked like disbelief. It was going to be a long evening keeping my attention off him and my eyes focused on everything else. Damn, he was fine.

"Enjoying the music?" he asked, gathering his hair back into a ponytail at the base of his neck. My fingers twitched; was it as soft as it looked?

When I smiled, I pressed my tongue over my fangs to keep from scaring the poor guy before his gig. Most people could recognize us since our coming out a generation ago, but there were those from smaller towns who had little to no contact with our kind. Somehow, Tom struck me as the sheltered type. Too bad he was my client; I'd *love* to teach him all about vampires.

"Not my job to be a music critic," I said, trying to sound nonchalant and failing miserably.

Tom grinned at me again. "Hopefully you can stay awake. I thought I heard you snoring a minute ago."

"I wasn't snoring. I was savoring." I realized what I'd said only after I'd said it but quickly followed up with sarcasm. "But I'll try to stay awake. One can only stand so much of that kind of warbling."

"Let me guess, screaming death metal?" Tom asked, raising an eyebrow.

"Ha, ha." I listened to other stuff, too. I couldn't think of anything specific, but I knew there was more.

"Stay here. I'm going to check the layout," I said, getting to my feet.

"Do I have to ask to use the restroom?"

I turned and smiled again. This time I didn't cover my teeth. "Yes. Just don't ask me to hold it for you."

Much to my surprise, Tom laughed and gave a mock salute before rummaging through his stuff again. I'd been going for intimidating, not funny, but whatever kept him safely in line was fine by me.

The club had two exits, a unisex restroom with three stalls, and two side rooms: one holding an office and the other an employee locker area. Stacy walked in when I was double-checking the lock on the staff room window. She frowned in annoyance then touched up her lip-gloss. In the harsh fluorescent lighting, she looked even worse. Her skin had a yellowish tinge and her hair looked like it hadn't been washed in quite some time.

I looked down at my hands to find them covered in black grease from the window. With a sigh, I joined Stacy at the sink and turned on the faucet. After a second of delay, the water came out full force at all angles, soaking everything, including my white shirt.

"F-ing great!" I spat, wiping water off my face with the back of my hand.

"It's broken," Stacy said, re-twisting a curl around her finger.

"No kidding?"

I grabbed a wad of paper towels and managed to get the grease off my hands before peeling off my shirt and wringing it out over the evil sink. Stacy eyed me in the mirror, the smirk playing on her lips quickly fading. Maybe it was because I was standing in only my white lace bustier but most likely she was staring at my necklace.

"I thought vampires were afraid of crosses."

"Myth," I grumbled, giving my damp shirt a good, hard shake. "You don't have a hair dryer or anything I can use, do you?"

Stacy considered me for a moment then frowned. "Sorry, but I might be able to find something you could wear."

Lovely. I stood almost head and shoulders above the spongy girl but what choice did I have? Maybe she had a t-shirt or something. She opened random lockers and rummaged through them. Finally, she turned and offered me a lacy peasant blouse at least three sizes too big and tailored for a man.

"Really?" I asked, giving her a dark look.

"I could keep looking?" she added, tossing the shirt back into the locker without re-hanging it and slammed the door closed.

The next garment she pulled out was better, much better. It was a black satin dress with a very low-cut V-neck and what would probably be close to a floor-length skirt. Not something I would normally wear on the job but if I could squeeze into it and make a few adjustments, it just might work. Anything was better than the wet t-shirt competition outfit I was currently sporting.

"Go keep an eye on Tom," I told her, admiring the black satin.

"My pleasure," she nearly purred.

"Call me if there's any trouble!" I yelled as she left the room.

After unzipping my boots and pulling off my soggy jeans, I used more paper towels to dry the rest of me. The black was just sheer enough that my bustier had to go. Luckily, the dress was snug across my breasts so my girls wouldn't suddenly pop out if I leaned over or raised my arms. Nothing says unprofessional like a wardrobe malfunction. The skirt was fitted from the bust line to just above the knee, which made it hard to walk let alone run. Using my pocketknife, I cut the dress off at the knee then added a helpful slit along one thigh, making me glad I wore heeled boots tonight instead of my black sneakers or this would be a serious glamour don't.

Speaking of fashion disaster, my hair looked too casual for this outfit and the front dripped from my impromptu shower. Pulling out the elastic and running my fingers through created a mane of gentle waves that spilled over my shoulders and down my back. Most of my eye makeup needed to be wiped off leaving me a bit bare for something this formal, but there wasn't anything I could do about that. At least I was dressed for this place now.

I'd been gone too long and needed to get back to work even though I was sure Stacy had her eyes glued on Tom. If something went wrong, she was as helpless as he. When I yanked open the door and looked around, Tom was nowhere to be seen.

"Damn it all," I cursed under my breath, heading for the restroom. My hand curved around the handle just as it opened, nearly yanking me inside.

"Hey, I was beginning to wonder if I'd scared you away. Stacy said... Wow, you didn't get dressed up for me, did you?" Tom eyed my dress appreciatively, lips curving into a devilish grin.

His question threw me for a second. While I had been doing everything possible not to think of him as a possible boy-toy, the thought he might be attracted to me had never crossed my mind.

"No, and that's beside the point. I need to know where you are at all times."

He put his hands in his back pockets and shrugged. "I didn't want to embarrass you by walking in while you were changing."

"I'm pretty hard to embarrass. Don't leave my sight again," I warned, poking him in the chest to emphasize my point.

"I promise to be a perfect gentleman for the rest of the evening and, as penance, I'll play the song I wrote for you."

"I bet you say that to all the girls."

Was he flirting with me? And more importantly, was I flirting back? I needed to lay down a few ground rules before this went any further than playful banter. My explanation was interrupted by a strangled shriek from behind. I spun around, putting myself in front of Tom like a shield. When I found the source of the noise, I relaxed my posture.

"What did you do?" Stacy cried, gesturing wildly.

I had no idea what she was talking about until she dropped to her knees and started fingering the new hem of the dress. "Oh, I can pay for a replacement."

"But it isn't mine," she sobbed.

Obviously, the dress hadn't been hers, but I didn't stop to think of how the owner would react to my modifications. I bent down to help her to her feet, which was not as easy as it sounded lest I pop a seam or rip the slit I'd added. "Will the owner of the dress be here tonight?"

She shook her head, eyes filled with tears. "Then you don't need to worry about it. I will either buy a replacement or leave money with the bartender. I'll even write a note saying I found and borrowed it, okay?" I asked and she reluctantly nodded.

The club opened at eight on the dot, but people didn't start filing in until quarter to ten. My seat at the bar provided a perfect view of the main door and the stage where Tom was mingling with the early arrivals. Only one guy approached me but scurried off when his date emerged from the restroom looking less than thrilled. I just sipped ginger ale and made easy money.

At the strike of ten, the sound guy announced Tomás River to a half-full club. The first set was too pop for my taste. I tuned out the music and wondered why he wasn't singing the darker, more powerful stuff from earlier.

Patrons filtered in and out as the night stretched on. The earlier crowd had been older and almost all couples, the later arrivals were younger and mostly women. I kept a close eye on the small group of vampires that sauntered in at the end of the first set. Outwardly, none of them looked dangerous but the hunger that flashed in their eyes at the sight of Tom, while understandable, gave me reason to pause.

After a twenty-minute break, Tom settled on stage as the lighting changed to a red smoky hue. The first few notes told me he was switching to the stuff I'd first experienced during sound check. Goosebumps raised on my arms and my pulse jumped in anticipation.

I really had to focus on ignoring the mesmerizing sound so I could watch the rest of the room. After two songs, I realized everyone else was just as engrossed in Tom's music as I was. His songs were dark, stirring, and pulled at everyone's emotions. It was as if he could reach into their souls and pull out their deepest fears and desires.

Shortly after midnight he began thanking everyone for coming, suggesting this would be one of the last songs. I suddenly wondered if he'd already played the song for me and I'd missed it. Then, I mentally slapped myself for believing he'd actually written a song for me.

"I apologize this song is still a little rough. I've been working on the melody for a while but didn't find the inspiration for the lyrics until tonight," Tom explained.

Hearing this, I sat up a little straighter, forgetting once again that I was working when he plucked those first few eerie notes. This was the song I'd been savoring earlier but the lyrics were different this time.

> *How long have I searched for you,*
> *but you still can't see me.*
> *My music calls to your soul,*
> *but you still can't hear.*
> *Golden eyes stare,*
> *yet see right through me.*
> *I bring you my heart in pieces.*
> *Lifetimes passed since I first looked upon your face.*
> *My eyes have never been the same.*
> *Your red-stained lips never have touched mine.*
> *All I do is dream of that day.*
> *I bring you my heart in pieces.*
> *I long for when you will finally call my name.*
> *The day you'll tell me that you're mine once more.*
> *My guardian angel, save me from myself.*
> *I bring you my heart in pieces.*

Tom repeated the last verse twice more then let the last chord slowly fade to nothing. In the silence that followed, you could have heard a pin drop. I shook my head to clear the mist filling my brain as everyone applauded.

As vain as I was, there was no way the song was about me. Tom must have had his heart broken by a vampire when he was younger and seeing me tonight rekindled the memory. I'm sure it would have worked on bubble-headed Stacy, but I was not that naïve.

Everyone seemed to want to leave at once. I pressed toward the stage so I could keep a better eye on my client. Half a dozen females, most of which were vampires, surrounded him. I guessed more than one was sure he'd written the hauntingly beautiful song for them. That thought was another punch to my ego.

I rested my hand on his shoulder to let him know I was close if he wanted to escape or someone decided to get a little too friendly. He turned at the touch and grinned at me before turning back to his adoring fans. His smile never faded as he signed a few cocktail napkins and received a couple of hugs followed by insinuating whispers and phone numbers. He seemed to revel in it, eating up all the fawning. I, on the other hand, was on pins and needles every time someone touched him.

As good as I was, if someone punctured his lung with a knife during a hug, I would be too late to stop it. However, none of these women looked dangerous, plus the amount, or lack, of clothing they were wearing led me to believe no one was carrying a concealed weapon.

"Thank you, ladies, for coming. I'm playing at the Red Rock next weekend but I really do need to pack up." Tom tried to make a gracious exit while still encouraging his admirers.

The women reluctantly dispersed and I let out a sigh. "At least you didn't die."

Tom, who had been beaming, suddenly deflated. "Did you even hear the song?"

"Like I told you earlier, I'm no music critic but I kept you safe and that's what's important. Besides, everyone was so entranced, even if they had wanted to hurt you, they couldn't."

A hint of a smile returned. "Does your employment extend to helping me haul this equipment to my truck?"

I cocked a hip and folded my arms. "Would a pack mule wear something like this?" He spent longer than necessary considering my frame, which made me rethink my previous statement. "For you, my dear Tom, I'll make an exception."

It took far less time to disassemble and pack everything than it had to set up. The bad disco pop music playing through the sound system may have been another reason. At least it was my reason. Paid by the hour, remember?

After I'd placed the last of the equipment in the back of an ancient white pickup, I found Tom standing a few feet away regarding me with a strange look on his face. Out of habit, I looked over my shoulder in case some behemoth was sneaking up to clobber me over the head. There was nothing except an empty street and the vacant lot beyond. Huh, he had been looking at me.

"Do you think you can make it from here or do I need to follow you in case of any post-gig stalkers?"

"You can follow me home," he said, unlocking the driver's door.

"Let me just run in and grab my stuff." I took a step away then stopped. "Actually, since we are still technically at the club, you need to come with me."

Tom slid his hand into mine as we entered the club. I'm not sure which surprised me more: that he did it or the fact I let him. We really needed to talk about the rules. I was his protection damn it, not his date.

As we entered, I spotted Stacy at the bar with my clothes and leather jacket.

"Thanks, Stacy, and don't worry about the dress. I'll have a check sent over first thing tomorrow."

She looked exhausted. "Janelle will be furious. Thankfully, I have tomorrow night off so I can avoid her wrath."

Tom took the most roundabout route across town to his apartment. The building was in a shifty neighborhood; no wonder he wanted me to follow him home. I was surprised he got all of his equipment loaded before the show without getting robbed.

I parked in a handicapped spot and flipped on my hazard lights before running back to his truck. "You want a hand getting this stuff inside before I take off?"

That same deflated expression flickered across this face again. "Sure, but you might want to move your car."

"Don't worry, I put up my security decal. No one would dare tow someone from Geo's."

Lucky for him, I carried nearly everything, really working for my paycheck now and my self-penance for flirting. Of course, he lived in a fourth-floor walk-up. If any of his neighbors from below happened to step out and glance up, they were in store for quite a view. At least I had worn full coverage panties.

He unlocked the door and flipped on the light to reveal an eclectic living room. The place itself was just as run down as the outside but Tom had decorated it in modern, utilitarian furniture. Somehow the cinderblock and two-by-four bookcase seemed to fit his personality as did the worn-out Seventies vintage couch complete with duct tape. Instead of a TV, a line of guitars hung along the long wall. I hoped he had good renter's insurance.

He stepped on the heels of his shoes to remove them then went around the open half wall into a tiny kitchen. "You want something to drink?"

"Actually, since you are safe and sound, my protection detail is officially over," I said, glancing at my watch to check the time.

Tom was smiling when he returned. "Great. Now that you're off the clock, you can relax."

Leaving was going to be far easier than explaining the rules, plus I had really hoped for a good review from this job. Other than the attack faucet, the night had gone off without a hitch. I hated to burst his bubble by telling him Geo's services didn't include happy endings. Even though, for reasons beyond logic, the idea had crossed my mind.

"If you want company, you have a pocket full of phone numbers from adoring fans staring at their phones with bated breath."

Tom set his untouched soda on the counter and turned out his pockets, revealing nothing but a guitar pick and bit of lint. When I tilted my head in question, he explained. "What you didn't see, was me dropping them in the ashtray on our way back into the club."

"Ah, I see." I didn't really but he seemed to be waiting for some sort of response. "It was really nice meeting you, Tom."

"Please don't go yet. I'm always so wired after a gig. It's still early and you don't have anywhere to be."

I raised an eyebrow. "How exactly would you know that?"

"My agent booked you until closing, which gives me about an hour more of protection."

"True, but once you're at a private residence I deem safe, I'm free to leave." I inched toward the door.

"Then don't stay because you're being paid, stay because we could be friends," he said, his voice hopeful.

"Listen, Tom. You seem nice and all, and I'm sure you're going to hit it big soon but this," gesturing between the two of us, "really isn't going to happen."

"You're not allowed to have friends?"

"Yes, I can have friends but I'm not allowed to socialize with clients. If I gave you the wrong impression, I apologize."

"Are you sure you didn't listen to the song?" Tom took a step closer and I instinctively took a half-step back.

My heeled boots made us nearly the same height. Tom was just tall enough I had to look up to stare into those pale blue eyes. That hypnotizing quality of his music had seeped into his speech, making it hard for me to think clearly. He was really gorgeous, and I hadn't had a boyfriend, or even one-night stand, in a while.

"I heard it." I was annoyed when my voice quivered slightly.

He brushed my cheek with his fingertips. "And?"

As if my body had a will of its own, I leaned in when he tipped his head toward mine. Our lips brushed and I tasted his breath. That's when I stepped back and lowered my head with a sigh. My body screamed for my mind to shut up and ignore reason, making my decision that much more difficult.

"Tom," I said, focusing on his mismatched socks. "I could get fired. I can't..."

He took my hand in his. "Arabella," he whispered, and my knees felt weak.

Before I did something I shouldn't... Well, more than I already had, I pulled my hand from his and dashed out the door. It took everything I had in me not to look back at his apartment before climbing into my car. I punched my steering wheel and cursed before slamming my foot down on the accelerator and squealing down the dark street.

So much for my good review. Only I could screw up such an easy job.

# Chapter Two

Time for more Vampire 101. Drinking blood isn't required for our survival. Vampires eat food just like humans but once we've tasted blood, the thirst for more can be overwhelming. There are those who give the rest of us a bad name by going on killing sprees or picking up underage girls befuddled by movies and silly vampire romance novels. Humans do the same horrible things but for some reason it's worse when a vampire does it. It doesn't make sense to me; it's just the way things are. I went nineteen years without a drop, which was amazing considering how many boyfriends I had during my stint with braces. But I digress...

My first time was accidental, and it scared the living crap out of me. I was in college, as was my very human boyfriend. Vampires go to college too; I even managed to scrape together an associate's degree. During a fairly hot and heavy make-out session, I bumped my top teeth into his bottom lip, splitting it open. We, however, were too distracted to notice until I tasted the sweet cinnamon flavor.

I didn't rip his throat out or anything quite so graphic but once I'd had a taste, I wanted more. Possessed with a single-minded purpose, I nipped him all over, greedily taking more than I should. Lucky for him, vampire saliva numbs the pain, at least for humans. Fortunately, he noticed when he started getting lightheaded and called my roommate for help.

My roommate, also a blood virgin at the time, had been better warned than me about the effects of blood. She had to physically restrain me while her boyfriend took mine to the hospital. He ended up getting a blood transfusion and needless to say, never spoke to me again. Since then, I've only dated other vampires and even that had been a while.

When I fled Tom's apartment, my motivations were deeper than the fear of losing my job, not that my employer stood for that kind of behavior. The last person who slept with a client not only got fired but was also banned from any form of personal protection employment for life. Geo had a long reach. This seemed to be the only thing I was good at, so I was going to do everything possible to stay in the business.

Geo paid me for my job at Club Opal and informed me of a glowing review, which had been a pleasant surprise. Maybe Tom felt guilty for coming onto me. As a reward, Geo granted me the pleasure of being an after-school babysitter for some spoiled rich girl the remainder of the week. Saturday finally arrived and I was more than ready for a well-deserved night off complete with two movies, a tub of ice cream plus a box of microwave popcorn. Did I mention vampires have raging metabolisms? Another perk unless you aren't within five minutes of a convenience store or kitchen. Blood might not be a necessity but food definitely was.

When I dropped my grocery bag on my kitchen counter, my phone dinged from my back pocket indicating a voicemail. Weird, I hadn't even heard it ring. I unlocked my phone and pressed speaker before unloading the perishables.

My boss's scratchy voice filled the room. "Arabella, we have a last minute no-show. Jake is sick again... On Saturday night... Go figure. Anyway, I need you at Red Rock no later than nine."

I closed my eyes and rested my forehead on the cold countertop. My boss knew the secret of bypassing a call and going directly to voicemail so he didn't have to hear our excuses for not taking last minute jobs. I was going to kill Jake! This was the third time I had to pick up the slack for him on a weekend. After a week of watching Ms. Princess shop and get manicures, all I wanted to do was put on my fuzzy bunny slippers and watch a bad action flick.

Once upon a time, I had been a waitress at the Red Rock Bar and Casino so I was very familiar with the layout. I pulled on a black tank top and light-colored flannel over the blue jeans I was wearing.

My hair was already pony tailed and I had no time to change it. I listened to the message once again for any additional information before heading out.

It wasn't until I pulled into the parking lot and read the marquee that I remembered who was playing tonight and why Geo hadn't been specific about whom I was supposed to be protecting. The big black block letters, hanging somewhat skiddy-wampus, spelled out: Tómas River. I was officially in Hell.

I rubbed my temples and took several deep breaths before getting out of the car. Could this day get any worse? The lot was already packed, which meant I would have to do my primary sweep with the place already filled with loud drunks. Lovely. Jake owed me big time.

Cigarette smoke poured out of the casino when I opened the doors. Lucky me and my heightened senses. My enhanced vision was no help against the noxious, gray haze and flashing strobe lights. This place was a full one hundred and eighty degrees from the Opal. My boots stuck to the floor as I made my way across the room. Mismatched plywood tables were haphazardly arranged to face the narrow stage in back. The only reason this place could claim to be a casino was the row of slot machines along the far wall.

It was no big surprise to find Tom surrounded by a handful of big-breasted women trying to 'help' him set up. I suppressed a sigh and joined them.

When Tom caught my eye, he grinned. "Arabella! I thought they were sending a guy or are you just here for the show?"

"It's your lucky night." My smile was forced.

The women on stage exchanged looks before glaring at me in unison. I sighed and moved my shirt so they could see my badge. Two looked relieved, while the others continued to stare me down to test if looks really could kill.

"Same drill as last week, Tom," I called, making a quick perimeter sweep with my eyes.

"I wouldn't have it any other way," he answered and something in his tone made me uneasy.

Red Rock was harder to secure than Opal but two very large bouncers stood at the only entrance/exit. Can you say fire code violation? But again, unless Tom had some psycho-stalker fan, he needed about as much protection as the chair he was sitting on. I tipped my head to the bouncers and they nodded in recognition.

I forced myself to ignore the music, played in the same order as last week. However, when he played the first few notes of the last song, I found myself staring at him like there was no one else in the room. Unlike last week, when I had been sitting above and behind him, he now stared directly at me and sang like I *was* the only one in the room.

When the last note faded away, the crowd erupted and we were back in the smoky, crowded bar. I took the last swig of my ginger ale and walked to the stage where I watched the bubble-headed fans fall all over themselves and all over Tom. I had to escort one very drunk woman to the bouncers because she was becoming a falling object hazard.

It took longer, most likely due to the larger crowd, for Tom to bow out and begin to pack up. This time I didn't help. I just watched the stragglers get hammered or leave in newly found couplings. There were going to be several people with some serious morning-after regrets tomorrow. I, however, refused to be one of them.

"Could you give me a hand?" Tom asked, motioning toward the jumble of music equipment.

I nodded and picked up the heaviest items. Once again, there was an awkward moment beside his truck but this time I didn't offer to escort him home.

"Goodnight, Tom," I said once he stashed the last piece of equipment in the truck bed.

"You're not going to follow me home?" He acted genuinely surprised.

I frowned. "We both know that's not a good idea."

"How about we go back in for a drink then?"

I shrugged my shoulders. "Sorry, I've got a date."

"What's his name?" There was something strange in Tom's voice. Jealousy maybe?

No need to mention my 'date' would be on my TV screen. "Not that it's any of your business, but his name is Chuck."

"Which movie?" he asked with a sly grin.

Damn, I wish I were a better liar. "That's not important. What's important is my job is done and I'm going home."

"I could follow you."

"You could try," I said, sauntering to my car. What the hell! I was flirting again.

There was no way his old truck could keep up with my muscle car, but hey if he was bored, let him have at it. I've put in a lot of effort to be unsearchable so he couldn't do a quick internet search to track me down. His truck was already idling behind me when I started my car, making me reconsider my challenge.

I may be immune to towing while on the job, but I was just as likely as the next person to get a speeding ticket. Luckily for me, I knew where the cops liked to hang out on Saturday nights. There were only two speed traps on my route home. Poor Tom wouldn't even be a speck in my rearview mirror by the time I made it to the first one.

Once we were out of the parking lot, I pressed my foot to the floor. The engine roared and my car took off. Over the glorious sound, I heard a terrible whine. I glanced in my mirror and saw Tom's pathetic truck becoming smaller as the whine disappeared. When I looked forward again, I slammed on my breaks and swerved into the oncoming lane to keep from ramming into the back of a battered station wagon.

Trapped behind grandma's beast, Tom quickly caught up. I could see him smiling in triumph when I looked back at the next stoplight. The confidence in his smile made me rev my engine. When I glanced back again, I could see him laughing. Suddenly, I realized I wanted to not only see but hear it as well.

He honked his horn when the light changed and I stalled my car. I hadn't stalled a car in years. This was beyond embarrassing. Why was I letting this guy get to me? I tried to ignore the rumble of his truck as I made my way home. He was surprisingly good at catching me despite my attempts otherwise.

I sighed in defeat as I pulled into my driveway. There was only room for one car, so Tom parked on the street. Right where everyone could see I had company at all hours of the night. Lovely! I'd be jobless by morning.

Tom opened the car door for me before I could get it myself. "Thanks," I mumbled.

"Do you have popcorn?" Tom asked as we walked to my front door.

I paused in the spot where my porch light should be shining if it hadn't burned out months ago. I could see his face perfectly but I doubted he could see me very well. My God, he was pretty.

"I can't date clients."

"Who said this was a date? Can't two people watch action movies and eat popcorn together?"

"Ah, hell. Why not?"

My house was no Taj Mahal but I loved it. It reminded me of an old country cottage with little curved windows and arched door frames. I'd painted the walls in bright colors and decorated with dark wood pieces. None of the rooms were big but it was just me. I hadn't expected company, so I hurried to the bathroom to pull down all my unmentionables still hanging to dry.

I tossed them in my bedroom closet and closed it just as Tom rounded the corner. "Nice place," he complimented.

"Thanks," I said, kicking a pair of underwear I'd dropped in my rush under the edge of the bed. "You walked right past the TV though."

I motioned for him to go first, still unsure of how I would react if I stood too close. Luckily, he headed back to the main room without too much prompting.

"You can pick." I tossed him the two movie rental boxes and headed to the kitchen to make some popcorn.

"I hope you like butter," I called after placing the flat, white bag into the microwave.

Tom appeared in the doorway, once again blocking my exit. I busied myself searching for a clean bowl big enough for the three bags I planned on popping. I normally ate two by myself and I wasn't going to shortchange myself because someone barged in on my night of fun.

"I don't have much in the way of drinks but you can help yourself to whatever is in the fridge," I said as I kept my plastic-ware from avalanching down onto my head.

When I finally extracted a bowl and managed to keep everything in the cupboard, I turned to find Tom standing immediately behind me. I jumped in surprise and dropped the bowl.

"Don't do that," I said, bending to retrieve it.

"Did you like the changes?"

His voice was all weird again and even being prepared, I began to lose myself. "You changed the song?"

His hands found my waist and he pulled me a step closer. He hummed the melody and began to sway. After a moment, he sang softly.

*Lifetimes passed since I first looked upon your face*
*My eyes have never been the same*
*Your red stained lips barely touched mine*
*All I do is dream of that blissful day*

The microwave dinged, dragging me back to reality. I stepped away and pressed the button for the door, black acrid smoke furling out. I turned, gestured for Tom to step aside, flipped on the range hood, and ran to open a window. As gross as burnt popcorn was, I was glad for the distraction. How the hell did he do that?

Once the majority of the smell and haze was gone, I closed the window so the house didn't get too chilly. Early May in Montana wasn't known for being overly warm. I put the next bag into the microwave and set the time for a minute less than the last bag.

"No distractions or we'll never get any popcorn." I laughed but it was forced.

"Well, what do you think?" Tom asked, stepping close again.

"I think you're overstepping your 'friend' boundaries," I said, taking a step back.

I had no problem getting the next two bags of popcorn popped and the movie started. The problem was paying attention to what was happening on the screen. Tom sat on the couch, so I stretched out with my stomach on the floor where he immediately joined me. It was easier to share the popcorn, but he was pushing the personal space issue again. Our hands brushed more than once while sharing snacks and the contact seemed to linger a bit longer each time.

During a particularly raunchy sex scene, Tom got up to get us some sodas. I heard him pop one open and fill a glass. Cursing instantaneously followed the sound of the second's cap snapping off. Without thinking, I jumped to my feet and ran to help. I got there just as he pulled the whole roll of paper towels onto the floor while trying to rip off a sheet with one hand. His index finger was cut and dripping blood onto my floor.

I inhaled sharply at the sight. Big mistake. The scent of the blood hit me like a battering ram and I clutched the counter in restraint. Tom wrapped his wounded finger and lifted it above his heart. I finally pulled myself together enough to bend down to gather up the puddle of paper towels, keeping as far back as I could while still being in the same room.

"Are you okay?" he asked me.

"You're the one who's hurt," I snapped but when I opened my mouth I could taste the scent in the air. "No, I'm not, but I will be."

Tom lowered his hand, opened the wad of paper towels, and grimaced. "Got any bandages?"

"Let me see," I answered, took a deep breath, then took a step toward him.

Tom moved the towel to reveal a long, jagged cut running around his index finger. "A bandage isn't going to help." After another deep breath, I continued, "But there is something I could do."

I reached out for his hand again, but he flinched away. "Oh, now you're afraid? Do you want my help or not?"

After a moment's hesitation, he extended his hand. Have I mentioned vampire saliva not only numbs but heals as well?

I tried to focus on what I was trying to accomplish, not what I was about to do as I lifted his damaged finger to my mouth. The blood was still flowing freely and ran down to his wrist then onto my hands. I could feel the frenzied bloodlust starting to surface but I tried my hardest to repress it. Like I said, it's been a while.

It was a good thing too. Since nearly killing my human boyfriend six years ago, I'd only had vampire blood, which wasn't nearly as appealing. Tom's blood tasted not of cinnamon but more like bitter dark chocolate. I didn't even realize blood tasted different from human to human.

When I finally released his hand, my heart was pounding, and my breath came out in gasps. I kept my eyes lowered but I could see his finger was almost completely healed. Only a tiny raised pink line remained where the ragged tear had just been.

I could feel where his blood had dripped on my hand and I longed to lick it off, but I was too afraid of how it would repulse him. He was so quiet; I bit my lip to keep tears from falling. I was a freak!

Imagine my surprise when Tom lifted my trembling hand toward my mouth. "Don't waste it. It's better when given freely."

I lost it and sucked every inch of my hand to make sure I didn't miss any. Then I was somehow in his arms, kissing him. He lifted me so my legs wrapped around his waist and carried me to the bedroom.

Strange or not, the frenzy for blood normally leads to an insatiable need for sex. Despite my best efforts to dissuade Tom from anything more than friendly behavior, a soda can was my undoing. I'm sure my boss will love that one.

I fell asleep wrapped in Tom's arms, listening to him whisper the words of my song. Was being unemployed really that big of a deal? Remember what I said about morning after regrets? I hate it when I'm a hypocrite.

# Chapter Three

Tom was still asleep when I slid from bed in the morning. I wondered if anyone saw his truck parked in front of my house all night. What the hell was wrong with me? I should've called Geo last night and told him he could cover for Jake. To be honest, even if I had remembered Tom was playing at the Red Rock, I wasn't fooling anyone that I'd skip a time-and-a-half paycheck.

Sunday is the day most people go to church, clean their houses, or visit in-laws. I, on the other hand, had the joy of a weekly staff meeting from nine to eleven. Believe me, this was one staff meeting I could happily miss.

After brushing my teeth and attempting to detangle my hair, I tiptoed back into the bedroom. The closet door screeched when I slowly pulled it open. It was childish but I was hoping to get out of the house before he woke up. No such luck. Tom lifted his head from my pillow and smiled at me, dark hair mussed from sleep.

"Good morning," he said, half sitting up and tucking his arm behind his head to lean against the headboard.

No one had the right to look that good in the morning. I shook my head and began searching in my closet for something. Oh yeah, a clean shirt. He came up behind me, swept my hair aside, and began kissing my neck. My eyes fluttered closed, and I leaned back against him.

"I, um, have to go to work?" The words were very difficult to get out.

"Call in sick," he whispered against my ear, making me shiver. I couldn't help it, a moan passed my lips and I heard him chuckle.

"Unless you're dead, everyone has to show up for Sunday morning staff meetings."

"Call in dead then." Tom unhooked my bra.

"Are you planning on supporting us both?" I asked, stepping away.

Tom gave me a disappointed look and sat on the edge of the bed while I finished dressing. He was in no obvious hurry to leave.

"There's coffee in the cupboard to the left of the sink. Help yourself to whatever you find in the fridge. I'll be back around noon," I said, tucking in my shirt.

"I could cut myself again." He gave me a sly look.

I climbed onto his lap before kissing the tip of his nose. "Don't tempt me."

The drive from my house to Geo's Security wasn't long enough to fully clear my sex fogged brain so I drove around the block pretending to look for a better parking spot. Trees blossomed and flowers bloomed everywhere I looked. It made me wish I had a green thumb. The downtown association had really stepped it up this year.

After two passes, I finally pulled into the same spot I'd spied when I approached Geo's initially. I couldn't procrastinate any longer since I still needed to fill out my timesheet for the teen princess job before the meeting if I wanted to get paid on time. I didn't have a desk but counters and shared computers were available for doing various job related paperwork. I could do it online but my home computer was embarrassingly old and painfully slow. Other employees showed up in sweats either hung over or bright-eyed and bushy tailed. I kind of hoped I looked somewhere in between and not the guilty, nervous wreck I was.

My boss, Giovanni or Geo for short, waddled in a few minutes before nine with the stack of next week's assignments. His greasy comb-over was almost distracting enough to miss his hairy paunch hanging over his too long, too stained trousers. You'd never guess his shrewd business sense from his appearance, but he treated his employees and clients well and that's what really mattered. Geo's security had twenty-something full time employees, all of which were finding a spot for this week's meeting. I shot Jake a dirty look from across the room. He didn't look sick to me.

"Someone enjoyed themselves last night," a husky voice said over my shoulder, making me jump. Cassie, another vampire and recent graduate from the newbie stage at Geo's, kind of adopted me after I started. Despite our nearly eight-year age difference, she was the closest thing to a best friend I had.

Rather than starting out in security like I had, Cassie had tried her hand in everything from legal aid to dance-fighting to hydroponics before finding her calling at Geo's. Her drop-dead gorgeous smile usually stunned any would be threats, giving her time to defuse the situation.

"Morning Cass," I whispered back.

"I expect full details after the meeting," Cassie whispered in my ear as Geo started.

He rattled on and on about a new client I would never meet then about how we were still filling out our time sheets incorrectly. After his rant, he started passing out individual schedules.

"Arabella," he called, looking over the sea of faces for me.

I snagged the sheet away from him and gaped. Only four jobs this week, all nights, all for Tómas River.

"Uh, Geo. Can I talk to you about my schedule?" I asked.

"Sorry Ara, nothing else is open. Just suck it up and I'll see about getting you more stuff next week."

Most employees grabbed their assignments and headed out; a random few hung around to socialize. Even though we all worked for the same person, we rarely saw one another other than at this weekly get together. The majority of people seemed to linger this week. My indiscretion felt like a neon sign across my forehead as I waited for Cassie to join me by the coffee maker.

"So... Vampire or human?" she prompted. "I passed your place last night and noticed you had company but no lights on."

"I don't want to talk about it," I mumbled, pouring myself a cup of brown sludge.

"You didn't kill anyone did you?" she asked a little too loudly.

Several heads turned and I grabbed her arm to steer her away. "I don't want to talk about it *here*."

Cassie's mouth formed an 'O' of understanding before following me out to the parking lot. Somehow, she'd managed to park in the slot next to me even though I'd arrived twenty minutes earlier. She leaned against her car and tilted her face toward the sun, making her long white-blonde hair spill down her back.

"So, when do I get to meet this mystery guy?"

I groaned. "Oh Cassie, I've messed up big time."

Her eyes popped open and she stared at me. "You did kill someone!"

"No, I didn't kill anyone but almost as bad. I slept with a client," I confessed.

She closed her eyes again and went back to absorbing the sun's weak rays. "Don't beat yourself up too much. Everyone's done it at least once. Just make sure you don't get assigned again. Easy as pie."

"That's the problem," I said, holding up my schedule. "I can't seem to get away from this guy."

Without opening her eyes, she asked, "Do you want to?"

Her question stopped me. I didn't want to stay away. Hell, I hadn't wanted to leave the first night, but I did what needed to be done. Life sucks. I pushed off my car and unlocked the door.

"I don't want to get fired, Cassie, but I think I might really like this guy." I shook my head. "What about Marco? He got blacklisted for sleeping with a client."

Cassie's eyes opened and she gaped at me. "Um, Marco didn't sleep with a client. He kidnapped and raped a client. He doesn't work security anymore because he's doing serious time. Geo downplays it because the whole affair nearly ruined his business. Come clean with the boss. He'll understand."

Her truth-bomb about Marco was more than my brain could process so I deflected back to the topic at hand. "What about Dr. Blackwood? He was a client. How's that going?"

Cassie's carefree expression slipped for a second and I regretted my question. "It's not. My trip to visit Stan in California made it clear neither of us are ready for anything serious."

"I'm sorry, Cass. Forget I brought it up. I've got to get back home."

"Oh my God, he's still there?"

I cringed. "He was when I left."

A wicked grin spread across her face. "He's human, isn't he? Never mind, stupid question. If you're protecting him, he must be."

"Hey!" It was true but she didn't need to rub it in.

"Sorry hon, but only the big guys protect other vamps. Get your butt in your car. I've got to meet the guy who is brave enough to give blood to my sweet Arabella."

While I'd taken my time getting to Geo's, I'd hurried home hoping to give Tom a heads up before Cassie started her interrogation. My heart sank a little when she parked her two-door Speck where Tom's truck had been when I left this morning. There was a car I recognized parked in my driveway, forcing me to park on the street as well.

"Hi, sis," a voice called as I opened my front door.

My sister, Acacia, was sitting in the living room on some stranger's lap who was wearing more makeup than she was. The white foundation made his Latino coloring look weird, especially where it ended in a jagged line just below his chin. My only sibling was taking the stereotypical approach to vampirism. She only wore black, hid from the sunlight, and acted as if humans were beneath her. My sixteen-year-old baby sister: the Emo vampire poster child.

They were watching the movie I had forgotten about last night thanks to the damned soda can. Well, watching was a relative term. In reality, they were groping each other while the movie played. When they stopped swapping spit and he turned to face me, I noticed his golden eyes.

"Do Mom and Dad know you're skipping church?" I gave lover-boy a pointed glare.

"I told them I was sick so I could spend some time with Raphael," she cooed, running her finger down his cheek.

My parents were raised Catholic and by proxy, so were us girls. Remember my fancy crucifix? They were still trying to repent for whatever sin they must have committed that led them to produce two vampire daughters. No matter how many times I tried explaining to them it was all genetics, they were sure it was some moral wrongdoing which gave them genetic freaks for kids. Their Catholic guilt had them dragging us to church every Sunday trying to beat the devil out of us.

"Does Raphael know you're a junior in high school?" I asked as I continued to glare at El Creepo.

At my question, Raphael shot to the other side of the couch and began mumbling something about needing to be somewhere. Cassie held the door open for him as he nearly ran from the house.

"Thanks a lot." Acacia scowled.

"That's what I'm here for." I called, heading to the kitchen. "Don't make me regret giving you a spare key to my house."

I heard my sister get to her feet and stomp in after me. "How come you can have strange men stay at your house and I can't even bring over a boyfriend?"

Obviously, Tom had still been here when my lovely sibling had arrived. No wonder he'd run away. I ignored her and continued poking at leftovers trying to find something I could feed both Cassie and me. Acacia could fend for herself. Maybe if I didn't offer lunch she'd get the hint, but I doubted it.

"First, this is my house so I can do what I want. Second, I'm an adult. Third, if your boyfriends weren't nearly twice your age, I might consider letting you entertain them here."

Acacia plucked a banana from my fruit bowl. "At least my boyfriends aren't stupid humans."

I slammed the container onto the counter, causing the lid to pop off and slosh soup everywhere. "There is nothing wrong with humans, Acacia! Stop acting like you're better than they are."

She slowly peeled the banana and took a bite. 'Whatever' she mouthed through a mouthful of food.

"Cass, do you want soup or pasta?" I asked, trying to ignore my annoying sister.

"Whatever, I'm not picky."

I knew my friend was both answering my question about lunch and supporting the end of my constant argument between my racist sister and me. After Acacia finished her snack, she lifted herself onto the counter and peered at my reheated soup. Instead of offering her any, I took a bite and feigned ecstasy even though it was mediocre at best.

Acacia handed me a folded note. "He told me to give you this."

"Did you read it?" I asked and she shrugged.

It took everything I had not to slap her silly. Instead, I read the message. Tom had really nice handwriting, kind of like calligraphy without the fancy pens.

*Thanks for the movie. Hope you like the changes I make for tomorrow night. ~T*

"What does that mean?" Acacia asked after reading over the top of the paper.

"None of your business!" I snapped as I crammed the note into my back pocket.

"Touchy, touchy. When was the last time you had a decent meal?" she asked, tasting my soup.

I snatched the spoon away. Of course, she was referring to blood and not actual food. There was no way I was going to tell her, but I couldn't help but recall the taste I'd had last night. A blush must have risen to my cheeks because she gave me a knowing smile.

"Sweet. Maybe humans are good for something. You haven't smiled like that in a while."

"Go home, you little mutant, or I'll tell Mom about Señor Romance."

She hissed at me and stomped out of the room. Cassie joined me in the kitchen after I heard my sister peel out as she headed for home. I knew my friend had heard the entire conversation from the living room. You didn't need to be a vampire or even in the same house to hear whenever Acacia and I went at it. The little brat was so infuriating!

"Don't be too hard on her. She's just trying to find her place. You remember being a teenager. It wasn't that long ago for you," Cassie counseled.

"I don't remember being such a pain in the ass." I threw my arms in the air.

"Well, she has big shoes to fill. Maybe if you didn't scream at her every time you two were in the same room, you'd see how much she looks up to you."

"Now you sound like my mom. Do you want the soup or should I nuke the pasta?"

"I think I'll stick with the pasta. It didn't get contaminated by Raphael's spit."

"Good point. Now I don't want soup either," I said as I dumped it down the drain.

# Chapter Four

"Welcome to the Salty Dog. AAARG!" the host hollered at me as I walked through the door.

I did *not* get paid enough for this crap. Tom played at a pirate themed bar and restaurant tonight. He was lucky he was so damn cute or I would have pawned the job off on someone else just to keep from coming here. If he didn't complain, I would. This place was so beneath him.

The interior of the Salty Dog looked like the hold of a ship. Every inch of the place was straight out of a cheap pirate theme park. The décor consisted of neon palm trees, more ships-in-a-bottle than I could count, fishnets complete with fake fish, and an army of creepy plastic parrots. Everywhere you looked, one of those demonic birds was staring you down. I repressed a shiver. Damn birds.

The waitresses wore pirate wench costumes while the poor bartender had to suffer an eye patch that he constantly switched from eye to eye so he could actually see his customers. I was more worried about the freaky birds than the patrons tonight.

I hadn't seen or heard from Tom since yesterday morning. The awkward morning after feeling had fully sunk in. What if he treated me like a leper now that he had time to think about what happened? It might be easier if we both forgot about it.

When Tom appeared a few moments later, his whole face lit up as he spotted me. I couldn't help but smile too and had to keep from running across the tacky restaurant to where he stood. Oh man, I was screwed.

"I guess my agent took my demands seriously," Tom said when I helped him with the second load of equipment.

"You asked to play at this freak show?"

He shook his head. "No, this was a favor for a friend. I meant booking you for my protection detail."

When he leaned in for a kiss, I turned my head and pretended to pick a piece of lint from his shoulder. "I think we should avoid PDA while I'm on the clock."

Tom gave me a disappointed look. "Hmm, maybe having you as my bodyguard wasn't such a good idea."

I whispered, "But I do so enjoy guarding your body."

"Pay attention to your song tonight. I think you'll like it." Tom's eyes shone with pride.

The gig in pirate-topia ended at ten when the restaurant closed. Thank God for small favors. Since I now knew what to look forward to, I was glad I wouldn't have to wait as long before I lost myself in the addictive music.

Wait, I needed to focus on my job. If I missed the song, I could get a personal encore afterward, which seemed like a safer option for both of us. You never know, I could get distracted and a flock of plastic birds might decide to attack.

I really needed to find a way to explain the situation with Tom to my boss before he heard it from someone else. There was no worry about Cassie saying anything but there were a bunch of Geo's employees who didn't like me very much. Maybe I should figure out the situation with Tom first. My hormone-fogged brain could just be tricking me into believing Tom and I had something real.

There weren't any pop songs tonight, to which I was grateful. I wondered why he kept playing those when the others were so much better. Instead, Tom played some grittier songs before transitioning into the dark mysterious stuff I really enjoyed.

As I scanned the crowd, I realized I recognized a few faces from the last two gigs. It appeared Tom was accumulating some repeat fans. At this rate, he'd be able to book the places he wanted and then...

Then someone with clout from the music business would hear him and whisk him away to the big city. Once that happened, he'd get a real security detail and forget all about me. I tried not to get myself down as I half listened to the music and gauged the crowd. Once again, no one obviously hostile was present.

Try as I might when the last song came on, I was pulled in by its allure. Luckily, so was everyone else.

*How long have I searched for you,*
*but you still can't see me*
*My music calls to your soul,*
*but you still can't hear*
*Golden eyes stare,*
*yet see right through me*
*I bring you my heart in pieces*
*Lifetimes passed since I first looked upon your face*
*My eyes have never been the same*
*Your lips touched mine tasting my very soul*
*That blissful day fills my dreams*
*I bring you my heart in pieces*
*I long for you to love me the way I've always loved you*
*The day you'll tell me that you're mine once and forever*
*My guardian angel, save me from myself*
*I bring you my heart in pieces*

Watching Tom interact with the slutty groupies was almost more than I could stand. But like the professional I was, I sucked it up and did my job. I stood, gritting my teeth and hovering like a vulture as girl after girl whispered innuendos and pressed their phone numbers into his hand or, if they were really bold, directly into his pocket. Curse my genetically advanced hearing. It was wrong but I wanted one to go too far so I'd have an excuse to knock her teeth in.

When one of the waitresses took a little too long with her hug, I tapped her on the shoulder. "Time to go."

She sneered at me and adjusted her grip. Tom reached up and unlocked her arms from around his neck, which made her pout in a very unattractive manner. After another disparaging look my way, she walked away swaying her hips so much I was afraid she would fall over.

Instead of waiting to be asked, I began gathering up equipment to carry out to Tom's truck. I didn't consider myself a jealous person but it was too much watching women prettier than me flirting so openly with him. Usually, my competition wasn't paraded in front of me night after night.

When everything was packed up and we were standing beside his truck, Tom asked, "What's wrong?"

"Nothing," I mumbled, mad at myself for making such a big deal over something I had no control over.

"If it's about the song, I can change it back."

"No, no, it's not the song. I just... Forget it, okay?" I said. "Am I lugging this stuff up four flights of stairs tonight or what?"

At this, Tom perked right back up. "I've got a surprise for you."

"Really?" I raised my eyebrows.

Tom's place was a little neater than last time. He, like me, obviously enjoyed the flexibility of living alone, where you can be as messy as you want when you wanted. He'd tidied up the living room and I could smell lemon scented cleaner.

"Ah, how sweet. You cleaned your house," I teased.

Tom cleared his throat. "Well, yeah, but that isn't the surprise. This is."

He handed me a thick sheet of ivory paper with a fancy logo at the top. After scanning it, I had to fight to keep the smile on my face. Someone had already noticed Tom's music. In my hand was a formal invitation from one of the major record labels on the West coast for an on-site audition.

"I want you to come with me," he said, excitement radiating from him as he beamed at me.

"Tom, this is so amazing. I knew you'd be discovered in no time." I tried to mimic his enthusiasm but it fell short.

"But?" he asked, retrieving the letter and putting it back on the coffee table.

"You'll need real security once you get a contract, and they're crazy if they don't sign you on the spot. I'm more small-time muscle, not really equipped for that level of protection." I smiled sadly at the truth.

Tom caressed the side of my face. "That's not what I meant. I wasn't inviting my bodyguard. I was inviting *you.*"

That's what I was afraid of. I was falling for him, hard, and knew the longer I prolonged this, the more it would hurt when it ended. He might think I'm something special now but once he mingled with models and movie stars, my allure would quickly fade. Just because I was a vampire didn't make me special. If he wanted one, there were far more beautiful and interesting ones out there.

As I looked into his eyes, I wanted to go with him to soothe his nerves before the audition, to celebrate with him afterward, or to just be there. The song that would make him famous was my song only because he told me it was. In reality, it was just a wonderful arrangement of words set to a mesmerizing melody that stirred my very soul. The sadness must have been clear in my eyes because when I opened my mouth to speak, he put his finger to my lips.

"You don't have to decide tonight."

When he kissed me, I felt a tear run down my cheek. It wasn't fair. I wanted this but as much as I hated it, I had to admit Acacia was right. Although vampires were nearly genetically identical to humans, the two didn't belong together. They were just too different. Tom and I were just too different.

"Don't cry, Arabella," he whispered against my lips.

I hadn't realized tears were freely falling as I lost myself in his sweet kisses. I pulled back and lowered my head. However, when I tried to step away, Tom's hands tightened around my arms holding me fast.

It took me a minute to realize even with my advanced strength, I couldn't break away. "How?" I began.

"Nothing is going to change, Arabella." Tom blinked and I saw the faintest hint of gold in those blue eyes. "Well, maybe just one thing."

His grip relaxed and I subconsciously rubbed where his hands had been. No human had ever been able to restrain me. Was I losing my strength? Or was I wrong about Tom being human?

"Please don't look at me like that," Tom said, turning away.

"But it isn't possible, your eyes..." I grabbed his shoulder and tried to turn him so he faced me, but it was like trying to move a boulder.

"You're first generation, Arabella. With each generation the differences get more dramatic, or in my case they change completely."

I didn't understand what he was saying. Two vampires couldn't have children. Something in our messed up DNA kept us from procreating. I used to joke it kept us from taking over the world. The mutation was either silent in one or more of the parents. Meaning half our genome came from a full human.

Tom wasn't finished nor was he looking at me. "I'm seventh generation, which means my ancestors found the one other vampire with compatible DNA. My father told me I'd know, from the moment I laid eyes on her, I'd know my match. Haven't you wondered why it's so hard for you to stay away?"

I groped behind me for the battered chair. Once my trembling hand found it, I sank into it so I didn't fall. He was right of course. I barely knew this man yet the thought of losing him made it hard to breathe.

When he turned to find me sitting, he knelt in front of me. "I can use my music to read emotions; to know what people want to hear. I know you feel its pull. You feel it more strongly than anyone else because of who you are."

It dawned on me then. "That's how you know so much about what I, I mean, what we are. Why do you hide it?"

Now I was really being hypocritical. Acacia was racist against humans; I was racist against vampires. I'd been hiding it my whole life as best I could. Contacts never agreed with my eyes, so I pretended in every other respect. I ignored the lure of blood, spent most of my time with humans, and downplayed my other abilities. The complete opposite of my sister who embraced who she was. I treated it like a handicap.

Tom touched my hand and I flinched. He had to work to get them unclenched, as I seemed unable to do it on my own. Once he had one free, he lifted it to his lips. I stared at his face, my brain still whirling with this new information. Tom seemed to have all the vampire traits without the outward signs that went along with them.

He kissed each fingertip then my palm. "It's sweeter when given freely." His lips were against my wrist.

I jerked back to reality. Nothing had to change! I wasn't a freak to him. He was asking for my blood just as he'd given his to me. I remembered the sweet taste and realized it was the most wonderful thing I'd ever tasted and it wasn't even human. My heart began to pound and my breathing increased.

The desire in his eyes both scared and excited me. Would my blood affect him as his had me? I wanted... No, I *needed* to know.

"I give it to you," I whispered.

I felt his teeth break the skin of my wrist as he closed his mouth around it. There were no words to describe the sensation. It was like nothing I'd ever experienced. He took more than I had the previous night, but I didn't care. I'd give it all if I could feel this euphoria forever.

At some point, my eyes closed and I fell against him. His lips left my wrist and found mine. The faintest trace of blood still on his breath sent me over the edge.

"Give this to me," I panted.

"It's yours, always and forever," he said, eyes searching mine.

I grabbed him and pierced his neck with my teeth. The warm richness filled my mouth and I savored it. It tasted different from last time, not so bitter with a hint of something I didn't recognize.

I found this time I could pull away before I took too much. "It's different."

Tom gathered me into his arms. "Because my heart's finally whole."

# Chapter Five

Two weeks had passed since Tom's confession. I'd worked his protection detail no longer feeling insecure about his ever-growing herd of groupies. No matter what they promised or begged, I knew he was going home with me. We'd even set it up so no one's car sat in front of each other's places overnight, not that we ever slept apart. While it seemed like we were racing forward at breakneck speed, something about knowing we were meant for each other made time meaningless.

Today, however, I was sick with worry. My boss had called me for an impromptu meeting on my day off. As careful as Tom and I had been, I had a feeling Geo knew about our little affair and I was about to get read the riot act, or worse, fired.

I sat in his office facing his decrepit desk, waiting for him to get coffee before writing me my pink slip. I fidgeted as he took his time; the chair groaned in protest as he sat due to his ever growing weight. He lit a cigarette and inhaled deeply before speaking.

"Arabella," Geo began in a disappointed tone. "I got a call from Tómas River yesterday."

"Oh?" I asked innocently. He gave me a stern look and I backpedaled, "I didn't misrepresent the company in any way. Nothing inappropriate happened while I was on the clock."

He held up his hand to stop my babbling. "You're not in trouble. Tom explained everything. I just wish you'd come to me. I could have assigned someone else and this wouldn't have been an issue."

"So, I'm not fired?" I blurted out.

"Of course not." He laughed. "For crap's sake, I met my first two wives while on the job."

"What exactly did Tom tell you?" I asked, still confused.

"He said you two met and started seeing each other before I assigned you to him. Once you found out you'd be working with him, it was too late to find a replacement and he convinced you not to say anything so you wouldn't get in trouble," Geo explained. "That's what happened, isn't it?"

"Sounds about right." I smiled, thinking Tom was a genius.

"I gave him a good tongue lashing for it too. I run a respectable business and can't have word getting out Geo's is a front for peddling ass." I nodded in agreement but he continued, "Speaking of which, you have your two weeks off. When you get back, I'll have a new schedule for you. Tom *won't* be on it."

I covered my confusion about the approved vacation I didn't remember requesting by getting to my feet. "Thanks for being so understanding, Geo."

"Just don't let that guy break your heart. You're too nice a girl for a rock star. You need a stable guy, someone in management."

"Ah, Geo, I didn't know you cared. Isn't it against company policy for employees to date?" I grinned. "Besides, aren't you still married to wife number four?"

"Five, actually, but you're not my type, too damned skinny. Now get your scrawny ass out of my office," he said as he stabbed out the last of his cigarette.

I made sure all my paperwork was finished considering I now had two weeks off. Somehow, I think Tom had something to do with that too. No complaints here; I don't think I've used a single vacation day since I started.

The sun shone, brightening my mood further as I headed downtown. I was supposed to meet my mom for a late lunch after what I'd assumed was my appointment to get canned. Mom was a part time realtor; a job she'd picked up once Acacia and I were both in school. She had been the one who found the house I was currently living in and got me a sweet deal to boot. My parents were far from wealthy but we hadn't gone without, or if we had, I'd never noticed.

We were meeting at her favorite little bistro. With the gorgeous weather, I hoped she'd snagged an outdoor table. When I arrived, she waved at me from the patio. Great minds obviously think alike. Mom and I looked similar, but she was prettier with pale green eyes I'd kill for. Her petite frame made her look delicate and she was about a head shorter than I was.

"Hi sweetheart," she greeted me with a hug. "Hope you don't mind, your sister's joining us. She's in the restroom."

I repressed a sigh and hoped my smile didn't slip. "How did you convince her to sit in the sun?"

Mom smiled, laugh lines showing around her eyes. "It's punishment for getting in-school suspension, again."

"Ah, I see." I took a sip of my lemon-flavored water to keep from saying what I really thought.

"Arabella, your sister tells me you have a new boyfriend. A nice human boy?" Mom asked.

Obviously, Acacia had run home and told Mom I had some strange man in my house as a way of getting back at me for scaring off Raphael. I'd planned on telling her about Tom at lunch today anyway. It would sting Acacia to find out I indeed had a new boyfriend to tell Mom about, rather than having to explain away a one-night stand.

"Acacia must have told you about Tom."

"She couldn't remember his name." Mom smiled, her happiness was clear then faltered. "Stop hovering in the shadows and get over here, Acacia."

"Tom River. He's a musician," I explained, and I saw her eyes tighten. "Not all musicians are junkies or womanizers."

My mom would never say anything negative about anyone, but she was about as easy to read as my menu. Acacia and I had gotten our stubborn opinionated qualities from her but our ability to voice them from Dad.

"Speak of the devil," I said when Acacia finally shuffled to the table, glaring at the sun as if it was shining just to spite her.

"I'll get a sunburn, Mom," she whined.

"There's sunscreen in my bag," Mom answered then turned back to me. "Your sister was just telling me about Tom."

"Is that the guy that stayed at your house the other night?" Acacia perked up.

"We fell asleep watching movies," I explained, giving her a dark look.

I loved my mom but her view of reality really sucked sometimes. She still believed all girls were virgins until their wedding night and I wasn't going to be the one to tell her otherwise.

Acacia stirred her water with her finger. "He's pretty hot, for a human."

"Acacia!" Mom blushed a deep crimson.

"It's okay. Tom's not exactly human," I started hesitantly.

Both my sister and mom looked at me like I'd lost my mind. Obviously, my feelings about other vampires were clearer to my family then I realized. Tom told me I could tell my family about him but he didn't want the general public to know.

"So, he's not the guy with the dark hair?" Acacia asked.

"Oh no, that's him."

"But he's got blue eyes!" she nearly squealed.

I rested my elbows on the table and covered my face with my hands. I'd planned on explaining everything to my mom without commentary from princess Goth. My new, wide cuff bracelet slid down from my wrist and my mom gasped.

Shit. I'd worn the stupid thing so she wouldn't freak out. Nothing says you're hiding a vampire bite like two round bandages, thus the bracelet. While vampire saliva sped healing, repeated trauma seemed to reverse the effects. Tom and I had been sharing blood almost every night since his confession. Therefore, I had two perfectly round marks about the size of a pencil eraser on my wrist.

"Oh sweetheart, he's not hurting you, is he?" Mom started wringing her hands.

I shoved mine under the table. "No, Mom, he's not. I'm sorry you saw that. I know it bothers you."

"I think it's cool," Acacia said, pulling back the tablecloth to get a better look at my arm.

Mom stood and muttered something about the bathroom. I knew she was having one of her vampire-induced panic attacks, so I let her go. After some deep breathing and washing her hands fifteen times, she'd come back as if nothing happened. Sometimes it was just better to pretend what Acacia and I were didn't scare the crap out of her.

"What do you mean he's not exactly human? Either he is or he's not," Acacia asked, then scooted closer to the table in an attempt to get out of the sun.

"It's complicated. He's a vampire, but not like us," I explained, lowering my voice.

She leaned in resting her chin on her hand. "Which explains those luscious blue eyes."

A flash of jealousy surged through me. It must have shown in my face because Acacia looked frightened and sat back. I'd watched dozens of girls flirt with Tom at the clubs but when my sister even hinted, I'd nearly bit her head off. What's up with that?

I cleared my throat and relaxed my shoulders. "Yes, that explains the blue eyes."

Acacia continued to stir her water and lick it off her fingers. "Does he have a brother?"

"Yeah, but he's older and they don't get along."

"Huh, sounds like us." She shrugged her shoulders then continued, "How much older?"

I looked to the heavens for strength. "I have no idea. What part of, 'they don't get along' was confusing? They don't talk and Tom doesn't talk about him."

Acacia lifted her eyebrows and mouthed, 'alrighty then'.

When Mom returned, she was the radiant smiling woman who first greeted me when I arrived. The waitress scurried over and took our order. Mom slapped Acacia's hand when she refused to stop playing in her water. I bit my lip to keep from laughing.

"When are you bringing Tom over so your father and I can meet him?" Mom asked.

I was amazed she kept her voice steady, but that's how Mom handled things: internally. She'd go home and cry then pray for me to find a nice human boy. However, being the sweet person she was, she would welcome him as long as I wanted him in my life.

"Well, he's going to LA in a few days for an audition..."

"Whoa, whoa, whoa!" Acacia interrupted. "Tom River? As in Tómas River?"

Mom and I exchanged a look while my sister seemed utterly unable to form coherent words. "He, he played at my school assembly. Arabella, you've got to introduce me. Emmy will never believe it!"

"Okay," I said drawing out the y. "As I was saying, when he gets back, we'll check our schedules, but I know he's eager to meet you and Dad."

"I can't believe it! He was at your house, then at my school and I didn't recognize him. I am such an idiot."

My sister rattled on and on, berating herself, not like I corrected her or anything. I was pretty sure she was less than welcoming when she invaded my house and met him by accident. I briefly considered ensuring she would be gone when I brought Tom over for the 'meet the parents' dinner. It might be cruel but when had that stopped me before?

Tom was more than eager to meet my parents; he was downright excited. Kind of struck me as odd, considering how he never talked about his family. More importantly, he'd already met my less than adorable sister. Most guys would have run away screaming but then again, Tom wasn't like normal guys.

# Chapter Six

"What do you mean, you want me to meet your parents?"

"They'll be disappointed if we're so close and don't visit. Besides, you already have the time off," Tom explained.

While he was doing cartwheels about dinner with my family, I was a little more hesitant. Tom didn't seem too fond of his and I found that worrisome. He seemed to get along with everyone, but I knew from personal experience family was different.

"About that, next time how about you let me ask for my own time off?" My voice shook as I tried to rein in the anxiety.

Getting two weeks pre-approved time off gave me no excuse not to go with him to LA for his audition and some alone time. I'd been genuinely looking forward to it until he dropped the bomb about meeting his parents.

"Sorry." He shrugged, not looking very sorry at all. "I already had Geo on the phone."

Remembering how he'd saved my ass at work, I gave him a quick peck on the lips. "You're mostly forgiven, but don't ever do it again."

He gave me a lop-sided grin. "It's not my whole family, just my parents. My sisters are out of the country and Victor is never home."

The way he said his brother's name was as if he felt contaminated by every syllable. Whatever happened between them was deeper than Acacia's and my petty squabbling. I wanted to ask but every time I tried, he'd either change the subject without really answering or distract me until I forgot. He was far too good at distracting me than I'd like to admit. Who was I fooling? I enjoyed every minute of it.

"When?" I asked, slouching further on my kitchen chair.

"Sunday night. My father insisted we stay at the house rather than waste money on a hotel."

I stretched my arms across my kitchen table and hid my face against them. I felt ill. Not only would I have to withstand a few awkward hours over dinner, now I had to *stay* with them. This kept getting better and better. I hadn't met many of my previous boyfriend's parents since most of the relationships were over well before then. It couldn't be as bad as I was imagining, could it?

"You okay over there?" Tom asked, rubbing the back of my hand.

I lifted my head and rested my chin instead of my face on my arms. "What if they don't like me?"

"Is that what you're worried about?" He laughed. "They'll love you, just like I do."

His words stopped me mid-rise. He'd never told me he loved me, other than in my song but that's not the same. He hadn't actually said the three little words but it was close enough to make me stop and notice.

"Don't look so surprised," Tom said, sitting back. "You must know I love you."

He said it.

No roundabout insinuating, no mumbling, just straight plain English. Why was I still frozen in a half-laying, half-sitting position gaping like a fish? Didn't I love him back? I thought I did but was it really love or the idea of love? It felt too soon to tell or maybe I was resisting, knowing all too well the pain of bad breakups.

I opened and closed my mouth twice but couldn't find anything to say. I know, me speechless? Call the freaking presses. Why didn't I say I loved him back? It would have been the smart thing to do but instead I just did a deer in the headlights impression.

Tom's smile never wavered. Instead, he took my hand and led me into my bedroom where he opened my closet. "Where's the dress you were wearing the first time I saw you?"

"I, I didn't keep it."

The black dress from Club Opal was currently residing in a landfill somewhere. After running from Tom's apartment, I'd ripped the knife-made slit all the way up. It wasn't worth saving since it was a little on the snug side anyway.

"Here it is," Tom announced, pulling out a green sundress I'd had for so long I couldn't even remember buying it, let alone still having it. Looking at it now, I wondered why I'd bought it in the first place. So many ruffles.

"But..." I began.

He lowered the dress and gave me an exasperated look. "You're killing me, Arabella! Have you listened to the lyrics to your song?"

Of course, I had. Every time he played it, I couldn't help but get pulled in plus he'd whisper the words to me as I was falling asleep. I could recite it word for word, but I had no idea what it had to do with my old ugly dress.

"You weren't talking about the black dress at the Opal?" I asked.

He held up the green ruffled nightmare. "This is the dress you were wearing when I first met you. Don't you remember?"

The expression he wore now was what I expected when I didn't immediately tell him I loved him back. Why was he upset about something I didn't remember? Duh, moron! It's because I didn't remember.

"The last time I wore this dress was at my college roommate's wedding five years ago."

I was still pretty human shy back then. The ex-boyfriend I'd nearly drained was at the wedding too and I'd spent a good share of the time keeping as much distance between us as possible. The rest of the event, I sat at the bar drinking ginger ale and feeling sorry for myself while everyone else was dancing and having a wonderful time.

I'd stayed after the bridal party departed to help my friend's parents clean up post-reception. A timid, dark-haired guy had approached me and asked me to dance. He didn't lift his eyes to mine, and I'd refused assuming he was human. I just didn't trust myself yet, being only months after my first taste. I'd cried all night afterward because I wanted so much to be one of the happy dancing guests, not the brooding vampire in the corner.

I snapped my fingers. "Oh my God, you! You were the guy who asked me to dance well after the band quit playing."

"I was the one you turned down." He grinned.

"Hang on," I said. "Did you know it was me at the Opal?"

Tom blushed slightly. "To be honest, I asked for you specifically. I don't really have an agent and have no need for personal security."

"Stalker much? How did you know I worked in personal security?" I asked.

"I saw you at an event a couple months ago and overheard you worked for Geo. I guess I saw it as my second chance. You should wear this when you meet my parents."

"Oh, Tom, it's hideous. I wouldn't wear it to a '90s costume party. I promise to buy something nice to wear but please allow me to burn this thing so it can be put out of its misery."

Tom whipped the dress out of my grasp. "Never. If you don't want it, I'll take it."

"Green's your color but you may have to pad your bra to make it fit right." I laughed.

"Put it on and dance with me?" Tom asked, still holding it like a prized antique. I held out my hand and he began to pass it over but stopped. "Promise not to deface it?"

I rolled my eyes. "I promise."

He helped me pull off my blouse and yank the now too small dress over my head. I left on my jeans and striped socks. Fashion police arrest me now!

Tom took one of my hands and wrapped his arm around my waist. I looked into his beautiful blue eyes as we danced to unheard music. Why hadn't I said yes all those years ago? I hadn't been ready, but now I was.

"I love you, Tom."

"I know," he whispered.

• • • •

THE PLANE TOUCHED DOWN and Tom squeezed my hand in encouragement when the fasten seatbelts light flipped off. I felt grimy from the recycled air and wished I could shower and change my clothes before meeting his parents. However, we were headed straight there after collecting our luggage. Lucky me!

While we were waiting, I excused myself to the restroom to make do with washing my hands and face, as well as trying to tame my snarled hair. I'd bought a new green sundress almost the exact shade of the one currently hanging in Tom's closet. Nostalgia was one of his more endearing qualities. My sink and paper towel bath did little to soothe my nerves. Forcing a smile, I returned to where Tom waited by the baggage carousel.

The drive to his parents' house took almost two hours, even though I swear we only went thirty miles. Tom had rented a fuel-efficient, two door convertible sedan. I understood why when we joined the insane traffic. I could feel my shoulders burning and mentally kicked myself for forgetting my sunscreen. Who goes to California and doesn't pack sunscreen?

When Tom turned into a neighborhood with houses the size of churches, I gave him a sideways glance. His knuckles were white where he gripped the steering wheel and I wondered, despite his earlier optimism, if he was nervous about me meeting his parents too. He even jumped a little when I laid my hand on his leg but recovered quickly, wrapped an arm around me, and kissed the top of my head.

A tall, wrought iron fence, complete with a gate blocking the driveway, surrounded Tom's parents' house. It took him three tries to get the right code so we could get in. As we sped up the driveway, my heart began to hammer. I thought I was nervous meeting his parents believing they were normal but I wasn't prepared for this. The house looked bigger than my elementary school. Why was Tom living in a crappy apartment with a truck older than him when his parents were obviously loaded?

I flipped down my visor and frantically began fixing my windblown hair. My nose was already red from the sun. No matter what I did, my hair stood up at weird angles. Lovely. I can just imagine it now. *Hi, I'm your son's new girlfriend, the clown.*

"Relax," Tom said when he parked in front of what could only be called a mansion. "You're beautiful and they'll love you."

I tried to smile but I knew it came out a pained grimace. Tom slid out of the car and ran around to get my door while I fought with my seatbelt. Why couldn't I get it undone? Maybe it was because my hands were shaking too hard. Eventually I freed myself and Tom helped me from the car.

The massive double doors were dark cherry with stained glass in a very intricate pattern adorning the top. Tom didn't knock. He just pressed the handle and walked in, dragging me in behind him.

"Anybody home?" he called.

"Tómas," a female voice replied from above and to the left of us.

I turned to see the most beautiful woman I'd ever laid eyes on glide down a spiral staircase. Her dark hair cascading behind her, long enough it brushed the bottoms of her fingertips. Full red lips formed a rapturous smile, and her eyes were so dark they were almost black. This was the Hollywood version of vampires.

"You must be Arabella." Her tone wasn't quite so, how can I put it kindly, excited as it had been when she welcomed her son.

"Arabella Simon, this is my mother, Desdemona."

Even her name was gorgeous. She extended a porcelain hand complete with long red painted nails toward me. My stubby natural nails looked embarrassing but went along nicely with my wrinkled dress and wind tunnel hair. I probably looked like a hooker he'd picked up on the way in from the airport. His mother, on the other hand, was dressed in a black wrap-around dress, which hugged her frame as if she'd just stepped off the red carpet.

"It's nice to meet you," I managed to say.

"I've had your room prepared. Go freshen up before dinner," Desdemona prompted.

She'd turned her body toward Tom and addressed him as if I wasn't even there. This was going just swell. Tom gave her a one-armed hug while keeping a tight grip on my hand. I hadn't expected his family to run up and smother me with love but I wasn't prepared for the royalty-like house either. Tom and I were going to have a chat about sharing important details later.

I tried not to gawk like a country bumpkin as Tom led me further into the house. The room Desdemona had referred to was on the main floor all the way on one end of a very long hallway. There weren't any family photos or a brag wall like at my house. I inwardly cringed as we passed what looked like an original Monet, remembering the poem I'd written about fish in third grade hanging on my parents' wall complete with finger painted frame and gap-toothed school picture. First thing I was going to do when I got home was call my mom to tell her to take it down.

"Guest room?" I prompted, looking at the mahogany furniture and heavy ivory satin bed linens.

Tom dropped our luggage and sighed. "Nope, mine."

A giggle escaped my lips before I could stop it. "What, no Spiderman sheets and Ozzy posters?"

"I have those now." He laughed.

I laughed too. "I know!"

This was too weird. Tom didn't fit in this house or in this life. No wonder he wasn't close with his family. While he did dress up well, I'd only witnessed it once; this just wasn't him. Maybe he would be glad for my family's shabby, relaxed nature.

"I'm going to go move the car." He gave me a quick kiss. "Just relax, dinner isn't until nine."

Panic flooded me again. He was leaving me alone? "How do you know?"

"Dinner's always at nine."

When he pulled the door shut, I felt like the room was closing in on me despite the fact this one room was nearly the square footage of my entire house. There was an equally elaborate attached bathroom. Everything was dark green marble with gold fixtures. I wondered if they were gold plated. When I re-entered the bedroom, I expected Robin Leach to appear with a microphone in hand. My dad loved that old show about the rich and famous.

I rubbed the backs of my arms. The house was a little chilly after the blistering California heat outside. After digging in my suitcase for a sweater, I considered tracking down Tom. Being alone in this picture-perfect mansion was giving me a serious case of the creeps. My hand touched the door handle, but I hesitated when I heard voices outside.

"Oh Tómas, she's only a first generation. You are far too good to settle for someone like her," I heard Desdemona say.

"Don't do this," Tom said, their voices fading as they moved away. "I won't have this argument again."

Again? What the hell did that mean? I shook my head as my mind ran with so many possibilities, each more ridiculous than the next. Staying in the room suddenly sounded far more appealing than mingling with Tom's mother who obviously thought I wasn't good enough for her son. Maybe it was a mom thing, but I had my doubts.

My guess is Desdemona had brought it up just outside the door so I'd be guaranteed to hear. Lovely. So much for the 'they're going to love you' pep talk. For once, my lack of vampirism was working against me. Well one for one, dinner will probably prove to be two for two against the golden-eyed freak. At least I could be proud of a perfect score.

A shower sounded wonderful but I was too afraid I'd make a mess. Besides, Desdemona would probably burn anything I touched once I left, lest I contaminate their lives any more than I already had. This was going to be a long week and a half.

Against the far wall was an extra-long couch that looked the least intimidating of all the bedroom furniture. I kicked off my sandals, leaving them in the middle of the floor, and laid down. It was the most comfortable couch in the world. My eyes shut and almost immediately I began to drift to sleep.

I heard the door bump open then closed but I was too far gone to open my eyes. The cushions dipped as someone sat next to me. I snuggled up against the warmth and made an 'Mmm' noise and heard Tom chuckle. He brushed a stray hair from my face then gently stroked my cheek with the back of his fingers.

I jerked awake when the door slammed open. "Get away from her," Tom growled.

# Chapter Seven

Wait. Tom was sitting on the couch with me. Wasn't he? I scrambled up so quickly little sparkling stars punctuated my vision. As my head cleared, I looked from the person beside me to the one standing at the door and back. Once again, I found my mouth hanging open. What a lovely habit I've developed.

"Get away from her, Victor," Tom said again, taking a step further inside the room.

Victor? His brother. Twin brother. Identical freaking twin brother! Again, Tom and I *really* needed to work on his communication skills. Give me a little warning here! Someone needed to pinch me to wake me up from this bizarre nightmare.

The man was Tom's mirror except for his short hair - think cross between professional and Hollywood heartbreaker. He was also dressed in an expensive looking dress shirt and slacks, a shocking contrast to Tom's faded jeans and t-shirt.

Victor made no sign he planned on complying with Tom's request, so I slid down the couch to get away from him. Of course, the skirt of my dress slid all the way up my thigh in the process. Despite their looks, Victor gave off a vibe which made me feel dizzy and nebulous. I subconsciously rubbed the cheek he'd touched with the back of my hand trying to remove the contaminated feeling.

"Nice work, Tómas. Feel like sharing?" Victor asked, reclining back and spreading his arms along the back of the couch.

Keeping my pace even, I made my way to Tom, letting him put a protective arm around me. His eyes never left his brother. Any other time I would have stood my ground and told them both to explain what the hell was going on but the whole situation had me out of my element. I was in personal security for crying out loud, I knew how to take care of myself.

"What are you doing here?" Tom asked, his posture relaxing slightly once I was next to him.

Victor shrugged. "I heard my baby brother was going to be home so I decided to make it a family reunion of sorts."

"Baby brother? Vic, you're three minutes older than me."

Victor looked mildly amused. "Yet, you're still the favorite."

Tom ignored his quip and continued, "Alexandra and Evelyn aren't even here. If you leave, it would be the best kind of reunion."

Victor regarded his manicured nails for a moment before grinning at me again. "Are you going to introduce us?"

Tom said, "No" at the same time I said, "Arabella Simon. It's nice to meet you, Victor."

I was getting tired of this crap. My nap-addled brain had finally caught up with my annoyance. This week was going to be hard enough if they were at each other's throats, the least I could do was try to ease some tension by being a gracious guest. Don't laugh. I can be gracious when I need to be. If that failed, I'd just kick ass and take names. Nobody in California seemed to like me anyway and Victor was asking for it by touching me without permission.

Victor stood and walked toward us. "I look forward to getting to know you better, Arabella."

Tom jerked me out of the way as Victor reached out to touch my shoulder, or at least I think he was reaching for my shoulder. The thought of breaking his fingers crossed my mind but then I remembered I was trying to be gracious. How could someone who looked so much like the man I was in love with put off such an odd vibe? The air seemed permeated with vitriol and testosterone.

When Victor left, I waited ten excruciatingly long seconds before speaking. "What the actual fuck, Tom?"

"He wasn't supposed to be here. Mother must have called him." Tom was talking more to himself than me as he roughly began to unpack the suitcases, stuffing things randomly into a large chest of drawers.

I grabbed his hand to stop him. "We don't have to stay here. We're both adults. Just tell them you changed your mind. We can check into a hotel and forget this ever happened. After you answer a few questions."

For a second, it seemed like he considered it, then he sighed. "If only it were that simple. Besides, you haven't met the one person who will adore you."

"Don't bet on it," I mumbled.

"I promise to explain everything. I just thought I'd have more time." Tom sounded so pitiful I leaned in for a kiss.

After a long shower together and a nap, we headed back through the maze of opulence to the dining room. Even though I hadn't seen the kitchen, I could smell dinner. To continue my amazing first impression, my stomach growled as we entered the room. Please just kill me now.

Desdemona, Victor, and an equally handsome older man were already seated when we arrived. The man I hadn't met was the only one who stood and moved to greet us when we entered. His hair was dark brown and slightly graying at the temples and he had the same blue eyes as Tom, and Victor, but his had a beautiful ring of gold around them. Stifling a shudder at the thought of Tom sharing anything with Victor, I turned my attention to the smiling man in front of me.

"Arabella, this is my father, Lucian."

"It's nice to finally meet you, Arabella." He sounded like he meant it when he took my hand and kissed the back.

I unsuccessfully fought back a blush. Tom obviously inherited his smoothness from his father. Still holding my hand, Lucian led me to the chair to Desdemona's left. Not wanting to be rude by demanding to sit by Tom, I took the pro-offered seat. Glancing down at the massive amount of silverware, I was thankful I knew to work from the outside in.

The painful silence stretched as Victor leered at me. It may have been my imagination but it seemed like Desdemona shifted in her chair to increase the space between us, lest I rub my inferior genetics off on her. If I had been in any other situation, I probably would have put my arm around her. Tom and his father appeared just as uneasy as I felt. I nearly jumped out of my chair when two Hispanic women pushed through a swinging door with platters of food. Again, my stomach made a noise and I felt the blood rush to my cheeks.

"How's the case going?" Lucian asked Victor, breaking the thick silence.

As the food was served, Victor chuckled. "The one between the stripper who accused the banker of rape or the waitress suing the basketball player for falling on her at a game?"

Victor glanced my way and continued without waiting for an answer, "The banker has a solid alibi for the night in question but his refusal to provide a DNA sample looks bad. The basketball player looks like he's going to cave and make a deal. A video taken by someone a few rows up has gone viral, thus pouring on the pressure."

"Our Victor is one of the best defense attorneys in the greater Los Angeles area," Desdemona gushed.

I nodded, trying to look impressed, and hoped my smile didn't look as hollow as it felt. From the sounds of it, Victor was a lawyer that defended sleaze balls. Sounded fitting. I took a drink of water and gave Tom a pleading look. He raised his shoulders almost imperceptibly as if this was an old pattern.

Lucian turned to his other son. "When's your audition, Tom?"

Tom took a bite of whatever was on his plate before answering. I'd been eating out of politeness but I hadn't actually tasted anything. The second course came out and I smiled at the woman who set down my plate but she wouldn't make eye contact with me. I watched as another woman arrived, setting a glass of red wine in front of each of us. Again, out of my forced manners, I didn't refuse, even though I don't drink.

Seems like a strange time to mention this but you may have noticed I'm a big fan of ginger ale while at bars. I'd like to say it was because I was on the job and while that sounds good, it's not the whole story. Vampires, some more than others, don't metabolize alcohol properly. For those like me, a few sips and we're falling down drunk for hours. There are more vampires hospitalized for alcohol poisoning than any other medical emergency. We burn through food double time but alcohol just lingers. Go figure.

While I was commiserating on my alcohol intolerance, I'd missed Tom's answer but I already knew his audition was Tuesday morning. I focused on my plate to discover I was eating what looked like poultry with some fancy vegetables and heavily spiced potatoes. Nice. Too bad my mouth felt like it was full of cotton balls.

"Arabella, what kind of work do you do?" Desdemona asked pointedly, looking at Tom.

It took me a minute to swallow my bite. Nothing like talking with your mouth full to impress the fam. "I'm in personal security. It's how Tom and I met."

He beamed at me from across the table. Somehow, its normal affect was lost when I noticed Victor's smug grin. I desperately wanted to accidentally kick him in the shin but the table was too wide. If we had been at my house, I'd have stuck my tongue out but I was afraid Desdemona would literally die of shock.

"Are you available for private parties?" Victor asked and from his look I knew exactly what he meant.

From his grunt, I thought Tom *had* kicked him. "I work for a security company and don't do side jobs."

Conversation quickly strayed from me because I was obviously boring. I focused on my plate, cutting my food into really small pieces. I felt like a circus freak. Every time I looked up, Victor was watching me. Tom barely kept a civil tone when forced to converse with his mother and brother. However, he seemed to really enjoy talking with his father.

As I watched, I decided I liked Lucian. He and Tom were a lot alike. The only difference was while Tom openly shunned this life, Lucian seemed right at home. I found myself smiling as they bantered back and forth about some new movie. Somehow, I imagined Lucian could feel just as at home in my little cottage eating popcorn from a community bowl than in this fancy dining room. Maybe more comfortable.

"A toast," Victor said after staring at me long enough to make me fidget.

I picked up my water glass and Desdemona sighed. Maybe just a sip of the strangely dark wine wouldn't have me dancing on the table or telling everyone how much I loooved them. Oh yeah, I was a lover not a fighter when I was drunk.

My eyes flicked to everyone's glasses. Victor's had already been refilled twice but was once again almost empty, as were both his parents' glasses. As soon as a toast was mentioned, one of the women quickly refilled them all. Tom's glass looked as untouched as mine. I was surprised when my glass felt almost warm in my hand.

"To new beginnings. May Tómas finally become the star he's always wanted to be and for bringing Arabella into our lives."

Something about the look in his eyes as he was staring me down and when he said the last part, froze my brain for a second. Everyone raised their glasses and drank. I touched my lips to the glass, letting just enough slide past my lips to be cordial.

I recoiled at the taste of blood mixed with a bitter wine. Tom mouthed 'sorry' at me but Victor's smile just widened. The staff had been refilling the glasses from a rather large decanter throughout the evening. Exactly whose blood was in this wine? And more importantly, why hadn't Tom warned me about it?

That was the last straw. I had enough of Desdemona's judgement, Victor's lecherous stares, and Tom's omissions. Dropping my napkin on my plate, I shoved my chair back. Lucian moved to get to his feet, but I held up my hand.

"I'm not feeling well. Please excuse me." I pressed my hand to my stomach, hoping I didn't throw my dinner up onto the table.

No one said anything so I turned on my heel and marched out of the room. I heard a chair scrape against the floor and knew Tom would be right behind me. It was a good thing too; I probably couldn't make it back to his room without a map. Plus, we needed to have a serious chat. The fact I hadn't demanded he tell me everything this afternoon didn't make sense. Was I really that lovesick?

Miraculously, I found the right room and promptly headed for the bathroom to throw up. Over my retching, I heard the main door open and close. I grabbed a handful of toilet paper and wiped my face.

"Arabella?" Tom's voice asked.

"Give me a minute!" I snapped.

After pushing myself to my feet, I ran myself a glass of water to rinse out my mouth. The taste of the stranger's blood lingered so I scrubbed my teeth with my toothbrush until my gums hurt. I pulled the barrette from my hair a little harder than I meant to, ripping out what felt like half my scalp in the process. After a rough brushing, I went back to the bedroom to find Tom sitting on the couch.

Too mad to sit by him and too scared to mess up the bed by sitting on it, I crossed my arms and leaned against the wall. "I think you owe me an apology."

"I'm so sorry," he said, blue eyes pleading.

"What are you apologizing for exactly?" I pushed off the wall. "The fact your family lives in a house the size of my block? The fact you have a twin brother, and for reasons beyond me, you hate? How about the fucked up wine your family drinks at dinner? Or maybe you're sorry you brought me here at all?"

He opened his mouth to speak but I wasn't finished. "Some warning would've been nice, Tom. Rather than shutting down every time I asked about your family, one good rant would have at least given me an inkling of what to expect. But no, you led me here to be completely blindsided by all this."

"I should have told you. I was just hoping..." He let the sentence die off without finishing.

"Hoping what? They'd just welcome me into their open arms? I'd be so impressed by the wealth I'd go along with anything? I just drank a stranger's blood, Tom! Why the hell did you think I'd be okay with that?"

"Are you finished yet?" Tom asked.

"No, I'm sure there's something I forgot. Give me a minute." I refolded my arms.

"While you're coming up with something else I did wrong, why don't you sit your ass down so I can explain everything to you?"

Ah, he could be just as snippy as me. This was going to make for great arguments and even better make-up sex, if we somehow managed to survive this fight. I hesitated for a few seconds so he didn't think he had control of the conversation before sitting as far away as possible, which on this couch was a good six feet out of his reach.

"I don't even know where to begin," he said, sitting back and looking at the ceiling as if it held the answers.

"How about why you're living like a starving artist instead of the heir to a fortune?" Yep, I'd forgotten that one in my little rant but remembered before he could continue.

"Because I don't want this life, any of it. When I walked away, I wanted it to be for good. But no matter how hard I try, I keep getting sucked back in. I'm sure you could see my father and I get along, but I can't understand why he goes along with my mother's crap."

I nodded and tucked my foot underneath me to get more comfortable. I could tell this wasn't going to be a short explanation.

"My dad is only fourth generation while my mother is sixth. Most of the money comes from her side of the family. Not all genetically compatible vampires fall in love, some are pressed into marriage for the benefit of the species."

"Like your parents?"

"Oh, I know my father loves my mother more than anything or why else would he put up with all this? My mother only loves her position in life. Since she needed my father to further her place in it, she married him and produced the seventh generation."

He shifted his position on the couch, bringing us a few inches closer. "I didn't tell you any of this because I didn't think it mattered. This life isn't the one I've chosen. I can't and won't live this way. Like the blood-wine at dinner... That became tradition a couple of generations ago and now it's a symbol of the elite."

My stomach rolled at the thought and Tom must have noticed my green complexion. "Don't worry, no one died for the wine tonight."

I gasped. "Tonight?"

Tom closed his eyes and let out a breath. "For special occasions, like weddings, births, and milestone birthdays, the size of the gathering requires too much for it to be donated so..."

This just kept getting better and better. "Your family murders a human for special occasions? Please tell me the reason you hate your brother isn't something worse than what you've already told me. Oh, and thanks for the warning about the whole twin thing. Good thing your hair and sense of style is different or who knows what I might have done."

Tom's eyes hardened and it made me wonder what his brother had done. "Victor embodies everything I hate about this life. You heard him in there bragging about helping the corrupt get away with any wrong doings. He uses his wealth to get anything he wants: power, cars, women, everything."

Somehow, I knew there was more to it but I let it go when I saw how his hands were shaking. I slid a little closer and reached my hand toward him. He grabbed it and pulled me to him, burying my head in his chest and stroking my hair.

"I'm so sorry I brought you to this terrible place, into this ugly life."

Biting my lip, I knew Tom wanted to get out of this house just as much as I did. But unlike me, who could walk away from it and never look back, he was tied to it. It drained his very soul, making him the monster I once thought myself to be.

I pulled back and gave him a gentle kiss. "Everyone has a crazy family, Tom. Some are just more homicidal than others."

He gave a harsh laugh. "I should have told you everything before we got here."

"Yeah, you should have. I probably wouldn't have believed you but yes, Tom, you really should have."

"About Victor..." he began, but I cut him off. There was only so much I could absorb in one sitting.

"Your brother creeps me out. I'll be happy if we don't see him again before we leave. Now, I'm going to change into my pajamas. You are going to find me some crackers and ginger ale for my stomach. I know very well everyone in the house heard my tirade so there's no way in hell I'm going to go face them again tonight. Tomorrow, we are going to pack up our things and find a cheap motel to spend the rest of our vacation together."

"Actually, I have to stay here," Tom said, scooting away, "at least until after the audition. Then we can go somewhere else, even leave the city if we want."

"Why?" I asked.

"Because I promised my father I would. While he put himself in this mess, he's still my dad and I love him. Plus, I really want you to get to know him better."

"Just until the audition?" I could make it two days, couldn't I?

"Then we can go wherever you want," Tom agreed.

"Good. Fine. Now go get me something to eat before I start gnawing on the couch."

# Chapter Eight

When I rolled over in the morning, I sank further into the feather bed. If this thing weren't like sleeping on a freaking cloud, I would have deemed it a suffocation hazard. Tom and I had fallen asleep curled up together in the middle of the enormous thing, but I am kind of a wild sleeper. Therefore, it was no surprise when I woke up on my stomach, one foot hanging off the side. Rising up on my elbows, I frowned when I discovered I was alone.

With a heavy sigh, I flopped back down onto my pillow face first. Lovely, I was trapped in this lavish prison. After my deplorable behavior last night, I wasn't excited about facing his family alone. Even if the episode wasn't entirely my fault.

The doorknob wiggled and I snuggled further under the covers just in case it wasn't Tom. While my nightgown was ridiculously comfortable, it had been washed until it was nearly see-through. Tom never complained about it, but I wasn't sure I wanted to show anyone else. Much to my relief, Tom's face, complete with long hair, peeked around the door. This whole identical twin thing still had me on edge.

He entered carrying a tray holding a random assortment of breakfast foods, two glasses of orange juice, and a red rose tied with a black ribbon. His attempt at sucking up, much to my chagrin, was working beautifully. I couldn't help it; I grinned at him then rolled my eyes when he laughed.

"Bribery will get you everywhere," I whispered after a good morning kiss.

"I thought you'd be hungry after your lack of dinner," Tom said as I played with the rose.

"Ouch!"

I'd stabbed myself on a thorn. Before I could put my finger in my mouth, Tom had it in his. Let's just say breakfast was quickly forgotten and the make-up sex was just as good as I'd imagined.

"What are we going to do today?" I asked, spreading jam on a now cold piece of toast.

Tom frowned. "I was hoping to take you to the beach but it looks like it's going to rain all day."

"I'd settle for the pool."

Last night, I peeked out the window to find a huge patio complete with an enormous pool. From the looks of Desdemona's pale skin, she wouldn't be out sunning herself and I seriously doubted she liked the rain. I, on the other hand, loved rain, especially warm summer rain.

"My dad asked if I'd spend the day with him since we aren't going to stay as long as he'd initially thought."

"Okay. Once again, what are we doing today?" I asked.

"I was thinking of dropping you off at the mall."

"Do I look like a mall rat to you?" I raised my eyebrows.

He leaned forward and took a bite of my toast. Through a mouthful of food, he continued, "That's not a label I'd ever put on you. I got a call from the guys I'm auditioning with and they said we're invited to a club tomorrow night. I didn't notice anything for you to wear when I unpacked yesterday."

I pulled my toast away when he tried for another bite. "That's because you were too busy cramming our stuff into the dresser. To be honest, I didn't bring my little black dress or fancy shoes. I kind of thought this was going to be a casual thing. What about you?"

Tom closed his eyes and I saw his jaw clench. "Fortunately, or unfortunately depending on how you look at it, Victor and I are about the same size. Since he has a closet full of clothes in his old room, I was going to scavenge something rather than endure an afternoon of shopping."

"Thanks," I said flatly. "But you better have whatever you're wearing cleaned first. I don't want his funk getting on you."

• • • •

LUCIAN AND TOM DROPPED me off at an open-air shopping center a little after noon, promising to pick me up in three hours. Who needs three hours to buy a stupid dress? Maybe they had a movie theatre or something. Shopping was not my kind of fun. I would buy the first thing that fit and be done. After glancing at a few price tags, I needed to amend my previous statement: I'd buy the first thing that fit and whose price didn't rival my car payment.

Easier said than done. Every time I found something cute it was a couple hundred dollars or more. I snorted at a pair of flip-flops retailing for over two hundred dollars. The salesgirl gave me a dirty look. Who shops at this mall?

After deciding against a fancy eight-dollar coffee, I tried a little boutique with cute stuff in the window. Their prices, while still way higher than they should be, were more reasonable. I had almost settled on a simple silver dress with a braided black cord belt when I spotted something that made me suck in a breath. The strapless black dress called to me. I didn't care how much it cost. If they had it in my size, it was coming home with me.

Luck was on my side for the first time since I'd arrived in California. The dress fit like it was made for me. The bodice was form fitting down past the tops of my hips, doing wonderful things for my figure. The skirt was layer upon layer of satiny-soft lace ending in points just above my ankles but only attached where it met up with the bodice so when I spun it flared out to show plenty of leg. I splurged on a pair of matching silver and black heels and chandelier earrings. If I kept this up, I would need to take on side security jobs just to pay my credit card bill. But this was going to be a celebration, right?

All my reckless spending took less than an hour. Great. Now what was I supposed to do? The answer came swaggering down the walkway in front of me wearing a pale green linen shirt and black slacks with a matching suit jacket thrown over one shoulder. Damn, Tom needed to dress up more often. However, it wasn't Tom approaching and I mentally kicked myself for not looking close enough before giving him a beaming smile.

"Could I interest you in some lunch?" Victor asked.

"Are you going to be there?" I retorted, placing my hand on my half-cocked hip.

He grinned mischievously. "How else am I supposed to get to know my brother's new girlfriend?"

Gak. This wasn't about getting to know me; it was about pissing off Tom. I was not going to play his little mind games, so I walked around him. "I'll pass."

He, of course, followed and quickly fell into step beside me. "I'll make it worth your while."

What is it with the River boys that made them so damned persistent? Tom wouldn't take no for an answer either. I stumbled when the answer hit me. Identical twins have identical DNA. Wonderful. This wasn't just about sibling rivalry; it was about survival of the fittest. Please Mr. Caveman, club me over the head and drag me home so I can be the bearer of your demonic children.

"Like I said, not interested." I peered into the window of a shop not really looking at what was inside.

"Oh, come on, it'll be fun. I can show you how we really live." Victor almost purred at me.

I repressed a shudder and started walking again. I'd seen enough last night. "In that case, hell no."

Victor was laughing so hard, he had to stop walking. He was obviously not used to getting turned down or having someone be so blunt with him. Two girls from a store across the way were whispering and pointing at Victor. Why didn't he ask them to lunch and leave me alone? I kept walking in hopes of spotting a ladies room as an escape. I wasn't above hiding.

"All right Arabella, I give. Let me at least buy you a cup of coffee to apologize for last night."

I couldn't believe the nerve of this guy but at least we could drink our coffee in the well-lit and, more importantly, well populated food court. I wasn't sure if it was my security training or self-preservation kicking in but I did not want to be alone with this man. As much as I hated to, I motioned for him to proceed to the overpriced coffee shack. His triumphant grin made me want to punch him in the gut.

I ordered the most expensive thing I could plus a chocolate biscotti. Victor didn't even raise an eyebrow but I had a feeling my fifteen-dollar Grande double shot caramel whip latte wasn't above his budget. I would be pinging off the walls later from all the sugar and caffeine.

Victor waited for our order while I snagged a newly vacated table with an umbrella. The rain had faded to a drizzle but I didn't feel like having a shower with my drink. While I waited, I unzipped the garment bag holding my new dress and popped off the tags with my teeth. He whistled in appreciation when he set our coffees on the table.

"Damn," he said, eyeing my dress.

"Glad it meets your approval," I said flatly.

He chuckled. "You could've just borrowed something from Eve; you look about the same size. And I'm sure my brother is mooching off my stuff."

Huh, I wondered how he knew? Tom hadn't told me any more about his sisters than the rest of this family. Maybe my impromptu meeting with Victor could be useful after all.

"Tell me about your sisters. Alexandra and Evelyn, right?" I tried to remember.

"Lexi is the oldest. She lives in Italy, where Eve is visiting at the moment. Eve's the baby of the family and just graduated high school this year. They look a lot like our mother but have Lucian's coloring. Eve's about your height but not so... curvy."

I frowned at his comparison as he was once again eyeing my 'curves'. I thought it was interesting he used his father's name and not his mother's when describing his sisters. The family dynamic was solidifying more and more.

"Why doesn't Tom like them?" I asked then recoiled when I burnt my tongue on my lava hot coffee.

"Whatever gave you the idea he doesn't like them?" Victor asked, carefully sipping his drink after watching me scald myself.

"What he said yesterday about a family reunion," I said, gesturing like it was obvious.

"Tom likes the girls just fine. He's just not a fan of big get-togethers."

I wonder why? I stifled a shudder remembering what he said about special occasions. I dunked my biscotti in my mug while I thought about it. Victor continued to stare at me while I did my best to ignore him and people watch.

Once our coffees were gone, Victor scooped up my bags and offered his hand, which I pointedly refused. "How about I give you a ride home?"

"Maybe I like spending my afternoon shopping," I retorted, reaching for my bag.

Victor raised an eyebrow skeptically. "Somehow I doubt that very much."

I gave up on trying to get my bags as he kept them just out of reach. "Fine. I just don't want to go back to that house."

"Done," Victor said, offering me his jacket since the rain had picked up again.

I only took it because my yellow tank top was getting soaked. The last thing I needed around Victor was a see-through shirt. From the glances he kept sending my way, I almost wished my shorts were longer. His coat smelled really good, faintly of sandalwood and cologne, when I pulled it around my shoulders. He led me to the covered parking lot and pressed his key fob. The cherry red Aston Martin chirped as the alarm disengaged. Eat your heart out, Mr. Bond!

"No way," I whispered under my breath, not caring he could hear me.

The car was beyond beautiful. He opened the passenger door for me after stowing my bags in the trunk. I slid onto the tan leather seats and a low moan escaped my lips. I was a real pushover for a sweet car, especially a fast one. This was obviously very new since it, like mine, still carried the new car smell. When he turned over the engine, the car absolutely purred.

"Music?" Victor asked.

"Doubtful you have anything I'd listen to," I mumbled, annoyed at myself for forgetting who I was with while I fawned over the car.

"Feel free to flip through stations until you find something you like," he suggested while backing out of the parking spot.

He'd put his arm behind my seat when he backed out and hadn't removed it afterward. I leaned forward, avoiding his touch, and began playing with the electronic satellite radio screen. Deciding to be really evil, I chose a death metal station. Satisfied when the singer began screaming at a million miles an hour, I sat back with a smug look on my face.

Just as I'd expected, Victor put both hands back on the wheel and looked anything but comfortable. The next song wasn't nearly as angry and he began to smirk.

"What?" I asked.

Instead of answering, he flipped the radio off and scrolled through the menu on his mp3 player. When the same song which had just been playing on the radio started, I crossed my arms over my chest and slunk further down in my seat. I should have picked opera or something similar but that would have driven me crazy in my caffeine-altered state.

He laughed. "Sorry to disappoint you."

I ignored him and stared out the window. I'd never been to California before so as we cruised down the streets I marveled at the palm trees and the brightly colored exotic looking plants. The traffic was lighter here than on Tom's and my trip from the airport but travel was still slower than cold tar.

After a while, Victor turned off the main road and headed up to the hills. "I think you should take me back. Tom is going to freak out when he can't find me at the mall."

Victor lifted his cell phone from his pocket without answering me. After a few seconds, he began talking. "Hey Dad. I wanted to let you know I picked up Arabella at the mall. I'll have her home by dinnertime. Bye."

"Hey!" I exclaimed.

He hadn't even left time for a response. At least, if I went missing, Lucian knew the last person who'd seen me alive. I realize it sounds harsh but seriously, Victor gave off a serial killer vibe. You know the ones who use their good looks and affluence to lure young women to his secret lair. Where he tortures them until he gets bored and murders them. Maybe I need to stop watching action movies and start watching more chick-flicks.

When I shuddered at the thought of watching anything with a large-chested bimbo working through adversity to find true love, Victor gave me a wary look. Annoyed with the whole situation, I continued to pout and look out the window. Maybe if I wasn't having any fun, he would take me back. Yeah, right and maybe Desdemona would hug me when I arrived.

"Do you want to drive?" Victor asked, breaking the silence.

"How lost do you want to get?" I laughed without thinking. The last thing I wanted to do was encourage this man.

He chuckled and pulled off the road. "You can't get me lost. Besides, I'll give you directions."

I really wanted to drive this car, but I didn't want to give him the satisfaction of finding out anything more about me. When he opened the passenger door, I refused to get out.

"Come on, Arabella. I saw the way you looked at the car. You know you want to," he coerced then added, "I also happen to know there are no speed traps between here and my house."

That did it. I wasn't going to get a ticket for this creep but if I could abuse his car without reprimand, I was all for it. Without replying, I clicked my seatbelt release and got out, this time accepting his proffered hand.

After adjusting the mirrors and seat, I peeled out. Victor grabbed the dashboard as I threw my head back and laughed. He'd asked for it. I shifted and tore around a corner, dangerously close to the guardrail.

"I've only made two payments. Let's try to make it last through the third," Victor said as I whipped around another corner, gravel pinging the undercarriage as I hit the shoulder.

A mischievous grin slid onto my face and I could have sworn Victor paled slightly. Boo hoo. The big bad vampire was afraid of my driving. He didn't give me any directions as we wove back and forth up the hills passing only a few cars. The houses were getting larger and larger with the spaces in between growing as well.

"Slow down or you'll miss the turn," Victor said when we passed a hideous brick monstrosity.

I revved the engine once more before easing my foot off the accelerator. I saw the tree lined drive on the left before Victor could point it out. My right hand twitched toward the emergency brake in anticipation of scaring the crap out of him when I skidded us onto the drive.

"Not so fast, Speed Racer. It's the next one," Victor said, reading my mind.

I squinted ahead but only saw a sharp corner sign. There was no way I was going to risk flipping us over trying to skid into something I couldn't see. I might drive like a maniac, but I didn't have a death wish. I slowed to what felt like a crawl and took the ninety-degree turn, tires still squealing slightly.

"Home sweet home."

This house wasn't as monstrous as the ones we'd just passed but still rated on the holy crap scale. It was a ranch style, faced with stucco and river rocks. I pulled in front of the four-car garage and Victor pressed the automatic door opener.

Compensating for something, Vic? I expected it to be filled with other expensive cars. Instead, there was only an old Mustang up on blocks mid-restoration. The rest of the garage was full of random other crap like exercise equipment, two beat up motorbikes, and a collection of power tools. Total man cave.

As much as I hated myself, I couldn't tear my eyes from the Mustang. "What year?" I asked as I got out.

"Sixty-nine," he said, running his hand lightly over the primer-colored hood.

Once I was out of the car and watching him from further than arm's length, I realized I really didn't want to be here, especially alone. "That was fun. Take me back. Now."

Victor chuckled and headed out the open garage door. "The clouds are finally clearing up. Why don't you relax by the pool and I'll get us something to drink."

"Hey!" I called as he disappeared from sight.

I ran around the car and nearly slammed into him as I turned the corner. He reached out to steady me so we didn't crash to the ground. There was an awkward moment where his hands lightly grasped my upper arms. When I looked up into his eyes, I hesitated; they seemed a deeper blue than Tom's. He slacked his grip and ran his fingers gently down my arms, goosebumps raised at his touch. My head suddenly felt stuffed with cotton candy instead of, well, brain.

I stepped back. "Sorry. I don't mean to be rude but..."

Victor laughed and turned his back on me as he headed for the front door. "Yes, you do."

"That's beside the point! I don't want to relax by the pool or have a drink. I don't even want to talk to you. Take me back," I demanded.

He ignored me and went into the house. God, he was infuriating! I had two choices, sit out on the front step or go inside and keep making pointless demands. It was extremely hot and muggy now the rain had stopped and he probably had air conditioning. Frowning, I followed him inside. I expected opulence equal to his parents' house but his obviously expensive furnishings were minimal in a feng shui kind of way. The colors were shades of beige and dark brown with just enough metal and glass to keep it from feeling institutionalized. The scent of leather and sandalwood perfumed the air.

From my position at the door, I couldn't see Victor. There was no need to strain my ears to find him though, just the noise of clinking crystal and pouring liquid. I entered the stainless steel and granite kitchen to find him topping off two glasses of red wine. His kitchen was bigger than my kitchen and living room put together.

"I don't drink," I said flatly, leaning against the wall.

A grin twitched on his lips before he licked a drop of wine from his finger. "You just don't drink the right stuff."

Victor held out the glass and I raised my eyebrows, making no move to take it. He shrugged and walked past me. Maybe my bitchy attitude was finally starting to get on his nerves.

"Are you coming?" he asked in a jovial voice.

So much for annoying. I pushed off the wall and followed his voice. I stepped into a sunken living room with two full walls of windows looking out at the city below. I bet the view at sunset was breathtaking. Victor stood by a sliding glass door balancing the two glasses in one hand. Beyond him was a patio with a small pool feeding into a larger one.

Suppressing another sigh, I lifted my chin and walked past him and flopped very unladylike onto a lounge chair. Kicking off my sandals, I reclined and closed my eyes. Maybe I could take a nap before he got tired of me and took me back for another fun filled River family dinner.

I heard Victor set the glasses on a tiled table and pull a chair closer to mine. When I smelled the distinct scent of blood, my eyes popped open.

"What the hell?"

Victor had cut open his thumb with a pocketknife and was adding a few blood drops into each glass. "You don't know much about vampires, do you?" he asked before putting his thumb in his mouth to stop the bleeding.

As I mentioned before, vampires don't properly break down alcohol but what he said about not knowing much about vampires was true. Just like sex, my parents avoided talking about anything uncomfortable, and my genetic condition was on the far side of the uncomfortable scale. Probably why I nearly killed my poor ex-boyfriend the first time I'd tasted human blood. Learning by experience, both pleasant and unpleasant, was how I'd learned the little I did know about my band of genetic freaks.

I leaned away when he pushed one glass closer to me. "I know enough."

He closed his eyes and pinched the bridge of his nose as if fighting to keep calm. "You say you don't drink then had a conniption fit last night when you were given something you actually could. You need blood mixed with the alcohol so your body will metabolize it properly. Try it," Victor said again, lifting the glass for me.

Let's see. Drink alcohol I know won't agree with me while I'm sitting with a man who obviously has ulterior motives. Oh, and as a bonus, I get to drink *his* blood along with it. Riiiiiight. Just how stupid did he think I was?

The more I thought about it, the angrier I became. Despite my best efforts of protest, he'd gotten everything he'd asked for. Tom had the same uncanny ability to get his way as well. My thoughts went back to Tom's explanation about how vampire genetics changed from generation to generation. I'd thought he was referring to his eye color but maybe there was more to it. Goosebumps rose on my arms as a feeling of dread spread through me.

As if my body had a mind of its own, my hand reached out and took the wine glass. While my brain screamed for me to stop, I lifted the glass to my lips and swallowed a good mouthful. The wine was better than last night's with a hint of dark chocolate. Victor's eyes held mine as I moved as if under someone else's control.

He got up and sat next to me on my chair. It was as if I was paralyzed. He reached up and touched my hair then laid the palm of his hand on my cheek. My heart began to pound and tears touched my eyes.

"No wonder he chose you. You are so easy to control," Victor whispered as his hand slid down my face to rest on my shoulder, causing my tank top strap to slip down.

He leaned in and asked, "Do you give this to me?" His breath sent tingles all over my body as it caressed the skin of my throat.

I couldn't move. I couldn't breathe. When I blinked my eyelids fluttered in the ecstasy I knew would come if I told him yes. My breath came out in a gasp when his lips touched my neck in a whispering kiss.

"Do you give this willingly?" he asked again, tracing his fingertip along the vein in my neck.

I licked my lips and drew in a shuddering breath. My brain screamed 'no' but my lips whispered, "Yes."

# Chapter Nine

There was no pain when his teeth pierced my throat. A moan of ecstasy escaped my lips and my eyes fluttered closed. I heard the wine glass shatter when my arm dropped like a stone. Victor wrapped his arm around my torso, pulling me off the chair and against his chest. I hung like a rag doll, unable to resist, not that I even wanted to anymore.

In my passion-induced fog, my brain's will to fight slowly began to disappear. With every pull he made on my blood, I yearned for more. Euphoria exploded in my consciousness and I reveled in it. I was getting lightheaded but wasn't sure if it was because I had forgotten how to breathe or from blood loss. At some point, I stopped caring.

I fell back against the lounge chair and heard a loud splash. Was I in the pool? No, I didn't feel wet except for the hot sticky dampness on my neck and shoulder. Somewhere on the edges of my senses I thought I heard dogs fighting. Dogs don't like water; no, that's cats. Why are they splashing?

"Arabella! Can you hear me?" a slurred voice asked.

"Hmm," was the only thing my mouth could manage.

I felt pressure on my neck followed by excruciating pain. My eyes flew open but a bright light blinded me. My arms felt like lead weights when I tried to block the light. The pain was slowly growing and my stomach cramped in response.

"Gonna be sick," I mumbled.

Someone helped turn me onto my side before I threw up. The pain in my neck flared as I vomited. The dogs were still fighting but now they were screaming too.

"Arabella, hold this." The slurred voice lifted my dead arm and set my hand against my throat, but I didn't have the strength to keep it there. "Honey, you're going to have to try and help."

"Too tired," I sobbed. "Hurts too much."

"I know but you have to try." The voice was getting clearer but so was the pain.

He moved my hand again and this time I managed to keep it in place but when he let go, the pressure all but disappeared. My eyes had fallen closed so I forced them open again. This time the light wasn't as bright and I was lying on my side facing the pool. People were playing in it. Why were they playing when I was hurting?

"Shhh," I whispered at the noisy pool goers.

A third person jumped into the pool and began breaking up the game. Must be the person with the slurred voice. I hoped they weren't too drunk to swim. My desire to protect them made me push off the lounge chair so I could help, even though I was in no condition to do much of anything.

My cheek and shoulder scraped against the concrete patio as I fell; my legs didn't seem to work any better than my arms. I cried out when the pain in my neck flared again. Suddenly, there was shouting from the slurred voice and one of the players was getting out of the pool.

"Oh God, Arabella. I came as fast as I could." Tom's voice was frantic as he pulled me into his arms.

"You're getting me wet," I mumbled but stopped when my throat burned.

He moved to lay me down again. Wanting him to hold me, I reached out and only managed to smack him in the face. I needed his arms around me to stop the cold from permeating my body. Instead, I found myself lying on the concrete in a puddle of pool water.

After pushing aside my flailing arms, in a strained voice he said, "I've got to stop the bleeding. It's going to hurt."

He lowered his head, and I heard screaming. My screaming. Suddenly, my arms worked and I pushed in vain at his shoulders. The pain surged to a new level and I sobbed helplessly. I was going to die. Please let me die.

• • • •

"ARABELLA," A VOICE whispered.

"Hmm?" I breathed.

We were swaying in a slow back and forth motion making me nauseated again. I squeezed my eyes tighter and swallowed hard. My throat still hurt but not as much.

"You're safe now. I'm so sorry," Tom whispered over and over.

It was then I pieced together what had happened. Victor somehow tricked me into giving him my blood and he had nearly killed me. The dogs fighting in the pool must have been Tom and Victor. The slurred voice was Lucian, but it hadn't been his voice that had been slurred; it had been my hearing. I groaned and began to cry.

Tom held me close and stroked my hair. My stomach began to settle as I recognized the gentle sway of a moving car. My breath came out in gasps as I cried harder and harder. Everything was wrong. Victor had manipulated me without me knowing. What he had done was worse than rape. He had taken a part of me, taken part of my soul. My heart sank as I realized Tom could do exactly the same thing.

I woke up sometime later in the center of Tom's feather bed, too weak to move. Someone had dressed me in a pair of silky soft sweats and wrapped me in a blanket. I had no memory of getting from the car to Tom's bedroom, let alone changing clothes. My lips were chapped and my mouth was dry. When I turned my head, my neck pinched and I stifled a scream.

"Arabella, don't move." Tom held a cup with a plastic straw to my lips. "Here."

It took me a minute to remember how to use it. When I did, the strong taste of orange filled my mouth, causing me to choke and sputter a cough. Coughing was the most painful thing I'd ever felt, with the exception of having my throat ripped out earlier.

Tom put the glass down and pulled me close. I wanted to bury my face in his shirt and cry, but I needed to know the truth. It took me a few swallows before I could remember how to work my mouth.

"Tell me you never did that to me," I whispered, my voice hollow and raspy.

"I, I'd never hurt you!" Tom's voice was frantic.

"You know what I mean. Have you ever controlled me?" I tried to keep the sob from my voice but it snuck through on the last word.

Tom hesitated for a second before answering and I felt my heart break. He had manipulated me, just like Victor but instead of taking my blood, he'd taken my heart. I pushed against him, but I was so weak I couldn't have pushed a kitten away let alone a vampire.

"Listen to me. I never forced you to do anything you didn't want," Tom said, a sudden fierceness to his voice.

"How do you know?" I sobbed. "How would *I* know?"

He kissed my forehead and pulled me against him. "I can feel when you resist and I stop. That's why I didn't follow you the first night after the club. I wanted you to make the choice. I would never hurt you; you have to believe me."

"You should've told me. I don't know if I'll ever be able to trust my feelings around you again."

He lowered me back onto the bed and tucked the blanket around my shoulders. "I'll let you sleep." The hurt was obvious in his voice.

I didn't want to be alone but I didn't want him here right now so I closed my eyes against the tears and listened as he left. Of all the things he kept from me, this was the worst. I desperately wanted to believe he'd never made me do something I didn't want but Victor's ability to manipulate me so easily made me wonder. I stared at the ceiling through tears, wishing I were anywhere else.

When the door creaked open a short while later, I rolled away, not wanting to face anyone yet. I heard the light scrape of a chair on the hardwood floor and someone sit. Squeezing my eyes shut, I slowed my breathing and hoped whoever was watching me would think I was asleep and leave.

"Arabella?" Lucian's gentle voice was barely more than a whisper.

I rolled to face him and opened my eyes. He'd changed his clothes after the adventure in the pool, now wearing dark slacks and a polo shirt. His face looked like it had aged ten years since this morning. I bit my lip but didn't say anything.

"I can't excuse away what Victor did," he began. "We shouldn't have left you alone."

My voice still sounded raw. "What happened between them?"

Lucian gave me a sad smile. "The boys have always been fiercely competitive. There was a girl who preyed on that weakness. Tom saw it for what it was but not before it drove Victor nearly insane with the challenge."

He took a deep breath and folded his hands in his lap. "The girl saw Tom wasn't going along with her mind games and became obsessed with winning his affections. After a while, it worked. I honestly believe he loved her and she loved him, but Victor couldn't accept defeat."

"He killed her, didn't he?" I asked just above a whisper.

Lucian shook his head. "He made Tom watch as she begged for more. She recovered but it broke her mind."

I closed my eyes and swallowed hard, both horrified at the thought and understanding of it. I'd felt the need to give Victor everything and he was more than willing to take it. "What does any of this have to do with me?"

"My best guess is Victor sees Tom's happiness as his own failure. After all these years, he's still trying to best his brother."

"Why hasn't anyone done anything to stop it? Victor is not above the law. I, I could press charges-"

"And say what? He wouldn't have taken your blood without your consent," Lucian said with a bitterness I'd never heard before.

My head swam from the blood loss as I pushed myself into a half-sitting half-leaning position on the pillows. "But he made me say yes."

"You know that and I know that, but can you prove it?" Lucian opened his hands in a show of helplessness.

This wasn't fair. Victor was a monster and nothing could be done. Well, I wouldn't let him win this time. He may have stolen my blood but he couldn't control me. Given time, Tom and I could work through this.

I reached over and grasped Lucian's hand, he patted mine with understanding. "Don't tell Tom I told you. I just couldn't bear to see him lose someone he loves so much again."

He stood up and fixed my blanket before pushing my hair back from my forehead in a very father-like gesture. "Get some sleep. I'll tell Tom to bring you something to eat later."

When he turned his back, I blurted out, "Thank you, Lucian, for everything."

He half-turned, giving me another sad smile. "No, Arabella, thank you. I love my children more than anything in the world and seeing them happy is what every father wishes. I just wish one's happiness wasn't at the expense of other's."

I dozed off and on for the remainder of the day. Around sunset, I crawled out of bed and headed for the bathroom to take a bath. I felt contaminated but too weak to stand in the shower. Catching a glimpse of myself in the mirror, I froze.

My skin was ghostly white, dark circles heavy under my pale-yellow eyes. The contrast between my ashen skin and black sweats didn't help either. My lips were almost as pale as the rest of me. Good God, Victor had sucked the color right out of me. Literally.

Turning away from the specter in the mirror, I knelt to turn on the hot water in the tub and waited until steam started to billow around me. Keeping my eyes averted, I rose and snagged my hairbrush from the counter. After piling my hair into a messy bun high on my head, I dropped the sweats onto the floor. My hand brushed my bandaged neck and the desperate need to see the damage flooded me.

Shivering against the cold, I wrapped myself in a dark green towel and went back to the full-length mirror. Stark red against my ivory skin were four jagged scars starting halfway up my neck and ending at the curve of my shoulder. Thanks to whatever Tom had done, the ugly marks looked weeks old.

When I reached up to touch them, a strange mix of pleasure and pain swirled within me. Dropping my hand, I ran back to the toilet and dry heaved. There was nothing in my stomach left to lose. Victor had infected me. I knew even if I scrubbed my skin raw, his contamination would be inside of me.

I looked at the deep tub and considered sliding under the water until the pain went away permanently. Then, I remembered the promise I'd made to myself that I wouldn't let Victor hurt Tom anymore. After another shuddering breath, I stepped into the stingingly hot water, its bite reminding me I was still alive. And as long as I was, Victor wouldn't hurt the man I loved ever again. If it meant I had to kill him myself, I would.

# Chapter Ten

I woke the next morning to the sound of the shower. Tom hadn't come back to the bedroom before I'd fallen asleep. Lucian had brought more orange juice and a rather large bowl of chicken soup for my dinner around ten. He hadn't answered when I asked where Tom was. Considering how deeply I slept, there may have been a sleeping pill in my soup.

Sometime in the middle of the night, I'd felt Tom lay down beside me but I was too tired to respond. I hoped he hadn't taken it as another rebuff. Shifting in the bed so I could see the bathroom door, I waited. My stomach twisted, not knowing what to expect.

In between my conversation with Lucian and dozing, I had time to process what had happened. I wasn't angry at Tom anymore but his omission about his abilities hurt me deeply. If he'd just talked to me, I would have known to be on my guard with Victor. I didn't need anyone to save me but I needed to know what I was working with, or against in this case. I knew I loved Tom. He wasn't making me feel the way I do about him, about us. We could get through this together. We had to.

His hair was neatly pulled back when he finally emerged. I'm sure the horror was clear on my face as I took in the highly tailored navy suit that made him look too much like his brother. Tom's expression fell and he turned away.

While rummaging around in the dresser, he said, "Dad's going to drop me off. I don't know how long I'll be gone."

"Tom, I..." I began.

"It's okay, Arabella," he interrupted, his back turned, profound sadness still in his voice.

I threw back the covers and stumbled across the room. "No, it's not."

He looked down at my trembling hand on his arm but wouldn't meet my gaze. "I'll take you to the airport after the audition. You shouldn't have to stay here any longer."

"Damn it. Don't do this!" I snapped. "How are you going to wow them if you're doing your Emo impression? I'll be here when you get back, then we're going out and painting the town red."

His troubled eyes finally lifted to meet mine. I stepped closer and pressed my lips to his to convince him I was serious. For a second, he stood frozen then clutched me to him, kissing me back. When he pulled away and pressed our foreheads together, he was just as out of breath as I.

Tom stammered, "We don't have to go out. We can just leave. We can..."

I pressed my finger to his lips. "Stop babbling and pull yourself together. Yesterday is forgotten. Well, not completely but today is your day. I'll be here when you get back."

His eyes darted to my neck then back to my eyes. He kissed me once more. "I'll be back soon."

"You better be," I warned. "Who knows how much trouble I can get into in a place like this? Besides, I'm raiding Eve's closet for something to wear tonight. You couldn't pay me enough to go back to the mall."

"Upstairs, second door on the right. She won't even notice, half the stuff she's got in there has only been worn once and will never see the light of day again."

Herding him toward the door, I smiled. "Don't worry about me. I'll raid the kitchen then catch up on my tan. I bring new meaning to the word pasty."

He gave me another kiss at the door, putting both hands on my shoulders. "I love you, Arabella."

"I know," I said, giving him a smirk.

The big house was eerily quiet as I began to snoop. There was no sign of Desdemona, not that I was complaining. In the kitchen, I helped myself to some leftovers while sitting on the counter. I considered drinking from the milk carton but finished the pitcher of OJ instead. If Tom's mother came in, she'd see how uncouth I was but at this point, I just didn't care. I was tired of pretending to be someone I wasn't.

After my snack, I headed upstairs to Eve's room. I expected a replica of Tom's uncomfortably formal bedroom and was therefore unprepared for what I found. The large lavender and gold canopy bed was made but the room itself appeared to be in organized chaos; just like every other normal teenager on the planet. The vanity was covered in dozens of bottles of perfume, hair products, and makeup. Tiny Polaroid pictures of friends were stuck around the edges of the mirror. Books were piled everywhere, some open while others were stuffed inside as a type of bookmark.

Posters of teen idols covered an entire wall and half of another. Eve's entertainment center was open, revealing a huge TV and a stereo system my sister would literally kill for. The built-in shelves on one side were full of more books and hundreds of CDs. In the middle of the shelf was a picture of Tom and a girl I assumed to be Eve.

Eve's chocolate colored hair was cut short, not quite long enough to touch the tops of her shoulders. Victor had been right; she looked like a young Desdemona, only happier. She and Tom were laughing at the beach, hands full of sand dollars. It was the only family photo I'd seen in the entire house.

There were two doors inside the room, the bathroom and what I was here for, the closet. Of course, I chose the wrong one first. I gasped when I opened the closet. It was bigger than my bedroom then I realized it wrapped around itself, meaning it was twice as big as I'd originally thought. Good grief, it was a good thing I had all day to search in here.

Hell, I could've outfitted myself for my whole vacation and Eve wouldn't have noticed unless I happened to pick one of her favorite shirts. Then I remembered she too was on vacation and probably had all her favorites with her.

The first rack was nothing but t-shirts and tanks followed by jeans and miniskirts, each organized in a rainbow from dark to light colors. Can you say OCD? The backside had the 'nicer' clothes, not that everything in here wasn't nicer than everything I owned. My thoughts went back to my new dress trapped in Victor's trunk and I wondered if there was any way I could get it back. It seemed like an unfair death for something so beautiful and expensive. My wallet hurt just thinking about it.

After unzipping more than a dozen garment bags, I sighed in defeat. This really *was* going to take forever. It was like a cruel combination of shopping and hide and seek. Everything I'd found was either too business wear or too formal. I needed something to make me look good even in my current unnaturally pale state. Black was definitely out.

I tried on a teal backless number but it was too tight across the hips. The next dress I found was a deep sapphire and had promise. Its neckline was wide just resting on the tips of my shoulders with long flowing, sheer sleeves. The top was loose while the skirt was form fitting but stretchy enough to fit my hips. It was a little short for my normal tastes but it was the best thing I'd found so far.

I went to the full-length mirror and looked at it from all angles. When I lifted my hair, my eyes fell on the red marks on my neck. It was too hot to wear a turtleneck; maybe I could cover them with enough makeup no one would notice. The rest of my color was slowly returning but I still looked pale. My next stop was the patio beside the pool.

I tried on a few more dresses before deciding to wear the blue one. I draped the garment bag over my arm and thunked noisily down the stairs thinking I was the only one in the house.

"What are you doing?" Desdemona's accusation made me jump.

"What?" I asked, grabbing the banister so I didn't tumble down the remaining stairs and break my neck.

"What do you have there?" She pointed to the bag.

I tucked a stray hair behind my ear and continued down the stairs. "Tom said I could borrow something of Eve's to wear tonight."

"Really?" She put her hand on her hip.

"Considering the dress I bought yesterday is being held hostage in your other son's car, I think it's more than fair," I snapped.

She regarded me coolly as if all of this were entirely my fault. In her mind, it probably was.

I resisted the urge to roll my eyes. "Listen, it's obvious you don't like me. Fine, you don't have to. Tom and I will be leaving tomorrow anyway. Just suck it up and be happy for your son. He's about to become the biggest damn thing since peanut butter."

I thought she was going to explode. Her whole body trembled, red splotches appeared on her cheeks and her full lips tightened into a thin line. Maybe she wasn't used to being told off but that wasn't my problem. I had a date with a deck chair, Mr. Sun, and maybe a sandwich; I was hungry again.

When I walked by, her hand snatched out and grabbed my arm. "You *don't* deserve him."

I gave her a dark look but her grip didn't loosen. "I think Tom's old enough to make his own decisions. Now get your hand off me before I break your arm."

Desdemona's hand dropped in a flash but the hatred was still burning in her eyes. "You are undoing everything I've worked for."

I turned my back on her. "Don't care. I'll be on the back deck if you'd like to continue our friendly chat."

She hated me but I didn't care. I had a feeling telling her where I was going would guarantee she wouldn't go anywhere near the pool. A smile touched my lips at that thought. So much for playing the gracious guest.

A cold turkey sandwich and soda later, I lay out in the sun for a little over an hour, rotating constantly. I'd pulled off my bikini's straps to avoid strange tan lines. Just as I'd expected, no one bothered me as I soaked up Vitamin D.

After eyeing the pool, I decided against taking a swim. Yesterday's adventure with water was still too close to the surface. Instead, I took a nice cool shower before attacking my hair. I didn't want to pay for someone to do it for me, so I needed some time before Tom got home to get it just right.

The time in the sun helped my paleness. If nothing else, it put some pink back in my lips and cheeks. Too bad it made my new scars show up even more. Maybe I could use a scarf. I pulled my hair up into a fancy French twist and began searching for a curling iron. Yeah, right, why would Tom have a curling iron in his bathroom?

I tiptoed back up to Eve's room and snagged hers from the vanity where I'd spotted it earlier. I also poked around in her jewelry box for earrings, settling on some faux sapphire drops long enough to reach my shoulders. Damn, this girl had good taste.

I'd just finished my makeup when I heard the door open. "In here," I called, turning my head from side to side making sure everything was even.

Tom barreled in, picking me up and twirling me around. "Arabella, everything went great. They loved your song."

It made my heart swell to see him so happy. "I told you they'd love you."

After setting me back down, his smile slipped a little. "I told them I'd let them know if we would meet them later. I wasn't sure..."

"Tom, I'm fine." I skipped over and held out Eve's dress. "I found something to wear, got some sun, and pissed off your mother. Sounds like the only thing I have left to do is party the night away."

He looked wary. "I'd be happy just to go somewhere and have a quiet dinner."

I shook my head. "Not a chance. Like it or not, you're going to be famous. Better get used to being the center of attention whether I feel like a million bucks or not."

The club was packed when we arrived, but we didn't stand in line. Tom went right to the door and gave his name where they quickly ushered us inside. I could get used to this kind of treatment. I'd looped a wispy blue and silver silk scarf he'd found around my neck to help cover my scars. More for him than me because every time he saw them, he looked ill.

"Tómas!" a man in sunglasses and an obnoxious orange shirt called. His bottle-blond hair was long in the back but very thin in front and the top. He took off his sunglasses as we approached, revealing hazel eyes sparkling with delight.

"Mr. Redding, this is my girlfriend, Arabella Simon," Tom said hurrying us over to the loud man's booth.

Mr. Redding yanked my hand forward when I offered to shake his. "Ah, the inspiration for the billboard's next top song."

I tucked a wayward curl behind my ear. "Nice to meet you, Mr. Redding."

He made a disgusted noise. "Bob. Only my employees call me Mr. Redding."

"Okay, Bob then." I laughed as I slid into the booth next to Tom.

Bob snapped his fingers at a passing waitress who scurried over. "Champagne for everyone."

Before she could turn away, I added, "Ginger ale for me, please."

Bob made the same disgusted noise. "This is a celebration, Arabella."

"I know, Bob, but having me pass out within the hour wouldn't make it very fun for me, now would it?"

Bob laughed and slapped Tom on the back. "Feisty! I like that. How serious are you about my boy Tom here? Maybe you'd prefer someone in management."

I smiled remembering my boss's similar suggestion. "I'm pretty fond of him." I stole a kiss before continuing. "Besides, California isn't exactly my kind of place."

We followed Bob from club to club over the next few hours. At each one, he introduced Tom to more and more people. I almost had a heart attack when he introduced us to one of my favorite bands. Hopefully, I hadn't sounded too much like a babbling fangirl.

The last club had several other famous faces I recognized but by then I was past my star-struck phase. Bob excused himself to talk to the club's owner as Tom and I took our seats. It was hotter in here than the other clubs and the scarf felt like it was smothering me. I tugged on it again and Tom frowned.

"I'm fine, just a little warm."

Before he could respond, Bob put his thick hand on Tom's shoulder. "Ready to work some magic, my boy? They've got some extra equipment in the back. Give these good people something to look forward to."

I understood then. Bob wanted Tom to do an impromptu gig. I opened my mouth to protest but Tom only grinned. With an encouraging squeeze to my hand, he stood.

"You okay by yourself?" he asked.

"I used to protect your ass, remember? Go. I'm sure Bob will take good care of me."

Tom was gone about half an hour before Bob went up on stage to introduce him. The longer I sat here, the warmer I got. Tom was out of sight so I untied and removed my scarf, feeling instantly cooler.

The crowd hesitantly applauded and several people asked who was playing in loud whispers. I smiled knowing they were about to be amazed. Tom looked relaxed when he sat on the lone stool and adjusted his guitar strap. He looked so different in his black silk shirt as opposed to his long-sleeved t-shirts he normally wore on stage. I liked the change.

When I heard him strum the first few notes of my song, I smiled. He smiled back at me through the stage lights and dark club. There was so much emotion in his expression I almost missed what Bob was saying.

"Too bad you aren't taking to LA. Can you tough it out for the next two weeks?" Mr. Redding asked.

"Two weeks?" I asked, tearing myself away from the music.

"Tom didn't tell you? He's agreed to stay in the area for the next two weeks so we can get everything settled and start cutting some tracks. I've got some big plans for your boy."

"Oh," I said, turning back to the stage.

He hadn't said anything, probably because he'd anticipated my reaction. There was no way I could stay another two weeks. Two days had almost been the death of me. Not only would I lose my job, but I also needed to get away from his family until I came to grips with his past.

"I'm sure Tom can survive without me for a little while, Bob," I finally managed.

Bob laughed and clapped when the song ended. The crowd cried for an encore to which Tom happily obliged. This was his dream and had been long before I'd come into the picture. There was no way I was going to make him choose. I'd go back home while he began to live out his dream. Hopefully, I'd be a part of it when he got home.

I had recovered from my shock by the time Tom rejoined us at the table. His smile was infectious and he radiated joy. Rather than dwell on our impending time apart, I'd enjoy every minute up until then. His blue eyes narrowed when he looked at my now exposed neck. I slid out of the bench and pulled him to the dance floor as a distraction.

"Do you want to leave?" he asked as we began to sway to the slow song.

"No, but I can't stay here either," I said, resting my head on his chest so he couldn't see my neck.

"Bob told you." It wasn't a question. I nodded and heard him sigh. "I won't make you stay."

"Good because I think if I have to stay in your mother's house one more day, we'll kill each other. You need to focus on you right now. We have all the time in the world. Just promise not to forget me when you're famous?" I teased.

He lifted my chin and brushed his lips against mine. "Never."

# Chapter Eleven

I pulled up in front of my parents' house and parked. I'd been back from California for a week, one of the longest of my life. At this rate, I'd have to take a second mortgage to pay for my out of network calls. Tom and I had talked at least an hour every night. Geo made sure we had crazy unlimited on our work phones but personal use was restricted to emergencies only.

Tom was extremely busy with gigs and the studio time Bob had arranged. I, on the other hand, had almost nothing to do. Since my boss expected me to be gone another week, he had to scrape up a few pathetic assignments for me. There were no jobs tonight so I had agreed to go over to my parents' for dinner.

The dessert was still hot when I grabbed the pan from my passenger seat. Mmm, cherry cobbler. I hadn't seen my family since getting back. The normalcy of the quintessential US family would be a nice contrast to the insanity I'd left in California. I'd even promised myself to be nice to Acacia, if I could.

"Knock, knock," I said, opening the front door.

The sound of Acacia's viola cut off mid-note and Mom called to me from the kitchen. The smell of meatloaf and potatoes greeted me. It looked like someone was working on a scrapbook; the living room was an explosion of photos, colored paper, and stickers.

"I brought dessert." I put my white ceramic pan on the counter.

"Acacia, you have ten more minutes!" Mom called before the screeching started up again.

"She's excited to see you, you know," Mom said, giving me a hug.

"No, she's just hoping I brought Tom with me."

After returning the hug, I flipped a dining room chair around, straddling it. Mom gasped and crossed herself when she looked at me. I scrunched up my face at my absentmindedness. The temperature had gone through the roof this week so I was wearing a tank top and shorts. Which under normal circumstances wouldn't have caused her to react. It was the lovely red scars which had yet to fade that nearly made her faint.

I lifted my hand to cover them. "It's not what you think. I had a little accident on my trip."

She turned back to the stove and stabbed the boiling potatoes with a little more force than necessary. At least she hadn't locked herself in the bathroom; maybe she was getting better. When I heard her praying under her breath, I realized I thought too soon. She kept her attention on the potatoes long enough I decided to give her a few minutes alone to collect herself.

I got up and headed to Acacia's room, hoping she had something I could use to cover my neck. She was still struggling with her song when I rapped on her door.

"Hey sis, got a shirt I could borrow?"

Her room looked like it had exploded but that's the norm. It was the new paint job that caught my attention. Three of her walls and the ceiling were painted black with an overlay of intricate white and red designs. It looked really good.

"If I can stop practicing, you can borrow a shirt," she mumbled, playing the same five notes over and over.

"Not my call but since I just sent Mom on one of her panic attacks, I doubt she would notice." I pushed the door closed behind me.

"Whoa. What did you do?" she asked, laying her instrument carefully on her bed before running over to me.

"I... had an accident?" I said, annoyed that my explanation came out as a question.

I would have liked to warn her but she never took anything I said seriously. Her romanticized view of vampires kept getting in the way of a healthy dose of fear.

"Get attacked by a gardening tool or something?" she asked, poking me in the neck.

The familiar mix of pain and passion surged through me and I slapped her hand away. Her black-rimmed eyes grew wide and she stepped back, heading for her closet.

She handed me a black see-through button up shirt with a high collar. "Here."

"Sorry. My trip didn't go as well as planned," I said, pulling on the shirt.

She flopped down on her bed and began putting her instrument away. "Tom didn't get signed?"

"Oh no, they loved him. He's still down there getting the Hollywood treatment. It was his family that made the trip ultra-bizarre." She gave me a questioning look, so I continued. "He's got a sister a year older than you."

"Any brothers?" she asked, snapping her case closed.

"No," I said coldly.

"But you said he did," she almost whined.

I closed my eyes and took a deep breath and repeated my new mantra. *Be nice to your sister. Be nice to your sister.* How could I put this in a way she'd understand?

"He's way too old for you," I said, sitting next to her. My hand lifted unconsciously to my neck. "And not very nice."

Her eyes narrowed then widened in understanding. "Whoa," she breathed.

"You're telling me. Let's not talk about it so Mom can make it through dinner?" I suggested.

Acacia adjusted my collar to cover my scars a little better. "But his sister's cool?"

"I didn't actually meet her. She was visiting his other sister in Italy. I saw her picture though and pilfered from her closet."

"Are you coming to my concert next week?" she asked as she shoved her case under the bed.

"It's summer, why do you have a concert?"

"I'm in City Honors," she muttered while still kneeling on the floor. "Thanks for knowing."

Crappy sister guilt made my stomach clench. "I'll be there," I promised.

She gave me a wary look. "Where's this coming from?"

"Seeing how bad it can be, I'm thankful we're only moderately messed up. Now let's go help with dinner."

Like usual, Dad ended up calling to say he'd be late. He ran his own plumbing business, therefore worked when his clients needed him. No one made a big deal about it, as it had been that way for as long as I could remember. I was mildly disappointed though, hoping to spend time with him.

I was helping myself to another huge spoonful of mashed potatoes when Mom asked, "How was your trip?"

Acacia and I shared a look before I answered, "Hot. Tom's family is weird."

"Arabella says he's got a sister about my age. Maybe she'll come and visit," Acacia added, stealing a forkful of potatoes from my plate.

I pretended to stab her in the back of the hand before cutting a bite of her meatloaf and stuffing it in my mouth. Mom gave a satisfied smile as she watched us and I knew our diversion worked perfectly. Maybe, my sister and I could get along under the right circumstances.

"I'd like to meet this boyfriend of yours. When is he due back?" Mom asked while serving my dessert.

"End of next week," I said through a bite of boiling hot cobbler. She must have put it back in the oven.

"He'll be back for my birthday?" Acacia asked.

"Yeah, I guess he will. Are you doing anything special for your big seventeen?"

She shrugged. "Probably not. I'm grounded, again."

"If you'd quit skipping school to run around with those, those..." Mom trailed off but we all knew what she didn't say.

"My grades are fine, besides summer school is sooo boring. Look at Arabella, she didn't go to college and she's doing fine."

Taking another bite of cobbler, I amended her statement. "I did go. I just didn't quite finish as planned. There's a difference. You should go. You'll be able to do much more with your art if you get a degree."

She scowled at both of us. "I thought we were on the same side. Now you're ganging up on me!"

Acacia shoveled the rest of her cobbler into her mouth before shoving her chair back and stomping to her bedroom, where she slammed the door.

"I wasn't that bad when I was a teenager, was I?" I asked.

"Worse," Mom said, pushing her cobbler around. "Well, not about school, boys were another matter. And you know what kind of boys your sister prefers."

I was silent for a moment. "They're not all bad, Mom."

"I know," she said quietly then added, "I just wish she'd find someone closer to her age than yours."

"Thanks, Mom. I didn't realize I was old and decrepit."

She huffed a laugh. "That's not what I meant."

"I know. Just realize she's trying to find herself. If she finds a nice human boy, great, but don't be disappointed if she ends up with another vampire."

"Like you?" she whispered as a tear ran down her cheek.

"God, Mom! It's not like I'm dying. Tom's the most normal guy I've ever dated."

"But he hurts you," she sobbed.

I shoved back from the table and knelt in front of her. "He doesn't hurt me."

She turned her head away when I pulled open my shirt to reveal my scars. "Mom, he didn't do this. He loves me and I love him."

She looked up at me with tear filled eyes. "Then who hurt you?"

I flopped back onto my butt with a huff. "I don't want to talk about it."

We didn't talk at all while I helped clean up dinner. Music thumped from Acacia's room but neither one of us wanted to deal with her teenage angst right now. When we got everything washed up and put away, I heard the back door rattle.

"Dad's home."

Mom walked over to the fridge and began pulling everything we'd just put away back out to reheat for him. Her disappointment and unease were still clear on her face and in her slow, careful actions.

"Arabella! I was hoping you'd still be here when I got home," my dad said as he dropped his lunch pail on the counter.

"Hi Daddy," I said, taking a hug that rocked me from side to side.

My dad was tall and rail thin no matter how much he ate. Maybe he's where I got my metabolism and not my vampire genes. He had the same military cut since he'd enlisted right out of high school. His career in the army was cut short when he injured his back during basic training. Deep lines were etched on his face from years of worry about his two daughters, plus a lifetime of hard work. I thought he was the most handsome man on the planet with Tom a very close second.

He spied what was left of my dessert while Mom was microwaving a plate of dinner for him. "My favorite!"

I handed him a fork and we sat at the table. He ate right out of the pan. A right reserved for dads and grandpas only, except when you lived alone then you could eat however you wanted. I couldn't help but smile as he shoveled it in. We were a lot alike.

"How was your trip?" Dad asked.

"Fine," I said, shifting so Mom could move away what was left of the cobbler and put his plate of dinner in front of him.

He noticed her guarded mannerisms but waited until she disappeared into the back of the house to ask, "Okay, what did I miss?"

I sighed. "Same old, same old."

He frowned and took a bite of potatoes. "I hear your sister is taking it well."

Her music continued to thump in the background. "That wasn't my fault this time."

He chuckled and continued to eat. I lay the flat of my arms on the table and enjoyed the comfortable silence.

"When are we going to meet this new boyfriend of yours?" Dad asked.

"He'll be back next week. Hey, Acacia says she doesn't have anything planned for her birthday, do you mind if I put something together for her?"

He started choking and I pounded him on the back. "I really did miss something."

"Oh, come on, we're not that bad." He gave me a skeptical look and I relented, "Okay, sometimes it's bad but I'm trying."

"All right, if she can make it through the week without getting detention or being expelled, you can throw her a party."

"Really?" Acacia squealed, making us both jump. "Oh, thank you, thank you, thank you, Daddy!"

He waved her off when she kissed him on the cheek. "Good grief. Whose house have I walked into?"

Acacia turned to me. "You need to invite Sophie, Carlie, Chelsea, and Emmy. I'll give you their cell numbers. Oh, and no nuts; Chelsea is allergic to nuts."

Dad and I exchanged a look then both smiled. This was going to be an adventure, but I needed something to fill up my free time. I tried to focus as Acacia babbled on and on about who needed to be invited and what kind of cake she wanted.

When I unlocked my front door, my phone was ringing. I swore and ran around looking for where I'd plugged it in to charge. I found it at the same time the ringing stopped. The screen showed several missed calls. When it started ringing again, I almost dropped it.

"Hello?" I gasped.

"I thought you'd forgotten about me. I've called twice," Tom teased.

I flopped down on the couch. "I told you I was going to dinner at my parents' tonight."

"How'd it go?" he asked.

"Fine. I'm throwing a birthday party for my sister next Sunday. Are you going to be back?" I asked, swinging my legs over the arm of the couch.

"You couldn't keep me away a second longer than Saturday."

"Good because I'm considering finding a temporary boyfriend. I've got needs too you know," I teased.

"Don't you dare. I want you to be good and lonely when I get back."

"Not helping," I laughed. "What's new in sunny California?"

"Eve's home," he answered brightly.

"That sounds like a good thing."

"I was thinking about bringing her home with me for a visit. Maybe she and Acacia could get to know each other."

"Great minds think alike. I was mentioning the exact possibility to my sister this very evening. Too bad you won't be home by Friday; she's got a concert. I had no idea she was in the city's honor orchestra."

"Maybe I could get an earlier flight," he suggested.

"On second thought, that might not be a good idea. I plan on locking you in my bedroom when you get back. I don't want to have to explain that as the reason I missed her concert. This is the first one she's ever asked me to go to."

"If you keep making threats, I'm going to seriously consider catching the next flight out of here."

"Still staying at your parents' house?" I asked, trying to change the subject.

He sighed. "Yeah. Victor dropped off your bags from the mall yesterday."

My hand lifted to my neck and I sucked in a breath. "Did you see him?"

"No. He's been smart enough to avoid me. I can't wait to come home." He sighed again.

I liked the way he considered here home, rather than the house where he grew up. He'd mentioned his lease expiring at the end of next month. Neither one of us had brought up the topic of moving in together but I knew he wasn't actively looking for a new place either. My mother would have a fit. Not only would I be living in sin but with a vampire to boot.

"I miss you, too. Any ideas for the party?" I asked.

He was silent for a second and I could imagine his face scrunched in thought. "I'll ask Eve. She's a big party planner."

"Great. According to Acacia, I'm old so having someone closer to her age helping with the party will make her happy."

"Where are you having it?" he asked.

"I haven't started on the details yet. Maybe I could rent the Opal and possibly get a really good deal on hiring a recently signed musician to play a few songs. That would be a birthday to remember."

"I don't think you can afford me," he teased.

"Can we work it out in trade?" I suggested slyly.

"There you go again with your threats."

# Chapter Twelve

"You ready yet?" Cassie called from my living room.

I was in the bathroom fighting with my hair. I'd just finished a job and wanted to re-braid it after a scuffle in the park, which had turned out to be an annoying misunderstanding. Who knew the woman I was protecting had arranged a secret meeting with her *married* boyfriend? Why was he stalking us from the mall? More importantly, why doesn't anyone tell me anything?

According to the X-rays, I hadn't fractured his wrist but the ER doctor was pretty sure his nose was broken. He was going to have to come up with one hell of an explanation to tell his wife. Yeah, just call me the ass kicker of adulterers everywhere. Now I could look forward to another crappy review from a stupid babysitting job.

I gave up and left my hair down, just flipping a few strands over my shoulder to cover my scars. "Let's go."

The concert was at Riverfront Park open-air theatre. I had a picnic basket already stocked with finger foods and a bottle of sparkling pear juice. Cassie was supplying the blanket and company. Mom and Dad were going to be late since he had the truck and Mom's car was in the shop again.

We jumped into Cassie's tiny car and sped down the street. She sang along with the radio while I spaced out. Planning my sister's birthday party kept me busy during the day while the nightly phone calls with Tom had me literally counting the hours until his plane landed tomorrow.

"Are you coming to the party?" I asked Cassie.

"Are you kidding? If I don't see this boyfriend of yours soon, I won't be able to afford tickets." She laughed and I smiled.

Bob's promotion of Tom had spiraled out from local to national during the two weeks he'd been in LA. I'd even seen a clip of him playing at a club on the national news last night. However, seeing him on TV only made me miss him more.

"Did you get the club booked?" Cassie asked as she pulled into the parking lot next to the park.

"Yep. I now owe the bartender a favor plus Tom agreed to play there the following Saturday."

Everything was set for Sunday at the Opal. Soda and punch were going to replace the alcohol. I loved my sister but I wasn't going to get arrested for contributing to minors. The invitations had been sent, food had been ordered from Acacia's favorite restaurant, and she'd made it through the week without any troubles at school. Maybe she just needed the right motivation. Thus, why I was spending my Friday night listening to a high school orchestra.

We found a spot where we had a good view but not too close to the walkways or smelly food venders. Cassie laid out the blanket while I scanned the black and white clad musicians for my sister. Acacia wasn't as easy to find as I would have thought. There were several girls who looked like her with black hair and too much eyeliner, each looking like they were waiting in line for the next Emo concert rather than waiting to play Beethoven.

My mouth dropped open when I finally spotted her. She'd stripped her hair back to its natural color; the russet-gold shone in the late afternoon sun. The white dress shirt looked odd, considering I hadn't seen her in anything but solid black for as long as I could remember. The thick black eyeliner was still present but, hey, it looked good on her.

"Hey sis!" I waved.

Her cheeks flushed and she half raised her hand in my direction. What was this all about? An introvert my sister was not. I scanned the rest of the group looking for the few friends of hers I knew. Most of the group were boys, human boys. Hmm? No wonder my sister was out of her element.

"Where's your sister?" Cassie asked, pouring us both a glass of the fancy pear juice.

I pointed to where she was standing with her best friend Emmy. "The redhead standing with the short fashion-Goth."

Cassie raised her eyebrows. "When did she change her hair?"

I shrugged. "Beats me. Last time I saw her she looked like the other girl's clone."

The concert was fabulous. They played both classical pieces and movie themes. I was bummed Tom had to miss it. There was no point in trying to record it on my crappy cell phone. I'm pretty sure a potato would have better audio quality. After the intermission, there were groups of small ensembles and soloists. Emmy did a solo of something dark in a minor key, no surprise there. The sky was getting dark when the conductor explained he'd saved the best for last.

My mouth dropped open again when Acacia stepped forward. She introduced her song in an almost quavering voice then lifted her instrument. It was a medley of Celtic ballads. Her first notes were hesitant but then she let herself go. I couldn't believe how good she was! The crowd erupted when she lifted her bow and smiled.

Cassie and I jumped to our feet whistling and hollering. Acacia continued to smile and bow until the conductor ushered her back and thanked everyone for coming. We quickly stuffed everything in the basket and pressed against the crowd toward the stage.

When I found Acacia again, she was talking to a tall blond boy. She looked uncomfortable but smiled when he touched her hair before giving in to his friend's beckoning. I recognized the wistful look on her face as he walked away. When he glanced my way, I noticed his bright green eyes. This was getting more and more interesting. I'd have to ask about him later.

My sister was huddled, whispering frantically with Emmy, when I was finally within speaking distance. "Acacia, that was amazing!"

She smiled and a blush rose to her cheeks. "Thanks."

"You want a ride?" I offered then frowned when I remembered we'd brought Cassie's car with only two seats.

Acacia waved to someone over my shoulder. "Nah, Dad's here."

"There's my star." Dad put his arm around her shoulders.

"Daaaad," Acacia said, blushing even more but not pulling away.

"See you Sunday. Remember to dress up, this place is fancy," I said, holding the 'a' longer than necessary to emphasize the point.

"Nice job, Emmy. See you on Sunday," I said, giving the girl a light tap on the shoulder.

She gave me a look most teenagers gave their parents. It reminded me of when someone catches a whiff of stinky cheese or finds out their parents still have sex. Wonderful, I have officially joined the ranks of the old.

I was still reveling in my discovery of my talented sister when I unlocked my front door. Cassie had dropped me off at the curb and sped off toward her late night job with some high-ranking city official. Between the surprise of my sister's hidden talents and anticipation of Tom's return, there wasn't much chance of me getting any sleep tonight, even though I was feeling pretty exhausted.

I had taken several steps inside my front door before I noticed flickering candles on every flat surface. "Um, hello?"

I had a pretty good idea of who was behind this but I still smiled so hard my cheeks hurt when Tom poked his head out of the bedroom holding yet another pillar candle.

"You're home early," he said, pulling me into his arms.

"You too."

"I wanted to surprise you but I'm not done setting everything up," he said, offering me a rose from a vase on the table.

"I could go and come back later," I offered but not meaning it in the slightest. There was no way I was letting him out of my sight.

His grip tightened and he kissed me until I was lightheaded. "I'm not planning on letting go of you for the next thirteen hours."

"Thirteen? That's rather specific."

He laughed, running his fingers through my hair. "That's when Eve flies in. I think they frown on nudity at the airport."

I gasped when his hands ran down the side of my face and slid down my neck. The wave of desire almost completely eclipsed the pain I usually experienced when something touched my scar. Much to my surprise and disappointment, Tom's hands dropped and he stepped back.

"I'm sorry," he said, shoving his hands in his pockets.

My thoughts were a confused jumble as I reached for him. "For what?" I asked, still overcome with the lingering sensation.

"Your scars. I, I can wait until you're ready." Tom seemed to be forcing the words out.

I blinked in confusion. Had he confused my gasp of pleasure as pain? He hadn't hurt me. I *was* ready damn it! I'd been more than ready for two weeks. Why was he acting like this? Anger simmered as my brain cleared.

"If you don't get back over here in two seconds, I'm taking you to the floor, Mister. I don't know what your problem is but suck it up."

Tom looked at me like I was crazy. "I thought, I felt... I told you I wouldn't make you do anything you didn't want."

"Jesus, Tom! I was the one worried about trusting my feelings around you, not the other way around. What do I need to do so you know it's what I want and not what you want?"

He took a hesitant step toward me, and I relaxed my clenched fists. This is not how I'd imagined we'd celebrate his homecoming. The last thing I wanted to do was fight but he was being an over-sensitive idiot.

I flipped my hair back so my scars were visible and he flinched when his eyes dropped to them. "It happened and I won't pretend it didn't. I lived, Tom, but if you're too afraid to touch me, he wins. Don't let him win again."

Before I finished the last word, I was in his arms. We had the reunion I'd imagined but he wouldn't take my blood even though I begged him to. He willingly gave his but I knew it was too soon for him to take mine. The memory of him having to take it to save me was still too fresh in his memory. For now, sharing everything else would have to be enough.

• • • •

TOM WAS COOKING BREAKFAST when my phone rang. He really couldn't cook but wanted to try making pancakes and bacon. I'd already eaten two pieces of blackened pork to hide his mistakes. Hey, I liked bacon-dust.

"Hello?" I laughed, snagging another overly done piece.

"Can I invite one more person?" Acacia asked without any pleasantries.

She'd already invited almost fifty people. What had I gotten myself into? Good thing, Mom and Dad had insisted on picking up the tab for the catering. The club reservation and invitations had cost enough. Plus, I still had to go pick up her gift today.

"There isn't time to send out another invite, Acacia."

"That's okay I have an extra at the house. I can drop it off."

"Boy or girl?" I asked.

She hesitated for a moment. "Does it matter?"

Definitely a boy. "Older or younger than your ancient sister?"

Tom cursed as his pancake folded during the flip and I stifled a laugh. He was trying ridiculously hard and it was damn cute. Or maybe it was my shamrock apron he was wearing over his bare chest. Bare skin and frying bacon were not a good combination but he had to experience it for himself before he'd believed me.

"Younger," she huffed. "He's in my orchestra group. I mentioned Tom would be there and he got all excited and stuff. I thought it would be nice to invite him."

"Okay, okay. Don't freak out! I just didn't want a Raphael repeat at your party. Hey, it isn't that cute blond boy I saw you talking to after the concert, is it?"

"Ugh! You're as bad as Mom." She hung up.

"Trouble in teen paradise?" Tom asked, tossing another mangled pancake into the trash.

"I think my sister is falling for a human."

"Really?"

"He is pretty hot, for a high school kid." When he frowned, I gave him a devious grin. "She's luring him in with promises of meeting the famous Tómas River."

"Playing the celebrity card, huh? Should I be nice to this kid? Yes!"

He'd flipped the pancake perfectly this time and I rolled my eyes at his personal triumph. "He looked okay but boys only want one thing."

Tom turned to face me, putting his hands on my hips and pulling me close. "And what is that?"

I gave him a long suggestive kiss. "How long until your sister's flight lands?"

He looked over my shoulder to the wall clock. "Not long enough."

I let my breath out in a huff. They'd be staying at Tom's tonight since my tiny house only had one real bedroom and my foldout bed sucked. Tom, on the other hand, had a very comfy and sturdy futon. I snagged another piece of bacon and headed for the fridge before my hormone-fogged brain got distracted again.

"Your pancake's burning, lover boy," I called over my shoulder.

"Shit!"

I pulled the butter and syrup out of the fridge, pausing long enough to cool myself. He was just as distracted as I was. Running around wearing only my silk bathrobe probably wasn't helping Tom's concentration. It would be a miracle if we got to eat any of the breakfast *and* make it to the airport on time.

"You want me to drive?" I asked as I used a knife to cut my tough pancake.

"Could you? My truck wouldn't start and I had to use a cab to get here."

I rolled my eyes. "Maybe you should think about letting that thing rest in peace. It's done its time in the name of music."

"Nonsense. Bertha just needs an oil change and a new battery," Tom explained.

"Why am I not surprised you named your truck? But Bertha? You aren't naming any of our kids."

As soon as I said it, I wished I hadn't. Tom's fork stopped halfway to his mouth and his eyes met mine. He looked absolutely horrified. Dropping my gaze to my plate, I focused on the hard disc masquerading as food.

"You're not pregnant, are you?" Tom asked, his voice just above a whisper.

I nearly choked on my bite. "God, no! I was kidding about the kid thing."

He looked at his fork then put it down, the chunk of pancake still stuck to the end. "Oh, oh that's... good."

His tone didn't suggest it was 'good' at all. What the hell? We hadn't even talked about living together, let alone kids. Did he want kids? I didn't even know if I wanted kids. Ever! This was too much. I counted back to my last period in my head, twice. Maybe I was a few days late but I'd never been very regular.

"I think I'll jump in the shower," I said, pushing my chair back and trying not to run from the room.

I really didn't have time for a shower before we had to leave but I needed the excuse to be alone. I turned on the water and pulled my hair up so it wouldn't get wet. I yelped when I stepped into the frigid water.

"Are you okay in there?" Tom asked from the door.

Hell no, I wasn't all right! We were having a nice breakfast together and we jumped from a safe neutral topic right into waters I seriously wasn't ready for. "I'm fine. Just didn't want to meet your sister smelling like a yak."

Tom pulled back the curtain, making me jump back into the water stream, soaking my hair. "In that case..."

From the look in his eyes when he stepped in to join me, we were going to be late to the airport. At least we could use the excuse we were showering. I just wasn't going to bring up the fact to his sister we had been doing it together.

When he pulled me to him and breathed against the skin of my neck, the non-scar side, I knew we were going to be really late. It's a good thing he was strong because my legs gave way beneath me when his teeth broke my skin.

# Chapter Thirteen

"We got hung up," Tom explained again as I wove through traffic.

Eve's plane had been delayed at LAX, thank God, but had still landed over half an hour ago. He was on his cell phone with her now, telling her to relax and we'd be there in a minute.

"I can see the sign for the airport now. Just meet us out front so Arabella doesn't have to pay for parking." He paused for a second. "Yes, she's with me."

I heard a squeal from the other end of the conversation and smiled. Tom had warned me Eve was super excited to meet both Acacia and me. Good thing, too, because the first thing we were doing once we rescued her from abandonment was to hit the mall to buy a gift for my sister.

I curved around the drive circling the front of the airport, looking for the girl from the picture. I slowed when I saw a singular blonde girl standing with two bags at her feet.

"There she is." Tom beamed.

Huh, changing your hair color must be in style right now? I pulled against the curb and flipped on my hazard lights. Tom jumped out and engulfed his sister in a hug before scooping up her bags. I popped the trunk release, hoping they would fit in my nonexistent cargo space.

Before I could open my door, she jumped in and gave me a one-armed hug. "Hi Arabella, I'm Eve. I love your car! I wanted one but Mom bought me a stupid Mercedes instead."

"Hi Eve. I love it too."

Tom stood outside for a second before Eve remembered he was there. She jumped out and flipped the seat forward but made no move to crawl in back. I bit my lip to hide my smile as I watched him cram himself into my pathetic excuse for a backseat.

"I guess I'll sit in the back," he grumbled.

"Boys," Eve said as she moved her seat forward. "I need to get something for the party tonight. I looked through my closet and I had absolutely nothing to wear."

I glanced in the rearview mirror to meet Tom's eye and he gave me an 'I told you so' look. Flipping my hazards off and peeling out, I headed toward our tiny mall.

"Well, we need to go shopping anyway," I added tentatively.

"Can you drop me at my apartment first?" Tom almost pleaded. "I need to, um, clean up before Eve stays over."

"You should have done that last night," Eve said, turning around to kneel on her seat so she could see him. "Oops, I guess you were too *busy*."

I bit my lip again when I saw Tom blush in the rearview mirror. Eve was a pistol. I knew Tom hated shopping so I took pity on him. At the next light, I made a U-turn and headed toward his apartment.

"I've seen his place when he hasn't cleaned in a while, you *really* want him to at least take a stab at it before you stay there," I explained.

"Thanks," Tom said flatly from the backseat.

Eve flopped back forward and put on her seatbelt. "What is it with messy boys? Fine, we *girls* don't need you anyway."

"Do you want me to pick up something for Acacia from you too?" I asked when Tom leaned into my window for a goodbye kiss.

"Nope, I got her something she'll love while I was in California," he said, sharing a conspiratorial look with his sister. "Have fun shopping ladies. See you later for dinner."

He slapped the roof and I sped off. "Can I stay with you? His place looks kind of, I don't know, sketchy."

"I'd love you to stay with me but I don't have a guest room. Plus, Tom's place isn't too bad, on the inside," I encouraged.

"We'll see," she said, pulling down the visor mirror to touch up her lip-gloss. "You think your sister will like me?"

"I'm sure she will. The only person she fights with is me, other than our parents I mean. Besides, you seem to like the same music plus you're both..." I cast a sideways glance at her, "vampires."

Eve looked about as much a vampire as Tom but I guess that's evolution for you. I could tell now the picture on her bookshelf was several years old. She was prettier than her mother, if that is even possible. Her waist length golden hair contrasted beautifully with her dark tanned skin and dark chocolate-colored eyes. She was definitely more of a girly-girl than Acacia but my sister had been full of surprises lately.

"What are you wearing to the party?" she asked as we parked by the main entrance.

"The dress I bought in California."

Tom told me he'd had it cleaned after Victor dropped it off. It reminded me of my unpleasant incident with the evil twin, but it was my dress. Damn it, I paid for the stupid thing and I was going to wear it!

"I thought you borrowed my dress?" Eve gave me a sideways glance.

"I did and thank you by the way. Mine was otherwise occupied," I explained. I had no idea whether anyone had mentioned the altercation to her and I wasn't going to bring it up now.

"Ah," she said in an all too understanding way. Yep, she knew all about it.

"Well then, black it is. I'm a fan of white but it just doesn't go well with my new hair. I can't believe I'm a blonde Californian. What was I thinking?" She laughed and flipped a few strands over her shoulder.

"I like it," I said as we walked into the air-conditioned bliss.

"I did it to piss off Mom. Boy, did it work. She freaked out when I got back from Italy," Eve said as she browsed through a rack of miniskirts, "but she was still on edge from your visit."

I swallowed. I didn't realize I'd made such a great impression; maybe threatening bodily harm had been a bit much. Eve laughed at my expression and linked her arm through mine then led me to the next shop as if we were best friends.

We continued this way from store to store. She tried on more clothes than I'd owned my entire life but only bought a pair of socks and sweatshirt with a pink moose logo. Whatever floats your boat.

"Hey, Eve," I said, flipping through a rack of clearance jeans next to the dressing rooms. "I need to pick up something for Acacia's birthday and thought..."

"I'd love to help!" she squealed as she came out in her latest outfit.

"You have got to buy that one," I said as she shuffled barefoot to the three-way mirrors.

"It isn't too, you know..." she asked, turning to see it from every angle.

"If you don't buy it, I will. Damn!" I said, holding up her hair so she could see the back.

The dress was a deep, sparkly copper. The bodice wrapped around to tie at the hip then flowed into the skirt which fluttered around her ankles as she spun. Maybe the strapless top was a little old for her but she looked fabulous. When had I become such a prude?

She frowned at her feet. "What about shoes?"

The salesgirl swooped in, another following with jewelry samples. I took a step back and watched them fawn all over Eve. She lapped it up all the while making it very clear what she did and did not want.

Eve ended up with Grecian looking sandals that laced up her very tan, shapely legs. The necklace was cascading loops of copper, brass, and silver and, of course, the matching earrings. I hoped Acacia wouldn't feel outshined. Hell, I felt outshined when Eve came back wearing her sleeveless blouse and denim shorts.

I continued to flip aimlessly through jeans while Eve paid for her haul. I needed a new pair but the thought of trying on clothes made me shudder. Next week, I'd come back. Next week, when I wasn't with the super shopper from Hell.

When Eve greeted me, she had two silk garment bags over her arm, one of which she handed to me. "You're welcome."

"Huh?" was my brilliant response.

"Let's get something to eat. Those cookies I got on the plane were nasty," Eve suggested, ignoring my poorly phrased question.

I followed her, wondering what was in the other bag. They were both black so I couldn't peek without unzipping it. She ordered two veggie sandwiches and espressos for us from the Italian café.

Once we were seated with our coffees, she said, "You'll need to drop that off tonight so your mom can steam out the wrinkles before the party."

"What is it?" I asked as I finally unzipped the bag.

When I flipped it open, I was even more confused. Inside was an identical dress to the one Eve had just tried on but this one was a deep emerald green. I guessed the little bag around the hanger's neck held similar jewelry as well.

"You said you needed something to give your sister. Now she'll look like a million bucks tomorrow night."

"Oh! How did you know her size?"

"Tom said she was probably a size smaller than me. I sure hope it fits. Black goes with green really well so her hair shouldn't clash."

"Black? Oh, she doesn't have black hair anymore." When Eve looked exasperated, I quickly followed up, "Green also looks great with red. She's a redhead."

"Oh, even better. I hope she likes me." There was a hint of sadness in her voice I didn't understand. Maybe Eve didn't have many friends, which was difficult for me to fathom.

"She'll never believe I picked this out by myself," I said, zipping up the bag to protect it from our approaching lunch.

On the way back to the car, Eve suddenly stopped in the middle of the road, making the car waiting for us to cross honk in annoyance. I grabbed her arm and pulled her out of the way, wondering what made her jerk to a stop.

"Do you have any wrapping paper?" Eve asked, glancing back at the mall.

"Most likely."

I knew I had a bunch of gift bags stuffed in the back of my closet but birthday paper, I wasn't sure. The only thing I knew I had was the obnoxious reindeer paper I'd bought last year for Christmas.

"Good, I know Tom doesn't. He *always* sends me gifts wrapped in newspaper." She shook her head. "Boys."

Somehow, Eve convinced Tom she'd rather sleep on my couch than at his place without hurting his feelings. Maybe she just wanted to stay with a girl. I wasn't complaining, she was a hoot. If Acacia didn't like her, her loss. I wanted to keep her and send my angsty sister back to California in her place. Maybe a year with Tom's crazy family would straighten her ass out.

The three of us stayed up until after midnight watching a terrible vampire-alien movie that had us all laughing hysterically. Eve had made chocolate cinnamon pudding, which we'd all eaten straight out of the pot. I'd missed the end of the movie when Tom started licking the remaining chocolate off my fingers.

"What time do I need to get there tomorrow?" Tom whispered.

Eve had passed out on the couch while Tom and I were watching the late-night news. He and I were now having some alone time in the kitchen. Actually, I was sitting on his lap, enjoying his kisses that were becoming less and less gentle.

"The party starts at six and I have the club until ten," I whispered into his ear.

He shuddered and tightened his grip around my waist. "What time are you going to get there?"

I shivered as his breath caressed my cheek. "About five, I think."

Hell, I couldn't think of anything but him at the moment. When he laughed at my response, his breath tingled against my scars and I sucked in a breath. Instead of pulling away like he had last night, he quickly shifted me to his other knee so they were on the opposite side.

"Oh, just get a room, will ya?" Eve called from the living room. "You're killing me in here!"

I put my hand over my mouth to keep from laughing but Tom snapped, "Go to sleep, Eve!"

"Do you want me to take you home?"

"What's the point? Our intentions don't seem to bother her anyway," Tom said, shifting us so we were both standing.

"Just keep it down. A girl needs her beauty sleep!" Eve tried to sound annoyed but a giggle escaped.

"It's not nice to eavesdrop!" Tom snapped.

I slapped him lightly on the chest. "Be nice and put me to bed."

I heard a distinct laugh but Tom surprised me by throwing me over his shoulder and trudging through the living room toward the bedroom still grumbling.

"Goodnight, Eve," I said, peeking out from under my hair as we bounced past.

• • • •

"OUCH!" I SAID FOR THE hundredth time.

"Sometimes it hurts to be beautiful," Eve chimed in once again.

Maybe trading her for Acacia wasn't such a good idea. She'd tricked me into going to the salon with her this afternoon. Stupid me for thinking only she was getting her hair and nails done. Now I was pinned in a chair while some sadistic woman scalped me one hair at a time. I'd already endured getting my head wrapped in foil as if I was afraid of aliens stealing my memories. My tin foil helmet didn't protect me from the demon masquerading as a manicurist. Why do people pay for this kind of torture?

"When will Acacia get here?" Eve asked while the makeup artist added another layer of something to her already perfect skin.

"Three. What time is it?" I asked, trying to turn my head to glance at my watch. "Ouch! If you pull my hair one more time, I swear..."

"Arabella," she chided. "Perfection takes time. Plus, once were done here, Tom won't be able to take his eyes off you. Not like it's a problem anyway."

I smiled at this. Eve hadn't hidden her all too knowing smile in the morning when Tom and I emerged from my bedroom. Maybe that's why I'd let her drag me here without much protest.

Eve turned to the evil woman still yanking and curling my hair. "Is that enough time to make the birthday girl beautiful?"

"Speak of the devil," I murmured as I saw Acacia peer in the window at me.

She looked paler than usual, which is saying something for her. I knew for a fact she didn't like the pampering treatment any more than I did. But if I was suffering, so would she. Besides, if she was going to win over that hunky blond tonight, we were going to pull out all the stops.

Eve batted away the eye-shadow brush when Acacia came in. Her finger and toenail polish were still wet so she shuffle-waddled over to give her a straight-armed hug and kiss on the cheek. My sister looked at me for help and I just shrugged, earning me another yank from the mistress of hair torture.

"I'm Eve. Did your dress fit? Is it okay that we'll match? What color nail polish are you going to get?" Eve rattled off question after question.

I hid my smile when Acacia's eyes bugged out. She couldn't get a word in edgewise as Eve barked orders for the salon minions to descend upon their next victim. She went back to her makeup after another woman plunked my sister in the chair next to me after scrubbing her hair.

"Does she always talk so much?" Acacia whispered.

I knew Eve could hear and noticed a slight frown. "You get used to it." I laughed.

It wasn't fair. Acacia went through the entire process in a little over an hour while I had to endure it for almost three. Damn teenagers and their perfect skin and hair. My sister looked like a Goddess in a black skull shirt, matching plaid skirt, and knee socks.

I was chaperoning both girls to the club tonight. Mom dropped off Acacia's dress earlier this morning but got flustered when Tom came out of the bathroom sans shirt. Crap. I'd hoped they would have had a better first meeting. Mom left the house clutching a paper bag.

I cranked the air conditioning because Eve had a conniption fit when I tried to roll down the windows for the drive home. Heaven forbid our hair get mussed before we get to the club. Both girls were speaking a million miles an hour in my back seat. Oh yeah, they'd hit it off big time once my sister finally got a chance to speak.

We had half an hour to change, touch up our makeup, and get to the club. I would have no trouble but who knew about the crazy seventeen-year-olds in my backseat. Apparently, Eve hadn't turned eighteen yet.

My phone was ringing when I got to the front door. Damn it, why did I always drop my keys in my purse when I got out of the car? By the time I found them and got the stupid door open, the chime sounded indicating a missed call. Whoever called didn't leave a message.

A second later, Eve's cell rang. "What's up?" she answered, corralling Acacia toward the bedroom where our dresses were hanging.

"No, she can't pick you up," she explained while I filled a glass with water. "Because you can't see the bride before the wedding."

I choked on my water and nearly dropped my glass. Through my coughing fit, I heard Eve say, "Relax Arabella, it's just an expression, jeez! Tom, get yourself a ride share, you mooch. We girls have better things to do than schlep your ass around." I heard her toss her phone on the dresser and unzip a garment bag.

"Turn around!" Acacia said briskly.

I put my glass down and tried to stop coughing. When I went into my bedroom, the girls were standing on opposite ends, backs to each other while stripping off their clothes.

"Do I need to separate you two?" I asked.

"I just thought she needed help getting her dress on," Eve explained.

"We're all big girls here. I think we are capable of dressing ourselves."

To my amazement, Eve had nothing to add and was uncharacteristically silent while we got changed and re-primped. Whatever was bothering her seemed to have worked itself out by the time we got back into the car. I had to help them get in with their long skirts. Hell, I was going to need help getting out with mine being so tight across my hips. Time to lay off the cookies and go back to the gym.

Eve was cradling the gold wrapped paper square in her lap. According to Eve, my Christmas paper could double for birthday wrapping. Good to know. Her gift was obviously a book, but she wouldn't let me see before she'd wrapped it. Tom's gift for Acacia was also a surprise.

"Thanks for the dress, Arabella," my sister said when we pulled into the 'Employee Only' spot alongside Club Opal, "and the party."

"Don't thank me yet. Maybe your party will suck," I said, using the door as leverage to get out without ripping my tight skirt.

I helped Eve out first, who in turn helped the birthday girl out of my car. Acacia stumbled when her sandal slipped on the door runner. Eve caught and steadied her. I looked away when the girls stared at each other for just a little too long before stepping apart. Eve gave my sister the same wistful look Acacia had given Blondie after the concert. Did Eve like girls?

# Chapter Fourteen

I didn't have much decorating to do for the party as the club was swanky enough already. I bought one of those cheesy 'Happy Birthday' banners but the girls nixed it before I got it pinned to the wall. Acacia turned beet red and Eve burst into giggles when I pulled it out.

It wasn't long before Acacia's friends began showing up. It looked like my prom all over again but with a strange Gothic overtone. I suddenly wished I was wearing anything but black. In no time, giggling girls and tall boys all vying for attention had surrounded my sister. Eve joined me at the bar with a sigh.

"Good thing I know you and Tom," she said, snagging a bottle of water from the bar.

"Don't worry, once she greets everyone you two will be inseparable again."

I hadn't spotted Blondie yet; maybe Acacia hadn't dropped off the invitation after all. But her best friend Emmy hadn't arrived either. Speaking of fashionably late, Tom was still MIA. As I waited, my security training began to kick in and I wondered if Cassie and I would be enough to wrangle this crowd of teenage humans and vampires. So far, there was a pretty even mix. Come to think of it, where was Cassie?

"Can I borrow your phone?" I asked Eve.

She slapped it into my hand and slouched with her chin in her hand. I patted her shoulder in encouragement. I'd spent plenty of parties sitting on the sidelines so I understood how she felt. Hell, I got paid to do it now. Somehow, I didn't imagine Eve was used to being a wallflower.

I dialed Cassie's number. She answered on the second ring. Maybe it was time I upgraded to a phone that was actually useful.

"Yellow!" Cassie hollered in greeting, making me hold the phone away from my ear.

"Cass, where in the hell are you? I'm the only one running crowd control here."

"Hold your horses. I'm on my way, fashionably late and all that jazz. Some of us work you know," she teased.

"Thanks a lot," I grumbled. "Just hurry."

When I handed the phone back to Eve, she brightened a little. "Friend of yours?"

"Girl from work. She's helping me teenage wrangle tonight."

"You expect trouble?" Eve sounded nervous.

"Not really. Everyone goes to school together, with very few exceptions," I added, bumping her with my elbow.

She gave me a lopsided smile, which instantly brightened when Acacia bounced over with Emmy close behind. My sister's tiny best friend was in black from head to toe. Was she really wearing one of those hats with black veils people wore to funerals, a black silk dress, and combat boots? This girl was so weird.

"Eve, this is my best friend, Emmy," Acacia said, taking each girl's hands and dragging them off. "Let's go find a table where we can all sit together."

"Looks like someone's jealous," Tom said over my shoulder, making me jump.

"Hey, you." I spun on my stool so I could welcome him properly. After a kiss, he raked his eyes over my frame and twirled me in a little circle. "I need to give you an excuse to dress up more often."

I stuck out my tongue. "You're just imagining my dress wadded up on the floor."

He grinned and shook his head. "I am now. No wonder Eve wouldn't let you pick me up; we'd have never made it to the club."

"Did you have any trouble getting your stuff here?" I asked, looking at the lone guitar case by his feet.

He bent down to grab the handle. "This is it. I wasn't planning on anything formal, just a few acoustic songs and a round of 'Happy Birthday.'"

I frowned. "You'd better get approval from your sister and the birthday girl. They vetoed my banner."

"I told you they would." He snagged another kiss.

Before he stepped away, I pulled him back. "Hey, Tom, Eve doesn't like girls, does she?"

His expression wasn't surprised, just puzzled. "Does it matter?"

"Not to me." I glanced at the trio at a table just right of the stage. "I think maybe she likes my sister. Acacia has a crush on a boy she invited. I just didn't want Eve to get the wrong impression and end up with hurt feelings."

He followed my gaze to the three girls. Acacia and Eve were laughing but Emmy was giving Eve looks that if could kill, would cause her to burst into flames at any moment. Tom grimaced and waved when his sister caught his eye.

"I'll talk to her," he said, then gave me a peck on the cheek before taking the stairs two at a time down to where the girls were seated.

My parents had a small party for Acacia last night so I didn't expect them to show and embarrass her with any more family than her older sister. I was hoping the coolness of the party would help my image. However, once it made it around the room that Tómas River was here, I was all but forgotten.

"What did I miss?" Cassie asked, sliding onto a stool beside me.

"Other than my boyfriend's sister falling for mine and Tom becoming the center of the universe? Nothing," I said, realizing I'd taken up Eve's earlier slumped posture.

"Well, you look smoking hot, does that count?" Cassie commented.

I looked in her direction. "Back at ya. Let me guess, just something you threw on?"

"How'd you guess?" Cassie smiled, flashing her sparkling white teeth and batting her long lashes.

"Figures. I've been poked, colored, polished, and squished into this dress. You just roll out of bed, slip into something, and look like a runway model."

"So, Tom's sister has the hots for Acacia?" Cassie asked, changing the subject. "I can see why. She looks gorgeous."

It was true. Acacia's hair, done up in a fancy twist, was shining with tiny sparkles. Her soft, yet evening appropriate makeup played on her golden eyes perfectly. Even the emerald green of her dress made her shine.

"It *is* her birthday." I smiled.

The kids danced in the aisles as Tom played half a dozen songs. I was kind of disappointed when my song never started. He flashed me a look telling me I'd get a solo performance later.

Between eating a dinner of Thai food and the arrival of the chocolate cake from Hell, Tom took Eve aside. From the crushed look on her face, I knew what they had discussed. I wished he had told me about Eve before the party. She had been having such a good time too. Her smile was a little too forced when she rejoined Acacia and Emmy.

"Is she going to be alright?" I asked when he joined me at the bar.

"She'll be fine. Eve's a hopeless romantic. Love at first sight and all," he said, watching his sister pretend to have a good time.

"Wonder where she got that idea." I bumped him with my elbow.

"I think she likes boys too. Someday she'll find who she's meant to be with, just like I have."

I gave him a wary smile and shook my head. He was so sure about us, not that I was complaining or anything. We were great together, but it was hard to say forever when we'd only been a couple a short time. However, I wasn't going to rain on this birthday parade.

"Time for the cake. I'll light the candles and you need to lead everyone in a round of 'Happy Birthday'," I said, getting to my feet.

The two-tiered chocolate cake was from my favorite bakery. Good thing I had vampire strength or there was no way I'd be able to carry this down the stairs to my sister's table. Why did she have to sit at the bottom?

After half a matchbook and two burnt nails, I got all seventeen candles lit. I nodded to Tom who clapped to get everyone's attention. As soon as he started the song, I started carefully descending to Acacia's table. Her face was bright red as the song continued. I smiled when I saw Blondie had joined the trio of girls. He was sitting between Acacia and Eve, neither one looked upset about it either.

After the little scavengers more or less devoured the entire cake, gifts were pressed toward Acacia. It was amazing how much teenagers ate, both human and vampire alike. How did my parents afford to feed us? I sat with Tom on the rim of the stage while Acacia's friends jockeyed for whose gift she'd open next.

Tom waited until almost last before pulling a small, newspaper wrapped parcel from behind his guitar case. Eve and I shared a smile at the wrapping. I peered around the onlookers as my sister opened the paper as if it was gold. She held up a t-shirt then jumped to her feet and hugged him, bouncing up and down. Hell, she hadn't been that excited about the party and the dress.

I understood when she turned it around. The charcoal gray shirt had the logo of one of her favorite bands on the front along with signatures of each band member and 'Happy Seventeenth Birthday, Acacia' written on the back.

When Tom finally fought his way out of the crowd, I snuggled against him. "Nice job."

"It was Eve's idea," he confessed.

His sister had just handed Acacia the gold wrapped book. Eve tucked a wayward curl behind her ear and bit her lip as my sister carefully broke the tape with her newly manicured fingernails.

I knew my sister didn't read much so I wasn't sure how she'd react. To my surprise, Acacia threw her arms around Eve and kissed her on the cheek. She clutched the leather-bound book to her chest, taking one of Eve's hands in her own behind Blondie's back. Emmy looked ready to break down in tears but that's how she always looked so it was hard to tell the reasoning behind it.

I glanced at Tom who looked concerned as Eve beamed up at us. I leaned over to whisper in Tom's ear, "What did Eve give her?"

"A sketch pad with Eve's favorite poems written in the corner of each page. Most of which she wrote herself."

Acacia was nuts about her art, drawing on everything within reach. No wonder our parents had decided to give into her decorating her bedroom walls rather than grounding her every time she got creative in the middle of the night. My sister used to grab pencils, crayons, or permanent markers to sketch her latest inspiration on her boring white walls whenever the urge struck.

I wondered if she'd even seen the poetry inside Eve's book. Blondie got up to refill the girls' drinks and the two girls hunched over the book as Eve flipped to certain pages pointing and whispering. Emmy trailed behind the boy, clutching her own empty glass. It wasn't as if I didn't like my sister's best friend. I just had a feeling she was the instigator in a lot of Acacia's behavioral problems.

Shortly after nine-thirty, kids began to filter out. Emmy was one of the first to leave; neither her nor Acacia seemed too upset when they hugged goodbye. Maybe I'd been overreacting to her behavior earlier.

Cassie and I were sharing a piece of leftover cake when Tom came over to us. "Have you seen the girls?"

"You need to be more specific," Cassie teased.

I offered him a bite but he waved his hand. "Eve and Acacia. I haven't seen them in a while, Blondie either."

I put down my fork and stood. The last time I'd seen Acacia she was heading to the restroom but that had been quite a while ago. I took his arm and led him in that direction. I hated to ask but I was afraid of what I might find in the bathroom.

I had to strain to keep the accusation out of my tone. "Does Eve have the same ability as you and your brother?"

As soon as I'd asked, Tom froze in place, jerking us both to a stop. "No. Just us. She won't take advantage of your sister. Eve's not like that," he defended.

"Oh, I hope not."

I slammed the bathroom door with my fist. It was locked. Having been in there earlier, I knew it was a simple twist lock. Knowing I'd have to pay for the repair, I grasped the knob and gave a sharp twist. The lock gave under my vampire strength but the door didn't budge when I pushed on it.

"Just a minute," I heard Eve call.

I pushed on the door again but someone was braced against it. "Open the door, Eve."

"Just a minute," I heard both Acacia and Eve say at the same time.

Double shit. I took a step back and rammed the door with my shoulder. This time it opened enough I got my foot inside. In the mirror, I could see both girls were wrestling with their dresses.

"Jesus, girls, just let me in already," I cursed.

Eve, who had been barricading the door, stepped aside so I could get in. I immediately shut the door behind me but not before giving Tom a dark look. I wanted a moment alone with the girls before I took them home for a real tongue-lashing. However, the scene inside was not what I expected.

Blondie lay unconscious, half propped up against the wall. I dropped to my knees and felt for a pulse. Please don't let him be dead. His heartbeat was weak but still there. I eased him down so he was lying on his back.

"Tom!" I called.

The door burst open and he was at my side in a second. "Go get Cassie and take this poor kid to the ER. I'll deal with the girls. Tell the stragglers the party is over."

He got to his feet and rounded on Eve, who slunk back. Before he could speak, I snapped, "I'll deal with the girls. Just get Cassie."

Tom lifted his hand to point at his sister; it trembled for a second before he dropped it to his side and wrenched open the door. Over the boy's thready breathing, I heard Tom announce Acacia was feeling ill and the party was over.

Both girls leaned against the wall, neither looked at the other nor at me. I was so angry, I needed to wait until I knew the club was empty and this boy was safely on the way to medical attention before I opened my mouth. A few minutes later Tom and Cassie appeared. Between the two of them, they easily carried the still unconscious boy out of the bathroom.

As soon as the door shut, both girls began speaking at once. I held up a trembling hand to silence them. While I was cooling my temper, I had pretty much figured out what had happened. Eve had given Acacia a second birthday present: her first taste of human blood. When the blood lust was slacked, the sexual lust was left and Eve had taken advantage of that too.

"Acacia, gather up your gifts and put them in my car. Eve, you stay with me." They both started talking again but I held up a single finger. "And neither one of you say a word."

The three of us left the bathroom to find an empty club except for the bartender who gave me a questioning look. He'd most likely seen what appeared to be a dead body being carried out of the bathroom, which was now being vacated by three vampires, not that Eve looked like one.

"He'll be fine. Too many pulls off his pocket flask," I explained as I grabbed my stuff from behind the bar.

The bartender nodded in understanding then shook his head disapprovingly at the girls. I went down to help Acacia carry all her gifts and Tom's guitar case. God, I hoped everything would fit in my car. More importantly, I hoped Cassie hadn't driven her two-seater, which was now full of three people, one of whom was unconscious. There's a traffic stop I'd like to see explained away if my closest friend and boyfriend weren't the ones begin carted off for pedophilia. Please let Blondie be eighteen.

Once we got everything in the car, both girls moved to get into the backseat. Fine, I could watch them in my rearview mirror as I drove. I slammed my door hard enough the car rocked. Both girls' eyes went wide but they used their brains and kept their mouths shut.

I drove straight to my house, running two red lights in the process. At one point, I noticed Eve was holding Acacia's hand again but after the glare I gave her, she put both hands in her lap. I marched the girls inside and closed the door.

They stood together looking at the floor. "What. Were. You. Thinking?" I asked, each word punctuated with my anger.

Acacia looked up, her make-up smeared from crying. "We didn't kill him, did we?"

Eve touched her shoulder, but I slapped her hand away. "No, you didn't but you could have."

"I wouldn't have let her." Eve defiantly lifted her chin. "She said it's what she wanted for her birthday, and I knew I could give it to her."

"In exchange for sexual favors?" Eve's face burned red. "And you. How could you just go along with all of this?" I demanded to Acacia.

She looked at Eve's crushed expression and stomped her foot. I didn't even realize people did that in real life. "Stop it, Arabella! You're not Mom."

"You're right and it's a good thing I'm not. Can you imagine what Mom would have done if she'd walked in on you? Do you think she'd ever be able to look you in the face again? Did you think about that? Did you think about *anything*?"

I knew I was shrieking but I couldn't help it. "Acacia, I wanted your first time to be in a safe environment, to know what to expect. Not in some random club bathroom."

"I don't care what Mom thinks. She hates us for being alive. I'm tired of hiding who I am. Why can you have a vampire boyfriend who gives you scars when he takes your blood? What makes you so damn special, Arabella?" Acacia yelled back at me.

"Tom didn't do this to me," I said, gesturing to my scars. "His sadistic brother messed with my mind and nearly killed me doing this. Now every time Tom looks at me, he sees the damage Victor did and is still doing."

I saw Eve flinch when I explained. Maybe she'd been given the watered-down version of the encounter. The more I thought about it, the more I wondered if she had at least some of the twins' power of persuasion.

"Eve," I began. "How could you do this? You can't force someone to love you. What you did is no better than rape."

Acacia reached over and slapped me. "How do you know she took advantage of me? Maybe I took advantage of her? You don't even know me. How can you possibly know what I want?"

She was as mad as I was and just as stubborn. That's why we fought the way we did. Her last statement cut me deep. I really didn't know her anymore. Every time we were in the same room, we nearly ripped out each other's throats. I'd extended the olive branch but now it looked like I'd ripped it away.

"It's true," Eve said quietly. "Tom told me to back off and I did. I just wanted to give Acacia what she really wanted for her birthday. The other stuff was her idea."

I sunk down onto the couch and put my face in my hands. When I looked back, the girls were holding hands again. Okay, we'd deal with that last part later.

"Fine. It doesn't matter who started what. What is important is whether Blondie is going to press charges against you."

Eve fumbled in her clutch purse. "He can't. He signed a waiver." I took the scrap of paper from her trembling hand. "Victor told me to have anyone sign one before... Well, you know."

Of course, he had. My memory ran back to the day I spent with Victor and tried to remember if I wrote my name on anything. Nope, he was up shit creek if I came after him.

I handed it back to her. "Go and get changed. I need to take Acacia home." When both girls headed to the bedroom, I clarified. "Acacia bedroom, Eve bathroom. I don't trust you two yet."

As if trying to push her luck, Acacia gave Eve a deep kiss before slamming my bedroom door closed. Eve gave me a sad closed lip smile before silently closing the bathroom door. I closed my eyes and seethed. The phone rang as I was massaging my temples.

"Yes," I answered, trying to keep my voice in a civil tone.

"Prince Charming woke up enroute to the ER, ticked to find out his threesome happened without him. We dropped him off at the main doors of the hospital. If he refuses treatment, it's his own damn fault for making bad decisions," Cassie said flatly. "You need some help slapping those girls around?"

"No, but can you drop Tom off at my place? I think he needs to stay with Eve while I drive Acacia home. This is more complicated than I thought and I think I made it worse."

# Chapter Fifteen

Neither one of us spoke on the trip to my parents' house. Eve never made it out of the bathroom before I ushered Acacia out of the house; I think she was hiding. Hell, I would be if I were waiting for me. Somehow, my sister repaired her smeared makeup so she just looked tired rather than like someone who'd been crying. That would help the plan I had formulated as I drove through town. My sister just stared out the passenger window clutching Eve's sketchbook to her chest as if it were a lifeline.

The porch light was on when I pulled into our parents' driveway. I knew Mom was fast asleep but Dad would be reading the newspaper at the kitchen table just like he had been doing since I started going out at night. The familiarity of it should have been comforting; tonight, it wasn't. When Acacia moved to yank open the car door, I put a hand on her arm. She looked at it then glared at me.

"Acacia, listen..." I began.

"I'm a screw up, Arabella. They expect it by now. Why would my birthday be any different?" The hurt in her voice was clear through the anger.

"Okaaaay. That's not what I was going to say but whatever makes you sleep better. What I was going to say was there is no need to worry them over this. They worry about us enough already. If you'll let me help you, we can figure this whole mess out."

I didn't want her to be alone and make all the same mistakes I'd made. She was doing a good job of making new ones all by herself but I would try and help her with those as well. I knew this would push Mom over the proverbial edge. Not only were her daughters some sort of demonic rejects sent from God to punish her but now one was also a lesbian. Dad could take it but he didn't have to, at least not yet. I needed to start acting like a big sister and hope Acacia would take the help I never had.

My stubborn sister's glare softened slowly as if she expected me to continue. "You won't tell?"

"We are going to march in with all your presents, full of smiles. You are going to tell Dad what a fabulous sister you have, say you're tired, and get your ass in bed. Then you are going to come over tomorrow so we can have a nice long chat. Sound okay to you?"

"Will Eve be there?" she asked, turning the sketchbook over in her hands.

"I don't know but it doesn't matter. Do you think you can act like you had a good birthday?" I asked.

"Why are you doing this?" she asked, narrowing her eyes.

Because I'm a freaking crazy person. "Because believe it or not, I love your screwed up ass."

She nodded and we got out of the car. We lugged her treasures to the house where, of course, Dad held the door open for us. Somehow, we managed real enough smiles as Acacia made it through a cliff notes version of the party before claiming exhaustion and disappearing into her bedroom.

"You clean up nice," Dad said.

I looked down, only now remembering, I hadn't changed out of my party clothes, just traded my heels for a pair of ratty looking flip flops. Now there was a fashion statement. I felt like hammered dog crap. My shoulders drooped as the weight of the evening settled in.

"Teenagers are exhausting," I said, slumping into a chair at the table.

"You're telling me," Dad agreed, folding up the newspaper with controlled slowness. "So how did it *really* go?"

I puffed out a breath, not surprised we hadn't fooled him for a second. My eyes flicked toward the back of the house knowing

Acacia was sitting with her ear pressed to the door waiting for me to spill the beans.

"Fun, Dad, it was really fun. I never realized how cool my little sister could be." I rolled his empty coffee mug between my hands, keeping my eyes lowered. "We're going to try and get to know each other a little better."

He put his hand on the top of the cup and met my gaze. "You don't have to protect me from my own children. I love you girls no matter what."

I gave him a sad smile. "I know, Dad. This is something we need to work out together, bonding and all that crap. I'm a big girl, I can take care of myself."

"You always have, Arabella. Just let me know if I can help."

"Tell Mom the party was wonderful," I said, trying to sound hopeful.

He smiled, making the wrinkles around his eyes crinkle. "That, honey, I can do."

"Working tomorrow?" I asked, scanning the half-finished crossword puzzle. "Twelve down is: EMPATHY."

He scratched the remaining letters into the tiny boxes before answering my question. "I have an appointment on the North-side at noon."

"Perfect. Can you drop off Acacia at my house on your way?"

He nodded and I stood, needing to leave before I fell asleep at the table. Any other time, I would have curled up on the couch but I knew I had a heartsick teenager and pissed off boyfriend waiting for me at home. Maybe I should stay here, it would be easier but when did I ever do the easy thing?

Seeing no lights inside, I eased my front door open as quietly as possible. A thick pillar candle with three wicks flickered on the coffee table. Tom was sitting next to Eve's sleeping form, gently stroking her hair. Every now and then her breath would hitch as if she were still crying in her sleep. I felt like a monster.

Averting my eyes, I slipped out of my noisy shoes, leaving them just inside the door, and headed to the bedroom. Flipping on the bedside lamp rather than the bright overhead light, I struggled to reach the zipper on my dress.

"Let me," Tom whispered, stilling my hands.

I leaned against him and closed my eyes. This was going to be hard, harder than it should have been. I'd made it a mess by blaming Eve for everything. As much I adored her, I'd jumped to the conclusion she'd hurt my sister because of what Victor had done to me.

"Eve probably thinks I hate her," I whispered, turning to face him.

"I'll talk to her when she wakes up. She wouldn't look, let alone speak to me tonight. Let her sleep on it. It won't seem so bad in the morning."

I rested my head on his chest and breathed in his scent. "I hope so."

• • • •

WHEN I WOKE, I WAS alone. I hadn't done anything other than pull out the five hundred bobby pins from my hair and drop my dress on the floor before falling into bed. I was sure I looked like an extra from a B-rate zombie movie.

Avoiding the inevitable and uncomfortable conversation waiting for me, I did what I always did, procrastinated. I snuck as quietly as possible to the bathroom and turned on the shower. The temporary highlights that cost a fortune swirled down the drain when I washed my hair. Twice. Yeah, it was juvenile to waste time but I was preparing, or so I kept telling myself.

I'd forgotten to flip on the fan before I got in the shower so the bathroom was a steamy blur when I stepped out. I pushed the tiny window open and turned on the fan. After toweling off and putting on my robe, I was surprised to see the color was still in my hair. Huh, there had been a lot in the shower.

My brush stalled when I heard Eve and Tom's voices from the living room. The fan muffled them but if I concentrated, I could still hear most of what was said. I felt bad eavesdropping but maybe it would help me prepare for my conversation with Acacia later.

"She doesn't hate you, Eve."

"Yes, she does," Eve answered. "You didn't see her when we got back last night. She was so mad."

"She wasn't mad. Okay, she was mad, but she was more worried than angry," Tom explained as I sat by the door to hear better.

"Things are different here, slower and in my opinion, better. You are used to unrestrained instant gratification. Mom's sheltered you from the real world. That's why Dad sent you to Italy."

"No," Eve said angrily. "They sent me to Italy to find a nice boy with old blood. They're ashamed of me for not wanting to carry on the family line."

"Ouch, not so hard." Tom almost yelped and I wondered what they were doing besides talking.

"Sorry," Eve mumbled. "So, she doesn't hate me?"

"I know for a fact she doesn't," Tom said. "And forget Mom and her world domination plans. You can be with whoever you want, Eve."

I smiled at this. Desdemona hated me just because of my genetics. It wasn't any fairer than forcing Eve to ignore her feelings just so she could pop out the next generation of super vampires.

"Oh Tom, it was amazing." Eve sighed. "Acacia is the best kisser ever."

"You've got it bad, don't you?" Tom chuckled.

"As bad as you have it for Arabella." Eve laughed too.

When I shifted, my elbow knocked against the door and the conversation stopped. Shit, I was so busted. I rattled around in the vanity as if looking for something. When I closed it, Tom was giving me a knowing smirk through a crack in the door.

I tried to ignore him and brush my hair but he pushed the rest of the way in and shut the door. When I swept my hair to the side so I could brush underneath, his hands wrapped around my waist and he kissed my neck.

"How long were you listening?" he asked.

"I wasn't listening," I said, not meeting his eyes in the mirror.

He gave me a little nip just behind my ear, making me shiver. "Liar."

I turned to face him, and he slipped his hands inside my robe and pulled me close. "How long did you know I was listening?"

"Since you plunked down on the floor. Just because I don't have your gorgeous eyes, doesn't mean I don't have vamp hearing."

I tried to scowl but my grin slipped through. "Flattery will get you everywhere."

"Yep. I'm taking Eve car shopping. Can I borrow yours?"

"Eve's buying a car?" I questioned. "Just how long is she planning on staying?"

"The car's not for Eve, it's for me. I think Bertha has finally given up the ghost." He explained, "Eve's ticket is open-ended. She's been accepted to UCSF for this fall but she's on the fence about California."

"Oh." What did that mean? "Sure, you can take the car, just fill it up before you bring it back."

"You still owe me for playing last night," he said, pinning me against the sink. When I leaned in for a kiss, he stepped back. "My turn for the shower. Go talk to her."

I rewrapped my robe and huffed. It wasn't fair distracting me then sending me out into non-buffered territory. When he turned his back to turn on the water, I caught a glimpse of his hair in the mirror and burst out laughing.

"That's what you were doing? Playing beauty shop?" I laughed.

He reached up and touched the pink ribbon before pulling it out and tossing his head to undo the fancy French braid. "Yeah, it helps her relax when she has something to do with her hands."

"I can braid your hair anytime you want," I offered, still laughing.

He frowned then grabbed my wrist, pulling me against him. "I prefer your hands busy elsewhere. Now, if you want to talk to her before Acacia gets here, get your naked ass out there before I pull you in here with me."

I stuck my tongue out at him but pulled it back in before he grabbed it. Sneaking a look at him as he pulled off his shirt, I skipped across the hall to my room to get dressed before facing Eve.

"I made coffee," she said when I entered the living room still tucking in my shirt.

She had been sitting on the floor but jumped up the second I emerged. Her eyes avoided mine as she raced to the kitchen. Maybe I had been harsher than I thought last night. With a defeated sigh, I followed her.

Her hand trembled, making the glass carafe tinkle against the ceramic mug as she poured the coffee for me. I could smell something baking in the oven. Damn, I had slept like the dead this morning.

"Thanks," I said, trying to meet her eye.

"I also made muffins but they're not done yet. Do you like blueberries? You must because I found the mix in your cupboard. I hope you don't mind I went through your cupboards," she was babbling and seemed unable to stop.

"Eve. Eve, stop," I said, putting my mug down and taking her hands.

"I'm sorry. I just wanted everything to be perfect." Eve still wouldn't look at me.

I lifted her chin. "I'm not mad at you. Well, maybe a little but I'm more confused and worried. A lot got thrown on my plate at once last night."

Eve relaxed her shoulders a little. "Yeah."

"Okay. Why don't we sit while we wait for those muffins? And no, I don't mind you going through my pantry. Just don't let your brother cook," I said slightly louder as the shower had just turned off.

"Hey!" was his only rebuttal.

I lowered my voice. "I'm planning on using his leftover pancakes as door stops."

A giggle escaped Eve's mouth but sadness still touched her eyes. "I can sleep at Tom's apartment if you want. I need to stay until at least Thursday or the airlines won't let me use the frequent flyer miles."

"Eve, I want you to stay where you want, for as long as you want." When she perked up more, I hated adding the next part, "Acacia and I are going to work on some rules today and I expect both of you to follow them."

Eve lifted her chin as if accepting my challenge, whatever it was. "Okay."

"Okay," I agreed and promptly jumped, spilling my coffee when the oven timer chimed.

# Chapter Sixteen

Acacia wore a faded black t-shirt and jean shorts when Dad dropped her off at my house. Eve and Tom had left about an hour before to go car shopping. Therefore, we were trapped in the house together. Alone. This should be interesting.

"Grab a soda and follow me," I instructed after waving to Dad from the door.

I headed to the unfinished room at the end of the hall. It was eight by ten feet with no closet and a pathetic excuse half circle window near the ceiling. There wasn't even a light fixture, just a place to screw in a light bulb. I had been using the room as overflow storage but there wasn't much: just my vacuum cleaner, an old treadmill, mountain bike, and half a dozen boxes I'd never opened after the move three years ago. They were obviously filled with priceless treasures I couldn't live without.

The walls were primed but never painted. The floor, on the other hand, was the same finished prefab hardwood as the rest of the house. It would make a great guest room, now that it looked like I might have real guests. This hadn't been on my mind when I asked my sister over last night but it would give us something to do together.

"Do people actually use these?" She slurped her soda and gave my treadmill a poke with her foot.

"It's Mom's. Do you think she might want it back?"

If I could mount a hanging bike rack in my tiny shed, that would leave only the boxes of junk and my vacuum homeless. Taking my hands from my hips, I bent over to grab the first box.

"Grab one and bring it out to the living room," I ordered.

She grumbled something unintelligible as I set the first box in an out of the way corner in the living room. She was carrying the smallest one in one hand, still sipping her soda when I turned around. *I'm not going to yell. I'm not going to yell. I'm not going to yell!*

"In exchange for keeping my mouth shut, you are going to help me remodel my spare room."

Her face went devoid of emotion. "That's blackmail."

"Yep, and I'm not above it. It will give you a chance to learn something from me and I can be the adult supervision while Eve is staying here."

Her eyebrows went up in surprise. "You're not going to keep me from seeing Eve?"

"Why would I do that?" I asked, brushing past her to get another box.

"But you said..." she began, following behind me.

"You need to stop being a shit just to piss everyone off and think about where you want to be. I don't want you to ruin your life or hurt Eve while you figure it out."

She eyed me suspiciously as I handed her a box of what felt like bricks. What the hell did I have in there? It wasn't important. I'd have the girls go through them later. Give them a chance to make fun of me.

I motioned with my head for her to take the box to the living room. "I told Eve we'd settle on the rules before she got back."

"What rules?" she asked, shifting the box so she could walk.

"For one, no more human blood, at least until you can control yourself. Also, you girls betrayed my trust last night and have to earn it back. Therefore, unless you are in a public place or under adult supervision you two won't be alone together."

"What do you get out of it?" she asked.

"I get to know my sister and make sure she doesn't end up in jail, or worse." I gestured to the empty space. "And I get help with this room."

"What can I do?" She slurped her soda again.

"First, stop making that noise," I said, swiping away her can and taking a drink without all the extra noise to show it was possible. "Plus, I need help painting and picking out décor."

"Really?" Acacia sounded hopeful.

"Really. Oh, and one more thing, I don't want you breaking that poor girl's heart just so you can prove something. You made quite an impression on her and she means the world to Tom and, therefore, to me as well."

Acacia chewed on her bottom lip while doing a slow circle. I could see the wheels turning as she considered the possibilities for the little room. She moved to one end and walked heel to toe counting her steps figuring out the square footage. I already knew but this was part of her process; I'd seen her do it before.

"Let me guess, no black?" she asked after she measured the window with her hands.

"I'm not opposed to anything at the moment but no, I'd prefer it not be the dominant color. I want to encourage my guests to stay unless it's the rest of Tom's family then I'll just offer them the shed out back."

"Got a bed sheet you can sacrifice?" she asked after scuffing her sock on the nice wood flooring.

With those few words, our fragile truce was formed. I would let her be herself and she would at least listen to my limited vampire wisdom. Somehow, I imagined Tom would be providing more insight than I, but this was a lesson in learning for everyone. As long as the incident at the club stayed quiet, no one would be the wiser.

The trip from the hardware store back to the house via city bus was interesting. I had ten paint samples, dozens of different sized brushes, a roller, and pole for said roller, paint pans, and a roll of painter's tape. Acacia whined until I got the bright orange instead of the basic blue saying it repressed her artistic process. This was turning out to be an expensive bonding experience but it would increase the resale value of the house, if I ever planned on moving.

Acacia and I wore matching bandanas on our heads and managed to get paint all over our hands and arms. Maybe the fact we kept painting each other while the other wasn't looking had something to do with it. The important thing was we hadn't raised our voices at each other even once.

We had a swath of all ten colors on the wall when Tom and Eve returned. Through the open window, I heard the familiar sound of my car door slamming shut and a second unfamiliar one a moment later. Tom and Eve's voices filtered in and Acacia gave me a wary look from where she was crouching in the corner.

"I would suggest taking it slow," I encouraged as we headed to the front of the house.

Eve bounced in and wrapped Acacia in a hug before giving her a peck on the lips. Tom gave me a much more passionate kiss, tilting me back until I nearly lost my balance. I just rolled my eyes when he grinned at me.

"Come on, show me what you got." I gestured to the door.

He shot a questioning look between Acacia and me, and our paint splattered appearances, but when he opened his mouth to ask, I interrupted, "Nope, you first then I'll show you what we've been up to."

Eve dragged Acacia out by the hand. I hadn't seen her smile like that in a while, last night excluded of course. With a deep breath, I followed Tom outside, squinting at the sudden brightness. A shiny new black SUV sat in the driveway.

"Spending your signing bonus already?" I asked, bumping him with my hip when I recognized the luxury and hybrid logos on the back.

"He is such a scrooge," Eve complained as she pulled open the driver's door and hopped in. "I had to drag him from the used junk dealerships so he would get something that would last more than a month."

I opened my mouth to stop Acacia from climbing in too, afraid she had wet paint on her clothes but Tom swung me around for another kiss before pressing the key fob, making the hatchback open. The scent of new leather wafted out.

"You know I love that new car smell," I whispered, peering in at the pale gray and chrome interior.

"Can we take it for a spin around the block?" Acacia pleaded.

I frowned. She was pushing the adult supervision thing already but how much trouble could they get in driving around? I looked at the fold-down seats in the back and winced. Plenty. However, after getting an okay shrug from Tom, I nodded.

Both doors slammed in unison and the radio blared when Eve started up the SUV. I ran around to Acacia's open window while Tom closed the hatchback.

"Eve, Acacia doesn't have her license yet so she's not supposed to drive without a parent." When I said this, my sister slumped in her seat and her lower lip protruded.

"Hey, it's not my fault you keep getting kicked out of Driver's Ed."

"Where are we going?" Eve asked, grinning from ear to ear.

Acacia looked at Eve who was still adjusting the seat and mirrors then back at me. "How about to my school and back?"

"Sounds okay," I said. "Hey, let me go get my wallet and you two can grab something for dinner and maybe a movie."

"I've got it." Eve grinned. "You can get the next one."

She began to back out but I kept a hold of the open window. "Remember what we talked about and don't make me track you down."

Tom wrapped his arms around my waist from behind and rested his chin on my shoulder as we watched them cruise down the street. "You sound like a mom already."

Back to the kid conversation again? I exhaled and tried to push my heart back down from my throat. I hoped Tom didn't notice my lack of reply or that I stiffened. He was in a good mood and I was going to work as hard as I could to keep it going.

"Are you going to show me what you've been up to today?" he asked, giving me a kiss on the neck.

Glad for the change in topic, I wiggled free of his grasp and led the way back into the house. As Acacia and I worked today, a thought had occurred to me and I was glad we would be alone when I mentioned it, just in case it didn't turn out as expected. Taking his hand, I pulled him toward my spare room.

As we went through the living room he asked, "Where'd the boxes come from?"

"Just doing some Spring cleaning. Ta da!" I said, spinning around, arms raised over my head once we were in the spare room.

"Looks like an art project," he said tentatively, eyes drawn to the color tests on the wall.

"I'm finally going to finish this room. It's not exactly a bedroom but it could be a guest room. And maybe... somewhere for you to practice?"

It took a moment before it clicked but I saw the understanding in his eyes a second before he smiled. "I think my futon will look great in here."

I smiled back. It was crazy and way too soon but it looked like when Tom's lease was up, he'd be moving in. My parents were going to shit little green bricks. Maybe if I distracted them with my stupidity, they wouldn't notice what was going on with Acacia. Yeah, great idea. What's wrong with me?

"Let's not mention this to my mom and dad tomorrow night. I want them to like you."

"It's about time I met them."

I couldn't help but smile again and took a step closer. "Just behave. They're a little old fashioned."

Eve and Acacia returned about an hour later, just after Tom and I got the paint testers closed and brushes cleaned. The timing was so perfect I wondered if they'd been waiting around the corner for us to be done.

Ninjas versus werewolves was the theme of our movie tonight. I hoped it would be as funny as it sounded. Bad sci-fi flicks were much more entertaining than comedies in my opinion. Eve sat on the floor arranging the little white Chinese takeout boxes and chopsticks while Acacia fought with my TV and DVD player.

"What's in the boxes?" Eve asked, tossing her head toward the pile in the corner.

Trying to navigate my chopsticks, I flipped a piece of chicken out of the box and into my lap rather than into my mouth. I needed more practice with these stupid things. I stabbed the chicken piece and popped it in my mouth. Damn, it was spicy but oh so good. Tom grabbed my chopsticks and headed for the kitchen, hopefully to trade them for a fork.

"Old stuff I've been storing. If you two want, you can dig through it before I drop it off for donation."

Acacia expertly maneuvered a bite of rice and veggies into her mouth as if to show me up then asked, "Why would we want your old stuff?"

"I think it would be fun. You know, see what your sister's really like," Eve said.

"I know what she's like and 'fun' isn't the descriptor I'd use," Acacia replied, snagging a piece of chicken from my box.

Like the mature adult I was, I pulled the box out of her reach and stuck my tongue out at her. Tom reappeared and handed me the chopsticks. There was a folded-up piece of paper between them and a rubber band holding the two sticks together. Both girls stifled their laughter but fell into a fit of giggles when they looked at each other.

"Just ignore them," Tom said. "I'm sure they used these when they learned too."

Tom demonstrated the proper way to navigate my chopsticks with training wheels then handed them to me. I got my next bite to my mouth with no problem, grinning as I chewed.

"Thanks," I mumbled through my bite.

"Do you think," Eve began looking at Acacia for support, "I might be able to help with your project?"

"Sure, many hands make light work. How about you Tom, you want to help?"

He frowned. "I don't really like painting."

"Too much like cleaning," Eve teased.

He threw his napkin at her, which she ducked. "I have to do some work. I need to get sheet music sent off to Mr. Redding by the end of the week."

I had a couple of jobs during the day and one evening gig this week, too. We'd have to figure out what to do with Eve so she wasn't bored. Sneaking a glance at Acacia, I mentally added: and provide adult supervision.

The rest of the evening was Pick on Me Night. The movie was forgotten when the boxes were opened. The one I thought was full of bricks was full of books and old yearbooks. Does anyone really look good in school pictures? My side ached from laughing when the girls did a fashion show in some old clothes mixing the worst possible combinations. Didn't I throw anything away?

Eve put a stack of books aside for herself and Acacia snagged some shoes but otherwise everything else was getting donated. The only thing I kept was a well-loved, faded stuffed bunny. After a ride in the washing machine, it would be perfect, but right now it smelled weird. I guess Tom wasn't the only nostalgic one.

# Chapter Seventeen

Eve spent the day at Tom's apartment, saying she wanted to relax and read while I escorted a lawyer and his client to and from the courthouse. Since the proceedings were closed to the public, I had to sit outside and pretend I couldn't hear everything through the doors. I didn't care about the civil suit, nor did I plan on talking to the press but whatever.

My job was to make sure they got in, traveled to and from lunch, and then home safely but otherwise I was left to my own devices. I snagged part of a discarded national newspaper hoping to find a crossword puzzle to fill my time. The place was empty except for courthouse staff but I kept one eye on my job while trying to keep from dying of boredom. I either needed to push for better runs or get a different job.

The horoscopes and crossword weren't in the section I had so I scanned the minor headlines. Nothing grabbed my attention enough to warrant reading the full articles accompanying the colorfully worded titles until I got to the back page. Victor's smiling face stared back at me. His law firm had been hired to defend some big shot actor accused of murder. Lovely.

I folded the paper roughly enough I ripped it, making the bailiff standing sentry duty outside the courtroom frown in disapproval. After another glance around the hallway, I went back to trying to make shapes out of the cracks in the tile floor. This was going to be a really long day. Why hadn't I brought a book?

Tom was finally meeting my parents tonight. When I'd mentioned Eve was visiting, Mom went into full hostess mode. Poor Acacia was trapped in the house with her. They'd be cleaning and cooking all day long. As boring as this was, you couldn't pay me to swap places with my sister. I caught another disapproving look when the bailiff caught me grinning like an idiot.

Unlike Tom's family who ate late, dinner tonight was planned for seven. Tom and Eve were going to swing by and pick me up. I think he wanted to show off his new SUV; too bad my dad wasn't much of a car buff. I hadn't gotten a chance to go for a ride yet, so I was excited.

I, once again, was supposed to bring a dessert. Eve had pestered me until I gave in and let her make it. Since I had to work all day, she didn't have to try too hard to convince me. When I slid into the SUV, I saw the covered pie carrier on the backseat next to her. She must have gone shopping because I knew Tom didn't have anything that domestic. His kitchen supplies consisted of three different sized plates, a conglomeration of mismatched silverware, one partially melted spatula, a small baking sheet, and one old nonstick pan. My favorite was his bowl collection made up of old butter and whipped topping tubs.

"Here goes nothing," I said when we pulled into my parents' driveway behind the car and truck. At least Dad was home.

Mom appeared at the door, wearing her ladybug apron, when we all piled out. I'd even dressed up in a nice blouse and skirt, mostly because I didn't want to look like a slob next to Eve, who once again looked radiant. Tom had put on a dark green button-down shirt with a relatively new pair of jeans and pulled his hair back.

I slid my hand into his as we made our way up the walk with Eve trailing happily behind. "Hi, Mom."

"Come on in," she greeted.

The living room had been cleaned but the photo album explosion was still in full swing. Acacia was trapped against the far wall behind a maze of pictures and albums scattered and stacked all over the floor, couch, and table.

"Acacia, I thought I told you to have this cleaned up by now," Mom chastised.

"This *is* cleaned up."

"Mom, this is Tom and his little sister, Evelyn," I said once we were inside.

"It's so nice to meet you, Mrs. Simon, and please call me Eve," Eve said, handing Mom the covered dessert. "Do you mind if I stay in here and help Acacia?"

"She needs all the help she can get," I answered, and we stuck our tongues out at each other.

"Stop it girls." Mom laughed. "Go ahead and try to pick your way through the mess. I'll call you when dinner's ready."

Tom and I followed her into the kitchen where I could see Dad out back with the grill. He was wearing his 'Kiss the Cook' apron and giant fish mitt while flipping what looked like pork chops. Why had I dressed up again?

"Come on." I pulled Tom to the back door. "I'll introduce you to my dad."

Mom handed me a plate. "Take him this. Those chops should be done by now."

"Mom says stop burning the meat," I called as we stepped out back.

"Arabella!" Dad gave me a hug before turning to Tom. "And you must be Tom."

"Yes, sir. It's nice to finally meet you," Tom said, shaking my father's hand after he took off the ridiculous looking mitt.

"I'll go see if Mom needs help finishing up," I said when both men began inspecting the grill.

Shaking my head at the allure between men and roasting meat, I went into the house to find Mom slicing up veggies for a salad. "Need any help?" I asked as I swiped a radish.

Mom looked from side to side. Dropping her voice, she said, "Emmy stopped by today. She and your sister had a big fight. I think it had something to do with Eve. Do you know why Emmy doesn't like Eve? She seems like a polite enough girl."

I could think of several reasons why Emmy didn't like Eve but none I would share with my mother. "Maybe Emmy is just afraid Eve is going to steal her friend."

She smacked my hand when I reached for another radish. "That's probably it. It just sounded like it was about some boy at the party. I thought maybe Eve had flirted with Emmy's boyfriend or something."

Okay, maybe I needed to talk with Acacia about this little argument. "I didn't even know Emmy had a boyfriend."

"Pig's done!" Dad announced, holding the platter up like a shrine while Tom held the door open for him.

"You're so crass. We have guests," Mom fussed, wrestling the plate away from him but accepting his kiss on her cheek with a smile.

There was no need to call the girls for dinner. They appeared at Dad's proclamation of food, but Mom sent them off to wash their hands. I filled water glasses while Mom put the finishing touches on the salad. Eve and Acacia sat in the two folding chairs on one side of the table, looking too short, while Tom and I sat opposite with my parents sitting at either end.

"Tom, what do your parents do?" Dad asked while passing me the green beans.

"My mother does a lot of volunteer work and my father's in accounting," he answered.

Why didn't I know what his parents did for a living? Probably because Tom never gave me straight answers when I asked about his family. I quickly rearranged my frown when my mom gave me a puzzled look.

"Is that what you're planning on doing, Eve, following in your father's footsteps?" Dad asked.

Eve promptly began to choke on her water. That question had so many possible answers only half of us at the table knew about. Acacia patted her back until Eve stopped sputtering, her face bright red.

"No. I'm thinking about majoring in Literature," she said once she finally stopped coughing.

"Where are you going to school in the fall?" Mom asked.

Eve glanced at Tom before answering. "I've been accepted to UCSF, Washington U, and Dartmouth but I haven't decided. I might take a year off."

"Those are good schools. Your grades must be excellent," Mom said, looking pointedly at Acacia.

She had been pushing her food around on her plate to make a design. "My grades aren't too bad. It's just my attendance that sucks."

"Where are you applying?" Eve asked and when Acacia shrugged, she continued, "Wouldn't it be fun if we ended up at the same school?"

Tom and I exchanged a look when Acacia perked right up.

"Where's Emmy applying?" I asked.

When Acacia met my gaze, her annoyed look told me to mind my own business. I raised my eyebrows letting her know I knew about their little argument this afternoon. She quickly averted her eyes and began cutting her food into even smaller pieces.

"She talked about a place in Oregon and the local community college but her grades suck so who knows if she'll even go," Acacia said.

"I can help you with your personal statements," Eve offered. "I have a bunch of templates I can send you."

My parents looked absolutely thrilled at the prospect of Acacia even considering college. Conversation was easy as if we were all old friends. Why couldn't my 'meet the parents' dinner have gone as well? Instead of dwelling on it, I just enjoyed the easy comfort as we ate.

Since the living room was a disaster, the adults went out back while the teenagers cleared the table. *Na, na, na, na, na!* I got to be one of the adults. It was about time too. If I'd known bringing a guy home meant no after dinner clean up, I'd have done it ages ago. Thinking back on my previous boyfriends, maybe it wasn't such a good idea.

"Will you have to move back to California for your music, Tom?" My mom asked once we were settled.

I hadn't even considered that. I was too busy enjoying the right now. He must have noticed my reaction to the question because he took my hand in his before answering.

"I hope not. I like it here and your daughter didn't really take to the city," Tom said, giving me a half smile.

"Arabella says you're renting. If you're going to be staying in the area, you should seriously consider buying." I could tell 'Mom - the Super Realtor' was emerging.

Tom glanced my way but started talking before I could come up with an excuse. "Arabella is finishing her spare room so we..."

I stopped him before he irrevocably ruined an otherwise perfect evening. "He's not ready to buy, Mom, and I promise not to let him get another realtor. Let him figure out what to expect before he gets into something he's not ready for."

My parents exchanged a look but didn't say anything. Damn. I wasn't fast enough, or my excuse was too lame. It was obvious Tom was about to say we were moving in together. The uncomfortable silence we'd been able to prevent now hung thickly over us.

"Why don't you ladies go see if we can have some of that mystery dessert, while Tom and I have a little chat?" Dad offered.

I jumped right up but my mom hesitated, as if not sure what he was playing at. With a nod of encouragement, she got to her feet and we headed inside. I was glad I was leading because the girls were looking a little too friendly when I came around the corner. I shot my sister a nasty look and they headed to opposite ends of the kitchen.

The four of us had the rest of dinner cleaned up in no time. Other than putting the plates in the dishwasher, the girls hadn't done much of anything while we had been outside. Well, I'm sure they were doing *something* but nothing that involved cleaning.

Eve had made a fancy looking blueberry cream pie for dessert. My dad went on and on about it, having a second helping bigger than his first. He and Tom hadn't said anything about their private chat but nothing in their body language indicated it was negative in any way. They had come in laughing and I heard the tail end of an embarrassing story from when I was little.

"Acacia, can I talk to you for a minute? In your room?" I whispered when Eve insisted on helping Mom clean up the dessert dishes.

She gave the room full of people a longing look before following me to her miraculously clean room. While she turned to close the door, I flipped on her stereo, adjusting the volume so we could hear each other but not be overheard in the dining room.

"What was your fight with Emmy about?" I folded my arms across my chest.

Acacia flopped down on her bed and smoothed a throw pillow. "Nothing."

"Bull. Mom thought you were fighting over Eve stealing away Emmy's boyfriend but we both know that isn't true. So, spill it."

My sister chewed on her bottom lip as if deciding whether or not to lie again. "Nick told everyone I had sex with him at my party."

I frowned; Nick must be Blondie's name. That didn't explain why Eve had been part of the argument. I pressed on, "And?"

She flinched at my harsh tone. "And Eve forced him to sign the waiver."

Shit. This was what I was afraid of. Eve would be protected because of her sleazebag lawyer brother but Acacia wouldn't. If this was just a jilted boyfriend rumor, the threat was only to my sister's reputation, which would most likely disappear as soon as she graduated. I wasn't worried about that and I doubted she was either, having never put much stock in what other people thought. However, if parents got involved, it could get ugly fast.

A gentle knock at the door made us both turn. "Am I interrupting?" Eve asked tentatively.

"Come on in. This involves you too." I gestured for her to sit next to Acacia. "Apparently, Blondie is going to be a pain in our asses. He's spreading nasty rumors."

Eve tossed her hair over her shoulder in a gesture of dismissal. "He can't do anything but talk. He signed the waiver."

My temper flared and I had to catch myself so I didn't yell. "Acacia doesn't have a fancy attorney to bail her out of misunderstandings. I've worked enough harassment claims to know if you didn't have a witness to the signature, it's all he-said, she-said."

At this, Eve paled. Shit. Somehow, I didn't think this was going to be the end of this little problem. However, at that moment, Mom knocked and poked her head in.

"I'm home tomorrow. Eve, would you like to spend the night?"

Tom had come up behind her, we answered at the same time, "No."

# Chapter Eighteen

"**A**rabella?" Eve whispered through my door, "Are you awake?" Well, I was now.

Eve had insisted on staying at my house for the duration of her vacation, even though my couch was not the most comfortable thing for sleeping. Apparently, Tom worked on his music at all hours and she couldn't sleep at his place. Lovely, another thing to look forward to when he moved in. The thought made my heart skip a beat. Strange hours or not, I was looking forward to it.

"I'm awake. Come on in," I answered, rearranging the covers and flattening my sleep mussed hair.

Eve was showered, dressed, and carrying a mug of what I assumed was coffee when she entered. Her golden hair was pulled up into a neat ponytail and she was wearing one of Acacia's old t-shirts. We'd planned on painting the room today and from the looks of things she was ready to go. I sat up and took the coffee from her with a grateful smile.

The project had been slow going between my jobs and Acacia's summer school four days a week. We'd narrowed down the color scheme down and my sister had some rough sketches done for detail work. Eve and I found a dresser and full-length standing mirror in a thrift store that would be joining Tom's futon in the room.

"Did you decide on the colors yet?" Eve sat on the edge of the bed, tucking her foot underneath her.

"I think I like the lavender and cream combo best but I know Acacia is still rooting for the buttery yellow and melon." I sipped the coffee. Yum!

"Maybe we could do a combination of all of those." When I wrinkled my nose, she continued, "I have an idea but I kind of want it to be a surprise."

Eve had wonderful taste and we had agreed on most things so far. However, I was a little hesitant because she had a really hard time telling Acacia no. If I gave them free reign, I'd have a rainbow paint splattered mess. The goal was a nice guest room, not a teenage den of creativity.

"As long as it isn't all black or filled with rainbows and unicorns, I guess I'll trust you. Just don't let Acacia bully you into something you know I'll hate. We don't have time to redo it."

With a beaming smile, Eve hugged me. I had to juggle my coffee mug so we both didn't get scalded. After the hug, she jumped up and skipped out of the room. I shook my head and threw back the covers. The littlest things made her so happy. After stuffing my feet into my new fuzzy slippers, a gift from Eve, I followed her.

She was singing along with the radio while thumping around in the kitchen. During her stay, she'd been the perfect roommate. She insisted on doing the dishes and cooking on days I worked. After some basic mower instruction, she even trimmed my lawn. I hope her brother was taking good notes.

I joined in on the second chorus of the song. We ended up dancing around like idiots until we were laughing so hard we had to hold each other up so we didn't fall down. Why couldn't Acacia and I have this much fun together? Speaking of the devil, her face appeared in my kitchen doorway as Eve and I swung each other around again.

"Am I interrupting?" she asked, giving me an annoyed look.

"Acacia, I'm so glad you're here!" Eve dropped my hands and ran over to give my sister a big hug. "Arabella said yes to the plan!"

My sister's surly expression evaporated as the girls entwined their fingers and brought their foreheads together. Was my sister jealous of me having fun with her girlfriend or because we never had fun with each other? Either way, my approval of Eve's secret seemed to brighten her mood dramatically.

"Can we borrow your car?" Acacia asked. "I need to take Eve to the craft store before we can start." Acacia asked.

"Sure," I agreed, nodding to the key rack by the door. "I need to drink this to turn my brain on and change into some work clothes before we do anything."

The girls began talking at a million miles an hour so I tuned them out, focusing on my coffee instead. If they wanted my opinion on something, they'd ask. Trying to follow their conversations was beyond comprehension. I'd found this out the hard way. The one time I'd tried, I ended up with six jars of different flavored peanut butters and a migraine. Don't ask.

I was wearing my new camisole and shorts pajama set, another gift from Eve. Once again, I hoped her brother was taking notes. Remembering Tom however, made me frown. He was leaving for LA again on Monday and he wasn't sure how long he'd be gone. The plan was to move his stuff over tomorrow just in case his lease expired before he got back. We needed to finish the room, and fast.

It was serenely quiet once the girls left and I let out a sigh of relief at my brief moment of solitude. I found an energy bar and ripped open the package with my teeth on my way to the living room to enjoy my quick and quiet breakfast. There was a knock as I passed the front door.

"Lock yourself out again, Eve?" I mumbled around my mouthful of food.

My blood ran cold when I opened the door. The mug I was holding slipped from my grasp. Victor's hand shot out to catch it before it smashed at my feet. If I'd been prepared, I would have kicked him in the gut and slammed the door in his face. Instead, I began to choke on my energy bar.

I backed into the house so I could lean against the wall and gasped for breath. When Victor took a step inside, I continued to back further in and my coughing fit only worsened. Had I inhaled the entire mouthful? Granola in the lungs, not a good thing.

After Victor cleared the threshold, I held up my hand in an indication for him to stop. I wasn't the least bit surprised when he didn't respond to my pathetic attempt at keeping him from invading my house any further. Why the hell couldn't I stop coughing?

"Can I get you a drink or something?" he offered, raising an eyebrow and my mug.

I shook my head angrily and pointed at the open door. "Get out!" I sputtered through my never-ending coughing fit.

He just folded his hands in front of himself and waited for me to stop choking to death. However, he did stop where he was just inside my front door. His eyes did a quick sweep of the living room before returning his gaze to me, a small smirk on his face.

"Quaint, but I expected nothing less. Are you sure I can't do anything for you?" he asked, reaching out to me.

I flinched. "Go to Hell." The coughing made my request sound less insulting than I'd intended and I stomped my foot when he laughed.

"But I've brought you the answer to all your problems," he said, offering my coffee mug to me.

I snatched it away and took a drink. To my relief, I stopped coughing, mostly. "I don't know what the hell you're talking about but if you don't get out of my house, I'm calling the cops."

"That's not very nice." Victor shook his head. "But that's just how you are."

His gaze swept up and down my frame, taking in my skimpy pajamas and I fought the urge to cover myself with my arms. I knew for a fact my striped underwear was visible through the thin, light-colored fabric. This was my house damn it, I could wear whatever the hell I wanted!

"Going to the phone now," I warned, taking a step toward the kitchen.

By the time the cops got here, I'd be dead if that was his plan but I hoped he'd fall for my bluff and leave. Another step and I'd be able to reach my cell phone but I'd have to turn my back on him to get it. I may be unarmed but I still had a brain.

"What do you want?" I asked as icily as I could.

Victor tilted his head. "You know very well what I want."

At the sound of his liquid smooth voice, my scars began to tingle. With a gasp, my hand lifted to cover them, as if it made any difference. It took all my will to force my arm back down to my side.

"I never meant to hurt you. It's Tom's fault you have those," he said, motioning to my neck, sending a mix of pleasure and pain to my very core. My knees began to tremble but through sheer anger, I stayed upright.

"Stop it!" I shouted. "Get out of my house!"

He sighed and adjusted his shirt sleeve so he could look at his wristwatch. "I see you're going to make this difficult."

"No, I'm going to make you get your creepy ass out of my house!"

"Remember, you brought this upon yourself," he said as he turned and walked back out the front door.

As soon as he passed the threshold, I slammed the door shut then flipped both the handle and deadbolt locks. Those wouldn't be enough to stop him if he really wanted to get back in, but I did it to make myself feel better. Unfortunately, it knew it wouldn't work so I stood in front of the door, willing it to stay closed.

A few minutes later, I heard the ringtone for my work phone somewhere in the back of the house. My frazzled brain took a moment to recognize the sound and by the time I found it, the ringing had stopped. The number wasn't one I recognized but if it was work, it was important, especially since they left a voicemail.

I unlocked the phone and pressed the voicemail button and apparently the speaker button at the same time. Victor's smooth voice filled my house, freezing me in place.

"Your sister sure is cute. Do you and her both a favor and keep your mouth shut about our little visit today. I'd hate for anything to happen to her."

There was a brief pause and the message started repeating. I tossed the phone away and pulled my knees to my chest. I knew what Victor was capable of. Hell, I'd lived it. He was threatening to do that or worse to Acacia. She was out there, unsuspecting and unprotected. There was nothing I could do to keep her safe, especially huddled on my kitchen floor like a five-year-old scared of the boogeyman. As much of a bad ass as I'd like to think I was, Victor scared the crap out of me.

· · · ·

WHEN THE GIRLS RETURNED, I'd changed my clothes, braided my hair and, most importantly, pulled myself together. Their laughter when they opened the door allowed me to let out the breath I'd been holding not knowing if Victor would do something while Acacia was with Eve.

To my surprise, the girls weren't alone when they piled into the spare room where I'd been setting up. Tom smiled at me after sharing a conspiratorial look with the two teens. I did my best to smile back not knowing how it actually turned out.

"I'm here to rescue you from painting duty," he announced, helping me from where I'd been kneeling on the floor.

"Eve..." I began.

"You said it was okay. Besides, if you're here, it won't be a surprise," she explained.

Both girls put the gallon paint buckets they'd been holding on the floor and set two small tester samples on top. I frowned and inspected the labels to make sure they were the colors we'd agreed on. There was no Melon, in its place was Glossy Ebony.

Acacia rolled her eyes. "The sooner you leave, the sooner we can be done."

I opened my mouth to protest but Tom grabbed my chin and turned my head so I was looking at him. "They've run the idea by me and you don't need to worry."

"I can see you're all ganging up on me." I threw my arms up in the air. "Do I need to change before you drag me kicking and screaming from my own house?"

He cringed. "I was hoping you could help me pack?"

"I'm not really getting out of work, am I?" I teased.

Tom had offered most of his furniture to his neighbors but what they wouldn't take we were donating to charity or the dumpster out back. After swinging by the truck rental and moving supply store to grab supplies, we drove to his apartment.

I found myself chewing on the inside of my cheek and staring out the window when Tom asked, "You okay over there? Having second thoughts?"

Forcing a smile, I turned to face him. "You couldn't get that lucky."

He regarded me for a second longer before turning back to the road. I couldn't help but worry about Victor's threat. The girls had looked at me like I was crazy when I told them to lock up after we left. What did he mean, he had the answer to all my problems? At the moment, my life was pretty conflict free. He was the only wrinkle in my otherwise happy existence.

Tom's apartment looked sparse when we entered. He headed to the kitchen to get us some sodas while I began organizing different sized boxes. We still had to pack his music equipment, clothes, bathroom stuff, and random assortment of crap that would never again see the light of day. The majority of our time would be spent cleaning so he would get at least part of his deposit back.

He put his hands over mine when I began to fight with the packing tape roller. "It's going to take those girls a while. Why don't we take advantage of our time alone?"

Any other time I would have had a witty comeback or come up with the idea on my own. Because of my unexpected visitor this morning, I just continued to wrestle the large roll of tape onto the plastic holder.

I almost had it when the roll snapped to the side, making me run the serrated blade across the palm of my hand. Cursing, I dropped the entire thing on my foot and managed to cut open my toe as well.

Tom took my hand in his and inspected the damage. "Not exactly what I had in mind."

He swung his arm under my legs and carried me to the bathroom. After digging in the medicine chest, he produced a tiny bandage for my wounded toe while I washed my hand. After covering the gash, he stilled my hands and turned off the water.

"Are you going to tell me what's bothering you?" Tom asked, holding my gaze.

I dropped my eyes. There was no point in trying to lie to Tom, he'd know, but I couldn't tell him what was really bothering me. I wouldn't make this his problem; it was between Victor and me. I was a big girl and could take care of myself. Instead of coming up with some lame excuse, I closed my eyes and took a deep breath.

"I'm just worried about the girls. Do you think we should have left them alone?"

Tom chuckled. "If they plan on getting half of what they need to get done, they won't have time to even think about doing something they shouldn't. We, on the other hand..."

The faint tingle in my scar told me exactly what he was thinking and this time I didn't fight it. If I had, he'd know there was more to my strange behavior.

"Speaking of hands, are you going to help me with this or I am going to have to do it myself?" I asked.

With a mischievous glint in his eyes, he lifted my still bleeding hand to his lips. I let myself get distracted, almost forgetting my earlier worry. Tom was oh so good at distracting me and, considering he was leaving for who knows how long, I was going to enjoy the time we had. When he sensed my tension fading, he took full advantage of the fact there weren't any teenagers in the apartment.

As Tom dozed next to me, I tried to convince myself that while Victor didn't have any qualms about hurting me or my family, I had serious doubts he'd do anything while Eve was around. Why wouldn't he want anyone to know he was here? Why did it matter? I fell asleep still wondering what trouble he'd brought with him.

"Come with me," Tom whispered, rousing me from my nap.

I snuggled up to him and his arms tightened around me. "I can't."

"Yes, you can." Tom kissed the back of my neck. "We could get a hotel room and try introducing you to California again."

His breath on my ear made me shiver. "I can't just abandon my life. I have responsibilities, a job, a mortgage, Acacia to look after..."

I let my sentence trial off. It hit me then. Victor must have known Tom was leaving. That's why he'd come. This time I didn't need Tom to save me. I wanted this thing over so we could both move on with our lives. This time Victor would have no choice but to give up. If he wanted a fight, I'd give it to him.

# Chapter Nineteen

After reminding Acacia and Eve to be good, I jumped in my car for my weekly staff meeting. Tom and I'd run to the store a few days ago for some ice cream only to discover the girls showering together when we got back. Luckily, we'd arrived just minutes before my mom and could therefore run interference. Since that incident and Tom's threat to take Eve back with him to California on Monday, they'd been on their best behavior.

The lot was almost full by the time I pulled into Geo's Security. My boss had been better about my assignments lately and I was looking forward to a busy schedule, especially with Tom leaving tomorrow morning. After scanning the crowd for Cassie, I pressed my way to where she was sitting on a table in the very back.

"Hey Cass." I jumped up so I could sit next to her and lean against the wall.

"Hey back, I never see you anymore. When are we going to hit the town?" she asked, giving Big Creepy Al a sneer when he flashed her a gap-toothed grin.

"Looks like Al would *love* to hit the town with you," I teased.

"Pass," she answered flatly.

"Other than the workload I get today, I'm free. Tom's heading back to LA tomorrow."

"Sweet!" Cassie said then quickly clarified when I gave her an exasperated look. "Not sweet, he's leaving; sweet, you'll stop avoiding your friends."

"I know what you meant," I whispered back playfully when Geo cleared his throat to get everyone's attention.

"The city sent me the new rules and regulations for private security this week. You will receive a copy with your schedules and I expect you all to *read* them." I rolled my eyes and Cassie giggled. "There is some big corporate trial in town so some of you will be doubling up and will be on protection detail until the case is concluded."

I perked up at this hoping to get more info. Maybe that's why LA's finest asshole was in town. However, Geo was obviously not interested in the details, just the business opportunity, and changed topics without further elaboration. After a few minutes of his drawling on and on, Cassie and I began to play hangman on a scrap of paper.

I jumped when Geo started talking to me. "You've got some proficiency training to brush up on, Arabella. Here's your schedule and permit application."

He handed me a stack of papers and began shuffling his stack to find Cassie's. I glanced at the top paper and frowned.

"Concealed weapon permit?" I asked.

"Congratulations, you're being promoted. According to the new regs, anyone working after normal business hours is required to have additional protection. Your file says you passed your firearms training but you're due for recertification. Get it done so you can start work by Thursday."

I shuffled through my papers trying to find my schedule wondering what I was going to be doing late at night that would require me to carry a concealed firearm. By the time I unearthed it, Geo was halfway across the room.

"Oh shit."

"What?" Cassie asked, glancing at my schedule. "Hey, we'll be working together. I wonder what the case is about?"

"Doesn't matter. I'm not doing it," I said, standing.

Cassie yanked me back. "You've been whining about piss-ant jobs for as long as I can remember. Don't blow it now Geo's finally giving you a chance for something big. I'll take you to the shooting range if you're afraid you won't pass your proficiency exam."

I slumped against the wall. She was right. If I turned this down, Geo might not give me another chance in the foreseeable future. Besides, according to this, I'd have to be armed while working. I could be a professional and not let a little discomfort ruin my career. Plus, if all went well, I'd kill two birds with one stone, all while getting paid.

"I'll take you up on that offer for range time. I want to make sure my client feels good and secure while I'm around."

Unlike the folkloric tales of vampires, we don't burst into flames in the sun or melt in holy water. A stake through the heart works but that would kill pretty much anything. Other than being stronger and slightly faster, vampires were just as vulnerable as every other human on the planet. A strategically placed bullet was just as effective as anything else.

"Looks like some serious overtime." Cassie was still talking while I was commiserating on vampire mortality. "Good thing Tom will be out of town. He might feel left out."

"Oh, believe me, it's a good thing he'll be gone but it has nothing to do with feeling left out." I huffed a laugh.

Cassie narrowed her eyes. "Are you going to tell me what's going on?"

"I think I'll let you die slowly from the suspense. I need to get home before two teenagers decide that painting one room isn't enough." I grabbed my stack of papers and headed toward the door.

"I'll call and reserve us a spot at the range on Tuesday," Cassie called, and I waved without looking back.

My first stop was the sporting goods store. I didn't own a gun, having never really seen the point before now. It had been Geo's recommendation that I take firearms training when he hired me. Now, however, there was no way in hell I would take this job without one. The lie I told Cassie wasn't entirely false but having a weapon had nothing to do with keeping my client safe. Quite the opposite,

I had just been given permission to carry a gun while protecting the one person who was more of a threat to me than anyone was to him. Geo had assigned me as Victor's protection detail.

I hadn't expected Tom to be there when I got home. When I heard his voice from the back room, I stuffed my paperwork into the bag from the sporting goods store then put the whole shebang under the couch. I did not want to have to explain my purchase just yet.

"You're back," he said, taking me into his arms as I straightened.

I forced a bright smile. "Are they done?"

He smiled back. "You're in a good mood. Geo finally giving you decent jobs?"

"Something like that." I started toward the back.

I only got one step before he pulled me to a stop. "Close your eyes."

I gave him an exasperated look and he raised his eyebrows. "Close your eyes!" came a chorus from the girls in the back room.

"Fine!" I called then closed my eyes but kept the same put out look on my face.

Tom took my hand and led me slowly to the back. The smell of paint assaulted my nostrils and I stifled a sneeze. I could hear the drop sheet being gathered and the scrape of furniture against the hardwood floor. Had they finished putting in the furniture as well?

"Now!" Eve squealed.

I opened my eyes and my jaw dropped. The transformation was absolutely incredible. As I suspected from the noise, the new furniture was already in place. The dark walnut dresser and standing mirror sat along the long wall, which was painted lavender. The rest of the walls were the butter yellow. Tom's futon cover had been replaced with one that matched the new color scheme. Both girls were seated on it, allowing me to get the full effect without blocking anything.

Acacia had hand painted fancy scrollwork and exotic ivy print in ebony where the corners of the walls and ceiling met. Eve had written parts of her favorite poems in fancy calligraphy in contrasting colors on all four walls. Overhead, a new, lighted ceiling fan whirred almost silently.

"Well?" Eve prompted, unable to contain her excitement a second longer.

"It's perfect!" I blurted out. Both girls launched themselves off the futon, enveloping me in hugs.

"See, I told you she'd love it," Tom said, trying to stay away from the attack hug I was receiving. "Now, get changed so we can go out and celebrate. This room needs to air out or we'll all be suffering from paint fume induced brain damage."

When the girls scurried off to get out of their paint splattered clothes, Tom led me back to the living room.

"I bought you something." He reached under the couch.

I stiffened, hoping he didn't accidentally pull out my bag instead. A breath of relief escaped my lips when he put a little black one in my lap. He made no move to open it, so I turned it over and dumped the contents in my lap.

The first thing I noticed was the bright red rectangle. "You bought me a cell phone?"

He gave me a sheepish grin and held up a matching black one. "Now, we can call and even video chat with each other as much as we want for free. Couldn't do that with your old brick phone."

"Oh," I said, picking up the other thing that fell out of the bag. This one I recognized too but made no move to open it.

"I know you're not much of a jewelry person..." Tom began, taking the tiny turquoise velvet box from me and turning it over in his hands.

When he popped it open, I nearly gasped in relief. As crazy as I was about Tom, I was barely sure I was ready for him to move in and not in the least bit prepared for an engagement. Inside was an opal pendant, my birthstone, set in a delicate yellow-gold setting.

"It's beautiful. Help me put it on."

I lifted my hair so he could fashion the clasp. His hands trailed down the sides of my neck and rested on my shoulders. He gave me a kiss on the back of my neck before I let my hair fall.

"Now you won't forget me while I'm gone," he said.

"Not likely. All your crap's in my house," I teased, giving him a thank you kiss.

"You'll have plenty of time for that later," Acacia said, making me jump. "Let's go, I'm starving."

• • • •

*HERE GOES NOTHING.* I watched as Tom's plane lifted off. If everything went according to plan, I'd earn my promotion and be rid of the Victor problem long before Tom got home. If I could do it without Tom finding out about it, even better. My first challenge was Eve.

There wasn't much chance of her not finding out Victor was here. The town wasn't that big, and she had a lot of free time on her hands during the day. She'd taken a real interest in 'our little town' as she liked to refer to it. Going as far as to get the local newspaper sent to my house. It was only a matter of time before she either ran into him or saw something on the local news about the case.

The sky was still the pale gray of dawn when I pulled up in front of my house. Tom's SUV was parked on the street so Eve would have transportation and he didn't have to pay for airport parking. I found myself smiling at the prospect of having it there even after he got back.

Eve was still sleeping on my couch, since the guest room was still noxious from the paint even with the window open and the fan on. I eased the door open and tried to sneak through without waking her up. My plan was to tell her the news over breakfast, which gave me at least an hour to prepare before she woke up.

I decided to spend some time familiarizing myself with my new toy, AKA my fancy red cell phone. Eve and Tom had spent last night programming it and I'd tried to watch over their shoulders as she explained how to do everything. Since I'm not tech savvy, I quickly got confused and lost interest. I'm more of a hands-on learner.

I pressed the power button and was startled when it chimed. Tom's name appeared at the top of the screen. Okay, now how did I see it? I pressed the green icon that looked like a cartoon text bubble and smiled when '*I love you*' appeared. I started pressing buttons until I figured out how to respond.

Once I figured out how to type a message, I tried to come up with something to ease his separation anxiety. After a moment of thought I typed, '*R U GONE ALRAEDY?*' Our painfully slow banter continued back and forth during his layover then he promised to call once he arrived in LA.

I took a shower while I waited and when I stepped out of the bathroom, I heard Eve's voice.

"I'm not sure," she said in just above a whisper then gave me a pained smile. "I've gotta go. I'll see you later."

"Morning. You want some breakfast?" I asked, heading for the kitchen.

I heard her get up and pad in after me. "I'm, uh meeting someone for breakfast."

"Doesn't Acacia have school today?" I asked, measuring out the coffee grounds.

"Um..." she scuffed her toe on the floor.

I closed my eyes and exhaled. "Victor's your brother, too. Don't feel like you're being unfaithful by wanting to spend time with him."

She gasped. "You know he's here?"

I huffed a laugh. "He stopped by for a *friendly* visit yesterday, and you're looking at his protection detail for the duration of his stay."

When I turned to face her, she looked horrified so I continued, "Do me a favor and don't tell Tom or he'll be on the next flight home."

"But, but..." she started.

"Don't worry about me. I know how to protect myself. Just don't expect me to invite him over for dinner."

She gave me a wary smile and headed for the bathroom. That had gone better than I'd imagined but I could tell Eve was warring with her allegiances. I had no idea what Eve and Victor's relationship was like. It was too much to hope that she despised him as much as Tom did. Just another thing I'd have to deal with.

# Chapter Twenty

"Nice," Cassie praised as I inspected my latest hole-riddled target.

We'd been at the shooting range for nearly two hours and our time was almost up. I'd made the appointment for my proficiency exam for first thing tomorrow morning. Despite using a different gun than during my initial training, I was doing okay. Cassie was kicking my ass but she had a standing appointment at the range every week.

"It's better but not great," I murmured, sending another target flying to the end of the range.

"You need to relax. Chances are you'll never even have to unholster your weapon let alone fire it."

I smiled at this. When I arrived today, she had surprised me with a thigh holster. Obviously, she expected me to wear a skirt at the Federal courthouse, not that I'd have my gun on me while I was inside. Maybe she just wanted to get a rise out of the security officers when we both hiked up our skirts as we turned them over each day. With the exception of courthouse security, no weapons of any kind passed the sign-in desk. It was the coming and going protection that we'd be responsible for anyway.

The hour chime sounded just before I took my last shot. That was all the training I'd get before my test tomorrow. I hoped it would be enough. I'd checked the range schedule but there weren't any other openings between now and then. Cassie and I hung up our protective gear and headed out.

"You hungry?" she asked when we got to the parking lot.

I shrugged. "Sure."

My house guest slash roommate had almost completely abandoned me since yesterday morning. Eve had spent the entire day with Victor and left before breakfast again today. It was better

183

this way though. If she kept him company, maybe he wouldn't come looking for me. Yeah, right, and maybe I was the Queen of Sheba.

We took my car to a downtown pub for a late lunch. I loved this place with its dark wood wall paneling and historical pictures hanging amongst the neon signs advertising the local microbreweries. Since they'd switched to nonsmoking, it was my favorite place for a little bar food. A plate of spicy chicken wings and onion rings were calling my name. Cassie made a detour to the ladies' room, so I went ahead to scout out a table.

The lighting was really dim after being out in the sunshine and I was still blinking into the darkness when I recognized two of the patrons. My hope to turn heel and escape was cut short when Eve called my name and waved. I rearranged my features into the best smile I could manage before weaving my way through the tables.

"Do you want to sit with us?" Eve asked after giving me a quick hug.

"I'm here with Cassie and we need to talk about work stuff," I explained tentatively, knowing we probably wouldn't talk about anything other than my need to go back to the shooting range.

"Perfect. I was hoping to prepare a schedule with you before we meet with the judge on Thursday," Victor said.

He'd been sitting with his back to me when I walked up so I hadn't even looked at him as I approached and spoke to Eve. As much as I'd like to pretend he wasn't there, I turned and looked down at him. He was dressed more casual than I'd seen before in a yellow polo shirt and designer jeans. I stifled a shudder at his resemblance to Tom.

"There's Cassie!" Eve half-stood and waved her over.

"Hey Eve and uh..."

Cassie looked genuinely startled and confused when she focused on Victor. Between the different clothes and haircut, not to mention my standoffish posture, it was obvious it wasn't Tom sitting there but it was an easy enough mistake to make. I knew exactly how she felt and wasn't about to let her flounder any longer than necessary.

"Cassie Franzenburg, this is Victor River, Tom's brother and part A of our protection detail," I explained, folding my arms across my chest.

Cassie's mouth formed an 'O' of understanding as she shook Victor's hand. "Nice to meet you, Ms. Franzenburg."

"How do you know it isn't Mrs. Franzenburg?" Cassie asked slyly.

Victor gave her a satisfied smirk. "No ring."

"Very observant. May we join you?" Cassie asked, pulling out an empty chair and plunking down without waiting for a response.

Fine, I'd warn Cassie about Victor later. Hopefully, she wouldn't be too mad at me for letting her flirt so shamelessly with the man who had tried to kill her friend. I walked behind Eve and made a point of moving my chair closer to her before I sat. It didn't make much of a difference around the tiny table but I hoped Victor noticed.

Victor and Cassie continued their playful banter and I cringed when Cassie flipped her hair over her shoulder. Were we back in high school? I hadn't told anyone the details of my 'accident' in California. Being the good friend she was, Cassie hadn't pried. She knew if I wanted to tell her something, I would. Gritting my teeth, I turned to Eve and did my best to ignore the display.

"Am I flying solo for dinner again tonight?" I asked, snagging a chip from the plate of nachos. Chicken *and* jalapeños, sweet!

"Aren't you working tonight?" she asked, flicking a glance at her brother.

"No, I told you I was working this afternoon but would be home well before dinner," I reminded her.

"That's right." She took a long drink of her soda, keeping her gaze fixed on the table.

"All right, spill it." I sat back and folded my arms.

Eve gave me a defeated look and her shoulders slumped slightly. "If Tom hadn't moved everything out of his place I could have cooked there but... I know I should have asked you since it *is* your house but after you said... I kind of made plans to cook dinner for Victor tonight."

She was doing her nervous babbling routine again and I noticed Victor's attention had strayed from Cassie's story. Not enough for her to notice but she wasn't watching him like prey watches a predator. I leaned forward and put my hand on Eve's to stop her from saying too much.

"It's okay, Eve. I'll just go hang out with Acacia tonight." When she frowned and sank further in her chair, I continued, "Let me guess, she's going to be at my house for dinner too?"

"I wanted to introduce her to Victor." She adjusted her already straight silverware.

Great, now I had no choice but to be there. Not only did I not want him in my house, but I definitely didn't want him anywhere near my sister without me to protect her. Keeping a professional distance was going to be harder than I thought. Victor's gaze was on me as I tried to figure out a way to break up the plans without hurting Eve's feelings.

Much to my annoyance, I came up with zip. "Fine. What can I do to help?"

The corner of Victor's lip curled into a half smile and I scowled at him in return. Cassie, still doing her best to flirt, was somehow oblivious to the tension at the table. As soon as I'd admitted defeat, he turned his attention back to her with a brilliant smile that caused Cassie's brain to freeze and forget what she was saying. She was going to be pissed when I told her Victor was off limits for so many reasons.

• • • •

CASSIE WASN'T NEARLY as mad as I'd imagined, more disappointed, when I told her to back off. I hadn't divulged the details of what had happened in California, just that we had a less than friendly incident. After some deliberation, I didn't want her to overreact and accidently-on-purpose shoot him while we were on the job. She refused my invitation for dinner, which meant she was more embarrassed than she wanted to admit. Considering we were stuck with him for who knew how long, she needed time to nurse her bruised ego before having to work with him every day.

Eve assigned me to salad duty, which under normal circumstances would've pissed me off but tonight it was perfect. I wanted to do some cleaning before Victor came over. It wasn't about trying to impress him, more about protecting my privacy. The less he knew about me the better. Besides, Eve and I had done laundry and still had stuff hanging to dry all over the house. Ugh, I'm turning into my mom, the super hostess.

While Eve worked on some fancy pasta dish, I cleaned the house, putting away anything that didn't absolutely need to be out. I did, however, put out some of Tom's things. This allowed me to make a point about our relationship and get rid of some of the moving boxes. Between the time at the shooting range and house cleaning, I felt grimy from head to foot.

"I'm going to jump in the shower," I told Eve as I finished putting away the cleaning supplies.

"Mmm hmm," she mumbled, running her finger down the recipe again.

With a quick glance at the clock, I hurried to the bathroom. Victor was supposed to arrive in little over an hour. That gave me plenty of time to shower, get dressed, and mentally prepare for the evening.

I turned on Tom's tiny radio, perched beside the vanity's sink, before stepping into the shower. The warm water eased my tense muscles and I tried to relax. Somewhere between shaving my legs and using my deep conditioner, I began singing along with the radio.

After a few verses of one of my favorite songs, my mood had dramatically improved. When I opened the bathroom door to let out some of the steam, I could hear Eve still rummaging around in the kitchen so I went about getting ready. With a towel on my head and another one wrapped around me, I wandered into the kitchen wondering when Acacia was supposed to get here.

Victor stood tasting the sauce Eve had been fussing over for the last few hours. I whipped my head back to the living room in search of my buffer in the form of a teenage blonde. In my surprised haste, both towels began to slip.

"She went to pick up Acacia," Victor explained as I fixed the towel trying to slip off my head while keeping a death grip on the one around my body.

In my opinion, there was no reason to answer so I turned and headed for the bedroom for some much-needed clothing. It was stupid but I pushed in the button lock on the doorknob once I was in the sanctuary of my room. All the tension I had before my shower had returned a hundredfold. I leaned against the inside of the door and tried to gather my thoughts. Why had I thought dealing with Victor was going to be easy? And why had Eve left without telling me?

I threw on the first thing I touched but changed my mind when I looked down at the suggestive slogan on my shirt. I wasn't even Irish! After towel drying and running my fingers through my hair, I headed back into the war zone preparing for the worst. I found Victor making himself comfortable on my couch, flipping through a book. When I realized what book it was, I dashed forward and grabbed it.

Victor laughed lightly and crossed his legs, putting one ankle on his knee. "I didn't realize hair could do that."

He was of course referring to my junior high school yearbook photo. Hey, perms were popular! I'd thought I'd hidden the yearbooks after the thorough teasing from the girls but apparently not. Using the excuse of finding just the right place on my bookshelf to stash the incriminating evidence, I kept my back turned and tried to regain some dignity.

"I like your hair down," Victor complimented and I stiffened.

With a deep breath, I turned. "Look..."

He laughed, interrupting me. "Here it comes."

I glared at him. "If I had my way, I'd send your ass packing right now. Just know this, the *only* reason you're here is because I adore your little sister. Since she's staying with me and wants to see you, I'm being the bigger person and accommodating her, not you. Don't think for a second any of this has to do with you."

I paused for a breath and he just continued to stare at me with that amused expression. "Furthermore, the only reason I agreed to your protection detail is because I need this job. I won't let you or anyone else screw it up. Got it?"

"May I make a suggestion?" he asked, sitting forward and resting his elbows on his knees. I motioned with my arm for him to continue. "A truce, of sorts. I won't do anything to make you feel uncomfortable..."

"Too late. You're already here."

Victor let out an annoyed sigh and stood. "Okay. How's this? I won't try to sway you from your path with my brother or ask for your blood. That is, until you want me to."

"They'll be enjoying icicles in Hell before that happens."

Victor grinned. "I hear they are pretty common in Michigan, just not this time of year."

"You know what I meant," I snapped.

"Yes, Arabella, I know exactly what you meant." He held out his perfectly manicured hand. "Will you accept my truce or not?"

He seemed sincere enough but I didn't trust one thing this man said or did. The ulterior motives were still just below the surface, insinuated in his unspoken words. Having this truce, as much of a farce as it was, was a step in the right direction. Unclenching my fists, I reached out to shake his hand.

When my hand was in his, he tried to yank me forward but I was prepared. I stepped in, bent his wrist backward, and swept my leg under his. His breath went out with a whoosh as he landed face first on my hardwood floor. Taking advantage of his surprise, I put my foot between his shoulder blades and bent his arm around, effectively pinning him to the floor, lifting just enough to make him cringe.

"I'll take your little truce for what it is, a diversion. And if you ever touch me again without my permission, I *will* kill you."

"What's going on?" Eve's voice was an octave too high.

I looked up at her through the curtain of my hair. "I was just showing your brother he has nothing to worry about while under my protection."

Dropping Victor's arm, I stood and flipped my hair out of my face, no wonder I always kept it pulled up. Acacia gave me an incredulous look as Victor stood and dusted himself off before turning to face the girls. He had a red mark on his chin where he'd hit the floor and I didn't even try to hide my satisfied smirk.

"Acacia, Victor River," I introduced. "Vic, this is my sister, Acacia, and the same deal applies to her. Now, let me get you some ice for that chin."

# Chapter Twenty-One

I passed my firearms proficiency with flying colors. Due to the annoyingly detailed background check they'd done when I applied at Geo's, my concealed weapon permit was fast tracked. The tiny temporary paper card fit into the business card sized pocket of my new navy suit coat. My pistol was in my thigh holster, and thanks to the flattering cut of my skirt, was almost invisible.

Eve had jumped on the chance of taking both Cassie and me out for a little shopping with an unnatural amount of enthusiasm. That was where we'd spent the majority of the day yesterday. I'd ended up with three new skirt suit combos, two new pairs of jeans, and a sexy little sundress Eve wouldn't let me go home without. Cassie came away with two identical suits: one in black, the other dark brown. Besides looking great in everything she tried on, she was much better at telling Eve to back off. Eve made shopping a full contact sport and I had fallen into bed two hours earlier than normal and slept like the dead.

I was currently on my way to pick up Mr. Wonderful from his hotel. Victor had meetings with his partner at the hotel yesterday, thus freeing up Eve's schedule. Somehow, I think his step back had a little to do with my knocking his ass to the floor. It had made dinner an awkward affair, but I slept better that night.

Pulling into the 'check-in only' parking, I hung up my security decal. Victor had told me he wanted to get to the courthouse no later than two so I was pleased to see my dash clock read 1:35. Plenty of time to get there as long as he was where he was supposed to be.

After checking myself in the rearview mirror, I opened my door and headed inside. Victor was supposed to meet me in the lobby. I walked past the registration desk, straight to the plush sitting area complete with leather furniture and enormous rock fireplace. Much to my annoyance, no one was there.

"Can I help you, Ma'am?" a pimple-faced teen in a hotel uniform asked when I turned.

Resisting the urge to strangle the kid for referring to me as 'Ma'am', I let out my breath of frustration. "Was a guest by the name of River here earlier?"

"Oh, you must be Ms. Simon. He left a message at the front desk for you to meet him at his suite," the annoyingly helpful ingrate announced.

"I'm sure he did. Do you have a phone I can use?" I asked, following him toward the registration desk.

"Yes, of ccc-course," he stuttered after glancing at the red cell phone clipped to the waistband of my skirt.

"Please dial Mr. River's room."

The helpful teen had put the phone on the counter so I could reach it. However, at my request he moved it back to his side. After a worried glance at the older, pinched-looking woman entering something on the computer, he turned back to me.

"Mr. River unplugged his phone. He wanted all messages delivered to him personally."

"Of course he did." I felt the beginning of a migraine starting. "His suite number?"

"1468, Ma'am."

"Thank you, and *don't* call me Ma'am," was my parting remark as I headed to the elevators.

The canned music grated on my nerves as I rode up the elevator. I stepped off on the top floor and rolled my shoulders since they'd managed to tense up to the point of being painful. Lifting my hand, I knocked three times on the door marked 1468.

"Come on in, Arabella," Victor's muffled voice called from the other side.

I had no intention of stepping a toe on the other side of his hotel room door so I adjusted my stance, putting one hand on my hip. After about a minute, I heard movement and the door clicked open.

"Sorry, was it locked?" Victor smiled at me.

"You were supposed to meet me downstairs."

With a quick scan of his attire, or lack thereof, I knew there was no way we'd get to the courthouse by two. "Is clothing optional at the courthouse now?"

His tousled dark hair looked like he'd just rubbed it with a towel, possibly the same one slung low around his waist. I jerked my vision back to his face but he'd already noticed my wandering eyes. While Tom was long and lean, Victor looked like he used that exercise equipment in his garage, a lot. It wasn't that I was ogling him, the small tattoo at his hip caught my eye was all. Damn it, I missed my boyfriend.

"I thought we could hammer out my schedule together before we head over. My meeting was pushed to three." Victor turned away from the door. "Come on in."

"I'll be downstairs when you're ready." I marched back to the elevators, thankful one was still waiting so Victor didn't have time to catch me before I escaped.

I headed out the side door when I reached the lobby, unlocked my phone and scrolled through my programmed numbers for Tom's cell. I pressed the call button. He probably wouldn't answer but just hearing his voice on his outgoing message would be enough to reground me. To my surprise, he picked up on the second ring.

"Hi Arabella, what's up?"

He sounded so happy; I couldn't help but smile. "Just waiting for a job. Got my time mixed up so I have about an hour to kill. How's the weather down there?"

Weather? I was asking him about the weather? I closed my eyes and took a deep breath. It didn't matter what we talked about, just that I was talking to him and not the jerk upstairs.

"It's sunny but they don't let me out much during the day. I just finished with lunch and I'm heading back to the studio right now. Will you be home tonight?" he said as his phone crackled. "I'm coming up to a tunnel and might lose you."

"Okay," I said but my phone beeped as the connection was severed.

I kicked a misplaced stone from the manicured landscape across the parking lot; it hit a dark sedan with a dull thunk. Grimacing, I turned around and pulled on the door I'd just exited to find it locked. I clipped my phone to my skirt and trudged back around to the main door. Stupid hotel.

Victor didn't emerge until ten to three, most likely operating under the delusion I'd come back up to his suite. Happy to see I'd disappointed him, I got to my feet and met him on his way to the front door.

"Ready?" I asked, holding the door for him.

He'd put on a charcoal gray pin-striped suit and platinum linen shirt; his hair was now perfectly styled. In his left hand was a black leather attaché case. He looked every inch the powerful LA attorney he was. Besides his unfair powers of persuasion, he was the other side's nightmare. Who would have thought someone so handsome could look so intimidating?

I unlocked the passenger door so he could get settled before sliding into the driver's seat myself. He hadn't said a word since coming downstairs and I reveled in my small victory.

Once we turned onto the main road, he cleared his throat. "After the meeting with the judge, I'll be in consultation with my team until nine at a local law office who was willing to share their conference room. Dinner will be immediately afterward."

I nodded and focused on the road. His tone was all business. Perfect. That's what I was hoping for: a business relationship. I'd keep him alive, and he'd treat me like nothing more than the help. Under normal circumstances, this would have bothered me to be looked down on in that way but in Victor's case, it was ideal.

When we parked in the public lot, Victor frowned. "This isn't the courthouse."

I tilted my head. "Really? There isn't parking at the courthouse so we walk from here."

"Drop me off then," he said sitting back.

"No. If I drop you off, you'll be alone. I wouldn't be doing a very good job protecting you if I left you standing on the sidewalk."

"Alternate arrangements will have to be made for next week," Victor said curtly and pushed the door open, narrowly missing the car parked next to mine.

"Don't take your frustrations out on my car. No one gets to park by the courthouse after 9/11. I hope your fancy shoes won't leave blisters after a few blocks."

"I was more worried about yours," Victor said offhandedly. "You look very... professional today."

The compliment took me off guard and I looked down at my feet. Eve had insisted on matching heels for each of my new suits. I'd put in squishy insoles and moleskin on my heels this morning in preparation for the walk.

"Don't worry about me," I said, motioning in the direction of the stairs.

The afternoon was uncomfortably hot as we walked toward the courthouse. Since I was supposed to be protecting Victor, I walked on the street side, which was unfortunately in full sun. About a block before we got there, I pulled off my jacket and slung it over my shoulder. I expected a quip about my red silk camisole but I didn't even get a raised eyebrow. Maybe Victor was too focused on the case. Another point for me.

I spotted Cassie as soon as we stepped inside the well air-conditioned courthouse. Her white-blonde hair was fashioned into a French twist and her black suit only enhanced her porcelain skin. Next to her stood a tall, dark-skinned man with unnaturally white teeth.

After passing through security and turning over my gun and cell phone, I joined them. As I pinned on my temporary badge, Victor introduced us, "Arabella Simon, this is one of my partners, Christopher Griffin."

He nodded my way then fixed his eyes on Victor. "Shall we?"

That was rude. Chris obviously saw me as a necessary evil, even lower than staff. I wondered if it was my place in society he looked down on, or my genetics? One glance told me he was from an older generation vampire family. Not as old as the Rivers, the gold was still too pronounced in his brown eyes, but he still felt he was in elevated status. Cassie and I followed them through the maze of hallways to the judge's private chambers. There, they left us to twiddle our thumbs on hard plastic chairs as they had their meeting.

As soon as we sat, Cassie puffed out her breath. "Can we trade? While *Mr. Griffin* is super yummy, he's a holy nightmare. He asked if I would drop off his dry cleaning? Do I look like housekeeping?"

"At least you weren't propositioned for an afternoon roll in the hay." I scrunched my face as soon as I'd said it, realizing I'd opened a whole new can of worms.

"I *knew* there had to be more to this animosity between you and Victor. He wants to steal you from Tom, huh?" Cassie lowered her voice as an employee passed.

"I don't want to talk about it," I mumbled, smoothing my skirt.

"Well, if you aren't interested, mind if I take a stab at him?"

"Only if you use a wooden stake," I said loud enough to earn a scowl from someone making copies in a room across the hall. "He's got issues. Just let it go, Cass."

She leaned back and pouted. "I hate jobs like this, too boring."

"The pay isn't bad."

"Why do you think the Dream Team needs personal protection anyway?" Cassie asked, desperate to keep herself entertained.

"You wouldn't take a shot at them?" I laughed.

"Ask me that again at the end of the job. If my client continues to be his charming self, I might shoot him just to put myself out of misery."

We snagged a piece of copier paper and played hangman and squares until the men reappeared shortly after five. I was surprised to see a second set of well-dressed people exit along with them. My brain finally realized they were the opposing side's attorneys. The judge never made an appearance.

Victor and Chris were talking amongst themselves so Cassie and I trailed behind them to the front doors. Cassie headed out first to make sure everything was safe for us to leave. Chris looked pointedly at his watch and sighed as we waited for her okay. She was right; he was a nightmare.

"Where are you heading?" I asked during a lull in the men's conversation.

Chris gave me an annoyed look but Victor shook his head at his partner. "The law office is at 230 West Main."

"Ready for another walk?" When he raised an eyebrow, I continued, "It's about a block and a half the other direction from where we parked."

"All clear," Cassie announced cheerfully.

Christopher muttered "finally" under his breath and Cassie sent me a put-out look. Stifling a smile, I motioned for Victor to follow them outside. Cassie had parked in the garage also, so we got the privilege of listening to Chris gripe about the lack of infrastructure in our backward city. Twice, I saw Cassie's fingers twitch toward her hidden gun.

The law office was just as dull as the courthouse but at least there were windows. Cassie and I played 'name that car' while we waited. This was going to be a long assignment even if the case only lasted a few days. It was after nine-thirty when the conference room door opened.

"See you in the morning, Victor," Chris said, then walked past Cassie, forcing her to scramble after him.

"I thought you were going to dinner after your meeting," I said, following Victor to the main door.

"I am," he said cheerfully. "Where would you like to go? My treat."

I stopped in my tracks. "You don't seem to understand how this works."

Victor carefully laid his suit jacket over his arm and adjusted his case. "You escort me to and from the hotel for the duration of the trial. I'm going out for dinner, therefore you are coming with me."

"Eat in your room," I said flatly, heading for the door.

He caught my arm but immediately dropped it when I stiffened. "Sorry, forgot about the no physical contact rule. One can only take so much room service and their exorbitant prices. It would be my pleasure if you'd join me for dinner, no strings attached."

"Vic, with you, there are always strings attached. But since I need to eat too, I see no reason why we can't find a nice, well-lit public place to eat."

Victor's smile was forced, suggesting he had something more intimate in mind, but to his credit, he kept his mouth shut. We picked up my car and headed to a nicer pizzeria. Unfortunately, it appeared to be rented for a wedding reception or something.

"The concierge recommended a nice French restaurant on Front. Is that far?" he asked when we got back into the car.

I knew the one he was referring to and no, it wasn't far. It was also a very intimate and expensive place, plus it happened to be one of my favorites. If we could get a table in the main dining room, I'd feel comfortable. With a sigh, I backed out and went around the block so we could head back in the direction of the restaurant.

"This is better," Victor said, holding the door for me.

The maître de flashed us a bright smile when we entered. "Welcome, do you have a reservation?"

I opened my mouth but Victor was too quick. "Yes, River for two."

I pressed my lips together and started to turn. Victor's hand brushed the small of my back and he whispered, "Don't make a scene, Arabella. I'd hate for you not to be welcomed back to your favorite restaurant."

I sidestepped out of his reach. "How did you know I liked this restaurant?"

"Eve told me. She's taken quite a shine to you." He gestured for me to follow the maître de up the stairs to the private tables.

I knew I should have stood my ground and taken him back to his hotel, but I really didn't want to be banned from this place. Damn him for putting me in this situation.

"Can I get you anything from the bar while you wait for your server?" the maître de asked.

Victor scanned the wine list and I rolled my eyes. "Sparkling water," I replied.

"And for you sir?"

"A bottle of your best red, and two glasses," Victor said, not even trying to hide his smug smile.

I lifted my menu so I didn't have to see his face. My grip tightened when he chuckled. They'd changed the menu again so I had to flip it back and forth to find my favorites. Risking a glance in his direction, I found Victor's hands were folded on the table and he was watching me.

"What?" I demanded.

"Do you ever wonder what would have happened if you'd met me first?"

"I'd have run screaming." I turned back to my menu.

"Somehow, I doubt that very much. We have a lot in common, you know," Victor said.

Again, I lowered my menu. "Except for the whole psychopath thing, we're practically identical. Can we talk about something else?"

Our server appeared with my sparkling water and Victor's bottle of wine. She poured him a small sample, which he tried then accepted the rest. I let the poor girl pour me a glass too, even though I had no intention of drinking. She took our orders and disappeared.

"I've never backed down from a challenge," Victor admitted.

"I've heard," I answered, wishing I still had my menu shield.

"Can we start over?"

I pulled back the neckline of my suit coat revealing my scars. "What do you think?"

Victor sat back and swirled his wine goblet. "I already told you that was Tom's fault. I would have stopped."

"Right," I said, reaching for my wine glass. "Stop it," I said once I realized what I was doing.

Victor gave me a rueful smile. "I can't help it. You're just so open."

Of course I was. Why else would I be sitting here? Victor was too crafty for me. Well, I just needed to work harder.

"Arabella," Victor called but I'd already started down the stairs.

"We'll take our orders to go," I said to our waitress.

Victor was quiet as we drove to the hotel, our dinners in little white cartons on my back seat. It was clear now that despite my tiny victories, Victor wasn't going to back down. If I didn't need this job so bad, I'd call Geo tonight and have Victor reassigned.

I made Victor wait in the entryway while I did a quick sweep of his suite before bidding him goodnight. To his credit, or bruised ego, he just nodded a farewell. Next week would be better.

Thanks to our country's birthday, I had a nice four-day weekend ahead of me that would, if I had any say in it, be Victor free. We traded cell numbers and I marched happily to the elevators knowing my fancy French dinner was waiting for me in the car, plus Tom would be calling any minute.

# Chapter Twenty-Two

The sound of my alarm jolted me awake Tuesday morning. It took me a minute to figure out where it was. I must have fallen asleep lying with my feet on my pillow waiting for Tom's call, a call which never came. This was the first time he'd missed a call but he said they were keeping him busy both day and night.

The long weekend had been relatively uneventful. The family and I watched fireworks from my parents' roof, preceded by a neighborhood BBQ. Eve and Victor had watched them from his fancy hotel suite. They had spent almost all weekend together whenever the attorneys weren't working on the case. I missed hanging with Eve but it gave me a chance to do some cleaning and just lounge around. Even after a relaxing few days, I was dragging. I was lucky to see past ten all weekend before my eyes slammed shut. God, I really was getting old.

I rolled over and pressed the snooze button then rubbed the sleep from my eyes. It had been a long night. What little sleep I had gotten had been plagued with nightmares of Victor. Through my blurry vision, I squinted at my clock. 6:02 AM. Ugh, this job was going to kill me.

The hot water stung my skin as I leaned against the shower wall. Despite the scalding hot water, I shivered. Forcing my eyes open, I went through my morning routine trying to shake the disturbing dream I'd been having. The one my alarm had mercifully saved me from continuing.

After braiding my hair and putting on my new maroon suit, I snuck out to the kitchen. Eve must have set the automatic timer because the coffee pot was ready and waiting for me. I filled my to-go cup and snagged one of the muffins Eve had baked yesterday afternoon. She'd told me she felt guilty for spending so much time with Victor while still staying at my house.

Grabbing Tom's keys, I headed to the door, but Eve's soft call made me detour to the living room. "Go back to sleep. I'll be home early tonight and we can have dinner together," I whispered from the doorway.

"Will you come to my birthday party?" she mumbled, and I wondered if she was still asleep.

"Of course, now go back to sleep." I tucked the blanket around her shoulders and she sighed contentedly.

As I drove through town on my way to pick up Cassie, visions of my nightmare returned. I could see Tom lying helpless as blood poured from his torn neck, red bubbles burst at his lips as he mouthed my name. I remembered my cruel laugh as I turned my back and walked willingly into Victor's waiting arms.

The blare of a horn jerked me back to reality and I stomped on the gas. While we'd been waiting for the attorneys on Thursday night, Cassie and I had devised a plan so the Dream Team didn't have to walk the three blocks to the courthouse twice a day. We'd travel together to and from the hotel, then one of us would escort them inside while the other parked the car and hoofed it over as fast as they could. This plan worked to my advantage too, since I wouldn't have to escort Victor alone anymore.

Cassie looked as tired as I felt when she literally fell into the passenger seat. "You are never going to guess what I did last night."

"Nope, but I bet you're going to tell me," I said, stifling a yawn.

"Oh, you brought me coffee," she crooned.

I slapped her hand away from my to-go cup before lifting it to my lips for a long satisfying drink. "I need this more than you do."

As soon as I put both hands back on the wheel, she snatched it from the console and took a drink. "Mmm."

"Brat," I mumbled. "Are you going to tell me why you look like you've been up all night?"

"I think I'll let you die slowly from the suspense," Cassie replied, using my comeback.

The hotel lobby sitting area was once again empty when we arrived. I clenched my jaw and marched toward the elevators. It was too early for this crap.

"I'll go get Chris," Cassie said once we were in the elevator.

"So, now it's *Chris*. What happened to Mr. Griffin?" I asked as she pressed 8.

She gave me a sly smile. "He called me last night and we had a little chat over dinner. He's not quite the nightmare I envisioned, quite the opposite actually."

The doors slid open and she sauntered out. "You did not!"

"Oh yes, I did." She winked as the doors started to close. "See you downstairs."

Great. So much for comrades in arms. I was planning on her despising our clients as much as I did. Now she'd be too busy salivating over Chris to even notice my conflict with Victor. My plan to use her as a buffer evaporated faster than I'd come up with it. Once again, I was heading to Victor's suite, alone.

This morning he was dressed and ready to go when he opened the door. "I'd invite you in but I already know the answer."

I nodded in reply and motioned for him to go ahead of me. As soon as I'd seen Victor, my nightmare hit me full force, twisting my stomach into knots and making my heart pound. It had felt so real. He gave me a sideways glance when I stood as far as possible from him in the elevator.

"You look tired." Worry touched his voice.

"Thanks," I replied.

"Tom didn't call?"

Much to my annoyance, I stiffened, giving him an answer without meaning to. "Not that it's any of your business but I didn't sleep well."

His frown deepened and when he spoke his tone was angry. "It damn well is my business. How are you supposed to protect me if you're falling asleep?"

I planted my feet shoulder width apart and put both hands on my hips. "You don't have to worry about me, Vic. I'm damn good at my job."

After adjusting his jacket's lapel, he smiled. "I don't doubt your ability. It's your willingness that concerns me."

The way he said 'willingness' made my skin crawl. Luckily, we'd reached the lobby so I could put more distance between the two of us. I wasn't surprised Cassie and Chris weren't down yet. Keeping Victor in my peripheral vision, I headed for the sitting area.

"Would you like some coffee?" Victor asked, diverting his course.

I followed him to the complimentary breakfast area. "I've got some in the car."

"Do you suffer from nightmares often?" he asked while opening a couple of sugar packets.

"Must have been something I ate." I leaned against the counter to watch the elevators. *Come on Cassie, where are you?*

"Or maybe something you didn't," he suggested.

I whipped my head around to face him. "Vic, it's too early for your crap."

"Not a morning person?" He chuckled. "Tom's been gone what, six, seven days? While he's not feeling the effects of your absence, I am willing to bet you're starting to notice his."

"And what is that supposed to mean?" I folded my arms across my chest.

Victor moved so he was leaning on the counter beside me, close enough his arm brushed mine. I was too distracted by his confusing comment to notice he'd once again invaded my personal space.

"My God, hasn't Tom taught you anything?" He took a sip of his coffee, grimaced and reached for another sugar packet. "I'll try to use an analogy you can understand. If first generation blood is like regular gas, second and third is more like high test. Now Tom's blood, like mine, is all that more potent. Considering how long you've been enjoying my brother's blood, your body's gotten used to the extra benefits it provides."

I glanced away from him and stared once again at the unmoving elevators. Tom hadn't told me this but he hadn't been too forthcoming with vampire knowledge either, not that I'd spent much time asking. As much as I'd like to tell Victor where he could shove his ridiculous theories, the more I thought about it, I *had* been feeling more run down the longer Tom was away.

"I could help you with that little predicament," he offered.

I pushed off the counter and reached for my cell phone. If Cassie didn't get her ass down here in the next five minutes, we'd be late. As I scrolled through the programmed numbers for her cell, one of the elevators numbers began to descend. That had better be them.

"If you don't want my help, you could always ask Eve, but I should warn you she hasn't been able to separate sex from blood yet. I, on the other hand, have no problem separating the two," Victor explained.

"Let me guess, in my case you'll make an exception."

The memory of him taking my blood flashed through my head and with it the feeling of uncontrolled passion. I felt my cheeks warm and I hoped he misread it as anger.

By the smirk on his face, I had a feeling he knew exactly what I was thinking. "Only if you want me too."

Fuming, I rounded on him. "I'm sure I'll manage without your help."

Victor downed the last of his coffee and tossed the paper cup in the trash. "Fine by me, but if I feel you aren't performing your duties as my protection due to extreme exhaustion, I'll be forced to contact your employer for a replacement."

"You're not going to break me down," I said.

The elevator doors opened, revealing Cassie and Chris heading our way. In my relieved distraction, Victor leaned in to whisper in my ear. "You haven't seen anything yet."

The ride to the courthouse was silent. The men sat in back while Cassie and I kept an eye out for any possible threats, not that either of us expected any. We'd prearranged for Cassie to escort the men inside this morning. I needed some time to calm down before having to sit in the courtroom all day for jury selection.

I joined Cassie in the gallery a few rows behind where Victor and Chris were set up at one of the two attorney tables. The other attorneys were already present as well: a portly man and a very attractive woman in a suit that was less than professional. It looked like it would be more appropriate at a strip club than in a courtroom. Even so, they both still looked dingy compared to Victor and Chris's Armani and Versace suits.

I had been curious to see Victor in action in the courtroom but his info dump this morning had me too distracted. I forced myself to stay focused on my work as the potential jurors filed in a few at a time. Luckily, Cassie was bright eyed and bushy tailed once she had emerged in the hotel lobby and scanned the crowd with much more care than I had.

"You want to talk about it?" she whispered, keeping her eye on a big guy in a trench coat sitting right behind our clients.

"About what?" I was watching the doors as more and more people filed in.

"Whatever happened this morning between you and Victor?" Cassie said.

If I hadn't been looking in his direction, I wouldn't have noticed Victor tilt his head slightly in our direction. We'd been speaking just above a whisper but, even over the rumble of conversations, I knew we were close enough for him to hear every word. Maybe I should tell Cassie everything but I didn't want to dump my problems on her any more than I wanted Tom to fly back and rescue me.

"Nothing happened. I'm just tired is all." My eyes narrowed when I saw Victor's mouth curve into a small smile and all of a sudden, the spacious room wasn't big enough for the both of us. "I'm going to get more coffee, you want some?"

When I turned back to Cassie, she regarded me with concern. "Sure. You'd tell me if you needed me, right?"

"I told you, I'm just tired. Caffeine will fix me right up. Can you hold down the fort?" I asked, standing.

"Me against a hundred defenseless, sleepy prospective jurors? They don't stand a chance." She laughed and the guy sitting in front of us turned and snuck at glance our way. Cassie bared her teeth menacingly, which made him turn around quickly.

Coffee didn't help and jury selection was boring, at least when the prosecution was up. No surprise, Victor was defending a national company with a local office that had been charged with knowingly endangering its employees to hazardous working conditions. I read the synopsis of the case in the paper last night while waiting for Tom's call.

It was hard not to be impressed by Victor's ability to dominate the room. I could tell the other side had no chance. One woman broke down in tears when he asked her if she had any personal qualms with sending a father of two to prison for the rest of his life. His next victim was nearly tearing her clothes off in an attempt to keep herself on the jury; the other side quickly dismissed her.

The afternoon drug slowly by as each side sent away more and more people. It was almost four when they finally announced the twelve poor souls and two alternates that would be trapped here for the duration of the trial. Trench coat man was one of the lucky selected; another was a clone of the woman who began to disrobe in an attempt to stay. At least it was a diverse crowd, not that Cassie and I would be in the courtroom after today anyway.

"What do you bet, juror number five's boobs fall out sometime during the trial?" Cassie whispered, making me nearly inhale the sip of coffee I'd just taken.

Victor turned his head at my coughing fit and I gave him a salute saying I was okay. He gave me an amused smirk before turning around, telling me he had heard what caused the fit. Cassie pursed her lips to keep from laughing so I glared at her.

Once I'd finally stopped, she continued before I took another drink. "Where are we going to dinner tonight?"

"What?" I said a little too loud, several people turned to stare at me.

"Chris said we were all going out to dinner tonight," Cassie whispered.

"I'm eating at home with Eve tonight. You can take Chris wherever your little heart desires."

She frowned. "Arabella, I can't take them both by myself. Geo would skin me alive."

I closed my eyes and took several deep breaths to ground myself, and more importantly to keep from yelling. "Don't make me do this. I'm having a hard enough time..."

"Please rise for the jury to exit and remain standing until you are dismissed by the judge," the bailiff announced.

From the look on her face, Cassie was bursting to ask me to finish my statement. I, on the other hand, was glad for the interruption, seeing I'd almost put my foot in my mouth yet again. Keeping my eyes anywhere but on Victor, I racked my brain for any excuse to call it an early day, but I was just too damn tired to come up with anything.

It took a few minutes for the attorneys to gather up all their paperwork and shut down computers. Being the mature, responsible adult I was, I ditched Cassie and nearly ran to the bathroom. When I emerged, the three of them were waiting for me.

Chris still looked at me like I had some sort of contagious disease. I wondered if it was the fact that I wasn't using Victor's services as Cassie was now enjoying his or if he was just a jerk. My guess was the latter. Folding my arms, I stomped to the security desk. Not waiting for Cassie, I pushed through the double doors and scanned the outside. The late afternoon sunshine and fresh air helped calm my nerves and I took my time walking back to the parking garage.

Once I was in the SUV, I turned my cell phone back on. There were two messages. The first was from my mom asking if I could come over this weekend; the second was from Tom. His calm, relaxed tone seemed to seep to my very soul.

"Hi. Sorry I didn't call last night. We lost track of time at the studio and when I got back to the house it was after two your time. You must be working since your phone is off. I miss you and will do my best to call you tonight. I love you."

I listened to the message twice before exiting the parking garage. God, I was so tired. As soon as I pulled up, my three passengers filed out of the building. Much to my annoyance, Victor slid in beside me.

"I think everyone's decided on the Depot for dinner. Is that alright with you?" he asked, fastening his seatbelt.

I rolled my head so I was facing him. "No, I'm not feeling well. I'm driving you back to the hotel then going home. I don't give a flying fuck what you do afterwards."

I threw the car in gear and floored it. Cassie put her hand on my shoulder but I shrugged it off. I needed to be alone or at least away from Victor. As much as I hated to admit it, he was right. I was exhausted and now I knew the reason and the possible solution, I was pissed.

No one said a word as I blasted through town. Victor put his hand on the dash to steady himself against my erratic driving. The gesture only angered me more. When I slammed on the brakes at a red light, I heard Chris curse. When I whipped my head around to tell him to shove it, my vision blurred and everything went black.

# Chapter Twenty-Three

"**S**he's fine, Eve. I'll take her home as soon as she wakes up."

My eyes were unable to respond to my command to open. The most I could do was flutter my eyelids. I was lying on my back on what felt like a bed. That didn't make sense; I'd been driving. When I tried to move, I heard the voice again.

"Looks like she's coming around now. We'll be there soon," Victor's quiet voice explained.

When I felt a hand on my face, I flinched away the best I could. "Oh right, the no touching rule. You'll just have to forgive me for carrying you up from the car then."

I licked my lips and felt the pull of sleep. "Won't happen."

"That's my girl." His hand brushed against my hair. "Are you going to reconsider your earlier refusal for my help or am I going to have to find a new bodyguard?"

"Go to Hell." My speech was slurred and my body felt like it was floating.

Victor's frustrated sigh pulled me back as I was about to succumb to sleep again. I needed to wake up and get away from him. He'd talked to Eve; she knew where I was. After swallowing, I tried again to open my eyes. Everything was a dim blur but I thought I recognized Victor's hotel suite. Oh shit, I *really* needed to get out of here.

"That's better," Victor encouraged as I rolled onto my side and tried to push myself to a sitting position.

"Shut up. I'm leaving," I slurred.

My attempt to get to my feet failed miserably and only managed to throw me against something solid and warm. Strong hands kept me from falling on my face then helped so I was once again sitting on the bed. It took me a second to realize I was leaning against Victor.

"I think you void your death threat if you're the one touching me," Victor's breath shifted the hair by my temple. There was a hint of pleading in his voice when he continued, "Please let me help you."

"Where's Cass?"

"Probably in Chris's room."

Victor must have given her a pretty convincing excuse to make her leave me with him. I should have told her everything that happened between us but I was so sure I could handle this myself. I frowned and tried to push away again. It was about as effective as my attempt to get to my feet. What was wrong with me?

"I told you it would only get worse," Victor answered my unasked question. "I could make it all go away."

A tear of frustration escaped the corner of my eye and slid down my cheek. "No."

Victor reached up and brushed it away. "Would it change your mind if I told you Tom gave the okay?"

"Liar," I mumbled, realizing I was slipping under sleep's influence again with my cheek resting in his soft hand.

"I called him after you passed out. There was no way I was going to take the blame for wrecking his new SUV *and* putting his girlfriend in the hospital."

"Wrecked the... Is everyone okay?" I sputtered, suddenly feeling more awake.

"Everyone's fine. You rear-ended a semi-trailer when you passed out. Don't you remember?"

"No." I lifted my hand to rub my face.

When it fell like dead weight, Victor caught my wrist. Despite the lethargy, my pulse began to race. I needed to get away before something happened. If only I could get past this sleepy haze enough to call Eve so she could come rescue me.

"Are you always this stubborn?" Victor still held my hand in his.

"Always, and you're touching me again," I said, unable to pull from his grasp.

Victor shifted so he had one arm around my back to steady me, our bodies now pressed together. "I promise I won't do anything but give you what you need."

My eyes had fallen closed again and I pushed them open, eyelids fluttering weakly. I felt like I could sleep for a week straight. Maybe that's all I needed, a few hours of uninterrupted sleep. If he'd just let go, I could lie back and drift into unconscious bliss.

"I offer it freely," Victor whispered, and I felt something wet touch my lips.

The taste of his blood filled my mouth and I couldn't help myself, I took it. As I pulled on the sweet elixir, I felt my strength slowly return and with it, other urges began to surface. I tried my hardest to repress the feelings that were starting to replace my exhaustion. When he mentioned Eve hadn't been able to separate blood from sex this morning, I realized I couldn't either. There hadn't been any reason to, and in my ignorance, I hadn't even considered the possibility of one without the other.

"You have no idea how good that feels," he nearly moaned, sending a spike of pleasure to my core.

"Shut up," I growled.

If I didn't think about what I was doing, I would be okay. I could just take what I needed then leave. Self-loathing could crush me later when I was safely locked in my own bedroom. I felt him try to pull away but I held fast. Not yet. I needed a little more. With a sudden jerk, my hands were empty and lips cold.

"Don't be greedy," he scolded lightly, voice thick with emotion.

I opened my eyes to find his face inches from mine. My breath came out in gasps, not a trace of exhaustion left. His pupils were dilated almost eclipsing the blue irises, and I could see he didn't want to separate the blood lust from any other lust either. Damn it, I needed to leave!

Victor pulled back, giving me the choice of just how far I'd take this. Other than my normal reaction to blood, my thoughts were my own. He wanted to see how strong my will was without his power of persuasion influencing me. It was a test I was failing miserably.

"This is wrong," I panted.

"Not if it's what you want," he whispered leaning in.

I met him halfway. Our lips touched hesitantly at first but soon they became desperate and hungry. His arms pulled me against him, fingers pulling my blouse from my skirt. I didn't resist when he lifted me to straddle his lap, instead I wrapped my arms around his neck. I tried to pull his shirt up but it was too well fitted. With one good yank, the buttons scattered in all directions leaving nothing between us except my silk camisole.

Victor's lips whispered kisses down my neck, finding my scars. Just his breath against them set me aflame. The thought of him taking my blood, to feel that exquisite rapture again, made it hard to breathe. His hands were so soft as he ran them over my back and the outside of my thighs, pushing my skirt up even further.

My cell phone's tinkling ringtone made me jump. I took a shuddering breath and reached toward where it had been placed on the nightstand. Victor's hand closed over mine as if to tell me to ignore it. I needed this distraction to clear my head. Surprisingly, he didn't resist when I lifted the phone and pressed the button to answer.

"Hello?" My voice shook.

"Arabella, are you okay? I'm pulling into the parking lot right now." Eve's hysterical voice was so loud I had to pull the phone away from my ear.

"I'm fine. Thanks for coming to get me," I said.

Victor slid me off his lap and stood as soon as he'd heard Eve's voice. He walked toward the window, rolling down the sleeve of his shirt, most likely to hide any evidence of what had happened, not much he could do about the now missing buttons. His silence spoke volumes as he kept his back turned and stared out the window.

"I'll meet you in the lobby," I said before I disconnected.

I stood and rearranged my clothes. My hand touched Victor's shoulder in a gesture of thanks. Suddenly my back was against the wall, his weight pressing into me. His lips covered mine with such longing and desperation, but my senses were coming back. I lay the palms of my hands against his chest and pushed gently. He stepped away and turned back to the window without a word.

When I made it to the lobby, Eve's hug nearly yanked us both to the floor as she flew at me. The few people milling around gave us strange looks. I gently extracted myself from her grasp but she refused to let go of my hand as we walked to my car.

"I was so worried when Victor called me, then when Tom told me what I'd have to do. I didn't think I could, so I called Victor back. Do you still need it because you look okay? Maybe Victor can come and help but that might make Tom mad. Well, madder than he already is."

Eve was babbling uncontrollably and my head was beginning to pound. "Just take me home."

She clamped her mouth shut and drove straight to my house. The traffic lights were blinking, indicating I'd been out for several hours already and morning would come way too soon. My earlier tiredness was starting to creep back in and I wasn't surprised when Eve had to shake me awake.

"Arabella, wake up. We're home."

I peeled my eyes open and stared at the dark little sanctuary of my house with relief. Eve helped me with my seatbelt and into the house where I collapsed on the couch.

"Let me help you to bed then..." She looked suddenly uncomfortable.

"You don't have to give me any blood, Eve. I'm just tired. Tell me what I missed."

Eve flopped down next to me and launched into her side of the story. Apparently, Victor had called her as soon as I'd passed out. He told her he was taking me back to his suite so I could rest. She was so worried about me she'd called Tom, who had flipped out and threatened to fly back immediately. About half an hour after they'd hung up, he'd called back and told her his flight would take too long and she'd have to give me the blood I needed. That had scared her so she'd called Victor back and told him he'd have to do it.

Somehow, I knew Victor's confession that Tom had given permission for me to take his blood was a lie. I thought back to his wording; he hadn't said Tom had okayed *his* blood, just agreed that I needed someone's. My stomach clenched when I realized what I had almost done; what I *had* done.

Victor had, of course, offered to take care of me and made Eve promise not to worry Tom anymore. She'd even called and told Tom I was doing better. There was no doubt in my mind while Victor had given me the choice, he'd forced Eve's hand this afternoon. The truth was she probably hadn't even realized it. Eve was sobbing by the time she finished retelling her side.

"Why don't you go to bed? I'm going to call Tom," I said, giving her a hug.

"But it's so late," she almost whined.

"I need to hear his voice before I can sleep. I'll see you in the morning, and thank you, Eve. You did everything right."

After a few more weak protests, she headed to the spare room. She must have moved in this afternoon while I was gone. I'd wanted so much to spend the evening eating dinner in the living room with her while watching some horrible movie. Instead, I'd blackened my soul.

My hands shook as I tried to dial Tom's number. I kicked off my shoes and hung up my suit jacket as the phone rang. The zipper on my skirt was stuck and I cradled the phone between my shoulder and cheek to get it undone.

"Arabella," Tom's frantic voice answered. "I'm at the airport. My flight leaves in an hour. I'll be home before you wake up."

*Home.* Tears filled my eyes and for a moment I couldn't speak. "You don't need to come home."

"I'm so sorry. I had no idea you'd pass out. Eve said you were in a car accident."

"I'm fine. I was stopped and rolled into the back of a semi. Your SUV is the one you should be worried about." I tried to keep my voice steady.

"You don't sound okay."

"Victor took..."

"What does Victor have to do with anything?" Tom interrupted.

I took a deep breath and sank onto my bed, resting my forehead in my hand. Somehow through all this, Eve had kept her promise to keep the fact that Victor was in town from Tom. In my current fragile state, I'd gone and blown it all to hell.

"He's here. I've been assigned as his protection detail," I said quietly then listened to him mutter a string of profanities I hadn't even been aware he was capable of.

"Why didn't you tell me?" Anger seeped into his concerned tone.

"Because I don't need you to rescue me, Tom. I survived twenty-five years before I met you; I think I can handle a few weeks without you here to protect me."

"Tell your boss to reassign you," Tom said.

"No, I need this job. I got a promotion to get it and I need to prove to Geo that I can do this. I won't let Victor ruin my career too."

The last thing I wanted to do was fight but I also didn't need him to swoop in and rescue me either. I had bigger problems to deal with. I needed to come to grips with what had almost happened in Victor's suite before I faced Tom again. Hell, I needed to figure out what had happened before I faced myself again.

"I'm coming home," he said resolutely.

"No, you're not. Have some faith in me. I'm stronger than you think," I said, trying to convince myself as much as him.

"Did Eve... Are you both okay?" he asked tentatively.

"We're both fine." I hated myself for the lie by omission. "I'm still really tired. Go back to your parents' house. I just wanted to let you know I was home safe and sound before I crashed."

"Are you sure? I'm already here, ticket in hand."

"I'm sure." I tried to smile, hoping he could hear it in my voice. "I love you."

"I love you too. I'll be holding you in your dreams," he said before we disconnected.

The tears I'd been holding back burst forth and I dropped my phone on the bed. I tipped over onto my pillow and buried my face, not wanting to wake Eve. She'd been through enough today.

As exhausted as I was, I couldn't fall asleep. My mind was pulling me in a thousand different directions. What if I *had* met Victor first? Would it have mattered? While I was drawn to Tom, the pull toward Victor was a hundred times stronger. And now I had the choice, who would I choose?

I rolled onto my stomach and mashed my pillow into a tall mound. I'd choose Tom. I already had. I loved him and he loved me. So why was I having this internal battle? Victor had tried to kill me! He only wanted me as a way to hurt his brother, right?

If he hadn't given me the choice to stop tonight, I'd have said his pursuit was only about besting Tom. But he *had* let me choose, then let me walk out the door. As much as I told myself it was because Eve was there, I wasn't completely convinced.

I flipped over and looked at my alarm clock. Wonderful, if I somehow managed to fall asleep in the next five minutes, I'd get a grand total of three hours of sleep before I had to face Victor again. My body screamed for me to rest but my mind wouldn't quit.

Instead of trying to block the memories from tonight, I let them crash over me. The taste of Victor's blood, his lips pressed against mine, his soft hands caressing my bare skin. After a while, my memory gave way to dreams. In my dream, I didn't answer Eve's call but as dreams sometimes are, no answers were given.

# Chapter Twenty-Four

C assie drove the following morning since Tom's SUV was at a body shop awaiting, what were mostly, cosmetic repairs. She'd borrowed her neighbor's van to schlep around our clients. When I opened the passenger door, the cup holder held two fancy coffees and in my seat was an almond croissant.

"How are you feeling this morning?" she asked, pulling away from the curb.

"Fine," I mumbled.

Eve had woken me up after listening to my alarm beep for almost ten minutes. I had slept right through it. My blood shot eyes and dark circles made me look even worse than I felt. However, my tiredness was nothing more than a lack of sleep. Victor's blood had undone the deficit of Tom's absence, but I knew it was only a temporary fix. One step at a time, I'd cross that bridge when I got there.

"If you need a sick day, I could call Al to cover for you," Cassie offered.

I picked an almond off the top of my pastry. "I'll be okay."

"You're not mad at me for leaving you?"

"Of course not, Cass. What were you going to do, stand around and watch me sleep? Victor... He... I'm fine."

"Did you call Tom?" I nodded and after another pause, she asked, "Sure you're okay?"

We'd pulled into the parking lot of the hotel effectively ending any further personal conversations. I pushed open the door and looked up to the top floor. I wasn't okay. I still had no idea what I was going to do but I had a job and that was my priority.

Much to my surprise, Chris and Victor were sitting in the lobby with to-go cups of coffee when we walked in. They gathered up their things and headed our way.

"Good morning, Arabella," Victor said.

I didn't meet his eyes. "Morning."

Chris ignored me as usual, maybe more after my little breakdown yesterday. I could have sworn I heard him sigh in relief when Cassie went around to the driver's side, but I was too tired to care.

The two men talked amongst themselves in the backseat while I stared out the window at nothing. It was Cassie's turn to drop us off at the courthouse. Good thing too because I wasn't sure I'd make the walk from the garage. I stumbled when my heel caught a crack in the sidewalk. I would have fallen on my face but Victor reached out and steadied me.

"Thanks," I said, straightening up and flicking the spilled coffee off my hand.

It was only after we'd made it through security that I realized I didn't react negatively to his touch. Somehow, I had a feeling he'd already noticed. We headed toward the courtroom in silence. The men went in while I took up residence on a bench just outside. Victor turned back for a second before following Chris, as if he wanted to say something but his partner urged him inside.

Cassie showed up a few minutes later with my forgotten breakfast. "Thanks."

"At least we don't have much to do today except hold this bench down with our asses. I won't tell if you need to take a nap on my shoulder," Cassie offered.

I smiled. Cassie was doing her best to cheer me up. I unwrapped my breakfast and took a big bite; the delectable apricot filling was a wonderful surprise. She was a good friend. Leaning back, I closed my eyes and enjoyed my breakfast.

The jurors filed past us into the courtroom then about fifteen minutes later filed back out. From their hushed whispers, no one seemed to know what was going on. I could hear raised voices inside but they were too muffled to understand.

"What do you think is happening?" Cassie asked.

"Maybe number five's boob popped out and they can't decide whether to put it on the transcript or not." I was feeling slightly more alive after food and coffee.

Cassie snorted a laugh but quickly stopped. I turned to see the juror in question walking by. She pulled the top of her low-cut blouse up slightly, which did absolutely nothing to contain her more than ample cleavage. My face burned and I turned away from her. Could today get any worse?

Just before noon, the bailiff dismissed the jury. Chris stormed out, followed closely by Victor who looked almost as unhappy. We scrambled to our feet and I was glad I hadn't taken Cassie up on the nap.

"What's going on?" she asked Chris.

"Our idiot client called the other side and made a deal without consulting us. One hundred and fifteen million dollars! Jesus, we would have gotten him off!"

I let my steps slow so I didn't have to hear his constant stream of expletives as he continued to berate his client. Even though I didn't look his way, I knew Victor had fallen in step beside me. The subtle scent of his cologne mingled with the silk from his shirt washed over me. I wanted to ask him about the case but wasn't sure I could talk to him.

"Chris is a little optimistic," Victor said quietly.

"Hmm?" I asked, still focusing forward.

"Our client was looking at prison time and billions in restitution. We could have gotten him probation but he still would have had to pay more than his deal," Victor explained.

"Oh."

"Have I been reduced to one-word sentences now?" he asked with a light laugh.

I felt heat rise to my cheeks. It was true. I hadn't spoken in more than single word phrases all morning. Bracing myself, I stopped and looked at him. Just as I expected, it didn't help. Instead, I sighed and resumed walking.

"Are you taking the next flight out of here?" I asked, forcing myself to at least be civil.

"I was hoping to spend at least another day with Eve before I headed back. Is it alright if I steal her tomorrow?"

"I'm not her keeper," I replied a little more harshly than I'd intended. "Sorry. I didn't sleep well again. We don't have any plans tomorrow."

We were waiting in the security line behind the jurors when Victor offered, "Can I take you to lunch?"

I closed my eyes and slowly exhaled. "Isn't that what got us in trouble in the first place?"

He laughed, a deep rich laugh that made a few people turn. "I guess it was. I'd like to spend some time with you too before I leave, if nothing else, to talk about what happened, or didn't happen, last night."

My hands shook as I signed my name in the 'out' column of the log so I could retrieve my belongings. I used the excuse of gathering them to put off replying. I moved forward to where Cassie and Chris were waiting for us just inside the exit doors.

"Do you want me to go get the car or can we walk?" Cassie asked when we joined them.

"Walking is fine with me," Victor said.

Apparently, Chris had already agreed because he started off toward the garage without waiting for me to reply. I'd forgotten to put the squishy insert into my shoes this morning so I leaned against the building to take them off. Victor half-smiled and shook his head.

"What?"

"Somehow you walking barefoot around downtown in a business suit doesn't surprise me."

My lips turned up into a smile too. "Let me guess, you wish your shoes came off so easily?"

He frowned. "I can feel a hole in the toe of my sock. What kind of a lawyer walks around downtown with his shoes in his hand and his big toe sticking out?"

The mental picture made me laugh. Cassie stopped walking and turned back to me in question. I waved her on as Chris was still on his oral tirade.

"That would probably make front page news around here."

I took mercy on Victor and sat in the back with him so Chris could continue to vent to Cassie on the ride back to the hotel.

"So, how about that lunch?" Victor asked when we all piled out.

I glanced at Cassie for help but she was already walking away with Chris. With my luck, she'd help him work out his frustrations all afternoon, leaving me stranded with Victor. I'd made up my mind and now I had to follow through.

"Cassie!" I called. When she turned, I waved her back. "Toss me the keys then give me a call later so I can pick you up."

When I had the keys in hand, Victor frowned. "I'm guessing that would be a no for lunch?"

"Thank you for what you did for me last night, but I think it's best if we stay away from each other."

All humor vanished from his face and when he spoke his voice was hard. "So that's it?"

"I'm sorry. I love Tom and that's not going to change," I said, taking a step back. "I'll let Eve know you want to see her tomorrow."

When I turned back to the van, Victor put a hand on my arm. "Let go of me." I tried not to put too much venom in my voice but it still trickled in.

His grip tightened and he stepped close enough to whisper. "You took my blood and gave me a taste of what might be, now you think I'll just let you walk away?"

Instead of pulling against his grasp, I tilted my body against his. "Yes Vic, that is exactly what I expect you to do. Get your hand off me or I'll shoot you."

He knew I was armed and hopefully my tone indicated the seriousness of my threat. There were other people in the parking lot and traffic whizzed by. His eyes narrowed and I felt my resolve begin to fail. It was then that I knew I had no choice; he had already decided for me. He wouldn't let this go. He wouldn't let me just walk away.

To my surprise, he finally released his grip. My arm tingled where blood rushed back to the spot where his fingers had been digging into my skin, four half-moon dents demarcated where his short fingernails had nearly punctured my skin. He straightened up and tugged his suit back into place before turning and walking to the hotel as if nothing had happened. My issues with Victor were far from over. I had no idea what his next plan would be, but I'd be ready.

• • • •

EVE DROPPED ME OFF at my parents' house Saturday morning before heading off with my car to pick up her brother. Victor had decided to stay through the weekend and had been monopolizing his sister's time. That was fine by me, at least he wasn't trying to weasel his way into mine.

Eve hadn't said what they had planned and I didn't really care. I made her promise to keep her cell phone on but I doubted Victor would do anything to harm his own sister. As far as I could tell, they didn't have any problems.

Acacia gave Eve a hug before she left. Apparently, the two of them decided a long-distance relationship would be too hard but they didn't want to lose their friendship. I'd missed a lot in the last few days. It was the most amicable breakup I'd ever witnessed. Both girls seemed content with friendship, so I was happy for them.

Mom had decided it was time to clean out the garage. That was why she'd invited me to come over. Dad was working so I guessed he booked a full day of appointments when he found out what Mom had on her to-do list for today.

The double car garage was packed from floor to ceiling on one side and the shelves that lined the rest of the walls were just as full. Some manual labor was what I needed to distract myself from my hellish week.

"Where do we start?" I asked, rocking back and forth on my heels.

"Let's pull some of those boxes onto the driveway so we have more room to work." Mom said as she pointed to the far wall.

"Do I really have to help?" Acacia asked, leaning against the open doorway.

"Yes, a good share of this is your stuff," Mom scolded.

I obviously got my pack rat habit from my mother. Most of the boxes were full of Acacia and my baby clothes and old toys. We made three piles: donation, garbage, and save. My sister kept putting everything in the garbage pile, so Mom delegated her to organizing shelves instead.

"I can't believe you still have all this stuff," I said as I opened yet another box of baby clothes.

"I keep hoping I'll get some grandchildren."

"Thanks, Mom," I muttered.

"You're not getting any younger. I was three years younger than you when you were born."

"Yeah, and married too," Acacia added, and I stuck my tongue out at her.

"You and Tom seem so perfect for each other. Maybe you finally found Mr. Right," Mom said, resealing the baby clothes box and moving it to the save pile.

"About that, when Tom gets back from California, he's moving in with me," I said tentatively.

She'd been bending over to put down the box but straightened up like a shot. Her hand moved to her chest and she took a few seconds to turn. Acacia and I shared an uneasy look.

"Well, that's nice," she said when she did finally turn. "It's a good thing he's already spoken to your father."

"Spoken to him about what?" I asked.

"Nothing, nothing." She pushed past me to grab another box.

"Mom."

"Arabella, I don't agree with your father on everything and certainly not about cohabitation before marriage but Tom seems very serious about you so if that is what you want, I won't stop you. You're a grown woman and I can't baby you anymore."

Both Acacia and I stood with our mouths hanging open. That was the most liberal thing I had ever heard Mom say. I half expected her to have one of her panic attacks when I told her about Tom moving in. She did, however, start barking orders for us to get our butts in gear. Not wanting to suffer her wrath, Acacia and I shut up and got to work.

Since we had no vehicle, there was no way to drop off the donation boxes once we were finished. The 'save' pile was neatly arranged in the back of the garage and on the shelves. There was also quite a substantial mound ready for the garbage truck. Acacia had disappeared on the pretense of making lemonade earlier and we were now trying to gag down the super sweet yellow drink. At least it was cold.

"Did Eve invite you to her birthday party?" Acacia asked.

It took me a second to remember then I laughed. "Yeah, but she didn't give me any details. I think she was still half asleep."

"It's at her parents' house at the end of the month," Acacia explained. "Apparently, it's going to be a huge event."

I had trouble swallowing my mouthful of faux lemonade when I remembered what Tom had told me about big family gatherings. The thought of staying in that house again made me shudder and I hoped my family assumed it was from the nasty liquid I was trying to drink.

"I told Acacia she could go but only if you were going to be there. She doesn't need to run loose in Los Angeles without adult supervision," Mom explained.

"I'll have to check with work but if I can get the time off, we can travel together."

As we were talking about details, a city patrol car slowly crept up the street. I gave it a casual glance and turned back to our conversation. All three of us stopped when it pulled into the driveway.

Two uniformed officers stepped out and walked toward us. They looked like carbon copies of each other with their military type haircuts and football player builds. I couldn't fathom why they were at my parent's house.

"Mrs. Simon?" The cop that had been driving asked.

"What can I do for you, Officer?" she asked, clutching her glass.

The second one turned to my sister and me. "Which one of you is Acacia Simon?"

"The one in the middle," Mom said, moving to stand in front of us. "What's going on?"

"Ma'am, your daughter needs to come with us," the driver said.

At this, I stood and shielded Acacia. "Why?"

"She's wanted for questioning regarding the attempted murder of Nicholas Allen," he answered. I reached out to catch my mother's arm as her knees gave way. "Ms. Simon, if you'd please come with us?"

"Is that really necessary?" I asked.

The two officers exchanged an exasperated look. "Unfortunately, yes. Mrs. Simon, you can ride with us if you'd like."

Damn it. Why couldn't Blondie just let it drop? I couldn't let Mom go with Acacia but I sure as hell wasn't going to let the officer twins drive away with my baby sister.

I turned to Mom who was still leaning on me for support. "Call Dad and meet us at the station. I know a good lawyer. This has to be a big misunderstanding."

Mom nodded weakly and slowly turned to where Acacia was still hiding behind us before hurrying to the front door.

"Mom," Acacia croaked, but I stopped her before she bolted after her.

"Don't. She can't handle it," I said then quietly added, "Let me fix this."

She latched onto my arm as I led her to the patrol car. When the officer offered to help her in, she shied away from his touch. After giving him a pointed glare, I slid in next to her. She held onto my arm and sobbed as we pulled onto the road. I grabbed my cell phone and scrolled for the one number I hoped I'd never have to call.

# Chapter Twenty-Five

**M**uch to my annoyance, Victor didn't answer so I left a brief, yet urgent message. Eve's cell phone went straight to voicemail, telling me she was either on the phone or had turned it off, even after her promise to keep it on. When we arrived at the police station, the cop riding shotgun steered us to an area where they took my sister's information and scanned her fingerprints. When they were done, the driver escorted us to what I assumed was an interrogation room. Above the industrial strength cleaner, I caught a whiff of body order and vomit.

"I'll be acting as her guardian until our parents arrive and I've already contacted an attorney," I said to the officer.

"I was just going to ask if you wanted anything to drink." He gave me a professional smile.

"No, thank you. The faster we can get this misunderstanding taken care of the better," I replied, returning the same fake smile.

As soon as the door shut, Acacia turned to me. "Nothing's going to happen to me, right? Eve said..."

"Shut up, Acacia. That mirror isn't there so we can check our makeup. Since you're with an adult, I'd bet my ass they're recording everything we say. Just keep your mouth closed and let me take care of this."

The minutes ticked by as we waited. My phone stayed painfully silent and our parents were still nowhere to be seen. Acacia laid her head on the table and stared blankly at the institutional gray wall. When the door opened, I jumped to my feet thinking it was our parents.

"Have a seat, Ms. Simon. I'm Detective Rogers. I'd like to ask Acacia a few questions." He offered his hand but I sat down without shaking it.

"We're waiting for our attorney," I said flatly.

Detective Rogers put a file folder on the well-worn table and pulled out the chair opposite us. He looked about ten or so years older than me. His dark brown hair was cut short, not as short as the officers that picked us up but close. His suit jacket was obviously off the rack since it was tight across his middle but hung down too far down over his hands. He had the look of someone who is overworked and underpaid. I knew the feeling but that didn't mean I liked him.

"We just need to get some things cleared up so your sister can go home," he offered.

"It was an accident!" Acacia blurted out.

I punched her in the arm before she could say anything else. "I'll think we'll wait for our lawyer, thanks."

With a satisfied smirk, Rogers got to his feet and tapped the folder once against the table. "That's all I needed."

When he opened the door, I caught a glimpse of my parents and Victor standing just outside. I scrambled to my feet and caught the door before it closed. "You got my message."

"Can I talk to you alone for a moment?" Victor asked.

"Don't leave me!" Acacia's voice was shrill with panic.

Both my parents rushed in and she fell sobbing into their arms. "Don't say anything, Acacia. We'll be right back," Victor instructed before closing the door.

"Thank you for coming so fast. Where's Eve? She's got the piece of paper the jerk-hole of a boy signed that will get Acacia out of here," I said in a hushed voice as he led us down the hall to a private area.

"Eve's on her way back to California," he explained, turning me so my back was against the wall.

"What?" I yelled.

"Keep your voice down. You need to teach Cassie how to keep her mouth shut between the sheets. She told Chris everything that happened at your sister's birthday party. He's got this thing about losing and was determined to find a case he could win."

"So he's taking it out on my family? You work with him, tell him to back the fuck off."

"Why do you think Eve's flying home? I got him to leave her out of it," Victor explained.

He hadn't let go of my arm after leading me down the hall so I shook it off. "That's it? Eve gets a free pass and my sister gets jail time. I guess it is all about who you know."

"I might be able to persuade the family to drop the charges if..." he began hesitantly.

"Anything. I won't let one mistake ruin my sister's entire life."

"That's what I wanted to hear." He lifted his cell and held it to his ear. "Chris? It's Victor. The thing we talked about. It's a bust. Tell the family there's a possible problem with the case. Nope. I'll be staying a little longer. See you when I get back."

As I listened to the one-sided conversation, it hit me. It wasn't Chris that had set this up but Victor. Eve had been sent away so she couldn't back up Acacia. He'd tried getting to me through blood and when that failed, he'd found the next best thing: my family. My desire to protect the ones I loved must be more evident than I'd realized.

"You son of a bitch."

His satisfied grin confirmed my suspicions. "I told you I had the answers to all your problems."

"The only problem I have is you and the ones you create in your selfish wake. I'll get Acacia out of this on my own." I turned away but he caught my arm again.

"Can you honestly afford an attorney good enough to beat me? You said you'd do anything to save your sister. Here's your chance to prove it."

"I hate you," I said through gritted teeth.

"Hate is a strong motivator. Go tell your sister she's going home. I need to have a word with Detective Rogers."

When I opened the door to the interrogation room, Acacia was nearly in Mom's lap and Dad had his arms around both of them. My sister's tear-streaked face looked up at me with such pleading. I'd promised to protect her at all costs and I wasn't turning my back on her now. It might take me awhile but I'd figure out how to beat Victor at this game. Until then, I'd be at his mercy.

Holding my voice as steady as I could, I said, "Victor's taking care of it. As soon as he speaks to Rogers, we can go home."

"What is this all about, Arabella?" my father asked.

Mom was stroking Acacia's hair and muttering soothing words when I glanced at her. Why hadn't I told him about this after my sister's party? Some warning would have been nice. Now I understood the reasoning behind Tom's omitted details. Sometimes it was easier to protect the ones we love by keeping them blissfully ignorant.

Keeping my eyes glued on Mom and Acacia, I answered him, "Just a misunderstanding, Dad. I've taken care of it."

My parents couldn't stop thanking Victor once we were all finally out in the parking lot. The longer I listened to my parents praise him for saving their baby girl, the sicker I felt. Acacia, who had finally recovered from her shock, took me aside, to which I was grateful.

"Arabella, are you okay?"

I forced a smile and smoothed her hair. "I'm just glad this is over."

"What about Eve? She's not going to get in trouble, is she?"

"You don't need to worry about Eve. Just do me a favor and be on your best behavior for a while. Somehow, I think life's about to get really complicated."

"Ready to go?" Victor smiled brightly while my mom put her arm around Acacia's shoulders.

"We'll see you two tomorrow night," my mom said.

"What?" I asked.

"We've invited Victor over for dinner tomorrow night to thank him." When I just stared at her like she was insane, she continued, "He's refusing any payment for helping us get Acacia out of this terrible mess. The least we can do is give him a decent meal."

"That's really not necessary, but I'd be lying if I told you I wasn't tired of room service." His comment made everyone laugh except me.

"Arabella? Are you alright?" my dad asked.

I pulled myself out of my funk. "Just tired, I think. I've had some long hours this week."

"That would be my crazy schedule's fault. I'll take you home," Victor offered and I stifled a shudder.

We didn't go to my house. Victor drove us back to his hotel instead. He had my car since he'd dropped Eve off at the airport. When he parked and got out, I stayed in my seat, arms folded across my chest.

"Don't be childish, Arabella," Victor said after he opened the door for me.

"Give me my keys so I can go home," I said in a flat tone.

"As stubborn as ever. It's a good thing I'm so patient." He reached over and released my seatbelt. "Come on. I'll order room service and we can pick up where we were so rudely interrupted the other night."

I turned to look up at him. "You honestly think I'm going to sleep with you to keep my sister out of jail?"

Victor shook his head and nearly yanked me out of the car. "You seem to have forgotten I have the power to make that decision for you."

"But you'll know it's all a farce."

"For now." He shrugged then continued, "I have faith that over time, you'll stop fighting and enjoy what I can give you."

"You have a very high opinion of yourself," I muttered, realizing then he'd led me from the parking lot to the hotel lobby.

When we arrived at his room, he handed me a silver gift bag. "Go take a shower and I'll order us something for dinner."

I looked down at my sweaty, dirty clothes and had to remember what I'd been doing today to get so filthy. The afternoon of cleaning out my parents' garage felt like a lifetime ago, rather than just a few hours.

"Order wine," I said before disappearing into the bathroom. Maybe if I drank enough, I could pass out or at least alter my memory enough to forget whatever Victor had planned for the evening.

I pressed the thumb-lock on the bathroom door and sat on the closed toilet. When I turned the gift bag over, the contents fell unceremoniously onto the floor. Figures. The black negligee was stark against the white and silver marble tile. At least there was a silk robe to go with the sheer lace nightmare.

The shower was a huge, tiled monstrosity with a clear glass door. I piled my dirty clothes on the floor and stepped inside, letting the hot water pelt me until my skin stung. After adjusting it to a more tolerable level, I took my time showering in hopes to be done when the food arrived thus prolonging the inevitable.

After drying off and wrapping myself in an enormous towel, I rummaged through Victor's toiletry case for a comb. There was one of those wall-mounted blow dryers by the sunken Jacuzzi tub so I dried my hair until it was completely straight. The complimentary hotel lotion smelled like an old lady so I replaced the cap and dropped it in the trash without using any.

With a quick scan of the room, I decided there wasn't anything else for me to waste time on. Victor's gift still lay in a pile on the floor, mocking me. I expected the lace to be stiff and itchy. Instead, the cool material felt more like silk, and, of course, fit perfectly.

The robe was barely long enough to cover my ass but it was better than having to walk out in something that would make a hooker blush. How could something so obviously expensive make me feel so cheap? Maybe it wasn't the lingerie itself but what it represented.

I adjusted the robe for maximum coverage and stepped out of the bathroom. From the lack of smell, I knew in spite of my procrastination, the food had yet to arrive. The lights were low and music was coming from somewhere. I jumped when I heard Victor's voice from the adjoining room.

"I'm glad you're home safe, Eve," he said then laughed at something she said. "I promise to be back before your birthday. I wouldn't miss it for the world. She's finally out of the shower. I'll give her the phone."

He offered me his phone while taking his time raking his eyes up and down my frame. I took the phone and crossed my free arm over my middle before turning away from his lecherous stare.

"Hey, Eve."

"Victor said Acacia was arrested. Is she okay?" The guilt was obvious in her voice and I wasn't about to add to it.

"She's fine. They let her go home." I sensed more than felt Victor approach me. "I'll miss you. Come back to visit anytime."

"You'll come to my party, won't you?" she asked.

"Nothing could keep me away." I tried to sound upbeat but my voice shook.

"Are you sure you're okay?" Eve asked.

"Tired. I'm going to eat a quick dinner and go to bed." My stomach twisted at the thought.

"I'll call you later. Bye."

"Bye," I whispered then let the phone slowly slide away from my face.

Victor took it when my arm hung limply at my side. With one hand, he swept my hair over my shoulder. His other hand wrapped around my waist, pulling me against him. I bit my bottom lip to stifle a gasp when his lips brushed just below my ear.

He chuckled at the knock on the door. "Hungry?"

Food was the last thing on my mind but if it helped put off Victor's boudoir plans, I was all for it. I waited until I heard the door click closed before I turned around. The smell of whatever he'd ordered made my stomach flip-flop but not in a good way.

My cell phone caught my eye when I entered the other room. Instinctively, I reached for it as if it could protect me. Victor was in the process of pouring us each a glass of wine.

"You won't be needing that tonight," he said without looking up.

"Tom's supposed..." I began.

Victor slammed the wine bottle down, sloshing the contents on the white cloth draped room service tray. "It's off."

Okaaaay. I set my phone back on the table and retrieved the wineglass Victor was holding out for me. My hand shook as I lifted it to my lips and I wasn't at all surprised by the faint taste of blood. So much for my plan to get wasted. Regardless, I drained the glass before putting it back on the tray.

Victor eyed me over his glass with amused interest. "I wasn't sure what you wanted to eat."

He lifted the lid to reveal a platter full of cold cuts, fruits, and cheeses; all things that could be eaten later. When he took another sip of his wine and replaced the cover, I knew exactly what he had in mind.

When he approached, I backed up. It wasn't my intention, just my survival instinct kicking in. As easy as death sounded, I had a feeling Victor didn't plan on killing me, at least not tonight. He struck me as the kind of person who liked to play with his prey first.

In my pathetic attempt to escape, I'd backed into the bed. Lovely. My breathing sped and my heart began to pound. Victor stepped close and tugged on the tie holding my robe closed. As he slid it off my shoulders, his breath caught.

"Even more beautiful than I'd imagined," he whispered.

When he tilted my head to the side, I looked up and blinked back tears. My drive to fight was evaporating and I knew my will was no longer my own. I hated the moan of pleasure that escaped my lips when his teeth broke my skin. Hated the fact there was no hint of pain like when I shared it with Tom.

One hand held me tight against him while the other ran slowly up my back before tangling in my hair. Unlike the last time he'd taken my blood, I felt him pull away after only a few seconds. The fingers in my hair pulled tight and his lips met mine. Body betraying my mind, I kissed him back.

My hands moved to pull off his shirt and I felt him smile against my lips before he pulled away, allowing me to complete my task. Once the shirt was off, he lifted me just below my hips, forcing himself between my legs. His lips trailed along my jawline toward my ear.

"Take it, it's yours." His voice was husky with passion.

I tilted my head to his neck and bit down. Hard. Blood filled my mouth as he lowered me onto the bed. The blood euphoria filled my being and all reason fled. My body's need for physical release rose with each pull. The question of what was right and wrong disappeared as I succumbed to desire.

If Victor heard me whisper Tom's name, he never let on. He was just as caught up in the ecstasy that followed sharing blood as I. As my hands ran over his body, I closed my eyes and imagined I was with the man I loved. Victor didn't feel the same as he drove us both to climax but I withdrew inside my mind, letting my memories overwhelm my senses. Victor might own my body and my blood but he'd never have my heart. That would always belong to Tom.

# Chapter Twenty-Six

The sound of the shower woke me from a fitful sleep. I was curled into a ball, gripping the blankets so tightly under my chin that my fingers ached. When I opened my eyes, I was staring at the curtains but they were too thick for any light to penetrate, messing with my sense of time. Every muscle screamed in protest when I pushed myself into a sitting position. I refused to dwell on the hows and whys of my pain as I pulled on the black robe.

My eyes fell onto my silent cell phone. Stumbling across the room, I flipped it over and pressed the power button. The familiar chime of a waiting voicemail message made my stomach clench in anticipation. I had to re-enter my password three times before I could unlock my phone to listen to my messages. The first was from Tom.

"Hi, it's me. I hope you're having sweet dreams. Sorry it's so late. Give me a call when you get this. They actually gave me the day off tomorrow or I guess it's today already. Call me. Love you."

Pressing repeat, I listened to it twice more. The water turned off and I reluctantly skipped to the next message. This one was from Acacia asking if I was okay and if she could come over while Mom and Dad went to church this morning. Pulling the phone away from my ear, I glanced at the tiny clock and cursed.

Geo's voice boomed in the background of Cassie's message. "Get your ass here ASAP. Geo is pissed. I'll do my best to stall but hurry."

I slapped my phone onto the coffee table and headed to the bathroom where I assumed my pile of filthy clothes still rested. My captivity was officially over. Losing my job was not part of this deal. As I reached for the handle, Victor pulled the door open.

"Good morning." He smiled as he dried his hair with a hand towel.

"I need my clothes," I said, trying to push past.

"What's the rush? You haven't eaten breakfast yet," he said, effectively blocking my path.

"In your infinite wisdom of turning off my cell phone and letting me sleep in, I slept through my staff meeting. Maybe if I get there before it's over, I won't get fired." I explained as he continued to shift so I couldn't get around him. "Get out of the way!"

He finally moved and I grabbed my stack of dirty clothes. They were better than nothing. There was no way I could drive home, get clean clothes and make it back to Geo's before everyone was gone. Maybe I could claim I'd gotten my days mixed up and was helping my mom clean her garage. One look in the mirror made me freeze; my hair looked like a haystack.

"In my defense, I had no idea you worked on Sunday," Victor said.

"You never asked."

He plucked a comb from the vanity but I snatched it out his hand and began attacking the snarled mess. Anger was a safe emotion; it kept me upright and moving. Tears filled my eyes but it was from trying to rip my hair out, not my emotional state. I wouldn't give him the satisfaction of seeing me cry.

"When will you be back?" he asked once I'd decided my braid was as good as it could get.

I wanted to scream 'never' but instead I walked past him to the main room. "Later."

"Give me a call. I'll be downtown working on your sister's case."

"My sister's case?" I slowly turned to face him.

He smiled ruefully. "The wheels were already put into motion. It's not like I can make the whole thing disappear. I'm good but not that good."

The gravity of the situation suddenly felt stifling and I had to brace my hand against the wall. It wasn't over. He must have realized

I'd look for a loophole to get away and this was his trump card. As long as Acacia's freedom was in jeopardy, I'd keep playing along.

If I didn't leave now, I'd probably punch something, like Victor. Pushing roughly from the wall, I headed for the door. Just before I slammed it closed behind me, I remembered my cell phone. Victor was holding it out to me when I came back in.

"Don't forget dinner with your parents tonight, Love," he called as I slammed the door.

•  •  •  •

THE LOT AT GEO'S WAS empty except for Cassie's tiny car and Geo's luxury sedan. Lifting my chin, I marched inside. Voices murmured from Geo's office so I headed straight there.

Smiling, I poked my head in the door. "Sorry, Geo, I totally spaced the staff meeting. My mom asked me to come over and help her clean out the garage."

Cassie turned to face me and Geo motioned for me to come in. I slid into the chair next to her and prepared for the worst. God, my life sucked.

"We have this meeting every Sunday. Same bat time, same bat channel. How is it you forgot this week?" Geo asked, mashing out the end of his cigarette in an overflowing ashtray.

"I said I was sorry. Must have gotten my days mixed up." I answered as cheerfully as possible.

When I glanced over at Cassie, she wouldn't meet my eye. This was bad. Geo got angry when people missed meetings but the mood in this room suggested something more than forgetting a weekly commitment.

Geo cleared his throat. "I know about the problem with your sister." I opened my mouth to protest but he silenced me with a look. "I also know you two are involved."

"It's a misunderstanding. I'm taking care of it," I said, trying to force the anger from my tone.

"Does taking care of it include spending the night with your client? I looked the other way with Tom but this seems to be becoming a habit with you."

Geo's disappointment was too much. I lost my composure and slammed my fist down on his desk. "It's not like that, damn it! I hired Victor to be Acacia's lawyer. Who said I was sleeping with him?"

Geo looked at Cassie then back at me. "Your car was outside his hotel all night and when you didn't show up this morning, I assumed..."

"Well, you assumed wrong. Thanks for thinking I'm a whore, Geo," I said then turned to Cassie. "And what the hell is wrong with you? Can't you keep your mouth shut?"

When I turned back to my boss his entire head was red. My verbal outburst was way out of proportion but the events of the last week plus the conclusions they'd jumped to just plain pissed me off. No matter what I did, everything kept getting worse.

"Just take a breath and sit down," Geo said, slamming me back to reality. "I don't know what's going on with you but deal with it or find another job. Cassie told me about the car accident, which you didn't report. I've been lenient with you but I can only do so much."

He shoved a single piece of paper across the desk at me. Cassie leaned over and handed it to me after I made no move to retrieve it. My hands were trembling so hard I had to put it in my lap to read it. I had one job this week, a grand total of about two hours. Fucking lovely.

"Really?" I asked, sounding way too much like my sister.

"And if you don't get your shit together, plan on getting a blank sheet next Sunday," Geo snapped.

Without replying, I grabbed the paper off my lap, half-crumpling it in the process, and got to my feet. The chair scraped the floor as Cassie rushed to follow me out. Instead of waiting, I headed straight to my car.

She grabbed my arm and swung me around as I moved to unlock the driver's side door. "What was that all about?"

"Thanks for telling Chris about the incident at Acacia's birthday party and obviously Geo as well. You have no idea what you've done."

"Then tell me so I can fix it. The way Chris talked about the party, it was as if he already knew all the details. I assumed you talked to Victor about it."

"Why would I? It was taken care of. Besides, I hate that man with a passion."

"He *is* a lawyer. I thought maybe you were asking for his professional advice. Don't blame me for this. If you get in trouble for covering it up, I'm just as involved as you are."

She was right. There were only six people who knew what had happened and if she hadn't told Victor, there was only one other person who could have: Eve. Knowing Victor, he probably pushed her until she revealed everything without realizing she was doing it. I kept blaming the wrong people for everything.

Exhaustion pressed down on me and I reached up to massage my stiff neck. "I'm sorry, Cass. This whole mess is more complicated than you know."

"You're working with Victor on Acacia's case?" she asked, turning around to lean on my car, obviously accepting my apology.

"Not exactly." I felt myself pale and saw her forehead creased in confusion. "I need to go. I've got to make something to bring to dinner at my parents' tonight. They're thanking Victor for rescuing Acacia."

"Why do I have the feeling it wasn't Victor who did the rescuing?"

"Because you know me." I yanked my car door open. "I'm really sorry for what I said. I was out of line. You're a good friend, Cass."

"We all have bad days, Arabella. Call if you need anything."

My house was painfully silent when I walked in. Eve's absence was like an oppressive weight as I headed for the kitchen to make some coffee. I went through the motions of the routine without thinking. All I wanted was a shower and memory eraser.

My work cell phone caught my attention as I headed to the bathroom. I unlocked it to see if I missed anything else. There were five missed calls from my boss, one from Cassie, and a voicemail.

Tom's voice filled the room when I pressed the speaker button. "Arabella, are you okay? I've left a couple messages on your cell and I haven't heard from you. Eve's home but she won't tell me the real reason she's back. Did something happen between her and Acacia? I'm starting to get worried. Maybe your cell phone died. Please call me when you get this."

Leaning my forehead against the wall, I closed my eyes and exhaled. What was I supposed to tell him? If I told him the truth, Victor would torture me by sending my sister to jail. If I lied, he'd know. I needed time to figure this out.

I unlocked my personal cell and sent him a text message. "GOT UR MESSAGE. IM OK JUST BUSY."

When I laid it on the counter, it started ringing. I pressed ignore and locked the bathroom door. The ring tone was loud enough I could hear it over the fan so I cranked up the radio before stepping into the shower. Between the water and the screeching guitar, my cell phone ring disappeared. Sliding down the wall, I let the tears I'd been holding fall. As much as I hated Victor, at the moment I hated myself more. If I hadn't been so stubborn about settling this on my own, I wouldn't be in this situation.

After a good pity-party cry, I pulled myself up and scrubbed my skin, trying to remove any trace of Victor's taint. He wouldn't be satisfied with one night. Somehow, I knew he had long-term plans for me, but that didn't mean I had to let it build up on my skin and weigh me down.

My cell phone chirped, indicating messages but I ignored it. Instead, I called my mom to find out what she wanted me to bring for dinner. She suggested dessert. Shocking. When she launched into a monologue about how wonderful Victor was, I made an excuse to get off the phone.

During my sob-fest in the shower, I decided I'd tackle this problem as if it were a job. Like Victor said, hate is a strong motivator and I'd use it to figure out how to use it to my advantage. My plan was to go along with this charade until I found a weakness then turn Victor's scheme against him.

I didn't dress up for dinner like I had when my parents met Tom. My old cargo shorts and V-necked t-shirt were the only comfort I'd have tonight. Well, those and Tom's necklace sparkling at the hollow of my neck. The pan of brownies filled my car with the rich scent of fudge as I drove to the law office Victor and Chris had used during their trial.

I blared the horn after I pulled up in front. Victor ran to the window and held up one finger asking me to wait. I gave him sixty seconds on the dot then blared it again. He wanted me? Fine, he'd get it all, the good and the bad.

He looked annoyed when he slid into the passenger seat and moved to put his attaché case in the backseat. As soon as the road was clear, I stomped on the gas. He was still half turned and was thrown partially into the backseat.

"In a hurry?" he asked, buckling his seatbelt.

"No, this is how I always drive. Don't you remember?" I took the corner fast enough the tires squealed.

"And you still have a license?"

"As far as you know."

"Did you call Tom? He left me a rather nasty message," Victor explained, and when I didn't respond he continued, "Your plan to distance yourself from him is brilliant. It won't be such a shock when you come back to California with me."

I slammed on my brakes at a yellow light. "What?"

"For Eve's birthday party. There will be no need to hide it by then."

"I'm not hiding anything." I tightened my grip on the steering wheel until my knuckles turned white.

Victor chuckled and leaned into my space. "Then why haven't you called him?"

The light changed and I stomped on the gas. Victor chuckled again at my silence. Going along with this was going to be the hardest thing I'd ever done. At least I had a deadline for when I needed to have this all figured out.

Eve's birthday party was scheduled for the last Saturday of the month, which gave me just under two weeks to find a hole in Victor's plan. I needed to do it in a way that might salvage my relationship with Tom. The opal necklace felt unusually heavy around my neck.

"I didn't take you for a jewelry person," Victor said.

"I'm not, just nostalgic," I answered, pulling into my parents' driveway.

I'd hoped my dad was out back grilling with his fish mitt again but Mom had pulled out all the stops. There was summer squash soup, roasted chicken and baby red potatoes in the oven and some fancy vegetable dish. She must have thought she needed to impress the big city lawyer. I, on the other hand, planned on pretending he wasn't even here.

Acacia's music thumped loudly but abruptly cut off when Mom banged on her door signaling we had arrived. After dropping my brownies on the counter, I headed in that direction. If Victor wanted to invade my life, he'd have to do it on his own. My mom had already grabbed his attention, allowing me to escape without too much trouble. My sister met me in the hall. She'd re-dyed her hair black and she shook her newly painted onyx nails to speed dry them.

While Tom looked like he fit perfectly in my parents' well lived-in home, Victor stuck out like a sore thumb. His light-colored button-down shirt and casual slacks made him look terribly overdressed. Other than my mom, who was still wearing her Sunday church dress, everyone else in my family was wearing comfortable weekend clothes.

I plunked down at the table and propped my crossed ankles on one of the corners. Acacia grabbed a piece of bread, tore it in half, and took the chair next to me. When she offered me the other half, I leaned forward and snagged it with my teeth. Mom was beaming at Victor but when she glanced our way, she went white as a sheet.

"Arabella! Where are your manners? We have a guest. Get your feet off the table!" she scolded then grabbed the bread and dropped it onto the plate in front of me.

I rolled my eyes and finished chewing before lowering my feet to the floor with an exaggerated thunk. Victor eyed me suspiciously and I grinned back. I'd been on my best behavior at the dinner at his parents', but I was now at home with no one to impress. He'd see just how uncouth I really was.

Dad kept uncharacteristically quiet during dinner. Mom and Victor did most of the talking, which was fine with me. The less I had to converse with Victor the better. In my current mood, I'd probably say something without thinking first.

Victor cleared his throat and turned to my sister, who was pushing her food around on her plate rather than eating. "You're going to need to change your hair back before the trial. The judge will be more sympathetic to the girl I saw yesterday."

"I thought it was over." Mom's fork clattered to her plate.

Victor took a bite of potatoes before answering; the wait nearly sent my mom into full panic mode. "Unfortunately, no. I convinced Detective Rogers Acacia was not a flight risk and the prosecution's case is tenuous at best. Since the accusation has been made, we have to follow through until charges are dropped."

He reached over and patted my mother's hand. "They will be dropped. I'll take good care of your daughter."

I glared across the table at him when he caught my eye. In his attempt to pacify my mother, he was threatening me. My parents' table was small enough I could have kicked him in the shin and I seriously considered it. However, when my dad pushed his chair back and left the table, it distracted me from my immature solution to a much bigger problem.

"Excuse me," I said, following Dad out back.

He walked to the west-facing fence and leaned on it. I took my time walking across the lawn. When I joined him, he put his arm around my shoulders and gave me a light squeeze. The stress was clearly etched in his face when he sighed and put both arms on the top of the fence again.

"This thing with your sister... It's a vampire thing?"

I slumped my shoulders. "Yeah, it's a vampire thing."

"I can't afford that fancy lawyer in there," he said after a while. "I doubt he'll be willing to continue taking payment in the form of Sunday dinner."

"Don't worry, Dad. I'm taking care of it."

"I can see that. How does Tom feel about his brother moving in on his girl?"

"Pretty obvious, huh?" I asked, turning to rest my back against the fence so I could watch the house.

"About as obvious as the fact you can't stand him."

I could see Victor standing in the dining room window watching us. "I'll take care of it. You have enough to worry about."

When I pushed off the fence, he caught my wrist. "It's a father's job to worry about his girls. Don't let the man in there mess up what you have with Tom. When Tom looks at you, he sees what he can give you, when *he* does..." Dad jerked his head toward the house, "he only sees what you can give him."

I gave him a sad smile and a hug. "I'm doing my best. We'll get through this Dad, all of us."

# Chapter Twenty-Seven

Thanks to Geo's lack of assignments, I found myself with little to keep my mind occupied all week. I'd been toying with the idea of pulling out the bushes in front of my house and putting in a flower garden for some time. Since Victor had invited himself to be my newest houseguest, the thought of working outside in the dirt sounded fabulous. At this point, I'd do just about anything to keep my attention busy and not spend time with my captor. Having a loaded weapon in the same house as a man I absolutely loathed was far too tempting.

After a breakfast of cold cereal and coffee, I changed into some old clothes. Still clad in his silk pajama bottoms and no shirt, Victor sat on the couch and punched keys on his fancy laptop. It was a good thing he had access to the internet through his cell phone or he would've been shit out of luck. My computer was so old, I wasn't sure it could even connect to the internet anymore.

"Where are you off to?" he called as I opened the front door.

"Gardening." I pulled the door closed before he could ask anything else.

The wooden shed in my minuscule backyard was full of random tools for both the house and garden. I'd painted it to match the house as soon as I'd moved in. It was home to my lawn mower and wheelbarrow; everything else was hung on the walls or leaned in the back corners. Dad had donated some of his old stuff, after explaining a good homeowner couldn't live without a few good tools.

After piling everything I thought I would need into the wheelbarrow, I pushed it around the house. Now, where to start? What did I want to end up with? This must be why I hadn't started this project, yet. I knew I wanted a change, but I had no idea what.

The red Dogwood bushes added a nice contrasting color to the yellow and sage house paint. Their thick branches were smashed together invading the yard, making it appear even smaller than it really was, which didn't take much. I lucked out by having the corner lot right up against a park so when I did have larger gatherings, we just spilled into the lush green the city kept looking beautiful.

After about an hour of trimming, I decided to pull out every other one and plant some flowering shade plants underneath. Deciding which ones to pull was the next challenge. All of them looked to have sturdy roots, which meant I was in store for some serious chopping and digging. Standing around wasn't getting me any closer to my goal, but it was prolonging the inevitability of going back inside.

The first bush came out without much trouble; the next one had roots that must have started in Hell. I cursed again as I hit yet another buried root with my shovel.

"Would you like a hand?" Victor's voice startled me.

"I've got it," I replied, attacking the root with my big garden shears.

I heard him chuckle and walk up behind me. "You don't like asking for help, do you?"

"That's because I don't *need* help," I grumbled.

"I didn't ask if you needed help, just if you'd like some."

When I turned to face him, he wore a pair of Tom's old jeans and t-shirt. Victor had picked up the shovel from where I'd left it against the wheelbarrow and now leaned on it while he regarded me. He looked like he was more than ready to help. My heart flip-flopped at the way his posture and mannerisms mirrored Tom's. Before I said or did something stupid, I turned away.

"What's the plan?" Victor asked as he dug the shovelhead under the root ball of the bush I had been fighting with.

It came loose with a loud crack. I bent to retrieve it and knocked off the excess dirt. The plan was for me to work on this project so I *didn't* have to spend time with him. However, a second pair of hands and someone else to run the shovel would get it finished quicker. As much as I hated to admit it, those bushes were kicking my ass.

"Flower garden," I said.

He must have noticed the pattern to my destruction since he headed toward the next bush to be extracted. "You continue to surprise me, Arabella. I have a hard time imagining you spending hours tending roses and pulling weeds."

Damn, he was right. Now that I thought about it, my brown thumb must be the real reason why I hadn't done this project. My mother was the flower guru, not me. I had a hard enough time keeping my few pathetic houseplants alive, let alone a garden. Hopefully, the nursery would have some suggestions for low-maintenance shade plants. A little landscaping bark should help with weeds too.

"You don't know much about me, Vic," I said, using the spade to cut the lawn back to where I imagined the edging would be.

"Tell me then. How about your favorites? You know: color, car, food, song, the works..."

"Dark blue, Mustang, caramel swirl ice cream, and 'I Hate Everything About You.'" Why was I answering his stupid questions?

"Was that last one your favorite song or a jab at me?" He laughed, stabbing the shovel down again.

"You pick." I hadn't even thought about that. Score for me!

"Gold, Mustang but only the classics, spinach lasagna, and 'At Last.'"

"What?" I turned to look at him like he was crazy.

"I thought it was only fair to give you my answers as well," Victor explained. "Maybe you'll discover we have more in common than you realize."

I went back to cutting the garden's edge with renewed fervor. The last thing I wanted was for him to know more about me, and I couldn't care less about his favorite things. He'd just tell me what I wanted to hear anyway. Best to ignore him and maybe he would get a clue.

After a few more failed attempts from Victor to further our conversation, we worked quietly, saying only what was necessary to get the job done. The bushes were cleared away by early afternoon and the grass pulled up to mark the new garden edge. The only thing left was to run to the nursery for the plants, topsoil, and edging.

"And off to the plant store," I said as we dumped the last of the stumps in the alley behind my house.

"I'll join you. You might need someone for heavy lifting," Victor said, wiping his hands on his, uh, I mean, Tom's jeans.

"I've got it. Besides, I'll probably stop at the grocery store on my way back."

"In that case, I'm definitely going," he said with a grin.

"Believe it or not, I can buy my own food," I said curtly.

"It kind of defeats the purpose of me cooking dinner for you if you buy all the food."

I stopped mid-step, remembering Tom's disastrous attempt at breakfast. My horrified expression must have given away my train of thought.

"Don't worry. I'm the best cook in the family. Where do you think Eve learned, our mother?" Victor said.

"Oh." I started walking again.

The gal at the nursery was far more interested in flirting with Victor than helping me find plants. After having to interrupt three times, I threw my hands up and stalked off, but not before accidentally-on-purpose ramming the flat bed cart into Ms. Unhelpful's ankle. After loading up half a dozen Hostas, some white flowering groundcover to replace the bark that made me sneeze uncontrollably and a roll of black plastic edging, I was done. My plan to leave Victor behind was foiled when he spotted me by the register.

When we got home from the grocery store, I let him lug in all the food while I headed straight back to the garden project. The radio mentioned a high chance of rain later. On top of the fact I had to work the next day, meant I needed to get these plants in the ground before they croaked. Hey, they deserved a fighting chance before I let them die.

Planting turned out to be the easiest part of the project. I fought with the curly edging for a while but refused to ask for help. Victor hadn't emerged after we'd gotten home, for which I was thankful. For some reason, watching him flirt with the girl at the nursery bothered me. From a distance, it was too much like watching those groupies flirting with Tom. Or at least that's what I kept telling myself.

Maybe I should take Victor out so he could find someone else to focus his attention on; someone to hang on his every word, like Ms. Unhelpful today. It was a good plan and might have worked, if he weren't so damn fixated on me. I still didn't understand Tom's fascination, but Victor's was just petty jealousy. There was really nothing special about me.

The clouds were threatening to burst by the time I finally finished putting away all the tools. I could literally hear the shower calling my name as I pushed the front door open. I made it two steps inside when the smell of chicken and garlic caught my attention, forcing me to detour toward the kitchen. Good thing vampires weren't hurt by garlic because I loved the stuff.

Victor was in the process of chopping up a bunch of spinach when I rounded the corner. The knife flew across the cutting board with the skills of a TV chef and I had to admit, I was more than a little impressed. He was so focused on his task he didn't even notice me until I snuck behind him to peer into the pot simmering on the stove.

"All done?" He stirred the cream sauce then held out the spoon for me to taste.

I stepped aside without accepting his offer. My small kitchen was suddenly too full for my liking. "I'm going to take a shower."

I guess telling me spinach lasagna was his favorite wasn't enough because that's what he made for dinner. As much as I hated to admit it, the pasta was the best thing I'd ever tasted. If I had been by myself, I'd have called the pizza guy after all the manual labor this afternoon. Muscles I didn't know I had screamed in pain. Time to go back to the gym.

The ever-present red wine was on the table. My full glass sat untouched, my own personal form of hunger strike. If the company was better, I might consider having a drink while enjoying my food. Instead, I sat with my elbows on the table and focused on cutting my food into really small pieces. I even did my best to imitate Acacia's slurping with my glass of water.

"Since we're trying to get to know each other, why don't you ask me something?" Victor suggested, sitting back with his glass of wine.

"Who said we're getting to know each other?" I asked around a mouthful of food.

Victor tipped his head and gave me an exasperated look. "Your bad manners aren't going to scare me away, Arabella. There must be something you want to ask."

There was, but I didn't think he would tell me the truth or, at the very least, he'd spin the answer in his favor. I wanted to know about the girl that led to the falling out between him and Tom. I knew there had to be more to the story than Lucian told me after my near-death experience. Without realizing it, my hand lifted to cover my scars. I left it on my neck and swallowed my last bite in an attempt to look casual and failing miserably.

"Why did you have to kill her?" I asked, reaching for my wine glass, hating myself for doing it, but managed to grab my water instead.

"Ah, Rachel," Victor swirled the wine in his glass. "That wasn't my fault, and she's not dead."

"Not the way I heard it."

"Tom told you? Let me guess, it was a romantic version where I stole her away and tortured him with it."

"Tom didn't tell me," I snapped.

"Lucian then..." He guessed then continued, "It's a long story. Why don't we move to the living room so we're more comfortable?"

I shrugged and started to gather up the dishes. We did a quick clean up, threw the leftovers in the fridge, and put the dirty dishes in some soapy water. Victor refilled his wine glass and brought the rest of the bottle into the living room.

I hesitated in the doorway. As much as I wanted to hear the story, I didn't want any wine. If I didn't have anything else in my hands, I knew I'd be tempted to drink it. For some reason, I really wanted a cup of hot chocolate. The teapot would take too long so I filled up a mug with some water and threw it in the microwave. My bulk container of cocoa mix lived in the back of my spice cabinet, mostly to keep me from drinking it all in one sitting. Victor came back into the kitchen when he heard me banging around.

"What are you doing?"

"Hot cocoa," I said as the microwave dinged.

He raised an eyebrow. "It's not really that kind of story."

"Suit yourself." I spooned in three heaping tablespoons.

"Is it any good?" he asked when I licked the spoon then poured in just a little more from the container.

"Better with cinnamon tequila but I don't have any... No, wait, Cass gave me some. It's in the cupboard above the fridge."

"Could you make me one?"

He sounded so pathetic. I rolled my eyes and grabbed another mug from the rack. "Since you helped me with those bushes and made dinner, I *guess* I could slave over a cup of instant cocoa."

While he was moving my basket of candles off the top of the fridge, I swapped the cup I'd grabbed for one that read 'Hot Chick'. Cassie had given me the cup and the bottle of booze for my birthday after we drank ourselves silly on this exact combination at her house last summer.

"Found it," he announced as I put the new mug in the microwave.

When I turned, he'd opened it and was taking a swig right from the bottle. "Thanks for sharing your backwash." I wrinkled my nose in disgust.

He offered me the bottle with a full body shake. It *was* tough stuff. I put it down but he shook his head.

"You want the story? Take a shot."

"Then I guess I'll just drink my chocolate and watch a movie," I retorted, feigning indifference.

The microwave dinged and I went about making the second cup. Only when I saw the two mugs sitting side by side did I realize I was even doing it. Victor was so frustrating when he did that! He'd figured out if my mind was open to something, he had no trouble pushing me to follow through, whether I was up for it or not. I really wanted to hear the story but the whole reason I made the cocoa was so I'd be coherent enough to hear it.

"Fine. One shot." I picked up the bottle and downed a mouthful.

Through my coughing and sputtering, he said, "And one for every time you interrupt."

"Deal."

I could keep my mouth shut, at least in theory. Victor sat next to me on the couch but not uncomfortably close. Since that first night he hadn't pressed for blood sharing or sex. I'd sat with my back to the arm and folded my legs so I was out of his reach. The bottle of cinnamon liquor wedged between my knee and the back cushions, just in case. In good faith, I'd added a splash into each of our mugs after we sat down.

"Rachel." The sadness in his voice startled me. "She literally danced into our lives during our first year in college. Tom and I were both in the same freshman English class. God, it feels like yesterday. Her hot pink t-shirt had ridden up above her jeans, showing just a glimpse of her pale skin and a portion of the tattoo on her stomach."

He turned to face me, a half-smile played on his lips. "Now I think about it, you look a lot like her. Rachel's hair was shorter and curly but nearly the same shade. Your eyes, though, identical."

I looked down, feeling uncomfortable under his intense stare. There was more to this story, possibly things I didn't want to hear, but I needed to know so I could understand. I took a drink of my cocoa, savoring its comforting burn.

"She sat in front; we, of course, were sitting in the very back. I know it's hard to believe but my brother and I used to get along. Tom nearly flipped his desk over trying to get to the front of the room. However, Rachel's friends surrounded her before we even got to our feet. When the instructor called roll, she twisted in her seat when Tom and I responded. Her big golden eyes studied each of us in turn before she whispered to her friend. My brother was so sure she was his. I know he told you about the whole compatible genetics but what he didn't consider was me."

"You can't call dibs on a person!" I blurted out.

That half-smile turned into a full mischievous grin as he reached for the bottle. "Here you go."

"Not fair! I need at least one freebie." I folded my arms and looked away.

"I'll make you a deal. You interrupt and take your shot, and I'll match you one for one."

I frowned. Now he'd started the story, I wanted to hear the end but I knew I'd never be able to keep my mouth shut the whole time.

If he were matching me shot for shot, neither of us would make it very far. However, I didn't want to be the only one getting sloshed. No blood in my personal liquor stash, thank you!

"Fine." I grabbed the bottle and tipped it up for a drink.

Victor did the same then launched back into the story. "For two weeks, both Tom and I did our best to ambush her coming and going from class with no luck. She was always surrounded by a group of friends or went an alternate route. Just when I was ready to stand up in class and introduce myself, the instructor put us in the same group. Once faced with her, I had no idea what to say."

"Was Tom in your group? Shit!" I took a drink without having to be told.

After taking his sympathy shot, Victor shook his head. "Nope, and he was livid. However, Rachel kept sneaking glances at his little group. When we finally introduced ourselves, she seemed disappointed I was in her group and not Tom."

I opened my mouth but caught myself before I spoke. The look on Victor's face made me stop, not the threat of more cinnamon death. He looked crushed. Had he really cared for Rachel? If that were the case, why on Earth had he tried to kill her?

"While I could diagram a sentence like nobody's business, I was hopeless when it came to creative writing and poetry. Tom, of course, excelled in this, too much like his music," he said bitterly. "It was after a significantly painful poetry section that Rachel approached Tom. The bastard couldn't stop rubbing it in."

Victor took a swig of his cocoa and rolled his shoulders back as if to ease the tension. "She'd been nice to me in class but it was clear she was much more interested in my brother. I called my father for advice but, like always, he sided with Tom. He told me there was someone out there for everyone and I needed to be patient. But I just knew she was meant for me."

"How could you know?" My voice was just above a whisper.

"I was practically invisible in our little class group so Rachel would talk about her time with Tom to her girlfriends. She mentioned how it didn't hurt when he took her blood."

My hand holding my cocoa began to shake and I whispered, "I don't want to hear anymore."

Victor took another swig of the cinnamon stuff, much longer than his others before handing the bottle to me. I accepted it and took my shot, only now noticing he'd missed my last interruption. When he turned back to face me, his eyes were glassy and slightly out of focus.

"But you haven't heard the best part." His voice was hard. "She dumped Tom and started showing interest in me. I couldn't believe it. Apparently, he'd done something to scare her off. Of course, I had no problem helping her pick up the pieces. How was I to know she was only trying to make him jealous?

"I can see it now but then..." He shook his head. "It was finally my turn. Tom had started his family legacy denial stage. I gave Rachel everything she wanted, fulfilled her every wish, and it filled me with joy because she was happy. Then one day, she just ended it.

Like you, she was incredibly naïve when it came to vampire knowledge. She'd become addicted to the power she pulled from our blood. Even though she didn't think she wanted us anymore, she still wanted that. Tom denied her when she told him she wasn't interested in anything else. He was the smart one."

He drained the last of his hot chocolate and only then noticed the cheesy logo. It got a huff of a laugh before he set it carefully on the coffee table. I looked down at my nearly full mug but wasn't surprised to see I'd ignored it. Leaning forward, I poured half of it into his empty cup.

"Thanks." He tilted it up to his lips and was silent.

The seconds ticked away on my wall clock. I counted two hundred before I opened my mouth. "And?"

Victor handed me the bottle, but I protested. "That doesn't count. You stopped the story." The bottle swayed slightly in his hand but stayed outstretched in my direction. "Fine, but the next time you stop and I have to prod you to keep going, I'm not taking a drink."

After his shot, he drained the now nearly cold cocoa. "Tom tried to convince me to let it go, that Rachel was playing us. He just couldn't stand she'd chosen me. It may have not been what he imagined as the ideal relationship, but it was enough for me.

Rachel and I had our casual relationship for almost a year before she suddenly broke everything off again. Tom and I had moved to our respective fields of study and we rarely talked anymore. A week later, I saw them together and lost it. He only wanted me to stop seeing Rachel so he could have her for himself. I tried to forget them, to listen to my father. I didn't need that kind of shit in my life."

Victor reached for the bottle again but I pulled it out of his grasp and shook my head. I needed to hear the end of this story and his words were already slower and starting to slur. My head felt like it was stuffed with cotton balls and my lips were tingling. One more drink and I'd be out cold.

"It was stupid but I invited her to my apartment, telling her it was a surprise for Tom. What I had planned was going to surprise him but not in a good way. Her mind was open, sensing no threat. Not as open as yours can be but close, it didn't take much persuading to get her to offer her blood. Somehow it had changed; it tasted so much better than it ever had before. I, I couldn't stop and she begged me not to."

Remembering when he'd first taken my blood and the euphoria it caused, I understood why she had asked. I wondered if he knew the reason for her plea?

I put a hand on his knee in a gesture of understanding. "Rachel is a person. She didn't belong to either of you and neither do I. Yes, our blood is compatible but I'm still my own person with feelings, hopes, and dreams. Just because you think..."

"Does it hurt when I bite you?" he asked, taking my hand in his so tightly my knuckles cracked.

"You're hurting me now." I tried unsuccessfully to hold my voice steady.

"Not as much as you're hurting me. Answer the question."

Victor's blue eyes were glazed from the alcohol but the desperate plea was still there. His version of the story was part truth, part perspective. This pursuit of me was much deeper than sibling rivalry. I had so many more questions but my brain was too scrambled from the story and the booze.

"No," I held his gaze as I answered.

His eyes narrowed. "No, you won't answer or no, it doesn't hurt?"

"Does it matter? I'm not an object to be passed around. I don't, and won't, belong to you or anybody else."

"And yet you're still here, with me."

I pulled against his hold. "Not by choice, Vic."

"Well, I'll just have to work on that, won't I?" he said softly, lifting my wrist to his lips.

# Chapter Twenty-Eight

My cell phone rang while I was in the middle of making my favorite Oriental soup for dinner. After adding another splash of soy sauce, I grabbed and pinned it between my cheek and shoulder before answering. Today had been Victor free and I was in a great mood due to my freedom, as temporary as it may be.

"Helloooo," I sang.

"Hey, you're home," a familiar voice said brightly.

"Where else would I be? Can you grab some green onions and freezer egg rolls on your way home?" I tasted my soup then added more drops of spicy chili oil.

"Sure, but I'm not sure how good they'd be by the time I got there."

The spoon stopped halfway to my mouth and I almost dropped the phone into the pot. I'd managed to avoid talking to Tom over the last few days between his insanely busy schedule and my sending him cryptic text messages. I let my personal cell phone's battery die so I wouldn't have to ignore the ringing when he called but Victor had charged it last night so he could keep tabs on me while he was out. Apparently, my lucky streak just ended.

When I'd answered the phone, I had assumed it was Victor. He had taken my car to meet with Nick's lawyers this afternoon. My brilliant sister had decided to take matters into her own hands. She'd gone over to Nick's house and started screaming at him through the door when his mother wouldn't let her in. Cops were called and as a reward, the judge had officially put her under house arrest and I wasn't any closer to finding a way out from under Victor's thumb. Eve's birthday was looming like an executioner's blade.

"Tom," I said, putting the spoon on the trivet and holding my hand to my stomach.

"Of course, who did you think it was?" He laughed.

"Um, nobody. How are things with you?" I recovered very poorly.

He hesitated before answering. "Busy. I had a few minutes and hoped we could talk."

Talk. Sure, I had loads to chat about. Unfortunately, I couldn't come up with one single safe topic. "How's Eve's birthday planning coming along?"

"She's dead set on having a costume party even though Desdemona thinks it's inappropriate. Which is probably why Eve wants to do it. I think they are currently in negotiations for a masquerade style party instead." He laughed, again sending a shot of pain through my heart. "Please tell me you'll be there."

"I've got the time off work already." I slid into a chair because my knees were turning to jelly. "Tell me how sunny California is treating you."

Victor had instructed me to tell Tom it was over when I finally did talk to him. As Tom regaled me with stories of long hours in a studio and even longer nights at clubs, my resolve began to crumble. My fingers found my opal pendant, which I worried between my thumb and forefinger. I mumbled agreements and made appropriate one-word answers when asked a question.

There was a moment of silence from his end. "Arabella, are you okay?"

I took a deep breath; here goes nothing. I was about to irrevocably damage our relationship. The next words out of my mouth would buy me more time but ultimately drive a wedge between us that I wasn't sure we'd be able to overcome. They were also the most painful lies I was sure I'd ever have to tell.

"Not really. Since you've been gone, I've had some time to think."

"That doesn't sound good." Tom half-laughed.

"It's not. God, I hate to do this over the phone but since I don't know when you'll be back... I've been trying to find the words to tell you, but..."

My words cut off with a sob. I couldn't bring myself to do it, but I had to. If we were meant to be together, we'd survive this somehow. After a few deep breaths, I locked my heart away.

"I think we should see other people, Tom. I'm sure you're lonely there and..."

"The only reason I'm lonely is because you aren't here. What's really going on?" Tom sounded more angry than hurt.

"I can't do this anymore. This thing between us, it's happening too fast. I need to take a step back," I managed, wiping away a tear that escaped the corner of my eye. Tom was silent for so long, I asked, "Are you still there?"

"So, when I called just now... You've already found someone else." It wasn't a question.

"I'm so sorry." He had no idea how much I meant it. I prayed he wouldn't ask the next logical question because my answer would determine whether my sister got to stay under house arrest or put into a juvenile detention center.

"Who?" His voice was harsh.

"Please, Tom, don't ask me that." My words were a strained whisper but I knew he could hear.

"I need to know, Arabella."

I closed my eyes and put my head in my free hand. "Victor."

The phone went dead and I felt a piece of my soul die along with it. My gasp of agony seemed to echo in my excruciatingly empty house. A single word was all it took to destroy the one good thing in my life. That's why I begged him not to make me answer.

My fingers wrapped around my opal necklace, the setting cutting into my hand, but I welcomed the pain. The smell of the soup suddenly nauseated me. I pushed myself to my feet and dumped the whole thing in the sink. Let Victor get his own dinner. I'd done my part for the day.

I stumbled blindly down the hall to my spare room where I folded myself onto Tom's futon. Wrapping my arms around a thick throw pillow, I put my head down and cried. Not a gentle sob but full body, throat wrenching cry. I'd hoped to have this solved before it got this far. I needed to get this out of the way because I wouldn't let Victor see this display of weakness.

Eve's poetry about endless love, understanding, and strength seemed to mock me as my tears soaked the pillow I clung to. She'd probably hate me when she found out what I'd done to Tom. Hell, I hated myself but it was only temporary and I had no other choice. Once this was over, he'd understand. Please let him understand.

Victor got home just before ten. I'd snuggled onto the couch to watch a DVD hours ago. I had no idea what movie it was or how many times I'd restarted it. It was part of my charade of having a normal day.

After he deposited all his stuff against the entryway wall, he came over to give me a kiss. It was part of his daily ritual, like a sick, twisted nineteen-fifties era sitcom. Despite knowing it was coming, when he leaned toward me, I flinched away. He chuckled under his breath and sat next to me on the couch. Too close. I swung my feet to the floor and scooted over.

"Bad day?" He unbuttoned the cuffs on his shirt. When I didn't reply, he continued, "I got a rather nasty phone call today."

"I'm watching a movie." I stared straight ahead at the screen without seeing anything.

"What is it about?" he asked, putting his arm over the back of the couch, resting on the top of my shoulders.

I slumped forward, putting my elbows on my knees. "Watch and find out."

"What's for dinner?" he asked as his hand rubbed against my back.

I jumped to my feet and stomped toward my bedroom. "Whatever the fuck you want!"

I made it halfway before Victor grabbed my arms and pinned me against the wall. Everything I'd done to prepare facing him tonight evaporated when he'd walked through the door. He was toying with me. That nasty phone call must have come from Tom, why else would he have mentioned it? Tom had called and left two messages for me during my breakdown; I'd deleted both without listening to them. The temptation to call and tell him the truth was too high.

"I didn't realize my brother had those kinds of words in his vocabulary," Victor said, holding my defiant gaze. "You did well convincing him. I wished I had been here."

The answer on how to solve this situation hit me like a ton of bricks. I'd spent so much time fighting him, he expected me to run at any second. My acting skills sucked but I was known for my stubborn and determined personality. Lulling him into a false sense of security would give me the leeway I needed. I'd have to be careful though. A complete one-eighty flip in my attitude would make him suspicious. Eve's party was just over a week away. That's all the time I'd have to go from completely defensive to mostly compliant. He knew me too well now to think I'd give myself fully to anyone, let alone him.

Dropping my gaze, I relaxed against the wall. "I'm tired."

Victor released his grip on my arms and I was afraid I'd blown it by not fighting back when he was obviously goading me into an argument about Tom. Pushing my hair back from my face, I looked up and studied his eyes. They were tight as if he wasn't sure what to do next. My show of submission had thrown him.

"If you'll get your ass out of the way, I'll go to bed," I prompted.

His half grin showed me I'd gotten away with it and gave me hope my plan would work. He stepped back and I slammed the bathroom door behind me for effect. Tomorrow I'd start my transformation from defiant bitch to sympathetic somewhat-willing partner. This afternoon I thought telling Tom it was over was hard, but pretending to fall for Victor was going to be twice as difficult.

• • • •

I WOKE EARLY AND STARTED breakfast, made from scratch waffles, eggs, and those little link sausages. It was part food for strength, part suck up for Victor not pushing me further last night. He'd come to bed long after I'd fallen asleep and I was surprised to find him sleeping beside me when I opened my eyes the next morning. It was the first night he hadn't pushed blood sharing since he'd told me the Rachel story.

The sausages were thawing in the sink and the waffle batter was resting when Victor appeared in the kitchen doorway. I wasn't the quietest chef, probably because I was used to living alone. Without saying a word, I walked over to the coffee pot and poured him a cup.

"Morning." I offered him the mug. "You working again today?"

He took it and pulled out one of the kitchen chairs to sit. "Only on my computer."

"How about a run?" I asked, checking the sausages.

"I didn't realize you were a runner," he said, spooning sugar into his coffee mug.

"Off and on. Got to keep my girlish figure and all that crap."

With a chuckle, he took a sip of his coffee then reached for the sugar bowl again. "I'm not sure you can keep up with me."

"Is that a challenge? Remember you're used to running at sea level, I've got home court advantage."

He regarded me for a moment. "My regular schedule is a five-mile loop in the hills around my house."

"Two and a half miles on flat ground shouldn't kill you then. I planned on making a big breakfast but it can wait until we get back."

I put the waffle batter and now-thawed sausages in the fridge. When I stepped back to close the door, I ran into Victor. He'd snuck up behind me. It took all my willpower not to ram my elbow into his gut when he wrapped his hands around my waist and pulled me against him.

"What do I get if I win this little race?" His breath was hot against my ear.

"I know what I want," I said, twisting so I could face him, resting my hands on his arms creating a little more space between us. "For you to work your legal magic so Acacia can come with us to Eve's birthday party."

This was a major part of my plan. If I could get the girls together and Blondie's signed waiver, Acacia would be home free and so would I. Tom was a big part of the plan too and I hoped he would forgive me for what I had to do in the meantime.

Victor's brows furrowed in frustration. "I'm not sure I can swing that."

"I thought you said you were good?"

His arms tightened, pulling me against him again. "I am."

The silk pajama bottoms did little to hide where his thoughts were headed so I wriggled away. "Finish your coffee and I'll get dressed."

Winning the race was only the first step. It would be up to Victor's legal wrangling to get the okay for Acacia to come with us to California while on house arrest. I'd sweeten the deal by giving him what he wanted after the run. God, this was going to be a long week.

# Chapter Twenty-Nine

The phone rang four times and I was just about to hang up when someone wrenched it from the cradle. I held my cell away from my ear to protect it from all the noise as it clattered to the floor.

"Hello?" Acacia sounded like she'd been running.

"Who has the best sister in the world?" I couldn't help but smile at my own question.

"Let me guess?" she said flatly.

"Oh, if you don't want to go to Eve's birthday party you can just keep flipping me that crappy attitude..." I began but her squeal cut me off.

"Arabella, you are the bestest sister! How did you do it?"

There wasn't any way I was going to tell her the details of the last few days. A shudder racked my body before I could stop it as the memories flashed back. Victor had taken to my slow warming all too well.

"It wasn't me. Well, it was my idea but Victor did all the work. He'll be your chaperone during your stay in California."

"Sounds lame. But hey, can I call you back? I need to call Eve and tell her the news." Acacia sounded like she was going to burst with excitement, which was something for her.

"Sure, but could you do me a favor? Can you have her tell Tom I'm sorry and it's not what he thinks?"

"Why don't you tell him?"

There was no accusation in her tone and it made me worry about how she'd respond when she found out what I had done to keep her out of jail. I'd blackened my soul by pimping out my body and blood but in the long run, it was a small price to pay.

"Please just do it and call me later so we can decide what we're getting the girl who has everything for her birthday."

Part of my plan, and the fact Victor's eagle eye constantly watched me, was I couldn't communicate with Tom in any way. Since his two unanswered voicemails, he hadn't tried any further contact. It hurt but it also helped with my plan. As long as I could convince him my affair with Victor was a sham once I got to California, we'd be okay. If not... Well, I didn't want to think about that yet.

I only had one more day before we headed south. As time inched ahead, I worried Victor wouldn't be able to get permission for Acacia to come with us. Or maybe he'd waited until the last possible moment so I'd continue to be agreeable to his demands.

The sound of the shower vanished and I mentally prepared myself. Over the last few days, I'd discovered Victor and I indeed had many things in common. The question of what would have happened if I'd met him first crossed my mind several times. However, there was no going back, no such things as second first impressions. Once I'd found out about his past and his current views on the superiority of vampires, it would have been over regardless.

"Did you call your sister?" Victor asked, sticking his head out of the bathroom.

"Yep, and she nearly hung up on me so she could call Eve with the good news." I grinned.

"Looks like she's not the only one excited."

If he knew the real reason I was excited, he wouldn't be smiling. I was nearly counting the hours until I saw Tom again, to have his arms wrapped around me, the sound of his voice whispering my song as I drifted to sleep. I turned away, arms wrapped around myself, and closed my eyes to savor the memory. If I listened close enough, I could almost hear it.

Wait, I really could. My eyes popped open and I ran into the bathroom where the little radio was softly playing. I pushed around Victor and flipped the volume wheel, flooding the room with my song. Cradling the tiny device in my hand, I stared at the black speaker and drank in the music.

Once again, the song had changed somewhat. Not the words this time, to which I was grateful but several stringed instruments now accompanied Tom's guitar, as well as the thump of bass and drum lines. The studio mixing had altered Tom's voice slightly but in a good way. Not as good as when he whispered it to me, but close. It was truly the most beautiful thing I'd ever heard.

When the announcer came on, I realized how my reaction must look to Victor. Shit! Had I just undone everything I'd worked so hard to accomplish? I turned the volume down before placing the radio back by the sink, keeping my eyes lowered.

"Like that song, huh?" Victor asked.

"Yeah," I mumbled and tried to sidestep out of the bathroom.

He angled his body to block the door then lifted my chin so I was looking into his eyes. "I'm not stupid, Arabella. I know you still care for him."

My heart leapt from my chest and my mind scrambled for an answer. Victor had known I'd been faking everything. I was out of my league; I'd be trapped with him forever. When I opened my mouth to protest, he made a hush noise and brushed a strand of hair from my face.

"I also know you now see we are meant to be together." He leaned in to give me a peck on my lips, still half open in shock. "I hate to steal Eve's thunder but I think her birthday party is the perfect opportunity to announce our engagement."

Hold the phone! Engagement? Victor's verbal threat was moving toward a legally binding agreement at light speed. It felt like I'd been kicked in the stomach. I'm sure the shock was clear on my face. This unexpected revelation was most definitely *not* part of my plan.

"Don't you think it will seem a little sudden?" I stammered.

Victor put his hands on my hips and pulled me close. "Not at all. My older sister found the man she was supposed to be with and they were married within the month. If you ask me, Tom was just asking for me to steal you away by putting off marrying you."

"Maybe he knew I wasn't ready for that level of commitment," I bristled.

Victor shrugged as if it didn't matter what I wanted. "I've called my jeweler in LA and your ring will be ready when we arrive."

"My what?"

"Nothing too ostentatious but I wouldn't want my friends' wives to whisper behind your back."

"I'm not wearing a ring." I pushed his hands off me and ducked under his arm to get out of the bathroom.

My escape was brief; his hand encircled my wrist after only two steps. "If you want your sister to come with us, you'll wear it."

I closed my eyes to repress my anger. My voice was quiet when I spoke. "I can't do this, Victor. Just let me go."

"With all the progress we've made? Once you're home with me and away from other distractions, you'll see you've made the right choice."

Turning slowly, I raised my eyes to his. "Vic, you're not giving me a choice."

The phone rang again, making me jump and interrupting our conversation. Whatever he'd planned for a rebuttal disappeared with the annoying noise. Victor tugged me along by the wrist as he angled toward where I had dropped my phone on the couch. My gut twisted when he answered then handed it to me. It was as if he owned the place. In all actuality, I'd probably given him the idea that he did.

"Hello?" I answered tentatively.

"Acacia just called me with the news! Are you going to have a chance to pick up a costume before you leave or are we going shopping when you get here? Did you get the invitation yet?"

Victor let go of me and I slumped against the wall as I listened to Eve's excited babble. Obviously, the argument was over and I was stuck once again. As I watched Victor's retreating back, I seethed with hatred. In my personal hell, I'd missed what Eve had said.

"What was that?" I forced myself to focus.

"I said," I could almost hear Eve roll her eyes, "Tom is going crazy without you. Now are we going shopping together or not?"

"Since we don't have anywhere here to shop for your Gothic Masquerade Ball, I guess you get to torture me with another afternoon of full contact shopping." As soon as I'd said it, I wished I hadn't. My anger toward Victor made my tone harsher than I'd meant. "I'm sorry, Eve. I would love to go shopping with you and Acacia."

Her response sounded hesitant as if she were trying to figure out what she'd done wrong. "I have an appointment at an exclusive shop tomorrow evening. Do you think Tom will let me have you for a few hours?"

With a sigh, I answered honestly. "That won't be a problem."

For whatever reason, it appeared Tom hadn't shared the fact I'd ended it with him and started seeing Victor. Maybe he had to see it with his own eyes for it to be real. A surge of hope to salvage our relationship rose up in me until I remembered I'd be coming to Eve's party with an engagement ring. I longed to ask if Acacia had given her my message but I was all too aware of Victor's presence in the next room.

"What do you want for your birthday, Eve?" I asked, trying to keep my tone natural.

"You're already giving it to me. I just wanted both you and Acacia to be here to celebrate. Oh, I've got another call coming in. I'll see you tomorrow. Bye."

"Bye."

"Another shopping event with Eve?" Victor asked.

"It's not polite to eavesdrop," I said curtly, grabbing my car keys.

"Where are you headed?"

"Out," I said, reaching for the front door handle. When I heard him draw a breath to protest, I interrupted. "I'll wear the ring. Just make sure you remember I'm only doing it because I have no choice, not because I want to."

I slammed the front door closed behind me without waiting for a response. Luckily, he didn't try to follow. I needed time to think and re-work my plan. I had less than twenty-four hours before I was either back in Tom's arms or forever trapped with Victor.

• • • •

ACACIA AND I WALKED down the crowded mall in silence. One of the stipulations of the house arrest was my sister couldn't go anywhere without one or both parents present. Obviously being an adult wasn't enough for her to be alone with me, that or Victor had suggested against it, thinking I'd run off with her. God, I was tired of his mind games.

Mom was catching up with an old friend in front of the knockoff fragrance store. The combinations of floral, spicy, and musky smells coming from the store was making me nauseated. My sister and I moved down the mall to an empty bench still within view of the required 'adult supervision'.

"Any ideas for Eve's birthday present?" I asked, plunking down on the bench and slouching in a very unladylike manner. Mom shot me a disapproving glance so I straightened up slightly.

"I made her something," Acacia said as she watched a couple of teenagers prance toward us looking like clones of this year's hottest pop star. "I decorated a journal with some of my art, you know, for her to write her poetry in."

"Then why did you want to come with me?"

She turned to face me. "Because if I have to sit in that house for one more minute, I'll go crazy."

"I thought you went out with Mom yesterday."

"Yeah, three hours at the nursery. It was worse than the open house she dragged me to last weekend. Honestly, how long is this going to last?" She sat forward and put her face in her hands.

I reached over and rubbed her back. "Hopefully everything will be settled before we get back from California."

Acacia dropped her arms. She had an incredulous look on her face when she turned back to me. It was now or never. I had to tell her what was going on, edited for age, of course. Who knew if I'd get another chance without Victor hovering?

Licking my lips, I shot a glance at Mom who was still enjoying her gossip-fest before I started. "Acacia, listen to me. Things are going to get really complicated when we get to LA. Everyone needs to believe I've broken up with Tom and now engaged to Victor. Do not, under any circumstances, let Victor get you alone."

She opened her mouth to protest but I pressed on. "Please do this for me. Everything will be back to normal afterward." *I hope.*

My sister stared at me, her forehead scrunched as she tried to figure out what I was saying. I flicked my gaze back to Mom; she was heading this way. The time I had to convince Acacia was over. There was nothing else I could say without piquing Mom's interest or worse, her intense worry.

"Arabella, sweetheart, you're bleeding," Mom said, pulling a handkerchief from her purse.

When she held it to my lip, I realized I'd been biting it in anticipation. Acacia still wore a confused look as she studied me. I dabbed the white linen square to my mouth and realization crossed her face.

I shook my head almost imperceptibly and darted my eyes toward Mom to keep her quiet. She huffed angrily and got to her feet then hurried down the mall. We rushed to keep up with her as she rounded the corner and stomped into the bookstore.

Mom gave me a questioning look; Acacia wasn't much of a reader. I shrugged and followed my sister's retreating back as she headed further and further into the store. The shelves were at least eight feet tall and the music was almost too loud. It was then I realized what she was doing.

"Uh, Mom, what was the title of that book Dad was talking about?" I prompted.

"The one with the elf quest? I can't remember." She frowned.

"Why don't you go ask at the info desk? I'll keep an eye on Acacia. She probably wants to get Eve a book on poetry or something."

As Mom hurried off in the other direction, I headed to where my sister had disappeared around one of those tall shelves. She was sitting cross-legged in the middle of the aisle when I found her. We were in the Art History section and, best of all, alone.

I eased myself to the floor beside her and let out a breath. "I was hoping it wouldn't go this far."

"What the hell, Arabella? Victor's behind this? What did I do to piss him off enough to want to send me to jail?" Her anger was clear even though she was whispering.

"You didn't do anything. This is between Victor and Tom, you just got sucked into the middle of it."

"What does he want?"

I flinched. "Me. I know it sounds stupid but..." I started, but she cut me off.

"It's not stupid. Any guy would be crazy not to want you." She looked down at her hands and added even more quietly, "So, you're with Victor to keep me safe?"

I closed my eyes. No matter how I answered, Acacia would feel responsible. Rubbing my sweaty hands on my jeans, I decided to be honest with her. If she didn't understand, she might not go along with my plan later.

"I'm with Victor because it's the right thing to do right now. He would have found a way to get to me regardless. I won't let anything happen to you but you need to trust me. When I tell you to, you are going to have to do exactly what I say, when I say it. Think you can handle that?"

She nodded then looked up, eyes wide. "Eve's going to be pissed."

"What?" I asked, thrown by her sudden change of topic.

"It was supposed to be a surprise, but Tom is going to propose to you at her party. She's even lined up the band to play the perfect song. I think she's more excited about that than her actual birthday."

Oh, crap. Eve was going to hate me for breaking her brother's heart and ruining her party. No wonder Tom hadn't said anything to her about the breakup.

"When did she tell you this?"

"This morning when I told her I was coming. Why?"

My heart began to pound and I couldn't stop the smile as it spread across my face. This was perfect. It was as if Tom knew my plan without me having told him anything. He was going to make me choose between him and Victor in front of everyone at the party. No wonder Victor wanted to have a ring on my finger before we arrived. It was going to feel so good to throw it in his face.

"You ready?" I asked, pushing to my feet.

"So, what are you going to give Eve for her birthday?" she asked.

"Exactly what she wants."

# Chapter Thirty

"Thanks for picking us up, Eve," I said from the back seat.

She had no idea how pleased I really was or the real reason behind it. Victor had his car in long-term parking so we parted ways at the airport. He must have thought I was trustworthy enough not to run off with Acacia under Eve's supervision. Little did he know, he'd given me the perfect opportunity to put my plan in motion.

"I was afraid if I didn't, Tom would steal you away and you'd have nothing to wear to my party." Eve waved another car in ahead of us as we tried to merge onto the freeway. "Are you staying at the house?"

"I have to stay with Victor. *Judge's orders*. Arabella is staying with me because your brother is a creeper," Acacia explained.

Eve caught my eye in the rearview mirror. "Do you want me to stay with you?"

"Thanks, but that won't be necessary." I didn't want to ruin her birthday any earlier than necessary.

I broke eye contact and stared out the window at the flashes of color from the brightly painted houses and more cars than I could count. As long as she didn't ask, I wasn't going to volunteer the information about my 'relationship' with Victor. Thankfully, after an uncomfortable pause, the girls began tittering about party details. Their high-pitched voices were normally like grating my eyeballs on a rusty cheese grater. Today, I let the sound relax me as I watched the cars creep past us.

When the car stopped, I jerked awake, momentarily disoriented. The uncomfortable twang of the pinched nerve in my neck told me I'd fallen asleep. The girls were already halfway out when I pulled myself together enough to follow. I rubbed my eyes with the palms of my hands and yawned loudly once I was on the sidewalk in front of a swanky looking shop.

Eve and Acacia headed straight in as if I wasn't even there. Maybe Eve would be so preoccupied in finding my sister's dress she'd let me do my own shopping. Hey, I could dream a little. She turned and motioned for me to hurry. How could someone so sweet and cute have such an evil twinkle in her eye? I'd seen it before when she tricked me into going to the salon before Acacia's birthday party.

Soft music played from invisible overhead speakers as we entered. When the door closed, the noise from the street disappeared. Plush white carpet muted our footsteps as we headed toward an elegant looking woman clad in black from head to toe. Her black hair shone like polished obsidian under the fancy lights, her lipstick was such a deep red it was nearly black as well. She made Goth look good. The woman embraced Eve and gave her air kisses on both cheeks.

"Here they are." Eve gestured to us with a wide sweep of her arm.

"Uh, Eve, don't you need something too?" I asked as the woman walked around us like a vulture.

She giggled. "I ordered my dress ages ago. Today is all about you two. I just hope we have enough time."

"Plenty of time," the woman answered as she pulled Acacia's shoulders back to correct her posture, making her gasp.

"Just put everything on my account, Giselle," Eve said as she headed to a small table containing a decanter of ice water and bite-sized snacks.

Giselle's deep smoky voice would be perfect in a jazz lounge. "Who is first?"

"Why don't you take Arabella? That way Acacia and I can browse," Eve suggested.

When Giselle turned her wicked 'I want to eat your soul' smile to me, I felt goosebumps raise on my arms or maybe it was the overly air-conditioned shop. The faintest hint of gold in her green eyes told me she was a higher generation vampire. How many of them were out there? Was I so sheltered or maybe I just hadn't noticed until I was made aware such a thing existed?

From behind me, Eve called, "She'll need to match Tom."

My heart fluttered at the thought. Victor had impressed upon me how important it was that I make Tom believe I no longer cared for him, which was going to be extremely difficult since just hearing his name made my pulse race. Maybe if I just ignored him and let the ring I was getting tonight do the talking it would be enough. My left hand felt heavy at the thought.

"Yes, yes, you are the infamous girlfriend," Giselle muttered and I caught the slightest hint of an eastern European accent.

I followed the woman as she pulled hangers off racks at random and laid them delicately over her arm. When she started re-hanging them on the clothing rack in the dressing room, which was the size of my bathroom, I realized what she had picked out for me.

"Um, I don't think any of this is going to fit. Is there even an entire outfit in here?" I laughed, picking up an under-bust corset, but sobered when I saw her stoic look.

"Start with these and I will find you dresses," she said flatly and lowered the curtain that served as the door.

It only came up to my shoulders, so I gave the two teenagers giggling by the food cart a dirty look before turning to the eclectic assortment of clothing awaiting me, having no idea what some of it was. I skipped to the things I recognized and realized I'd never seen such an assortment of leather, lace, and chains. Acacia was going to be in heaven when it was her turn.

Giselle flipped back the curtain without a pause as I was struggling to zip up a red leather bustier. "Ever heard of knocking?"

She lifted her pale hand, complete with long, dark red tinted nails, and rapped her knuckles on the wall then handed me half a dozen more garments.

"Thanks," I muttered under my breath before giving up on trying to squish myself into the red leather torture device.

I flipped through the stack of dresses Giselle dropped off, marveling at the finery; everything was in shades of black, gray, or cream. Obviously, Tom's outfit would only match those colors. Butterflies began waging war in my stomach and I tried to focus on untangling a black silk and lace halter style dress from its velvet hanger.

The fabric whispered over my skin as I pulled it on over my head. The zipper was on the side, so I had to suck everything in and prayed I didn't zip myself. After adjusting my cleavage, I turned to the mirror and gasped. The girls heard my startled sound and hurried over as I turned to get a better look.

"Oh. My. God. It's perfect," Eve said, faking a swoon onto Acacia's shoulder.

"It's too long," my ever-optimistic sister added.

With a frown, I looked down at my feet to see two inches of silk and lace pooled on the white carpet.

"Excuse me." Giselle pushed into the room with a pair of black ankle boots with four-inch heels. "Put these on."

Careful not to step on the extra fabric, I sat on the chaise lounge in my dressing room and pulled on the soft suede boots. How had she known what size I needed? After a quick glance around the room, I noticed the sandals I had been wearing were missing. She must have swiped them in an attempt to finish the outfit without having to ask. Damn, she was good.

When I stood again, the dress's bottom hem just brushed the thick carpet as I made my way to the full-length, three-way mirror for the full effect. My ponytail looked ridiculous so I grabbed the elastic and freed my locks. After flipping my head down and giving my hair a quick toss with my fingers, I turned and smiled devilishly at the mirror.

The cream-colored silk, the exact shade of my lightly tanned skin, behind the black lace made the bodice's black lace appear to be painted on. Lifting my arms to move my hair, I turned to get a better view of the back. It was cut so low the two little dimples at the tops of my hips just peeked out. Thank God I'd continued going to the gym and started up my running schedule during my Victor imprisonment. There wasn't enough of this dress to hide any imperfections.

"Now, you need jewelry." Eve pulled me to a long display case full of fancy crucifixes and chains.

"I think I'll just stick with this." I touched my opal pendant.

"No," Giselle said with such determination we all turned. "I will not have an incomplete outfit leave my store."

Alrighty then. "I've got a silver cross in my..."

Giselle gave me a look that would have made a meeker person shiver but I only shut my mouth. This was part of Eve's birthday present, being able to play dress up with Acacia and me for her big party. The Goth woman steered me to a chair and began applying necklaces, earrings, bracelets, armlets, and big fancy rings. No one had the guts to tell her to back off so I let her bejewel me, all while thinking I'd decide what I would wear tomorrow without her supervision.

Once the crazy woman was satisfied, I had enormous silver disks of spider webby designs hanging from my ears, a black lace choker with a tiny intricate crucifix dangling in the front, and a large black stone ring that fit on my index finger. The ring was awesome, the rest was just too much for me but it made Giselle happy, so I let her put it all in a box.

Giselle turned her hungry eyes on my sister. "Now, it is your turn."

• • • •

"ARE YOU SURE YOU DON'T want me to stay with you?" Eve asked for the third time as we rounded the final curve approaching Victor's driveway.

"Nope, you need to get a good night's sleep before your big day," I said in the most upbeat tone I could manage.

It was a good thing it was dark because my face would have given away my terror of coming back to this place. The day of freedom had been absolute heaven but what was impending was nearly causing me to hyperventilate.

"I'll pick you gals up tomorrow at one," Eve said as she put the car in park.

"Your party doesn't start until eight. Why so early?" I asked, almost panicked.

"To get ready, silly. The makeup artist and hair stylists will be at the house at two-thirty. It will take a while to get through all five of us."

"Five?" Acacia asked as she opened the door.

"You, me, Arabella, Mom, and Lexi." Eve counted on her fingers as she made her way up the front walk.

"Your sister's here too?" I asked, cringing when I saw movement inside the house.

"Yep. You'll love her, Acacia," Eve said, taking my sister's hand.

Did that mean I wouldn't? I didn't know much about the last River sibling. The little I did led me to believe she subscribed more to Desdemona and Victor's view on life and vampire world domination. Hopefully, the mysterious Lexi wouldn't throw a wrench into my neat little escape plan.

"I was about to call Search and Rescue," Victor said, taking Eve in a big hug and giving me a knowing look, which told me he didn't trust me even under Eve's supervision. "But since I knew who was in charge of shopping, I was willing to give you another hour before I sent out the cavalry."

"I'll be back at one to pick up the girls," Eve said then turned to me, "unless you need me sooner."

"I promise to take good care of them." Victor's laugh sent a shiver down my spine.

Eve hugged Acacia then me. "I'm sorry you didn't get a chance to see Tom tonight. He said he's busy tomorrow afternoon so you'll both have to wait until the party."

Flicking a glance at Victor, I stepped back and forced a smile. "It's okay. I'll see you both tomorrow."

The panic attack I'd been fighting since we'd arrived hit me full force when Eve's headlights disappeared down the drive and Victor closed the door, effectively locking us in. The last time I'd been here, I'd almost died. The house looked exactly the same but the clean, organized living space that had once impressed me now felt like a feng shui prison.

"I'm going to bed," Acacia announced, her subtle way of asking the whereabouts of the guest room.

"Let me help you with that." Victor grabbed her skull and crossbones duffle bag and led the way to the opposite end of the house.

"I'll be there in a bit," I called and hated myself when my voice shook.

In my brain-scrambled panic, I headed to the living room in an attempt to distance myself from Victor. The lights illuminating the porch and pool slammed me into that painful memory. My knees began to shake and I had to reach out for the wall so I didn't fall. Oh, God, I couldn't do this.

Victor's voice made me jump. "Would you like something to drink?"

"Water?" I croaked.

Concern pinched Victor's brow and I knew my crumbled resolve showed clearly on my face. "Arabella," he whispered, reaching out to me.

Jerking out of his reach, I swore under my breath, knowing I was undoing everything I'd worked so hard to make him believe. "I can't do this anymore, Victor. This," I gestured between us, "and being here. I just can't."

When he reached out again, I stepped back but this time caught my sandal on the rug and began falling backward. Victor's hand snatched out and caught my wrist as I flailed uselessly. In a split second, I was pressed against him, his breath ruffling the hair around my face, my wrist still tight in his grip.

He reached up with his free hand and smoothed the hair out of my face. "I promise everything will be worth it. One more day and all your sister's legal troubles will be over."

"And what about mine?" I felt hot tears slide down my cheeks.

"I'll give you the world. All I ask is you give yourself to me." Victor's blue eyes bore into mine.

"I'm tired," I whispered, looking down.

His grip on my wrist loosened. I was surprised when my fingers began to tingle, meaning he'd been holding tight enough to cut off the blood supply. I balled my hand into a fist in an attempt to speed recovery and lessen the odd prickling sensation. When I opened my fingers again, Victor flattened my hand out, palm down.

"Just one more thing," he said quietly enough my gaze lifted to my hand as he slipped the platinum band on my third finger.

# Chapter Thirty-One

Desemona decided Eve was needed at home so she sent a car to Victor's for Acacia and me. I could tell my sister was impressed. Hell, I'd be impressed too by the gray stretch limo cruising its way back to the Rivers' home. That is, if I didn't know what was awaiting me at the end of this wild ride. As I tried to calm myself, I twirled the ring Victor had put on my hand last night. It felt like a lead weight, permanently cold against my skin.

"Let me see it again," Acacia said, pulling me back to reality.

I held out my left hand for her to inspect it for the fourth time this morning. Nothing ostentatious, my ass! The delicate platinum band held what I guessed was at least a two carat, princess cut, pink diamond solitaire flanked by two pear shaped smaller diamonds. I don't even like pink!

"Maybe you could accidentally lose it while washing your hands," Acacia suggested, letting my hand fall.

"Only if I washed my hands in the toilet. There is no way this gaudy rock would make it past the drain guard." I held it up as if she hadn't already seen the size of the diamond.

Acacia shrugged and slid across the seat to look out the other window. "Just trying to help."

I'd been a bundle of nerves all morning, snapping one second then tearing up the next. Acacia had taken it all in stride, probably thinking it was all part of my foolproof plan. The only problem was my plan was falling apart, just like I was. I'd thought I could fool Victor into believing he'd won. I hadn't. I'd thought I could face Tom. I couldn't. Feeling helpless was not something I'd ever thought I'd feel but right now I did.

A plan no longer existed. I'd go along with Victor's charade to save my sister then find a way out that hopefully didn't end in my death, or permanent loss of my sanity. Saving my relationship with

Tom was no longer a viable option. When we stopped in front of the Rivers' mansion, I was glad Tom was going to be gone all day. I wasn't ready to face him yet. Maybe I wouldn't ever be.

With a last second decision, I pulled the ring off and stuffed it in the pocket of my shorts. Acacia raised her eyebrows in question but my explanation was cut off when Eve yanked open the door. Her hair, dyed back to its natural chocolate brown with golden highlights, was done up in enormous rollers. It would have been hysterical if my mood hadn't been so sour. Maybe that's why her mother had insisted she stay home this morning; the dye job would have taken time Eve hadn't accounted for in her pre-birthday party primp-fest.

"Mom and Lexi are over at the caterers making sure everything is set. Come on! I want you to see my room," Eve exclaimed, pulling Acacia from the car.

With a quick glance over her shoulder, I motioned for Acacia to go ahead. Eve took her hand and both girls ran inside, leaving me alone in the car. The driver opened the door on my side and offered his hand but I waved it off as politely as I could.

In her haste, Eve left the front door open so I pushed it the rest of the way and walked inside. The museum-like quality that had made me so starry-eyed on my last visit had somehow lost its luster. Dragging my feet, I headed to the staircase to meet the girls in Eve's bedroom.

"Arabella?" a deep voice called as I lifted my foot to take the first step.

I closed my eyes and let out a breath. The one person I hoped to avoid had found me before I could escape to Eve's sanctuary. Rearranging my features, I turned and gave him a beaming smile.

"Lucian, how are you?"

He raised an eyebrow skeptically and I knew I was busted. "Do you have a moment?"

"Sure," I said flatly and followed him to a room I hadn't seen on my last visit.

He led me into a large office, most likely his. Books and portraits lined three of the four walls. I recognized a painting of what appeared to be a five- or six-year-old Victor and Tom but quickly glanced away. A large walnut desk dominated the space in front of a huge window, making up the remaining wall. Lucian motioned for me to go in ahead of him. I spotted a dark green leather couch and matching set of chairs and angled toward them. Somehow sitting in front of the desk brought back too many memories of the principal's office.

Once I was seated on the couch, Lucian sat next to me and shook his head. "Why are you doing this?" When I opened my mouth, he continued, "After everything that happened, everything I told you. Do you understand the depth of what you are doing?"

Hearing his accusing tone was too much. For some reason, I longed for Lucian's approval and friendship. He was the only person, besides Eve, in the River family who had accepted me for what I was instead of whatever had been decided by my genetics.

My breath hitched and tears poured from my tightly closed lids. "I am so sorry. I never meant..."

His arms wrapped around my shoulders and I wept against his soft shirt. He murmured soothing words and rocked me gently as I poured out all my frustrations in body shaking sobs. After a few minutes, I stopped and pulled myself back to a sitting position. He handed me a handkerchief for my eyes.

"Your shirt...." I began, seeing the black streaks from my mascara against the pale yellow of his shirt.

"Is the least of your worries. Now, tell me everything."

After a moment's hesitation, I did. I told him *everything*. My emotions swung the full pendulum from anger to desperation. Why hadn't I asked for help before I buried myself so deep I couldn't even see a way out? I knew the answer but I didn't want to accept it. It was because I'm the most stubborn person on the planet, always trying to save everyone else no matter what happened to me along the way. A strategy that had always worked, until now.

Lucian was silent for a few moments when I'd finished. He was holding the engagement ring I'd dug out of my pocket between his thumb and forefinger. His forehead was creased in deep thought and his blue-gold eyes were tight with worry.

"What are you going to do?" he asked finally.

My shoulders slumped and I shook my head. "Any ideas?"

He let out a frustrated breath. "Nope, and I hear Eve coming. Put that back in your pocket unless you want to let loose her wrath."

"There you are!" she exclaimed, throwing the door open.

"Your dad caught me on the way in and..." I began.

"Have you been crying?" she interrupted, rushing to my side.

"No. Well, yes, but I'm just worried about my sister. I didn't want to ruin your birthday," I lied. "Sorry you had to see this."

She bent down to give me a big hug. "You can tell me anything, Arabella. What are sisters for?"

She winked at her dad and I knew she was referring to me becoming her sister-in-law. Too bad the ring in my pocket was from the wrong brother. Lucian gave my hand a squeeze of encouragement before getting to his feet.

"According to my lovely wife, I need to get a haircut before the party so I will see you ladies later."

"Come on, Arabella, everyone's waiting for us upstairs." Eve pulled me to my feet. "You're going to need some eye drops to get rid of that red."

*They* indeed were waiting for us. Eve's bedroom had been transformed into a staging area for what could have easily been a fashion show. Two women, looking like they were ready for a beauty pageant themselves, manned the makeup tables set up by the stereo.

The racks of garment bags, which I assumed held our costumes for this evening, formed a semicircle in the center of the room. Eve had taken Acacia and my purchases home with her last night so we didn't forget them.

"Ouch!" Acacia hollered from the bathroom.

Eve and I entered to find my sister in a beautician's chair being tortured by an enormous woman in layers of lavender silk, making her look like an upside-down tulip. Biting back a laugh, I gave her the most sympathetic look I could manage before Eve pulled me into the main room.

That was where we stayed the rest of the afternoon. We moved from table to table getting colored, painted, buffed, and every other form of primping in preparation for Eve's big party. It was just after six when Eve's door opened and Desdemona and another woman glided in. I was getting the final coat of copper-colored polish on my fingernails and got a pinch from the woman doing the painting when I turned too far to gawk.

Alexandra didn't look anything like I'd imagined. I figured she would be another ravishing dark beauty like the rest of her gorgeous family. The oldest River sibling was, for lack of a better word, plain. Her brown hair was cut severely short and she was beyond thin, almost to the point of skeletal. Her eyes were dark like Desdemona's but other than that they hardly resembled each other. However, they moved with the same fluid and slightly predatory grace.

Neither woman looked in my direction as they headed to the bathroom where Eve was getting the final touches on her hair. Acacia was finished except for changing into her dress. Her red hair was piled in a loose bun on top of her head where it was draped with a string of shining black pearls. Tiny ringlets fell like red rain around her face and the back of her neck. The makeup artist had somehow made her heavy eyeliner look sophisticated. Her short nails had been touched up with their usual black and accented by elbow-length black lace, fingerless gloves.

I, however, demanded a more natural look for the evening. My hair had been put in the same giant rollers Eve had been sporting earlier. It now formed gentle waves cascading over my shoulders. Several black pearls were pinned in to keep my hair from falling into my face plus a few more just for show. My makeup, too, was light, just enough to 'enhance my natural beauty' according to the artist. I think she was afraid to put on too much seeing my teary face when I first arrived.

When Eve stepped from the bathroom, she absolutely glowed. Her hair was similar to Acacia's up-do but much more elaborate. Weaved into her hair were strands of white ribbons studded with diamonds and pearls. Her makeup, while heavy, made her even more beautiful. Or maybe it was her beaming smile that radiated her excitement for the impending party.

"Mom and Lexi are going to get touched up while we get dressed. Can you manage so I can help Acacia?" she asked me.

I raised my eyebrows in question and both girls blushed. "I actually do need help," my sister confessed.

"Let me know if you need a third person." I dismissed them, angling toward the rack of garments.

My dress was the only one with a dark maroon silk bag, making it easy to find. The girls zipped and unzipped several black ones until they found Acacia's red corset and black floor-length skirt combo. It always surprised me how good she looked in that color despite being a redhead. I guessed the lone white bag belonged to Eve. There were more dresses than people and I wondered if there was going to be a wardrobe change mid-night like those fancy Hollywood parties I read about in the tabloids.

I went into Eve's closet to change, half for privacy and half hoping to avoid having to interact with Desdemona. It was better, and easier, to be ignored by her than to face another possible fight. At the moment, my emotions were right on my sleeve and I couldn't be accountable for my words or actions.

The fabric of my dress was cool as I pulled it carefully over my head. My fingers trembled as I tried to tie my halter straps without catching my hair or damaging my still tacky nail polish. After the third try, my arms were burning from keeping them up so long. I put them down with a huff and shook them to restart normal blood flow before trying again.

"Let me help you." Desdemona's voice sounded immediately behind me, making me stiffen.

"Thanks," I said, holding up my hair. Her fingers were cold against the back of my neck and goosebumps rose on my arms.

"You've caused quite a stir, Arabella. My children's happiness means everything to me," she continued as she tied and retied the bow until it was perfect. "I expect you to be on your best behavior for my baby girl's party."

I nearly lost it. To her, all this *was* my fault. She'd warned Tom not to make the same mistake twice and from her standpoint she had been right. I'd done exactly the same thing as Rachel, worse actually. As much as I wanted to scream at her, to tell her the truth, I knew it would fall upon deaf ears. Nothing I said would make any difference because, in her eyes, I was beneath her.

When her hands finally fell away, I murmured another thanks without facing her. I waited until I was sure she was gone before turning. A sigh of relief slipped from me when I scanned the empty room. Without thinking, I put on all the jewelry Giselle picked for me along with Victor's ring before heading back out into Eve's room.

"Since you're ready, you can help us," Lexi said, even her voice was plain in a monotone sort of way.

"Let me just check on the girls before we head out." I started toward the bathroom where I could hear them giggling.

Lexi stepped into my path. "I'm sure they're fine. We need to set up the final touches. If you don't think you'll mess your nails, you *could* help."

It was hard to hate someone within seconds of meeting them but Lexi was just one of those people. I was wrong when I said she was plain looking. Now we were standing inches apart, she had a kind of sharp, pixyish beauty. Her dress of black satin draped loosely off her petite shoulders. When she turned away, I saw the top laced up the back. There was a slight bustle in her skirt, making her waist look unnaturally tiny. Next to her, I looked downright chunky.

"See you downstairs girls!" I called as I followed the two women out to the main house.

At the bottom of the stairs, Lucian was waiting dressed in a dusky gray tux. A dozen or so velvet hat boxes were neatly stacked beside him. When he caught sight of his wife and daughter, his whole face lit up. How could such a wonderful man be in love with such a bitch?

I realized suddenly that was my future. Trapped with Victor, taking solace in finding happiness any way I could. I stumbled at the thought but caught myself on the banister before I took out the two women gliding gracefully down the stairs ahead of me. Lucian's eyes clouded with concern and I gave him a weak smile letting him know I was okay. Desdemona and Lexi took his arms so I followed a few steps behind as we headed toward the back door.

The driver that had offered to help me out of the limo earlier passed us. I turned to see him grab three of the hat boxes. With a sigh, I turned and headed back to help.

"Want a hand?" I asked, catching his gaze, not a hint of gold to be found in his large hazel eyes.

When he met my stare, he quickly looked down. "Thank you."

I grabbed four boxes then remembered how he struggled with three and put one back, not wanting to make him feel any more uncomfortable. We made several trips and once the velvet boxes were securely placed on a silver and black draped table at the entrance of a huge white pavilion tent, I smiled in triumph. At his returning grin, I could tell he wasn't used to being treated as an equal.

Desdemona and Lexi buzzed around shouting orders as an army of people finished with the final touches of the pre-party prep. After peeking inside the boxes to find them packed full of fancy masquerade masks, I stared across the yard at nothing and spun Victor's ring nervously. One of the prongs grabbed the delicate lace on my dress. Before I could make it worse, Lucian appeared and took my tangled hand in his and freed it.

"Thanks," I whispered.

He held my hand in his and patted it, obviously trying to calm my nerves. Desdemona called to him and he gave me a half-smile before ambling over to where she waited. I resumed my slow, deliberate breathing to keep from hyperventilating in anticipation of the coming evening. Whatever the crisis was, Lucian solved it by opening his billfold.

The California heat wasn't helping my attempt at relaxing. There were ceiling fans circulating the air under the tent but I lingered just outside, not quite ready to get into the throng of it all. My hair felt hot against my back and I lifted my hands to fluff it.

"That's new," a familiar voice said, catching my left hand as I lowered it.

My head whipped around from watching the chaos inside the tent and my mouth opened into a small 'O' as I stared at Tom. I knew it was him at the sound of his voice and recognized every difference between him and his brother instantly. I couldn't believe I'd ever mistaken one for the other. I tried to pull my hand free but he held it fast. We stared at each other for what felt like an eternity but was probably only a few seconds before Lucian called for us to follow.

Without a word, Tom moved alongside me, linking his arm through mine, never letting go of my hand. I swallowed the lump in my throat and tried to remember how to breathe as I followed his lead blindly into the tent, unable to look away from his face.

# Chapter Thirty-Two

"Tómas, where are my husband and girls?" Lexi shouted from the opposite end of the tent, pulling me from my reverie.

He chuckled under his breath before answering. "Franco is getting them a snack before the party starts. Last time I saw them, they'd just found some raspberry sherbet in the freezer."

Lexi let out a strangled shriek, gathered up her long skirts, and sprinted passed us into the house. I would have wondered what was wrong with raspberry sherbet if I wasn't so lost in the sight of the handsome man beside me. My heart physically ached with love for him.

"Both my nieces are dressed in pristine white dresses and neither one is known for their table manners," Tom explained lightly then added. "You look beautiful."

His comment brought a blush to my cheeks and made my heart flip-flop. After a second of thought, my brow wrinkled in confusion. I lowered my gaze to where his hand covered mine, a faint smile tugged up the corners of my lips at the sight. He was acting as if nothing had changed. He hadn't tried to contact me since I broke it off, he'd seen and commented on the ring, and Victor loved gloating about his phone conversations with his brother. So, what the hell was going on?

"Tom," just saying his name made my pulse quicken. "Can I talk to you alone for a second?"

"I don't think that would be such a good idea, Love," Victor interrupted.

My breath caught and I tried to put more space between Tom and myself, but he held me fast to his side. I'd never seen such loathing in a stare and my stomach clenched when the brothers locked gazes. Something unspoken passed between them and it was

Victor who looked away first. I'd have said he'd lost the battle but his gaze met mine as if nothing happened.

"Shall we?" Victor held out his arm.

This time when I pulled away, Tom released his grip immediately. I couldn't bring myself to look at his face. Where his positive responses toward me made my heart race, the thought of seeing his pain was too much to bear, or worse, not seeing it. Instead, I linked my arm with Victor's and let him lead me away. After a few steps, I could have sworn I heard Tom sigh. I closed my eyes and let out the breath I hadn't realized I'd been holding.

"Didn't you and my baby brother look cozy back there?" Victor's tone was thick with sarcasm as we made our way to the opposite end of the tent.

I slid my arm from his and folded them across my stomach. "Stop it," I warned. "I'm wearing the ring and I let you whisk me away without a word. Don't goad me into an argument."

For a second, I thought he was going to laugh but my look must have silenced him. He glanced over my shoulder to where I assumed Tom still stood, before again meeting my gaze. His blue eyes sparkled with new triumph and a slow smile spread across his face.

"I spoke too soon," he said with a laugh.

He put a hand on my shoulder and turned me back the way we'd come. A beautiful blonde woman had joined Tom during our retreat. While this wouldn't have surprised me, their closeness did. He had one arm around the woman's waist and she was whispering something in his ear. His free hand reached up to brush her cheek in a very intimate gesture that made tears prick my eyes and my breath hitch.

I'd read Tom's actions all wrong. He wasn't acting like nothing had changed. He was acting as if he accepted my decision and moved on. I literally felt my heart break. My knees suddenly couldn't hold my weight and I fumbled for one of the black and silver satin draped chairs in front of me. Before I could sit, Victor put his arm around my waist and pulled me against him, his thumb gently drawing circles on my exposed back as his breath shifted my hair.

"We can slip out after Eve opens our present," he whispered in my ear before lowering his lips to kiss the nape of my neck.

I gulped back a sob and blinked furiously at the tears threatening to overflow. The situation was far worse than I'd thought. As I struggled to keep the tears from falling, I realized I recognized Tom's date as an up-and-coming actress from an action flick I'd seen last fall. Tom had moved on and I was trapped with Victor.

"Can you get me something to drink?" I asked, voice husky with emotion.

He pulled out a chair for me, into which I sank into ungracefully, then headed toward the bar. I'd drink whatever he brought. I just wanted to drown my pain and lose myself. Eve was going to come downstairs thinking everything was perfect until she saw Tom with that golden Goddess and me with Victor. So much for her birthday present.

When Victor returned, he handed me a champagne flute and held two masks with fancy handles. "Eve had special ones made for the family."

I took a sip of champagne without tasting it before examining the mask he'd handed me. It was in the shape of a swallowtail butterfly, glossy black decorated with silver and pearls. Nothing like the cheap paper ones I'd gotten at a New Year's Eve party a few years ago. Even the ones in the velvet boxes were nicer than the dollar store specials I'd had in the past.

Lifting it to my eyes, I snuck a glance to where Tom and the actress had been but they were no longer there. Most likely they had disappeared into the now arriving guests or off to a secluded place in the house so they could be alone. I tipped my champagne flute up and drained it.

"You might want to pace yourself," Victor suggested.

"What's the point? You're the only one who wants me here, besides Eve, who is going to flip out when she realizes what's going on. You're already planning a stealthy get-away after ruining your sister's birthday. Do you ever think of anyone other than yourself, Vic?"

By the end of my tirade, I knew I was shouting but I didn't care. Victor opened his mouth but I pushed to my feet and brushed past him. "I need to use the can."

The guests in my way parted as I stormed toward the house. I must have looked like a bitchy prom queen from Hell as I made my way out of the tent. Even the band looked up as I stalked past. I recognized the singer; I loved this band.

I opened four doors before finding a stupid bathroom. Unfortunately, the blonde actress was just leaving as I reached for the handle. We eyed each other for a second, sizing the other one up. I stepped back so she could go back to the party I was trying so desperately to escape.

"You must be Arabella," she said with a southern twang. "Tom's told me so much about you."

"I'd like to say the same but we don't speak anymore," I said, shouldering past her.

Her tinkling laughter made me want to deck her. "Of course, he doesn't talk about me. We've been friends since we were both knee high to a grasshopper. I doubt he even knew I had a crush on him since fifth grade, not that I could compete with you."

My blank look made her falter. Her smile slowly began to fade and she lifted her hand to her mouth. "You didn't think we were here together, did you?"

"Doesn't matter," I mumbled and turned back to the bathroom.

"Arabella." She reached out and touched my shoulder. When I turned again, she pointed down the hall. "He's waiting for you, Sugar."

When I realized my mouth was open, I snapped it shut and mentally cursed. That was one habit I was going to stop if it killed me.

She gave me a coy smile. "I see why he's so attracted to you. Go on. I'll go chat up Victor but I can only guarantee fifteen, twenty minutes tops before he comes looking for you."

Before leaving, she turned me so I was facing the direction she'd pointed. At the end of the hallway was Tom's old room. Had I been wrong again? My heart told my feet to run to him but my head kept my pace slow as I walked down the ever-lengthening hallway.

Hand poised to knock, I looked back down the hall again to find it deserted. My hand dropped and instead of knocking, I pushed the door open. Tom stood at the window with his back to me. I hadn't noticed before but he wore a pair of black satiny slacks and a loose fitting cream-colored shirt, contrasting nicely with his sun-kissed skin. His hair was tied in a simple black ribbon at the base of his neck, a few strands escaped as he rubbed it in a nervous habit I found endearing.

The door thumped closed as I pressed my back against it. Tom's hand stilled and he slowly turned. His expression careful as if he didn't believe what he was seeing.

"If you love him, I'll leave you in peace." His voice was tight.

I walked toward him, keeping my hands clasped behind my back. I had about fifteen minutes to tell him everything but I couldn't find the words. His eyes pulled me forward and I felt the slightest resistance brush my consciousness. He could feel my willingness but was pulling back his own desire so when I answered, it would be only my wishes coming forth. That was the one thing I had come to recognize during my time with Victor, except it was always in the opposite direction forcing me to do what he wished.

Tom took my hand in both of his when I laid it on his chest. His eyes searched mine with such longing as I whispered, "I wouldn't have come if my heart didn't belong to you."

Suddenly, his lips were against mine. The kisses were not the gentle ones I remembered but full of desperation, begging my words to be true. I tasted the salt of tears and wondered if they were his or mine. My breath came in a gasp when we finally pulled apart. Our bodies were pressed together; Tom had one hand holding me against him and the other tangled in my hair.

"I missed you so much, Arabella." He spoke against my cheek. "I was afraid."

He didn't need to finish; I knew what the unspoken words were. I'd felt the same when I'd seen him with the actress outside. His scent enveloped me and my head began to swim. How could this man hold such sway over me? I didn't care. I loved him with every fiber of my being and never wanted to be apart from him again.

"I was always yours." I tilted my head down in shame. "I only did it because Acacia needed..."

His fingers lifted my chin so I could see his eyes, tears brimmed, mirroring my own. "I know. My father called me this afternoon after your little talk. My hope had almost run out for us. Why didn't you just tell me?"

It all seemed so stupid now. If I'd just told him everything from the start, neither one of us would have had to endure such misery. Stubbornness was my biggest flaw and I silently vowed not to fall into its clutches again.

As much as I hated to, I took a step back, almost hurt when Tom didn't stop me. I pulled off Victor's ring and let it fall to the floor. The rug muffled its impact. I lifted my eyes to Tom's and closed the gap once more. He led me to the couch and we slid down together.

"I'm yours, forever and always," I whispered, turning my head up and to the side, exposing my neck.

Tom's fingers trembled against my skin as he pushed my hair back. My eyelids fluttered closed in anticipation as I felt him inhale and pull me close. A small gasp escaped my lips as I relished in the tiny pinch of his teeth breaking my skin, followed by the fire flaring deep within me.

After a few moments, Tom lifted his head. "I will *never* leave you again."

With a sly smile, I leaned in for another kiss. "I think I'll hold you to that."

My lips made a trail from his mouth to his neck as well. When my teeth broke his skin and the rich taste filled me, I let him move me onto his lap. His hands pushed my skirt up to my hips, calloused fingertips traced up and down my thigh as he whispered my name.

In the blood-induced haze, we made love. I'd almost forgotten how perfect we were together, neither one dominant, both relishing in each other's pleasure. Nothing else existed in that moment; our love eclipsed everything. I could hear the thump of the music outside as well as the sounds of the party now in full swing but it was as if my brain couldn't comprehend more than this moment in Tom's arms.

"We should get back," he said, and I realized I had almost dozed off while snuggled against him.

"He'll know," I whispered, clutching the front of Tom's shirt where I was resting my head.

Tom pushed us both up to a sitting position. "It doesn't matter. He can't hurt us anymore."

"What about Acacia? I can't let her suffer because of his unwillingness to let me go." Panic started to replace my earlier euphoria.

He repinned a black pearl in my hair. "Eve gave me the waiver. When the party's over, we'll go get it and the case will have to be dropped."

I closed my eyes in relief. Was it really going to be that simple? My plan about handling it myself seemed more and more selfish the longer I thought about it. All we had to do was wish Eve happy birthday, grab Acacia, get the waiver, and all our problems would be over.

Tom helped me to my feet then I made my way to the bathroom to fix my makeup and hair. Eve would be upset I'd ditched the party but even more so if I messed up her attempt at beautification from this afternoon.

When I returned, Tom was pinching Victor's ring between his index finger and thumb, a look of disbelief on his face. "Did *you* pick this out?"

"Do you even have to ask?" I asked, reaching for the obnoxious thing.

He stuffed it in his pocket before I could grab it. As he withdrew his hand, he lowered himself onto one knee. Even though Acacia had warned me of his plan, I wasn't ready for it. When I moved to kneel in front of him, he held up a hand to stop me.

"I've waited for you my whole life and I don't want to spend another second away from you. Will you marry me, Arabella?" In his hand was a simple gold band inset with three round diamonds.

When I found my voice, it shook. "Do you even have to ask?"

"I told you I would never make you do something you didn't want. Now answer my question before I change my mind."

I raised my eyebrows and held out my hand so he could slip the ring on. "You can't get rid of me that easily."

# Chapter Thirty-Three

N ow came the tricky part. Tom and I had to rejoin the party without looking conspicuous about both our departure and re-arrival. Our goal was to find Eve and Acacia, separate them then slip away without Victor catching on. There was no doubt in either of our minds he was searching for me. Honestly, I was surprised he hadn't found us in Tom's room already.

It killed me as I exchanged Tom's ring for Victor's before we parted in case he found me before we executed our get away. Tom left the room before me. I was to wait three minutes then follow. Those felt like the longest minutes of my life as I paced back and forth letting enough time tick by.

When I wrenched open the door, I nearly collided with Desdemona. "Why am I not surprised to find you here? Not content with only one of my boys? You want to have them both, just like that whore, Rachel."

This time I didn't have to take her snide remarks. "Listen lady, it's always been about Tom. I love him and he loves me. It's your other son who is obsessed with something he can't have. If you have a problem, talk to him."

"That's *exactly* what I plan to do. I'm sure he'll love to find out where you've been hiding." She reached out and grabbed my upper arm.

"What did I say about touching me?"

I slammed my head forward into her face and heard the telltale sound of cartilage breaking. To my surprise, instead of releasing me, her grip tightened, forcing her long nails through the skin on the inside of my arm and pulling me into the hallway. A second later, a pair of strong arms grabbed me from behind, effectively pinning mine to my sides, and lifted me off the ground. Pulling my legs in, I kicked out and caught Desdemona in the stomach, which sent her falling backward into the wall. When whoever had me pinned to their chest lowered me, I rammed the heel of my boot into their shin as hard as I could.

Unlike Desdemona's unwillingness to let go, this guy dropped me so fast I fell forward into a stumbling run. After only a few strides, my legs were completely tangled in my long skirt. No wonder I never wore dresses! I grabbed handfuls of silk and lace, hitched up the front to free my legs, and made a beeline for the party.

As I rounded the corner, the music slammed into me and forced me to slow as I entered the crowd. The once empty backyard was now swarming with glamorous guests. I dropped the material clutched in my hands and smoothed the front of the dress before entering the throng with a slow but determined pace.

Only after the guests surrounded me, did I dare look back toward the house. A guy that would have looked right at home in a pro wrestling arena appeared at the tent entrance. As he limped forward, I realized he must have been the guy who grabbed me from behind. While all the other Rivers' servants were humans, it appeared they employed vampires as bodyguards, evident by this guy's bright golden eyes. Or in the case of Beefy back there, first generation vampires were their idea of personal bodyguards.

I caught a flash of red hair and started toward it, hoping to find Acacia. In the confusion of dancing and mingling guests, I lost my goal and turned frantically only to find Beefy closing in fast. A group of what looked like male models materialized just ahead of me and I ducked behind them, using their height to hide behind. When I peered around them, Beefy looked confused. No one said all vampires were rocket scientists.

Someone grabbed my wrist from behind. I whipped around ready to fight off whoever it was. Eve's startled eyes stared back at me as my elbow aimed for her face. Luckily, I had enough time to stop or I would have given her a broken nose to match her mother's. She was sporting a white feathery mask that matched her ivory ball gown. It vaguely resembled her sister's, making them polar opposites in both color and personality.

"What are you doing?" she yelled over the music.

"Where's Acacia?" I shouted back.

"Last time I saw her she was dancing with my brother. Over there." She pointed.

Her brother, but which one? I grabbed her hand and dragged her in the direction she'd indicated. I couldn't see anyone resembling Tom or Victor but it didn't help that everyone was wearing fancy masks. No wonder Beefy could spot me a mile away; I was the only person without one.

When we reached the outer rim of partygoers, I bent down slightly to disguise my height; Eve mimicked my movements. The over-head fans were doing little to cool the now crammed tent. I lifted my left hand to push my hair from my face.

Eve grabbed my hand and squealed in delight. "He was supposed to wait until the song! Hold on, this isn't the ring he showed me."

Beefy must have heard her outburst because I caught a glimpse of his massive bulk moving our way. "I don't have time to explain. Who was Acacia dancing with?"

"Victor, but I don't understand..." she began but I grabbed her wrist and pulled her into the house.

My heels snapped loudly on the floor as we entered the painfully quiet space. Thankfully, she followed my lead without question. But where was I going? I angled toward her bedroom to give myself time to think. Unfortunately, we were intercepted at the base of the stairs.

"Mom!" Eve shrieked, pulling her hand from my grasp. "What happened to your face?"

Dried blood covered the front of Desdemona's dress as well as her upper lip and chest. It looked as if she'd made a futile attempt in cleaning up but abandoned it halfway through. Her eyes were already swelling and a purplish haze of the impending bruise crossed the bridge of her nose.

"Why don't you ask her?" Desdemona's harsh tone was diminished by the fact she sounded like she was suffering from a bad head cold.

Eve turned back to me with tears in her eyes. "Arabella, you did this? Why?"

"I'll explain everything when we find Acacia. Come with me, Eve, please," I said, holding my hand out to her.

"No," she planted her feet and folded her arms. "Tell me what's going on or I'm not taking another step."

"Yes, Love, why *don't* you tell us what's going on?" Victor's voice asked from behind me.

Could this get any worse? Tom and Acacia were MIA and I was surrounded by three pissed off vampires. There was no way to lie my way out of this, not with Desdemona's face as blatant evidence against me. My only option was to continue with Tom and my plan of getting out of here.

"Where's my sister?" I asked, turning to face Victor.

"Safe. For now, anyway."

"Take me to her," I said through gritted teeth.

"Of course." Victor nodded and offered his arm. "But first you owe me a dance."

I threw my arms up in frustration. "You have *got* to be kidding!"

"Eve picked out a song for you. Since you're ruining her party, you can do her this one small thing," Victor chided.

"*I'm* ruining..." I was so angry I couldn't even finish my sentence.

I turned my gaze to Eve; she'd removed her mask. Glistening tears slid down her cheeks, smearing her fancy makeup. Desdemona had her arms around her daughter's shoulders but her eyes were narrowed in my direction.

"Is it that important to you, Eve?" I asked, trying to catch her eye.

"Of course, it is," Victor said, capturing my wrist.

"Why don't you let her answer for herself? She's an adult now. Why don't both of you let her make her own decisions?"

No one spoke for a few seconds then Eve lifted her chin and met my eyes. "It doesn't matter."

I wondered if she meant the song or the fact she was officially an adult now. She'd spent her whole life trying desperately to please everyone and it was going to take a lot more than a birthday and my support to change that kind of behavior. If we made it through this, I was going to make sure she found the strength to get away from her crazy-ass family.

"Take me to Acacia, and I swear if you hurt her..." I began.

"I promised no harm would come to her as long as you behaved yourself," Victor said, then whispered when he pulled me roughly to his side, "but we both know you haven't."

"I'm coming too," Eve said from behind us.

"No, you're not. You are going back out to entertain your guests," Desdemona protested.

"The hell I am! Whether you like it or not, I love Acacia. I'm going with them to make sure nothing happens to her," Eve yelled back.

My heart swelled with pride as I heard her footsteps hurrying to catch up with us. However, I then realized I now had to protect not only Acacia and myself but now Eve as well. Deep down I knew Victor would do whatever was necessary to get his way, even if it meant hurting his own family.

# Chapter Thirty-Four

Victor insisted Eve follow us in her car. At first, I'd protested but having a second car was going to make our getaway easier. If there was a getaway. I sighed and stared out the passenger window of Victor's Aston Martin. I'd blown everything with my little tryst with Tom at the party. God, I was such an idiot.

The sunset sent otherworldly shadows everywhere as we drove through yet another suburb. There was no way he had the time to drive Acacia out here and get back to the party in time to intercept Eve and me before we could escape. What game was he playing now? The flash of blue and red lights behind us answered my question.

I waited nervously for Victor to pull over but he continued to cruise at the excruciatingly slow speed limit. Did he really think he was above the law? The flashing lights started to dim and I turned to see Eve's car idling by the sidewalk.

"Bastard," I muttered, knowing he'd set it up so she couldn't follow us.

"You are going to have to learn to watch your language. I'd hate for our kids to swear like sailors before kindergarten."

I folded my arms across my chest and slumped. "That's not going to be a problem. *We're* never going to have kids."

A genuinely satisfied smirk slid onto his face. "You think so?"

How long was he going to drag this out? It was obvious he wasn't taking me to my sister. For all I knew, she was safe and sound at the party wondering where the hell I was. Instead of completing Tom's and my plan, I was taking a tour of LA's nicer neighborhoods.

"Stop jerking me around, Vic, and take me to my sister," I snapped.

He glanced in the rearview mirror before flipping on his blinker and taking a right. We left the residential district and ended up in an area filled with boutiques and restaurants where you could only get a table at if you knew someone who knew someone. The longer we drove the angrier I got.

When Victor turned into the parking lot of a chic looking market, I lost it. "Enough! Take me back or..."

"Or you'll what?" he snapped, making me jump.

While Victor had been controlling and manipulative, I'd never known him to be aggressive. I knew he was capable of murder but it wasn't until I'd heard him just now, and saw the look in his eyes, that was I truly afraid of him.

He rolled his shoulders back and pinned with me a glare. "I'm going to grab a few things. I'd like to trust you to sit tight but you haven't done much to instill my faith in you tonight. Get out of the car and follow me like a good girl."

I opened my mouth to protest but his look silenced me. The store was practically empty and, from the dirty look we got from the cashier, closing soon. Victor grabbed one of the little baskets in one hand and put his other arm protectively around my waist.

"Caramel swirl, right?" he asked, leading us toward the freezer section.

"Ice cream!" I started and he shushed me. "I don't want ice cream, I want my sister, you fucking bastard!"

My final comment made a woman, who looked like she'd had more work done than Barbie, gasp. Victor flashed her a smile and with a blush at him and a disappointed shake of her head at me, she pushed her cart around the corner.

"You'll have her soon enough. I promise she's in no immediate danger, if you decide to go back to our original agreement."

We'd stopped in front of the ice cream section and I stared at the frosty glass; our distorted, ghostly reflections looked back. I couldn't do it anymore. I'd tried and failed. I loved Tom too much to hurt him anymore by becoming Victor's slave. There was only one way Victor would give up this insane pursuit of me. Unfortunately, that would require the death of one or both of us. I needed more time.

Gently extracting myself from his grip, I tugged on the freezer case handle. The chilly air swirled out like mist around my ankles. Once I'd dropped the pint of ice cream into the little basket, I stepped back to Victor's side and let him put his arm around me. A contented sigh escaped his lips as if he expected me to throw a tantrum in the middle of the store. Little did he know, I had no problem stating my opinions despite my surroundings.

I let him lead me blindly as he gathered a fancy loaf of bread, cheeses, a carton of orange juice, and two bottles of champagne. The woman at the checkout counter looked relieved at our swift shopping and more than happy to ring up our purchases so she could close up shop.

Victor got onto the freeway then took the exit I now recognized would take us back to his house. I guessed the party was over in more ways than one. We'd long since lost Eve so I had no back up. Who knew where Acacia and Tom were? Safe and together? I hoped as much as we drove up the dark hills.

We hadn't spoken a word during the winding drive to Victor's house. I was ready to scream in frustration when he parked in the garage then headed to the kitchen whistling a happy tune. I lagged behind, looking everywhere for a sign of Tom or Acacia. The more I looked, the more I believed they weren't here.

When I joined him in the kitchen, he was opening a bottle of champagne. "What are you doing?"

"Celebrating," Victor said as the cork popped, making me jump.

I threw my arms up and walked out. This was ridiculous! Victor must be insane if he thought I was going to just forget everything that happened tonight. My legs were tangled in my skirt again. I let out a small shriek of frustration then headed to the bedroom for my suitcase. I couldn't go find Tom and Acacia in this stupid thing.

Victor found me as I struggled to unzip the side without getting pinched. "Not that I'm complaining about you getting undressed, but you might want to hold off for a few more minutes."

I turned away from his smirking face and continued to fight with the stupid zipper, now stuck in the lace. "I don't really care what you think, Vic. I'm changing and then I'm leaving. Obviously, Acacia isn't here. I intend to find her and go home."

"Then you'll want to stay put. I'm sure she's on her way here by now." Victor explained.

I let my arms fall to my sides, hands clenched in fists and eyes closed to regain focus. "This is over, Vic. This little game, it's done. I'm leaving as soon as my sister gets here."

He still had that infuriating satisfied look on his face when I turned toward him. "Not only will you stay, but you'll want to."

Without waiting for a response, he turned and left the room. I didn't know what his plan was but nothing would make me want to stay with him. Abandoning my changing attempt, I grabbed a handful of material so I could walk normally and followed him. Despite my haste, he was exiting onto the back porch when I caught up with him.

This was the one place I'd avoided since I arrived. The memory was still too close to the surface, but with a deep breath, I stepped out onto the patio. The temperature was comfortably cool now in the late evening. Stars sparkled above, fading into nothing over the lights of the city below. Victor was sitting with his feet up beside the pool when my breathing was finally normal again.

"Have a seat." Victor patted the spot next to him.

I yanked off the obnoxious ring and tossed it to him. To my surprise, he caught it with one hand and pocketed it. "You'll have it back soon enough."

"Haven't you been listening to me? Are you so conceited you can't take no for an answer? I'm leaving and that's final."

Victor just smiled and shook his head as the doorbell chimed. I spun but only made it two steps before his hands grabbed me from behind. My elbow shot back hoping to catch him in the stomach but he was ready, holding me far enough away it didn't connect. As we struggled, his arms pulled me against him so we were facing each other.

After fighting in his grasp for another second, I spit in his face. He closed his eyes and sighed, letting go with one arm to wipe it off. In his distraction, I wriggled free but only made it a few inches before he backhanded me across the face. I stumbled, tangled in my skirt, and hit the concrete scraping my hand and arm.

"I see you've finally found your place, Arabella," Desdemona said, looking down at me.

She'd cleaned up the blood and changed her clothes but the damage I'd done to her face was clearly visible. Victor walked over and embraced her before returning to me. I swatted away his offered hand so he grabbed my arm and yanked me to my feet instead. I heard a deep, slow chuckle and saw Beefy leaning against the window watching us.

"Are you sure about this, Victor? She might not be the one," Desdemona asked.

"It's amazing I found both Rachel and Arabella. There is no way I'm going to risk the chance there isn't another vampire out there with compatible genetics. I won't let our family line die out because of something as trifling as this. Besides, I have faith she'll come around with the right motivation." Victor turned and gave me one of his beaming smiles.

Desdemona glared at me and I returned her black look. My arm was beginning to ache where Victor held it, while the other flamed from the concrete burn. I squirmed then gasped when his short fingernails dug in as he tightened his grip. Beefy pushed off the wall and headed back into the house still smiling like an idiot.

"You'd better get on with it then. I don't know how long Eve will wait before she comes looking for that trash, Acacia." Desdemona looked pointedly at me.

"Don't talk about my sister, you bitch," I spat. She gave me a disapproving sneer and shook her head before walking around us.

"That is no way to speak to your future mother-in-law," Victor chided. "Let's get your scrape taken care of before the rest arrive."

I let Victor lead me back into the house. Once we were in the bathroom off the master suite, he finally let go of my arm. My freedom was brief as he forced my scraped hand and arm under the hot water in the sink.

"Rest of what to arrive?" I asked through gritted teeth while he none too gently continued to clean my wound.

"Just Chris, Acacia, and your motivation," he said, then frowned. "Mother's not going to be pleased but it's the only way."

My blood ran cold. I'd assumed he was going to use my sister against me but it was clear Desdemona hated her as much as me. He was going to use someone she loved as my motivation. The only one with that kind of sway over both of us was Tom.

"You bastard. What did you do?" I demanded.

"Me? Nothing, not yet anyway. What *will* happen is entirely up to you," Victor said, lifting my hand to kiss the newly scrubbed skin. "There, all better."

He motioned for me to head back but I stood my ground. I wasn't going to make whatever he planned any easier; I was done pleasing him. If I weren't in this stupid dress, I'd kick him where the sun doesn't shine and run like hell. Unfortunately, I had a feeling I'd only make it to the end of the driveway before Beefy caught me. Plus, how would I get Acacia back?

Victor reached out for my arm again, but I lifted it out of the way while turning to head back to the bedroom. I folded my arms across my chest and Victor put his arm around my waist, pulling me close. It took everything I had not to ram my elbow into his chin.

"Acacia!" I pushed away from Victor and wrenched open the sliding glass door.

"Why did you leave me at the party?" she asked.

She was fine, still looking like a model from the party as she sipped her OJ from a champagne flute. As I looked back and forth between her and Victor, I realized my mouth was hanging open again. What the hell was going on?

"Come with me. We're leaving," I said as I ran over and grabbed her hand.

"What? Why?" she began then the little light came on.

She put her glass down and followed me. Victor was standing in front of the door, blocking our way. I opened my mouth to let him have it when I caught movement inside. He stepped to the side and pulled the door open in one motion. My breath caught and Acacia's grip on my hand tightened.

Beefy pushed Tom out ahead of him. His hands were bound behind his back and he landed face down on the concrete, bouncing slightly. I dropped Acacia's hand and ran to help him. Victor reached out for me but I somehow managed to shove him away. He landed with a quiet 'oof'.

Tom was facing away from me and I carefully turned him over. His face looked worse than Desdemona's. From the way Beefy was cracking his knuckles, I had a pretty good idea who had beaten him to a pulp. His left eye was completely swollen shut and a cut above his right eye oozed blood down his bruised and scraped cheek. When his one eye focused on me, he let out a sigh of relief but it stopped half way and turned into a groan of pain, leading me to believe his face wasn't the only place Beefy had used as a punching bag.

"Victor! What the hell are you doing?" Desdemona shrieked as Beefy held her back from rushing to her injured son's side.

"Relax, Mother. None of his injuries are fatal." He glanced at Beefy who nodded his head in agreement. "Arabella just needed a push in the right direction."

"Beating the crap out of Tom is not going to convince me to do anything, you bastard!" I shouted, holding Tom's head in my lap. I just couldn't look away from his broken face.

"How about this?" Victor asked.

I heard the sound of the gun being cocked and turned my head just in time to see the muzzle flash. Tom cried out in pain as the bullet tore through his leg. As quickly and carefully as I could, I laid his head down and pressed on the wound. Tears blurred my vision as Tom writhed in agony.

When Victor raised the gun again, I shielded Tom's body as best I could. "Stop! I'll do what you want, just don't hurt him anymore."

"Looks like I'm right on time." Chris's voice startled me from my attempt to put myself between Victor and Tom.

"Did I happen to mention Chris is licensed in the state of California as a non-denominational minister?" Victor asked as he grabbed my upper arm, pulling me further away from Tom.

He was going to force me to marry him? Like it would make any difference. If I hated the man before, it was a hundred-fold more now that he'd shot Tom. As soon as I could, I'd get the marriage annulled. There had to be more to this than just staking a claim via wedding rings.

Tom's voice pulled me from my personal thoughts. "She won't ever love you, Victor."

"That's the difference between us, brother. I'm not looking for a foolish romantic version of happily ever after. Arabella is one thing to me: a vessel for immortality."

I was only half listening to their argument. Acacia huddled next to a chair in a pathetic attempt to hide. Chris was laying some papers on the glass table as if nothing was out of the ordinary.

"Acacia, go inside and grab a towel to put on Tom's leg," I instructed in a harsh whisper.

When she straightened up, Victor turned the gun on her. "I don't think so. Sit in that chair like a good girl."

"He's going to bleed to death!"

"Then we had better get on with the formalities so Mother can take him to get some medical attention," Victor countered.

# Chapter Thirty-Five

Victor made Acacia stand to my left like a melancholy bridesmaid in this sick and twisted shotgun, er, handgun, wedding. She cried softly as Chris set up what looked more like a satanic ritual than a wedding altar on the round glass patio table. Two different marriage licenses were off to one side. There were also two silver goblets half filled with red wine, some sort of ornate ceremonial dagger, and one of those fancy calligraphy pens. The fact there was no ink in sight made me more than a little nervous.

Beefy had taken Desdemona into the house and given her something to knock her out. Personally, I hoped he used his fist but that's just me. She'd gone off the deep end when Victor had shot Tom. If the gunshot hadn't alarmed the neighbors, her screaming most definitely would have. I wondered if any of Victor's neighbors were close or brave enough to call 911.

Now her wails were silent, the only thing I could hear was Tom's labored breathing over the pounding of my own heart. Victor had forbidden anyone to call for help but instructed Beefy to put pressure on his leg to slow the bleeding. We were standing with our backs to them and when I tried to turn, Victor held me fast to his side.

My mind was reeling, searching for a way out of this, but came up blank. At this point, there was no way other than Victor's. I still didn't understand what he meant about 'vessel for immortality' but I had no intention of being anyone's vessel of anything.

"Ready?" Chris asked.

"No," I said at the same time Victor said, "Proceed."

Chris let out a breath. "I'm guessing we're doing the short version because of obvious time constraints. Turn to face each other and take the other's hands. Oops! I'll hold that for you."

Victor handed Chris the gun, who laid it carefully in front of him on the table, just out of my reach. "We're here today to join Victor Lucian River to Arabella Michelle Simon both in marriage and to each other for eternity. I'd ask if there was anyone who would object but considering the objecting party is unable to do much more than bleed, there's really no point."

Victor cleared his throat. "Stop screwing around and get on with it, Chris."

An involuntary shudder racked my body at Chris's description of the ceremony. This sounded a lot more complicated and permanent than 'til death do us part'. I snuck a look at Tom from the corner of my eye. Victor squeezed my hands so hard a gasp escaped my lips before I could stop it.

"Victor, do you take Arabella as your wife and sole blood partner?" Chris asked.

"I do," Victor answered with a smile.

Chris offered the dagger to Victor who took it with his right hand. My heart began to pound in my ears not knowing what was coming next. I jerked reflexively when Victor stabbed the point into the end of the third finger of my left hand. Blood immediately began to well and drip from the wound.

"The ring finger on the left hand is a direct path to the heart." Chris handed him the calligraphy pen and I now understood the lack of ink. "Victor, please sign your name in Arabella's blood here, then add a drop to your wine glass."

I tried to pull my bleeding hand out of his but he was stronger than me. The pen tip jabbed painfully into the same spot where he just opened it with the knife. I watched in horror as he artfully signed his full name on the demonic license. My shock made me pliable enough I didn't even fight when he moved my hand over the wine glass and massaged a drop into one of the goblets. I, however, quickly withdrew my hand when he put my fingertip in his mouth to stop the bleeding. With a chuckle, he raised his glass in a mock salute and drank.

After carefully inspecting both the license and wine, Chris turned to me. "Arabella, do you take Victor as your husband and sole blood partner?"

"Fuck no!"

Victor's face went blank for a second then he reached across the table for the gun again. "Clearly, as long as Tom lives, you won't see reason."

"No, stop!" I cried. "If I do this, will you let Acacia go?"

"I'll personally deliver the waiver to the opposition's lawyers," Victor answered.

"And Tom? You have to promise not to hurt him."

"Arabella, don't do it! You'll be bound to him," Tom started but Beefy backhanded him into silence.

"As soon as we're done here, you'll never have to worry about him again."

Something in Victor's eyes gave away his carefully worded answer. It was obvious now no matter what I did, Tom's life was forfeit. As long as he lived, Victor knew my heart would belong to someone else. He wouldn't risk losing his prize. Tears poured openly from my eyes and everything became a blurry smear. I heard Acacia's breathing hitch as she cried beside me. How had it come so far?

In a shaky voice, I turned back to Chris. "Go ahead."

"Arabella, do you take Victor as your husband and sole blood partner?" Chris repeated.

I swallowed twice against the tears. "Yes."

My heart broke completely when I heard Tom sob, "No."

When I moved to take the knife, Victor stopped me. "Don't try anything or I swear I will kill him and then force you to continue with the ceremony."

I nodded meekly and took the dagger from Chris, who picked up the revolver at the same time. It was all I could do not to stab Victor in the heart but I knew if I did, Chris would shoot Tom, and probably me. Instead, I pressed too hard on Victor's finger, not only puncturing the tip but slicing down the side as well. Unfortunately, it didn't seem to faze him, almost as if he expected it.

When I put the dagger back on the table and picked up the pen, Chris laid the gun down and pushed the license in my direction. I filled the tip with Victor's blood but hesitated over the paper. A single scarlet drop hit the page where my name should have gone. This wasn't going to end once the ceremony was over. Deep down I knew Victor would kill Tom once he was done using him as incentive, but how could I save him?

I turned to Tom and through tears mouthed, "I'm sorry."

His face, already contorted in pain crumpled as his heart broke along with mine. It was as if a part of him was dying already. My hand began to tremble and when I turned back to the paper another drop fell. I wrote an 'A' then lifted the tip.

"You need to sign your full name." Chris said as if his patience was wearing thin.

I let out a breath and rolled my shoulders back, planting my feet shoulder's width apart. Victor's breath eased out as I turned and rammed the pen toward his neck. My aim was off as he flinched back so the sharp tip penetrated just above his collarbone.

"Go to Hell!" I screamed then flung myself between him and Tom.

The sound of a gunshot and the fire of the bullet entering my side seemed almost simultaneous. I wasn't sure whose shocked cry was louder: Tom, Acacia, or Victor's. I heard another shot as I crawled with one arm to cover Tom's body with my own. Rough hands grabbed me and tugged me away from my goal. Somehow, I'd managed to keep the pen clenched in my hand and I swung it at my attacker.

Beefy began to scream as the pen embedded itself into his left eye, wrenching it from my grasp. His wails overshadowed the rest because of his closeness. Pain flamed across my side and stomach as I pulled myself toward Tom with one arm.

"I'm so sorry," I whispered.

I felt the blood soak through my dress as the pain flamed through me. If I had to die to save Tom, I would. Victor couldn't have me and if this was the only way, so be it. I just hoped Acacia had enough sense to get away during the confusion.

"Shh, help's on the way," Tom soothed.

"It will be too late for you, baby brother," Victor said from above us, the gun pointed at Tom's head.

"No!" I screamed as he aimed.

Instead of a shot, there was a primal scream that made Victor turn. Eyes wide, he swung the gun toward the source of the noise. His reaction was too slow as Acacia drove the silver dagger into his throat straight to the hilt. The revolver hit the concrete and I jerked in case it went off on impact, sending another wave of pain so strong I nearly passed out.

Blood poured from Victor's neck despite his hands pressed against it. A grotesque gurgling sound came from him as he stumbled backward toward the pool. The loud splash cut off the terrible sound and I closed my eyes at the sudden silence.

"Arabella, what do I do?" Acacia wailed, kneeling beside us.

"Help Tom. Call 911," I said softly, suddenly too tired for anything louder.

"Hang on, Arabella. You can't leave me now," Tom said, tilting his head against mine. His voice was strained as he began to whisper the words to my song.

# Chapter Thirty-Six

I expected death to be quiet and serene. Not mine. Obviously as good as I thought I had been during my life, it hadn't been enough to get a ticket into heaven. I mean, I hadn't been to church in over four years and had sex out of wedlock, but all in all I was a good person. Hadn't saving the lives of the people I loved counted for something?

Only Hell would be full of daytime soap operas and smell like bleach and stale vomit. The final bonus was the leaky faucet dripping in time with my heart. At least the last thing I'd heard was Tom's sweet voice singing my song.

That thought brought tears to my eyes. I'd left him when I'd died. I hoped he knew how much I loved him. And Acacia? She must know despite our petty differences, I loved her too.

It wasn't fair. I still had so much to do! Neither Tom nor Acacia were safe enough for me to leave them yet. Was Acacia sitting in a juvenile detention center awaiting trial for something she didn't do? Had Tom bled to death before help could arrive? And why was it so freaking cold in Hell?

A sharp pinch in my arm made me flinch. "Get away from me, minion of Satan!"

"I've been called a lot of things but that's a first." A woman's voice laughed. "Now, hold still so I can change this IV."

IV? Was food intravenous in Hell? Just another luxury I'd taken for granted when I was alive. No more ice cream. Wait, why did I need food when I was dead? I tried to open my eyes but they seemed glued shut. Had I been cursed with blindness but all the rest of my senses were fine? That sounded about par for the course.

A few moments later, what felt like a warm scratchy washcloth was laid across my eyelids. Once it was removed, I tried to open my eyes again, only to be blinded by harsh fluorescent lighting.

"Your little friend stepped out for a coffee. Do you want me to change the channel?" A blurry figure in aquamarine asked.

Everything cleared a little more when I blinked again. Every inch of me hurt and I didn't seem to have the ability to move anything but my eyes. The aquamarine blob I'd called the Devil's Minion waited patiently for my answer. She didn't look like a demon, more like someone's grandma, complete with little white bun.

"Does Hell have basic cable?" I asked, trying to move my fingers only to find them painfully stiff.

"Not sure about Hell, but we do. Anything in particular?" She laughed, making her entire body jiggle.

"Anything with car chases and explosions."

"I'd think after what you've been through, you'd want something less dramatic." Her voice was quieter as if she'd turned away.

It took me a second to figure out why it was so dark; my eyes must have closed again. At the sound of screeching tires and the deep gravelly voice of one of my favorite actors, I smiled. Maybe Hell wasn't so bad after all.

"I'll let the doctor know you're finally awake. You gave us quite a scare." Aquamarine Grandma said, giving my leg a gentle squeeze.

"Doctor?" I asked suddenly. "I'm not dead?"

"Not yet but from what I hear, your guardian angel has been putting in some serious overtime," she said before she disappeared.

The revelation of finding out I wasn't dead seemed to pull me fully into reality. The smell of bleach, Aquamarine Grandma, even the leaky faucet, AKA my IV drip, made sense. I reveled in the pain, knowing it meant I was still alive. A giggle bubbled out and before long I was laughing hysterically, which hurt like hell.

"Arabella!" Eve squealed as she ran into the room and grabbed me in a hug.

I gasped in pain but held her tight when she tried to move away. "Stop trying to please everyone," I said angrily as I hugged her back.

"Only if you stop trying to save everyone," she retorted, tucking her hair behind her ear as she stood beside my bed with a bright smile.

"I heard you were off getting coffee, where's mine?" I asked, trying to shift in the bed but everything from my shoulders down was dead weight.

"She wasn't getting coffee. She was staging a break-out attempt but abandoned me in the home stretch," Tom said from the doorway.

Eve scurried over to help him, looping his free arm over her shoulders. He looked unnaturally pale in his green and white striped hospital gown and robe, long hair hanging limply about his still bruised face. I'd have to amend my earlier statement about my dad being the most handsome man in the world. He was now running a close second. When Tom gave me a smile, I heard my heart monitor begin to race.

Leaning heavily on a crutch, he made his way to where I was trapped in bed. It was obvious he wasn't putting much burden on Eve as she helped him ease himself onto the ugly hospital chair. I tried to scoot closer but again it was as if I was paralyzed.

"You look like shit." I smiled as Tom took my hand, covered in tape and tubes, in his.

"You are still the most beautiful creature I've ever seen." He lifted my hand to his lips.

"I'll be in the hall keeping watch," Eve said before giving us some privacy.

Tom's eyes clouded as soon as she'd gone but I interrupted before he could say anything. "Where's Acacia?"

"With your parents," Tom said and after a second added, "The charges against her have been dropped."

Closing my eyes, I let out my breath. "Tell me what happened."

"You mean after your suicide attempt?" His voice was almost angry then he let out a shaky breath. "What you did was incredibly stupid, you know that, right?"

"Yep, I'm an idiot. Now, tell me what happened."

Tom put his hand on my cheek and I leaned against it, absorbing his strength "At least with you bound to Victor, you would have been alive." His voice broke on the last word. "Just promise you'll never do anything like that again."

"I don't ever plan on being in a situation like that again, so I promise," I said, holding up three fingers in a mock Girl Scout salute.

"When were you a Girl Scout?" Tom asked skeptically.

"For about thirty seconds when I was eight, are you going to tell me what happened or am I going to have to call my sister?"

The sadness clouded his blue eyes again. "Acacia cut the zip-tie securing my hands then called 911. I held you until they arrived. They said it was too late, that you'd lost too much blood."

His grip on my hand tightened but I pleaded with my eyes for him to continue. "I punched one of the EMT's because he wouldn't help you, he was too obsessed with my leg. Which is fine, the bullet passed through without too much damage. It hurts more than anything. Your heroic attempt landed you in sixteen hours of surgery. You died twice on the table but they brought you back. To me."

So, I *had* died, multiple times. I guess my stubborn streak was good for something. In my selfish rescue of Tom, I hadn't stopped to think how my death would have affected him. I was too worried about how his would affect me.

"Tómas?" Desdemona's voice sounded from the doorway, making me jump.

Her face hardly showed any signs of the damage I'd inflicted. Either I'd been in here longer than I realized or she was a magician with makeup. Her eyes met mine for a second then dropped almost apologetically. Eve lingered uncomfortably behind her.

"I'm taking Eve to visit your brother. We'll be back in a few hours to pick you up," she explained then turned back to me. "It's good you're finally awake, Arabella."

I hardly heard her attempt at kindness, still too stunned at her earlier comment. Victor was alive? How? Acacia had stabbed him through the throat! I saw him fall into the pool. A tremble shook my entire body and my heart monitor began to jump erratically.

Tom struggled to his feet and put his arms around me, but I couldn't stop shaking. "He's still alive?"

"According to Eve, he hasn't regained consciousness, but in a manner of speaking, he is."

I needed to pull myself together. So what if he was alive? I think I made my intentions about us glaringly clear. He *had* to leave me alone now, didn't he?

"He can't hurt you anymore, Arabella. I won't let him hurt us ever again," Tom soothed.

My thoughts raced back to the chaos. "Chris?"

I felt Tom shake his head. "Victor put a bullet between his eyes after he shot you."

That should have been comforting but it wasn't. Somehow, I'd assumed Victor had been the one who shot me. The unfinished ceremony flitted through my memory. Would he still try to bind me to him? As quickly as the trembling started, it stopped. A cold feeling of dread settled deep in my stomach.

"Victor's bound to me, isn't he?" I asked in a whisper.

Tom relaxed his hold and leaned back to look into my eyes. That shadow clouding Tom's mood darkened as he nodded. The rhythmic beeping accelerated and I hated the sound of my fear being broadcast so publicly.

"Am I...?" I tried to ask but the words died in my throat.

"No." Tom kissed my forehead then rested his cheek against it as he rocked me gently. "You got all heroic before you finished the ceremony."

"What if we got married? If I bound myself to you?" I began, frantically trying to come up with a way to sever any tie to Victor.

Tom just shook his head. "As long as you live, he'll be bound to you but what we have is stronger. Our love is stronger. You don't need to worry about him right now."

I nodded and hoped it was true. There was just one last question I was dying, ha ha, to ask.

"What did Victor mean when he said I was his 'vessel for immortality'?"

He slipped his hand from mine and sat back with a sigh. His expression was a mixture of pain and anger. I tried to reach for his hand but he stayed out of arm's reach. This whole limited mobility thing was really getting on my nerves.

"The only real kind of immortality one can have. He wanted you to produce the next generation."

Why hadn't I figured that out? Victor's conversation to Desdemona about continuing the family line came back to me. It made sense but Lexi had children and there was always Eve. Well, if Eve found her soulmate and that person wasn't a girl. If what Victor said was true about Rachel and I being the only genetic matches, my death could have taken Tom out of the equation as well.

"A son," I said quietly.

Tom nodded. "He was on his way to succeeding, too."

His standoffish posture suddenly made sense and I jerked in understanding. No wonder I'd been such an emotional wreck lately. "I'm pregnant?"

He shook his head and took my hand again. "Not anymore. The trauma was too much. You lost the baby."

I closed my eyes and swallowed. Tears welled in my eyes for the child I hadn't even known existed. Victor had destroyed yet another life. Even conceived for malicious reasons, the child had the right to live. A selfish moment slid over me and I was glad Tom wouldn't have to see Victor's and my baby.

"Age was hard to confirm," Tom began as he entwined his fingers into mine. "They told me seven to eight weeks."

A sob escaped my lips before I could stop it. Seven to eight weeks. There was no way the baby had been Victor's. We hadn't begun our twisted dance yet. No wonder Tom was acting this way, he'd thought Victor and I had slept together during my first trip to California. I opened my mouth to tell him this but hesitated. Would it hurt him worse to know the child had been his?

I'd gone from being the answer to Victor's future to being what held him back. Lovely. If he had been persistent before when he had everything to gain, what would he do if he had nothing left to lose?

Looking into Tom's blue eyes, I found the strength to smile. We could do this together. I'd put my superhero cape under the bed and ask for help instead of taking on the world alone. Whatever the future held for us, we'd achieve it together. And for once, I liked the sound of that.

# Don't miss out!

Visit the website below and you can sign up to receive emails whenever Melinda Call publishes a new book. There's no charge and no obligation.

https://books2read.com/r/B-A-JVKY-LKGMC

**BOOKS 2 READ**

Connecting independent readers to independent writers.

# About the Author

Melinda Call grew up in the Pacific Northwest and Mountain West of the United States. She loves her family fiercely, even the four-legged ones that don't speak clearly. Her hobbies include reading, gardening, and baking. Feeding the people she cares about is her love language. She talks too much and cries during almost every movie/TV show/commercial that she doesn't fall asleep watching. Even though she is a scientist by day, she whole-heartedly believes magic exists.

Check out Melinda's website to read about her crazy life, books, freebies, and for links to follow her on social media.

Read more at https://melindacall.com.